THE WAKEFUL GUEST

In beautiful Bavaria Delia found happiness and love, brittle as glass. Where there's a will there's trouble – sudden death and growing suspicion shattered her romance. Was greed for money behind that series of "accidents"?

By the same author

LADY ROSE AND MRS. MEMMARY
MOMENT OF TRUTH
OUR DREAMING DONE
WINTER'S GRACE
TURN AGAIN HOME
APRICOT SKY
THE LEOPARD'S COAST
FOR EVERY FAVOUR
DOVES IN MY FIG-TREE
THE COUSINS OF COLONEL IVY

Children's Books

JILL'S GYMKHANA
A STABLE FOR JILL
JILL HAS TWO PONIES
JILL ENJOYS HER PONIES
JILL'S RIDING CLUB
ROSETTES FOR JILL
JILL AND THE PERFECT PONY
PONY JOBS FOR JILL
A PAINTBOX FOR PAULINE

THE WAKEFUL GUEST

by

Ruby Ferguson

LONDON
HODDER & STOUGHTON

The characters in this book are entirely imaginary and bear no relation to any living person.

First printed 1962

MADE AND PRINTED IN GREAT BRITAIN FOR HODDER AND STOUGHTON LIMITED, LONDON BY C. TINLING AND CO. LIMITED, LIVERPOOL, LONDON AND PRESCOT

PART I

I

It was when I was actually in the hall waiting for the taxi with my luggage around me that my courage and determination evaporated and ran out through my shoes.

I didn't want to go.

It was ten past eight on a January morning, a discouraging hour at best, and the ghastly nature of the coming day loomed miserably before me. What had I been thinking of to let myself in for such a journey? Taxi to the station, train journey to London, somehow to get myself to the airport, check tickets, find the right plane—I had never flown before—and eventually land in the dark at Munich. Then to find an hotel for the night, and tomorrow morning a station and a train which would take me and my luggage—if I hadn't already lost it—to Dorfen where I might or might not be met.

Why does one, carried away by thoughtless enthusiasm, let oneself in for such efforts?

All through the preliminary preparations I had been blinded by pleasurable excitement. Now that The Day had come I could only think, how marvellous if a telegram arrived saying "Don't come. Arrangements cancelled", and I could go upstairs (looking disappointed for the benefit of Mother and Ursula) and take off my things and unpack, and run gaily down to wash cushion covers or do some other chore, usually irksome but suddenly delightful.

Ursula, on her two sticks which she managed so well, came out of the dining-room and saw me standing there.

"What's the matter with you?" she said. "You look a bit gloomy. Wishing you weren't going, or something?"

"Don't be silly," I said, furious at being read.

"You're twenty minutes too early. The taxi won't be here till eight-thirty. I told you there was no need to scamper through breakfast. It's nervous tension. Shall I get you a codeine?"

I brisked up a self-confident smile.

"I don't want one. You know I'm always ready too early for everything. It's a thing of mine."

"Well, it's pointless standing in the hall. You might as well come and sit down where it's warm."

We went into the sitting-room. The fire had been lighted and was blazing up, and though it wasn't giving out much heat it looked cheerful.

On the overmantel was one of those perpetual calendars in a silver frame, with knobs to alter the day, the month, and the year, for ever if necessary. It belonged to Ursula.

"You haven't turned the calendar up today," I said.

"I haven't had time yet."

It said January 7. She turned it to January 8.

"You haven't even turned the year up! It's 1949 now."

"Good heavens!" She twiddled the knob. "What would Father have said?"

Though Father had been dead for seven years, one or other of us was always coming out with this remark. Father had been a stickler for routine, for doing the same thing at the same time each day. At twelve fifty-nine he was always in the hall, watch in hand, waiting for the lunch gong to go simultaneously with the striking of one from the grandfather clock.

"The universe," he told us, "runs by method. A miracle of diurnal timing."

And now for a whole week not one of us had noticed that it wasn't 1948 any more. It showed how little the passing of time mattered in our house.

Mother came in, and began where she had left off.

"So it's come to this, Delia. I still don't know why you need to go. It isn't too late to cancel everything."

Hardening opposition was all I needed to put steel into me.

"But I don't want to cancel anything."

She stooped and "washed" her hands above the warming flames.

"I still can't imagine why a girl who has a happy home and a pleasant life wants to go dashing across Europe to a place she knows nothing about. It's only restlessness. You should fight against it."

"But I need a change. I don't want to spend the rest of my life in a rut. I told you, Mother."

"You talk like a girl in her teens." (Mother would never have used such a word as teen-ager.) "And it isn't nice to describe our home as a rut. You have a lovely life, and you've always found it well filled with activities, and you've got your Red Cross."

"Getting endless cadets through their first exams? It isn't enough."

She tortured her forehead into a score of wrinkles.

"I know what's the matter with you. You've got that idea of the young that everything away from home is better. You'll soon find out, dear."

"I'm not all that young, Mother. At least I'm old enough to find out for myself."

Ursula hugged her brown cardigan round her shoulders.

"I don't suppose you'll even like Ida von Mester. I remember her, you were too young. She had a huge, glittering personality."

She made the words sound revolting.

"She's my godmother," I said. "Mother chose her for the job, so she must have liked her once. She wants me to go and stay with her so she can see what sort of a person I am. What's wrong with that? She hasn't seen me since I was three."

"Stay with her!" My sister made a sarcastic face. "She wants you to live with her. You'll probably find yourself her companion-help. I didn't take to her and I was nine when she came here, old enough to know. She was worldly."

It was Ursula's worst epithet, not lightly bestowed but damning.

Mother looked downcast.

"Poor Ida changed very much. She was a nice girl when we were at school together. It was getting into the wrong sort of life, and marrying that German that changed her."

"He's been dead for years," I said. "And I shall have Eilys Mallins for company."

"You don't even know Eilys Mallins."

"She's Ida's other goddaughter and she's young. Of course I'll like her. . . . And I'll have some proper Red Cross work to do."

"Oh, don't mention that!" said Mother, jerking her head. "I don't want to think about it. You're quite mad. You'll catch something and lose your health."

The point of this conversation was that it was just a gramophone record which had been played over and over, ever since the day I got my godmother's invitation and decided to go. Everything that Mother and Ursula uttered on the subject irritated me to madness, yet you can't live in a groove for twenty-eight years without dreading to leave it and wondering how you will get along in the world outside. Especially when your groove is a pleasant one, insulated from the dangerous kind of life you read about in the newspapers.

Ursula and I had had an almost cloister-like upbringing. Up to the war we had maids, and spent our days doing light gardening, walking the dogs, reading, sewing, going out to lunch with neighbours and having them back. Once a week the wild excitement of driving the car eight miles into town to do a little shopping, change the library books, go to a cinema matinée, have tea and cakes at a café where we knew everybody and everybody knew us. When Father died it made little difference. With Mother we went on living like nuns, only with more comforts and self-indulgence.

The war was a terrible blow. Ursula caught it worst, they sent her into the A.T.S. She eventually found herself in devastated Normandy, where she contracted polio and was sent home with a life disability pension. As I was a Red Cross officer authority left me alone, because technically I was running the local sick bay. I spent six years keeping that place as clean as a whistle, and we rarely had a patient in the beds. Mostly I went there each morning in full uniform, dusted off imaginary dust, and sat knitting army socks and praying that the men at the anti-aircraft battery six miles away would start measles. When Ursula came back a war casualty and a heroine, Mother kindly tried to give me my share of the glory by reminding me that "they also serve who only stand and wait".

We all slipped back into the old ways directly the bells of peace rang out, except that we hadn't any maids and—except for a daily from the village—did the work ourselves.

I will say for Ursula that she was never a neurasthenic and she mastered her lameness very well. I could never compete with her in strength of character.

For interests outside the home we had visiting, and the eternal country wizz-wazz of getting things up for charity. We did some serious reading. We read the same books and discussed them. We studied languages and spoke French and German together until we were fluent. We sometimes worried because we weren't really educated, yet we steered nervously away from considering things like politics, economics, and world chaos. We never actually talked about anything that wasn't superficial, our real selves and feelings, for instance. This was due to our upbringing which had dinned into us that nice people never talk about feelings, because feelings are hardly ever nice and the ill-bred simply wallow in them.

Mother divided all people into two kinds, our kind and the others. For our kind, most of the troublesome things in life such as sex, social problems, psychological disturbances, and any questioning of the established order existed only to be ignored. Being Our Kind was not snobbish, it was an elegant state of mind. If we suspected in ourselves any human passions we shoved them down and jammed the lid on, ashamed of being so common.

If Ursula and I disliked the idea of becoming old maids we never talked about it. We had been brought up on the twin theories of what-will-be-will-be, and Mr.-Right-coming-along, and that seemed to cover the subject, or should. Ursula's encounter with the armed forces had, so far as I ever knew, left her unscathed. We had exchanged girlish confidences about a few mild flutters, hers with the doctor's August locum, which had lasted just as long as he was among us and no longer, and my own on-and-off affair with the local squire's son, which never quite came to an engagement and was so restrained on both sides that it eventually died of its own inertia.

An almost incredible life, a life of negative happiness? I had never asked myself that question. But now the break had come and it was my own doing, my own responsibility.

I thought, this is the actual moment. I am looking at something which of my own free will I am about to abandon, our sitting-room with its pale Chinese carpet, the Chippendale chairs, the pie crust tables, the bowl of Christmas roses, the Birkett Fosters on the wall, the baby grand in the corner where I learned to play Chopin and accompany Ursula's fiddle, the work stand under the window with Ursula's tapestry and Mother's trolley cloth, and my own knitting, and I am realizing that tonight there will only be two sitting in front of the fire stitching away and listening to the B.B.C. Symphony Orchestra.

I am thinking of my bedroom which I shall not visit again for a long, long time, the grey and blue room with the furniture I chose myself for my twenty-first birthday, and the bookcase with the mixed selection of books I adored, classics and poetry, collected over years and years.

I feel sick. I wish with all my heart that the beastly taxi would come.

"You know you needn't have put your coat on so soon," said Mother. "You won't feel the benefit when you go out. And you could have had that other cup of coffee. You're sure you have your passport handy?"

"Yes, thank you."

"Are you sure you've got—"

(I'm not sure about anything. I feel frightful. For two pins I'd howl like a werwolf. I wish this was a dream, at least I'd wake up.)

"If you don't like it there," said Mother as though she'd just thought of it, "or if anything isn't quite nice, you must come back at once. At once!"

"Yes, and don't have any silly pride about it," said Ursula. "I mean, thinking you'd lose face or anything like that. We'd understand. I've a feeling you'll be back soon."

"The one thing that reconciles me to it at all," said Mother, "is Ida's suggestion that she intends to do something about her will. That's why she wants to get to know you and this Mallins girl. She's rich, and possibly she'll divide it all between you. It would be a comfort for me to know you were well provided for when I'm gone and my annuity drops out. I should like to think of you and Ursula being able to live as you've always lived, without financial anxiety. These frightful taxes, and the value of money falling! Look at the poor Miss Elwins."

(The prospect of Ursula and me ever looking like the poor Miss Elwins was all I needed!)

"Perhaps Ida won't take to me," I said, grim and flippant at the same time. "Perhaps Eilys Mallins will inherit the lot. I'm not awfully good at getting on with new people."

"She can't help taking to you." Mother's confidence in her daughters was sublime if misplaced. "She can see at a glance that you are a really nice girl. They're rare in these days."

If it was possible to feel worse, I felt worse. But there was a noise on the gravel outside. The taxi had arrived, the moment of departure had come, and for good or ill I was off to Bavaria. Action at last.

We embraced and exchanged kisses, heavily flavoured with rue and this-need-not-have-been. Mother and Ursula had decided against going to the station with me; public good-byes were embarrassing.

"Don't forget," said Mother for the tenth time in three days, "to look out for Jean at Paddington. She'll look after you and she might go with you to the airport. And do be careful, dear—"

"Yes, Mother."

I got into the taxi and began the long series of wavings which at last carried me out of sight.

2

THE journey was no less tedious than I had expected. There was no soaring of the spirit when I actually got off the mark, such as should by all accounts be the reward of enterprise.

At Paddington I had no need to look out for Jean. Looking more like a kangaroo than ever with her narrow, inquisitive head, thin wiry superstructure, and over-developed base, she came loping along the carriages before the train stopped. She wore a green knitted pixie hat, a short coat of imitation leopard which would have sent my mother—"Only the real thing or nothing, dear"—into a fit, a skirt of purple tweed, and dusty black suede ankle-boots.

She insisted on bundling me and my luggage into her car and driving me to her Pimlico flat for lunch.

"No trouble, old girl. Left it all ready to hot up."

We set off in a series of forward darts and abrupt brakings. Jean was the kind of driver who grips her wheel with brutal pressure and holds it down as if she expected it to rise up and hit her in the eye. But we made Pimlico.

Over tinned tomato soup, fish pie, and fruit salad, she got down to discussing my plans.

"I got a shock when your mother wrote and told me what you were up to, and about meeting you. I didn't think you had it in you. But frankly, old thing, I think you're a bit mad to go off to this outlandish place at some old woman's whim."

"You make it sound more frightful than it is."

"Of course if your object is to break away from home—"

"It isn't."

She looked aggressive. "Of course it is. It's a normal reaction. You're normal, aren't you? It's high time, too. I'm all against repressed lives."

"Come off it, Jean," I said. "You make me sound like something out of a museum."

"No offence, old thing. I've always known that you lived in an artificial world. So did I, once. I broke away, and look at me now."

What I saw didn't seem to offer any cogent proof of the value of breaking away.

Jean went on, "But why on earth couldn't you just have come to London and trained for something and got a job? Not that it would be all that easy. You're not young and you're not really any good at anything. But I could have helped. I've got friends who are starting things and want partners. Bookshops, and decorating, and guidance bureaux, and students' hostels."

Being a partner in the enterprise of one of Jean's friends left me strangely unmoved. Who was to blame that I found myself looking at her over the coffee cups with a kind of loathing, she who had been my school friend, my best friend at fourteen?

"I do believe so passionately," she was saying, "in everything being free. Everything!"

"It certainly opens up prospects."

"That's why it does me good to see you showing a bit of initiative at last, Delia, though I can't say I'm in favour of you going Out

There. I could have fixed you up so nicely. And it's a long way for your first little spreading of wings, isn't it?"

"Is it? It's only a few hours from London, and I can come back if I don't like it."

Her eyes popped. "Oh no, no, old thing. You couldn't do that. That would be defeatism. Once you've started something you've got to grit your teeth and see it through. Never haul the flag down."

"Right!" I said. "You've got me in Bavaria for the rest of my life. I feel fine. What now?"

She looked at me, highly doubtful.

"Need you go today? Let's ring up and postpone your flight. You can stay here, I'll shove up the camp bed for you. I'd like you to meet a friend of mine who's running a—"

"No!" I shouted. "I'm going to Ida von Mester's. I wasn't sure before, but you've settled it for me. I want to start in on this tooth-gritting business, it sounds fascinating."

She said, visibly deflated, "Well, if anything does go wrong and you don't want to lose face, remember you can always come to me. I won't even say, 'I told you so.'"

"Thank you. That'll be a comfort."

She insisted on driving me to the airport, and she talked all the way about the mistake I was making. It wasn't worth arguing, so I let her. She wasn't nearly so good at it as Mother and Ursula. And I never wanted to see her again. So friendships die.

Jean proved to be deadly efficient when it came to dealing with tickets, luggage, passport, boarding card, and finding Gate B.

"There's nothing to flying," she told me. "In fact, old thing, it's damn boring. Do you want any food—magazines?"

"No food. And I've brought a book."

"You'll need it. There's nothing to see."

"Don't wait," I said. "There's twenty minutes yet."

"What, leave you? Not jolly likely. It's just at this point that novices develop nerves."

To be called out at last was bliss.

The flight didn't bore me, it was too much of a novelty, but landed at Munich stone deaf, and what with airing my correct, over-academic German, and not being able to hear a word that anybody was saying in reply, nothing was easy.

I was directed to an hotel, and spent a strange, unrestful night discovering the limitations of German bedclothes in midwinter and picturing my own empty room at home.

Next morning was better, very cold but bright and tangy, and I got myself to the station and into a slow train which eventually decanted me at Dorfen. I was actually here at last, and it felt a world and an age away from yesterday, from home, and Jean, and *The Times*, and our butcher's telephone number.

There was apparently nobody to meet me, certainly no one in sight who looked as if she might be Ida von Mester. I came out of the station and stood blinking in the sharp sunlight. The short approach was paved with the cleanest of white flags and flanked by lines of chestnut trees, all of a size, and looking like the guard of honour at a civic ceremony except that their clear, bare lines were even more impressive than gorgeous uniforms.

Beyond I saw the neatest of town squares across which glided a bus painted bright blue, and there were shops with deep roofs and fanciful eaves, a bandstand, a spruce traffic cop in white gloves standing on a black-and-white-striped podium, the whole thing like a toy town laid out on a flat table.

Dorfen. It sparkled in the cold, and smelt of woodsmoke with a dash of wine.

I wondered if I should wait, or take a car out to Ida's place. A driver approached me and asked my name. He had been sent to meet me. Gratefully I climbed in, feeling better and less unwelcomed.

We drove out into the country—real, deep country—and along a narrow valley with a handful of scattered houses which you could hardly call a village. There was hardly anyone about. I saw a deserted sawmill, and got an impression of thunder-green larches, their branches still untipped by the vivid shoots of spring. There was a lush, woody wetness in the air. I hadn't expected a place so solitary.

Then came Ida's house among lawns and pines, looking extremely Gothic, all gables and high stone-framed windows and elongated walls. The driver seemed delighted to have got me there at last, and hardly had the car ground to a stop at the steps below the big double doors than they flew open and Ida—it could be no other—rushed out and seized me.

"Dahling, you're here! Are you really, really Delia? What must you think of me for not coming to meet you! But the others are out and I did want to have a meal ready for you."

I had expected something flamboyant, but she was charming. Short, but with a taut, trimly rounded figure, she was amazingly well preserved for a woman who couldn't be far short of seventy. Her hair was ash-blonde and curled prettily, her make-up was quite magic, overlying all wrinkles and age-blemishes which were not actual furrows, her eyes were light grey, heavily fringed, and her manner was so vivacious that she couldn't walk, she tripped.

Her dress was unusual, slightly medieval, made of blue velvet edged round the neck, wide sleeves, and hem with fur, and over it she wore with casual gaiety a gingham apron.

She began to cope with the car driver, who at her bidding carried my luggage inside. Then she turned to me again, and carrying the welcome on from where it had left off, kissed me with enormous zest on both cheeks.

So this was Ursula's huge, glittering personality. She didn't seem to me at first sight to glitter, but she gleamed, a nicer word.

"You didn't have any difficulty in getting here, dahling? You do speak German?"

"In a school text-book sort of way."

"We speak English here mostly. It's good for the boys."

The boys? I didn't know that Ida had any family. If she had they must be fairly middle-aged boys.

"I'm just doing the lunch," she explained. "There's a fair on at some village and they did so want to go. Now come inside properly."

She linked her arm through mine and led me into a black-and-white-tiled hall with dim, Gothic-looking pictures on the walls—castles and gorges and thunderstorms—Chinese vases of towering size in niches, an enormous pinewood table richly carved, and matching chairs. And, happy sight, a log fire on which you could have roasted if not an ox a full-sized pig, in a stone fireplace through which you could have driven a small car.

"Now let me look at you properly—I say!" She poked a finger into the middle of her cheek. "You're nice-looking, but not in a smart, modern way, and you really are a bit fat!"

I wasn't pleased. Everybody resents being called fat, and my build was against my ever being slender. My mother—she and Ursula were delicately boned and tiny of frame—had always blamed it on Father's family.

"Now don't take me seriously. I like you so much already, and I hope you like me." She gave my shoulder a playful shove, and matched my slight frown with an enchanting smile which nobody could have resisted.

"I know I shall. Do you want me to call you—well, Aunt, or—"

"Dear, no! I'm Ida to everybody. Aunt? It makes me shudder. Now run along upstairs and pick yourself a room while I hurl a few things on the table." Seeing my look of surprise she added, "You can have any room in the house you take a fancy to, they're all clean. Except mine. I don't mean mine isn't clean, I mean it's the only one you can't have. If you want Jarzy's he won't mind turning out for you—he said so. Or Onkel. Or Gladys."

Resigned to bewilderment, I hoisted my grip bag under my arm, took a suitcase in each hand, and began to climb the broad staircase of polished pinewood. This led to a square landing with doors all round it. I opened the first I came to and saw a bare, wood-floored, sparsely furnished bedroom, clinically clean and containing a narrow, white-quilted bed. I wasn't drawn to it. It reminded me of the nursing home where I left my appendix. I closed the door and went on to the next room.

As soon as I opened the door I saw that this was Jarzy's room—or Onkel's. Who on earth were they? And Gladys?

The bed was strewn with hastily cast-off male apparel. There were books and music scores all over the place, a diving mask on the dressing-chest, and masculine hairbrushes on the window ledge. The gentleman had also tried his hand at wood carving, for propped against the looking-glass was a half-finished round tray with a design of grapes. It wasn't very well done.

I withdrew and crossed the landing.

The next room I barged into was Ida's, it couldn't be anyone else's. After the clinical one and the hobbies one this was Bourbon Versailles. I caught a glimpse of a white flowered carpet, an ornate fourposter bed with a pink velvet bedcover and cushions matching the pink canopy above, a crystal chandelier, a winged, brocaded chair, and a gilt dressing-table with mirrors sprouting all over it. The doors of a wardrobe, white picked out with gilt, stood open revealing racks foaming with dresses.

I backed out again.

Next to Ida's was another unoccupied room but I judged that it faced north and would get no sun, so I left it.

That was all on that landing. A flight of stairs led to an upper floor, but I had lost heart for exploring, so I returned to the first room I had inspected, dragged in my luggage, pulled off my hat and coat, and sat down on the white bed.

Frankly I was depressed. My chin felt to be resting on my toe-caps. Ida was kind and full of charm, but I didn't like the set-up, it smacked of the theatrical, of the corny cult of bohemianism. And outside the narrow stone arches of my window was an over-large wintry landscape with a twilight-of-the-gods suggestion about it which reminded me that I was in Bavaria where anything could happen.

"De-eee-lia! Lu-uuu-nch!"

Coldly I hauled myself off the bed and went along to the bathroom to wash before going downstairs. Somewhere away in the back of the house Ida was carolling the *Habañera* from *Carmen*, and I followed the sounds to a large kitchen with a scrubbed table in the middle.

Ida's idea of hurling something upon this table was breathtaking. She had hurled to good purpose enough for eight people, a cold duck, a slab of ham, a glazed meat pie, at least three dishes of salad, sauces, rolls, butter, cheese, fruit, cream, pastries.

"Sit down, dahling. Help yourself. You must be starving."

"I haven't seen so much food in years."

"We're lucky. We're all among the farms. Did you find a room?" She sat down opposite to me and began to load a plate.

"I took the first one at the top of the stairs."

"Oh yes? In my husband's time some famous guests slept in that one. There aren't any famous people any more, only newspaper names—people who spring up on a gimmick and flop down again. No real characters with real panache. If you've got a sense of atmosphere you'll feel fine in that room . . . oh dear, look at me in my apron!" She tore it off. "You're not used to me yet. Do you think it's sordid of me to entertain you in the kitchen?"

"Of course not. It's a lovely kitchen."

"Jarzy and Gladys did so want to go to the fair, and Onkel's at school. Myself, I love eating in the kitchen, but Gladys won't often let me. She's got a horrid sense of pre-war standards, has Gladys."

(Gladys? Jarzy? Who were they—the servants? And did Ida ever explain anything?)

The food was so good, I ate and ate.

"Now, tell me," said Ida, "how's your dignified mother? What did she tell you about me?"

I racked my brains to think of anything nice that Mother had said about Ida, but mercifully she saved me by rushing on, "Did she make a fuss about letting you come?"

"She wasn't very keen for me to come, but I wanted to. You see, I've always been at home, it was a break up."

"And—oh dear—wasn't your sister killed in the war, or something?"

"She only got polio. We've always lived quietly."

"H'm. How old?"

"Twenty-eight."

She let out a huge sigh.

"I feel younger now than I did when I was twenty-eight. When I was twenty-eight I'd been married for six years to such a pompous young man, a K.C.—my mother picked him for me, they did in those days—and was entertaining formally in Thurloe Gardens. No letting your hair down forty years ago in Thurloe Gardens, South Ken. Motor-cars were highly experimental in those days, and my husband got himself killed in one a week before I'd planned to run away from him. I was arranging the final details when it happened, and I realized that Heaven was bent on keeping me respectable.

Humphrey left me a lot of money, and I felt bad about accepting it, seeing another few days would have put me beyond the pale, but I stifled my conscience and took it. The worst of stifling your conscience, dahling, is that once you've done it you've already formed the habit."

I gave a doubtful giggle.

"I don't think you like me terribly," she said. "You haven't taken to me."

"Oh, I do—I have. You're just not what I expected."

"Nobody ever is. That's one of the beauties of life."

"Excuse me for interrupting you, Ida," I said, "but isn't something boiling rather wildly on the stove?"

She gave a glance.

"The soup! Gladys made it specially and I forgot it. Will you have some now?"

"But I've got to the fruit."

"So have I, but I'm going to have some. What does it matter?"

I passed without fuss from tangerines to minestrone.

"I can't think you've taken to me," I said. "I'm always at my worst with new people."

"Oh, but I have!" She made a sweeping gesture with the soup spoon. "I take to practically everybody, it's a weakness of mine. It's when you live a sheltered sort of life that you get choosy about people—'I like so-and-so and I don't care for somebody else.' The only people I never took to were the Nazis, and thank Heaven my husband was dead before they really got going."

"Where were you during the war?"

"Here, of course. Where would I be?"

"An Englishwoman? They let you stay?"

"I didn't count as an Englishwoman, I'd been here so long I was part of the scenery. And the local people like me, I'm one of them. Of course in the end the twerps chucked me into Auschwitz, but it was my own fault and I only had to stick it for a year."

"Ida! You were in Auschwitz and you survived?"

"Looks like I survived, doesn't it?" She selected a slice of pastry. "Unlike some camps we got a daily food ration and I wasn't on the extermination list. They pinched my dentures, the devils, I must have looked a hag. But what a dull subject! One thing I never do is talk about the past. It's the most ageing thing and it dates you. One simply can't afford to remember anything about the nineteen-twenties, and as for pre-1914—! People automatically think you're ninety. So I never start a sentence with 'Do you remember?' I don't—and if I did I wouldn't want to. Are you ready for coffee?"

"I'd love some."

She brought the percolator to the table and set it bubbling. The cups and saucers were exquisite, each painted with a different little mountain scene.

"Pretty," said Ida. "Von Mester family heirloom. Most of his family got wiped out in the war. And I haven't anybody of my own, you're the nearest—you and Eilys Mallins—and you're only goddaughters after all. But it's high time I made my will, and you two ought to come in for a tidy chunk when I pop off."

I put down my cup.

"Listen, Ida. If you talk like that you'll make me feel like going home. I couldn't stay here under the implication that I was hoping to please you, and get something for it in the end."

"But what nonsense!" She gave a trill of laughter. "There's a lot of money and I've got to make some arrangement, but I won't talk about it if you're as sensitive as that. Let's talk about something else. Men."

"Men! Heavens, why?"

Her eyes became like saucers.

"Heavens, why not? When two women get together and don't talk about men they must be ready for the undertaker. Tell me, have you got an affair?"

"Why—no—"

"Good. There's nothing like making a new start in a new country, leaving everything tidy behind and no danglers."

I couldn't bring myself to tell her that I hadn't even left a dangler behind, that there hadn't been any danglers. It was too shaming.

Ida warmed her hands round her coffee cup.

"We must find you a new man, you must fall in love. Not being in love makes a woman dreary. The worst of nice English girls is that they aim at being the sort of woman that men respect—and don't marry. You wouldn't be that sort, would you? Now me, I'm always in love, it keeps me young."

That doesn't surprise me, I thought. Now who can it be? This Jarzy? Not Onkel. You couldn't be in love with a man you called Onkel. But one more suggestion that this Gothic monstrosity of a house was a love-nest and I'd be off home like a shot.

"He's my lawyer," said Ida dreamily. "He's about twenty-five years younger than I am, though I told him I was forty-nine. This must be about the last love of my life, such a depressing thought. The utter end. Wait till you meet him—oh, just you wait."

"Does he live in this house?" I could believe anything.

"Goodness, no. He lives in Dorfen where he has a practice. It was so wonderful to find an English lawyer, and I believe he does very well. He came out with the British legal commission in '46. Now I shall have to think seriously about who would do for you."

"I suppose we couldn't talk about something else?"

She looked disappointed.

"I suppose we could. But you've got to have something to occupy you while you're here, and—"

"I've already done something about that. Through the Red Cross. I'm going to work part time at the refugee camp near Dorfen."

She stared.

"Oh. Oh, are you? I had a feeling you were going to turn out the noble kind."

"Not a bit." I was irritated. "I might as well do something worth while. I can't hang around. Of course I'll help in the house, and—"

"It's all very sad," she said vaguely, flicking back a stray curl. "Let's go in the drawing-room if you've finished. We'll leave the washing-up, somebody will do it."

Remembering the décor of her bedroom, I rather dreaded the drawing-room, but it turned out to be a pleasant surprise. A big, well-proportioned room, comfortable and attractive at the same time, with deep sofas and thick, soft rugs, and on a dais a magnificent grand piano.

There was an open grate with a fading fire. Ida darted over and began heaving logs from the basket and casting them on the fire, but when I tried to help she wouldn't let me. Every movement she made was quick and lively and had, I thought, an air of bravado, an assertion of youthfulness.

I sat down on the nearest sofa. Ida having stoked the flames sat back on her heels and pulled a splinter out of her wrist.

"One thing we do have," she said, "is tons of wood frightfully cheap. In fact you can do your own felling if you want to. Jarzy does quite a lot of ours."

I couldn't stand any more of this.

"You haven't told me who all these people are that you keep talking about."

"Oh, they're just the family. They belong here, like I hope you and Eilys Mallins are going to belong." She gave me a rather sweet, appealing smile. "The only insurance against a lonely old age, Delia, is to make people care for you while you still have something of yourself worth giving in return. I know a lot of old women who are very lonely. They couldn't be bothered with people when they had their faculties, and now they can't understand why people can't be bothered with them. . . . Come and look at our view."

She scrambled up and took me to the window. We looked down a deep, wild, wooded valley which ended in a mountain like a craggy wall.

"I've been looking out at that for thirty years, and now it's all going to be drowned."

"To be—what?"

"Drowned. They warned me about it ages ago, and it's to be quite soon now. They're going to flood the valley and make a reservoir."

"But your house?"

"Oh, the house will have to go too. Any time now."

"Aren't you very upset?"

She spread her hands. "It's no use blowing one's top. It has to happen. I get compensation which will help to pay for a new house nearer town. You'll probably like that better."

"But you—after thirty years—"

She didn't look perturbed. "I'm attached to the place, but what's the use of worrying? When you get to my age you stop being affected by practically anything."

"What an awful pity it seems."

She wound her arm through mine and nudged me affectionately. "What do you expect me to do? Run round in small circles sobbing? I've never bothered about the past and I'm nearly indifferent to the future as well. Let's have fun in the present, otherwise we might as well be dead. It'll take more than my house being drowned to get me down, though it is a weird thought. There used to be a village—you'd pass through it as you came—but most of the people have cleared out already."

"I thought it looked deserted."

"And further up the valley there's a handful of cottages. A few old people cling on, they've lived there all their lives. They think this reservoir is the end of the world. Silly old fools. They're going to be better housed. They've less to complain of than I have."

I stood looking down the valley, the sparkle of winter spraying it with lustre, from the hilltops to the dark green depths. Even the milky mist of distance seemed to glow in the utter stillness.

"It is so beautiful."

"There are other beautiful ones. Come back to the fire."

The warmth caught me and I gave a tremendous yawn.

Ida crowed with laughter. "I bet you didn't sleep much last night."

"Those German bedclothes. There must be an art in keeping both ends of you warm at once."

"You poor pet. Now you're going up to your bed at once for an hour's nap, and you'll be as gay as a robin when the others come in. I shall fill you two hot water bottles."

I jumped up. "Please tell me where to find them and I'll fill them myself. I didn't come here to be a nuisance."

She told me where the bottles were kept, and that there was always water boiling on the stove. When I came from the kitchen into the hall she was waiting there, kind and smiling.

"Have a good rest, dahling. Make yourself at home. Everybody does here."

3

I BET they do! I said to myself cynically as I slid the piping hot bottles between the sheets. How many more of them, making themselves at home?

As I took off my suit and shoes I felt a surge of protective feeling towards Ida, battened upon by a horde of creatures who took advantage of her hospitality. But all my thoughts were blurred by tiredness, and though the bed was harder and narrower than mine at home it felt a haven of rest, and in two minutes I was asleep.

I woke to the sound of running footsteps on the stairs, and voices as people passed my door. A woman's, light and high-pitched, said, "You oughtn't to have let me eat that second one. I was all right until—"

My watch said a quarter to five. Hurray, somebody was back, now they might make a cup of tea.

But when I had dressed and found my way down a babble of chatter was streaming from the kitchen, and arriving there I found it was Ida who was making the tea.

"Oh, here she is!" She flung out a happy hand to me. "Here's Delia."

The two people in the room, unintroduced, gave me small, guarded smiles like children who have been told to be nice to a visitor.

There was a fair young man with bright eyes, high cheekbones, an energetic nose, and a tumbling forelock, and a thin little woman, fortyish, with a face like a Pekinese and a bitten bun in her hand.

(Gladys and Jarzy? Nobody told anybody anything in this house.)

"How d'y'do," I said cagily.

"You are welcome, Dahlia," said the young man, turning me into an autumn flower.

"How d'y'do. I'm sure you're dying for some tea," said the woman in a social voice. "Did you have a good journey?"

"Not bad. I'd never flown before."

"Nor have I. But it's all the rage, isn't it?"

Ida filled a large cup and passed it to me, along with a plate of buns.

"Gladys bought these at the fair. Try them—they're nutty. What else did you do at the fair, Jarzy?"

"Oh, we did go on everything, and we ate hamburgers at a stall—"

"He made me have two," said Gladys. "The second one was a mistake. I—"

Jarzy interrupted artlessly, "There were a lot of American soldiers there. They were buying things for the kids. It was all pande-burly. We brought you a present, Gladys won it throwing balls."

"Here," said Gladys, producing a paper-wrapped parcel which contained a china cat with a sinister smile. "Isn't it cute?"

"For me!" Ida couldn't have been more genuinely pleased if it had been a diamond bracelet. "Oh, but he's divine. I'll never part with him. I shall call him Sigismund. Oh, thank you, my dahlings, how lucky I am! I love him."

The other two looked pleased.

"And now, Ida, dearest one," said Gladys, "if you will take Delia to the drawing-room, Jarzy and I will set about making supper."

"I can help," I said.

"Oh, no, you're a guest."

(What are you? I thought.)

Ida grabbed my hand. "They want to get rid of us. Come along." She whispered as we went, "Gladys is a wonderful cook and hates to be helped. I am not so wonderful, and anybody can help me—see?"

"I get the idea, roughly."

"Gladys looks after me all the time." Her expression was soft, backward-looking to something with meaning for her.

With her hand on the drawing-room door she said, "It turns so cold in the evenings—" and flinging it open, "Oh, the fire is lovely. I hope Onkel isn't late, he was coughing this morning."

"So Gladys looks after you and you look after Onkel."

"You're quite wrong. Onkel looks after all of us. He's the only truly balanced one, you'll see. He thinks before he does anything, I wish I could."

"Is Onkel an elderly man?"

"Oh, my dear, no, whatever put that idea into your head?"

In the distance it sounded as though somebody had put on a record, for a high, clear voice was singing.

"Do I hear singing?"

"That's Gladys, chopping the vegetables. When I want to annoy her I say that the only good thing about her is her *Vissi d'Arte*."

"She certainly is good."

It was one of those sexless, birdlike voices which can reach and sustain C in alt with effortless purity of tone, marred only by a tendency to trill for the sake of trilling.

"My skylark!" said Ida. She crossed the room and opened the piano, cocking her head on one side at me.

"I suppose you don't play?"

"Yes, I do."

"Really? But how wonderful! It's miraculous!"

"Lots of people do, you know."

"But I'd wished it so much." Her eyes shone with delight. "Gladys has had to play for us, but her playing has no style—I'd rather die than tell her so, poor pet—besides, we need her voice and naturally she can't give her best to both at once. I do the contralto myself, and Jarzy is a nice tenor and Onkel a baritone. When we can get Gordon it's terrific, he's a true bass, but—"

"Excuse me," I said, "but who is Gordon?"

"But, dahling, I told you! I must have done. Now come over here and play me something, I can't wait."

I sat down and played the first thing that came into my head, trying not to be put off by Ida standing at my side and beating time gently with the china cat.

"Brilliant," she said. "But no passion."

"There wouldn't be any passion in Mozart, would there?"

"Maybe not, but there should be detectable emotion, like wine in soup. And I've got a feeling, dahling, that you'd play Liszt, Rachmaninov, and Stravinsky in much the same way. You need awakening."

Trying not to feel annoyed I went over to the fire and began to warm my hands. She joined me and pressed my arm.

"Don't be hurt—please!"

"I'm not—really, I'm not."

"I think you play beautifully and I'm thrilled. So will Onkel be. Gladys's playing used to sear his musical soul sometimes."

I felt my shoulders shaking, I had to laugh.

"Ida, please, who *is* Onkel?"

"But didn't I tell you?" She took my hand and made me sit on the sofa beside her. "He teaches in a school in Dorfen. He used to be a teacher in Berlin, but he was anti-Nazi and a Jew so he didn't last very long, poor sweet."

"Oh. Did you come across him at Auschwitz?"

"Well actually, Gladys and I met him the day the Americans let us out—"

"Gladys too!"

She looked at me quite reproachfully.

"I must have told you that. Well, we were a motley mob. Onkel offered me his arm and I took it, and we've never been separated since."

"But why 'Onkel'?"

"It was ages before I even thought of finding out his real name. We had a young girl with us, and she called him Onkel, and it stuck. It's easy to remember . . . And now I shall get the music out, and you can run an eye over some of the scores."

A door slammed.

"That must be Onkel at last."

A man came into the room, short, rather stocky, with a fine head of tousled brown hair and one of those mild but noble Teutonic faces which one associates with the period of Wagner.

"My dear Ida, I am so late." He had warm, brown eyes and his smile was sunny. "The wheel of the bus went phut."

She seized his arm and brought him to me.

"Look, this is Delia."

He brought his heels together, picked up my hand and kissed it. It was the first time anybody had ever done this to me, and I liked it.

For one twinkling moment he surveyed me.

"Miss Delia, you are very welcome. I am yet another one of the family for you to know."

"The last?" I said, laughing.

"Do there seem to be so many?"

"What do you think, Onkel?" Ida broke in. "She plays the piano very well. Isn't that an asset? What do you think of her?"

He scrutinized me, grave and friendly. I tried not to feel like a museum exhibit.

"She is kind, she has nice eyes, and I like her very much."

"Thank you," I said. "I return the compliment."

He beamed.

"Then all is well, and in the hall is a heaven-sent smell of Gladys's casserole. I cannot wait to get some."

"He eats too much," said Ida, slapping him heartily on the stomach. "All Germans do. Let's make for the dining-room, supper must be ready."

Later, we all got down to the work of the evening, with me installed at the piano. Never was I so thankful to be a good sight-reader, as they pushed score after score on the rack before my eyes. To have failed would have been unbearable humiliation in the face of all this musical enthusiasm.

The four of them made a semicircle beside me. Absorbed, unwearying, they sang their way through great dollops of Verdi, Wagner, Gluck, Puccini. They sang bits of *Fidelio*, *Lucia di Lammermoor*, *Pelléas et Mélisande*, *Die Fledermaus*. They had a go at Benjamin Britten. I had never seen people enjoy themselves so much. Their virtuosity fed by success, they turned to solo work, and by the time I had accompanied Gladys in *Mi Chiamano Mimi* and Onkel in *Kennst du das Land*, and Ida and Jarzy had ripped off half a dozen of their favourite arias, it was long past bedtime, though nobody but I seemed concerned about that.

Did they do this every night? I wondered. And if they did, how long could a normal constitution stand it?

At last they came to a reluctant standstill. Ida flung her arms round me dramatically.

"Delia, it was wonderful, the most magnificent evening we have ever had."

"We must have tired you out," said Gladys kindly.

I admitted it had been a long day.

"You had better go to bed," said Onkel, "or tomorrow there will be nothing left of you to play at all."

4

I FELT as though I could have slept on a board, but actually it was a long time before sleep came. In spite of hot bottles the night felt bitingly cold, and this silence was deeper than any I was accustomed to. I heard a clock downstairs chime one, then two, and three, before I fell asleep. Then it only seemed a few minutes before a tapping on the door awakened me and the half-light of morning was in the room.

Muddled as to where I actually was, I called, "Come in!" and in marched Jarzy carrying a tray.

"Breakfast for Dahlia," he announced gaily.

I struggled up, grabbed my dressing-gown and pulled it round my shoulders.

"Oh, you shouldn't have troubled."

"It is no trouble."

He placed a chair beside the bed and put down the tray. There was a pot of tea, milk, fresh rolls, and plum jam.

"No butter," he said. "We use it all up last night."

"It doesn't matter." I poured a cup of tea. He didn't attempt to go, but looked round the room carefully.

"I shall shut you the window. It feels very cold in here."

"Oh, thank you."

"Your stove is out. But look—I see it has never been lighted. My own fault. You must have froze in the night."

"I didn't even notice there was a stove, or I'd have been quite capable of lighting it."

"I do it now . . . that is better, you poor thing." Casually he sat down on the end of my bed, and said pleasantly, "I hope the breakfast is what you like?"

"Breakfast in bed is a terrific treat."

I had been away from home two nights and it felt like a month. Here I was sitting up eating breakfast with a strange, good-looking young man perched on the end of my bed as though it were the natural thing to do. It was a whole lifetime and several worlds away from home.

"Onkel is off to school," he said. "I have not the job at present. In summer I farm, but in winter the farmers do not want me. I wish we had our own farm here, but it is no use if they will flood the valley. I do the washing-up and the cleaning and such."

"Excuse me," I said, "but could you tell me what nationality you are? You speak very good English."

"I am Polish."

"Could Ida have picked you up in a concentration camp too?"

"Not me. Only Onkel and Gladys."

"Tell me about Gladys."

"Well, she is governess to some family at the British Embassy in 1939, and she get left behind in the rush and finish up in Auschwitz. Me, I escape out of Poland in 1940 and get to England where I join the Royal Air Force and am posted to a Polish squadron. I tell them I am nineteen, but I am only sixteen, but I look nineteen. I am shot down over Mainz and put in an Oflag. I escape and try to get to Switzerland, but I am pursue and I lose myself. It is not so nice. I find myself here, in Ida's garden, and I am in bad way. Ida find me, she take—*took*, you will forgive my English grammar—she took me and she looked after me for three weeks in this house. Then they find me and shove me back in prison camp. And the worst is they send Ida to Auschwitz, for what she did for me. Now do you wonder I have love and gratefulness to her? We did arrange it that if Ida and me are still alive when the war is over we will come back here, and this will be my home. Well, we are lucky, we come, and this is it."

I had stopped eating while he talked.

"That explains everything. Now I know why you're all here. Of course you'd stick together after sharing such experiences. But I don't fit into the picture at all. How can Ida have any use for me—or Eilys Mallins?"

He looked amazed.

"But Ida talk all the time about her goddaughters. She is so proud. She tell us, 'These beautiful girls they will fill us with glamour in the house.'"

I giggled. "You've had one disappointment already. I don't know a thing about Eilys Mallins."

"But she has been here. Yes, for two days, one year ago. She is very prettiful and wizard. She and me dance all night in the hall with records, and the sun come up bright, and we are tired, but Gladys bring us coffee and we go on dancing, dancing. She is gay, like a film star, and so beautiful, and she make us all laugh."

I felt utterly despondent. The vision of Eilys as my kindred spirit had slipped several notches. I couldn't even compete, already she had beaten me hands down. I might bash the piano by the hour, but she—prettiful, wizard, and like a film star—could dance all night and charm the ducks off the water.

"I hope you're going to like me," I said doubtfully.

"But we do." His face held the frankest possible smile. "Your face it is a shop window and we like what we see in it."

I gave a titter of amusement.

"It depends what kind of a shop. It could be an impressive one, with a length of satin and one Old Master in a gilt frame, or it could be the homely kind, all dusters and aspirins."

"It is the grand one," he said gallantly.

"Thank goodness." I went back to my breakfast with some feeling of relief. "This jam is delicious."

"Gladys made it."

"What's her other name?"

"She is called Miss Jones."

"She would be!"

"How do you mean, please?"

"Just that it sounds right . . . You mentioned about the valley being flooded. What a weird feeling, to think this house will be at the bottom of a lake. Will Ida be upset?"

He looked thoughtful.

"We will have to arrange something to take her mind off it. Something funny and excitable. Me, I shall be glad to have a lake. I will get some fine swimming."

"You're a swimmer, then?"

"Yes, and I am a great diver also. I can stay under water a long time."

I put down the tray.

"Well, I can't stay in this bed a long time. Goodness, it's nearly ten. I must get up."

He jumped up and lifted the tray.

"You are not to hurry, Ida said so. You will rest if you wish. We tire you out last night with all that playing."

I smiled. "I enjoyed it. But I did rather wonder if you went on like that every night."

"Oh no. It was just to show that we admire your playing that we go on and on and do not stop." He twirled the tray and made for the door. "The stove will soon be hot. You will stay there till lunch if you want. Do not worry, I shall go to my chores."

In front of the hall fire a little later I found Ida. She wore owl glasses and was tugging viciously at a large piece of needlework.

"Hurray!" she cried. "You're up."

"I should think I am. It's half past ten. Can you find me something useful to do?"

"Certainly not, dahling. You're going for a lovely stroll up the valley to make you feel romantic."

"There's nothing like trying," I said. "But won't you come with me?"

"Good gracious, no. I never walk an inch if I can help it. I was brought up to think it gave you healthy ideas and thick ankles, though yours look all right. When Eilys comes you'll have company."

"When is she coming?"

Ida threw her needlework down in a heap.

"In about a fortnight. She's with her father at present, he lives at Cannes and she likes to make her home with him. She always was fonder of her father than her mother, though the court divided her equally between them when she was a child, if you know what I mean."

"Jarzy says she's very attractive."

Ida chuckled. "Jarzy was very taken with her. She's pretty and gay and chic, you'll like her . . . Now buzz along, and see if you can meet an exciting man riding a beautiful horse."

"Am I likely to?"

"Oh, I believe in expecting thrilling things to happen, even if they mostly don't . . . Where's my needle?" She kicked at the pile of linen on the floor. "I felt like sewing so I got out this Thing. Will you believe me, I started it before the war?"

"What is it?"

"Heaven knows, and I've forgotten. It's a bedcover or a curtain or something. But it's rich-looking, isn't it? It may come in for the new house. I'll tell you what! I'll take you in the car this afternoon to see it."

"You mean you've got a new house already?"

"Of course." She gladly pushed her sewing away. "We're going to have such fun moving in. I shall leave most of the old furniture here and let it drown. One way of getting rid of it."

My thrifty soul revolted.

"But isn't that dreadfully wasteful? There must be some poor people who—"

She made a face at me.

"Oh, don't you sound priggish! Poor people don't want solid, old-fashioned stuff, anyway. They like shiny mass-production stuff and imitation satin on their chairs. Nobody would say thank you for plain pine beds and chests. It can all swim!" She made a dramatic arm-sweep. "You children shall choose furniture in München for your own rooms, and I'll pay for it, and Gordon can be as broody as he likes about the way I spend my money. It's my business and I want to have fun, and why shouldn't I?"

"Perhaps you won't feel so bad after all about leaving this house?" I said.

She ran a hand through her blonde curls.

"I'm not feeling bad. You'll never get through life if you're going to tear yourself to shreds over the things you have to leave behind as you go. I had a good time here once, in the old days. Joachim was the gay sort, more the Viennese type than German, not a typical 'von' at all. He'd been a student in Vienna and made love to all the famous beauties. That gives a man style. We had fabulous parties here, but that was in another life, a different world. I've forgotten it already, and the house has nothing to do with it. There's fun today and there'll be fun tomorrow. Mind you, Joachim carried me over the threshold the day I married him, and it turns me up a bit to think of fishes doing the same, if you know what I mean . . . and if you don't go and have that walk it'll be lunch time. Now enjoy yourself, and don't think of anything sordid."

I turned up the narrow valley road. It was a biting cold morning, with silvery sunlight falling from the huge pale blue sky on an unyielding earth. Beside the road ran a stream, a ribbon of brown, white-flecked water, and on either side were hazel thickets extending to the slopes. Then the larch plantations began, standing like regiments, and above them were the bare tops of the hills, slightly silvered and swept by blue shadows.

Far beyond the valley wall were white mountains, and there lay Austria and the Alpine ranges.

I remembered all kinds of legends as I squelched over the emerald moss beside the stream. This was a land of trolls and fairies, there was something exciting in the tangy air, and something had happened to me. Freedom. I felt like a plant taken out of a small pot and put into a much larger one—or even an open garden—where it can spread and bloom. I had spread, I didn't know about blooming. Similes can be carried too far. But I had put out a leaf or two since I left England.

I came to a cluster of tiny gingerloaf houses beside a little *gasthof*-cum-shop. Two or three old people were about and greeted me with the old-fashioned *Grüss Gott*.

I found myself sitting on a pine bench inside the inn, with its sanded floor, huge fire, and half-door open to the wintry valley, and listening to the talk of this handful of old inhabitants who clung to their homes until they would be forced to leave before the flooding began.

They were all very sad about it. One old man who said he was over eighty told me he had been born in the house next to the inn, and had never lived anywhere else.

"But you'll have a new home to go to, won't you?"

Oh yes. Everybody was being provided with homes. Some had already gone to them. He himself was going to live with his son, not far away, he would be comfortable, but it wouldn't be the same. This spot, near the lion-shaped rock, was home, and if they drowned it it was still home, and nothing should keep him away from the spot.

I told them who I was, and that I too was living in a valley house, due for extinction. Oh yes, the *gnädige* Frau von Mester's house. She was well-known and highly thought of, as her husband's family had also been in that neighbourhood.

There were handshakes and stein-clinkings all round. I seemed to have cheered them up by the time I had to go. I hurried home to find the family eating lunch and reading the newspapers.

"I said you'd be late," said Ida. "And you look sparkling. What have you been up to?"

"Drinking the wine of the hills," said Jarzy, giving me a generous helping of veal stew.

"I've been drinking more than that. Pilsener. And I've been talking to some of the old people up the valley. They hate having to leave."

"But they're enjoying the drama of it," said Gladys.

"One old man was very distressed. Siebler, they call him."

Gladys ladled cabbage and dumplings on to my plate.

"Enough?"

"Enough for six. I ought to start slimming."

"Who likes thin women?" said Jarzy.

"I do. Almost the first thing that Ida said to me was that I was too fat. I'll never forget or forgive."

"I think you are just right," said Jarzy.

"Bless you. You're a nice person."

"If we have enough petrol," said Ida, "I shall take Delia to see the new house this afternoon. Have we any, Jarzy?"

"Enough for that little journey and more. But you be careful!"

"You and your precious petrol!" Ida winked at me. "I suppose you think we're popping off to Salzburg."

"I was not think of the petrol," said Jarzy. "I was think you drive like crazy."

"Delia can do most things," said Ida. "Can you drive, Delia?"

"I had my own small car at home."

"Hurray! Then you drive and I tell you everything as we go along."

5

I HAD expected a journey, but it wasn't more than a few miles. Out of the valley, and down a country road, and Ida cried, "There it is."

It was a big chalet with a good deal of timber in its construction, a steep-pitched roof, and carved wooden balconies, standing in a garden with a shrubbery and a neglected lawn, winter bare.

"It looks uncared-for and empty now," said Ida, "but do you like it? The others do."

"I think it's lovely."

I ran the car up the short drive and stopped in front of the big balcony and the front door.

"Gladys says it looks like an hotel," said Ida. "That's only because the paintwork's a bit lurid. I shall have it all scraped and turpentined. You wait till you see the inside. All wood, with that rich piney smell that makes you sleep well. And look at that hill-side behind! In the spring it's covered with primulas, millions of 'em, pink and red and yellow and violet. Do you know, Delia, it's the sort of house I've always wanted to live in, ever since I got myself stuck in London with Regency façades and wrought-iron gates. It's a dream coming true."

"Who did it belong to before?" I asked as we got out of the car.

"Oh dahling, some ghastly people. Regular Nazis. I hope they haven't left any atmosphere behind. After the war *She* disappeared, and they sent *Him* to prison at the Nürnberg trials. They say *She's* waiting in Switzerland for *Him* to come out. But we won't think about them. We're going to be so gorgeously happy here."

She ran up the steps, her bare bright head gleaming and her loose fur-lined coat swinging.

"Come on in—if I haven't lost the key—no, here it is."

We went into a panelled hall, empty and bare in a fading, greenish light.

"Do you think it's got possibilities?"

"I can picture us sitting here," I said, "with a big log fire, light flickering on the walls and dancing on the silver coffee pot."

"Dahling, how beautiful!" Ida clasped my arm in both of hers, and sniffed noisily. "That pine smell. Do you get it?"

"Yes, I do. It's like very good bath salts. Ida, it must have been an expensive house."

"Pooh!" She snapped her fingers and her eyes danced. "What does that matter? You all like it. We shall have fun here."

She led me round a big drawing-room, a narrow dining-room with fitted table and benches of pine, a small sitting-room—"Onkel can do his homework here"—and a huge German *küchen* which reminded me of a stage-set for *Cinderella*.

"Let's go upstairs," cried Ida, lit by excitement. "I can't wait for you to choose your room. My, my! Those stairs need polishing."

"I'll enjoy doing it," I said.

"Will you really? We shall all have to work like mad."

On the upper floor she flung open a door.

"Now this is the room I'm having. It has windows on two sides. I've always wanted a room with windows on two sides. It's going to be spacious and extravagant—like me."

Her enthusiasm was rather touching. It struck me that here was a woman of nearly seventy, for the first time in her life having her own house, the house she really wanted and could do as she liked with. No wonder she skipped bright-eyed from door to window, and examined cupboards with the excitement of youth.

"Come on, dahling, you next. You get your choice of the others."

"I wouldn't think of it," I said. "I'm the newcomer. Of course the others must choose first."

She gave a hearty stamp on the boards.

"Oh, don't be so noble! You'll spoil everything."

"I'm not being noble. Just fair. Gladys and Jarzy and Onkel all come before me."

She frowned. "The men will expect you to choose before them in any case."

"All right. If they want to be chivalrous let them suggest it themselves. But I won't take advantage. And Gladys has first choice anyway."

Ida swirled her big purple coat round her.

"What a lovely, sweet, unselfish nature you have, dahling. But you've made me feel so disappointed. I brought you on purpose to choose your room, and you won't."

I burst out laughing.

"Oh Ida, what an act you're putting on!"

She considered. "Perhaps you're right."

"I know I'm right. But if you really want a selection, I'm willing to go round and have a look."

We peeped into the other bedrooms. There really wasn't much to choose between them.

"I'm quite taken with the one over the dining-room," I said.

"There you go! Choosing the worst."

"It isn't the worst. There isn't any worst, they're all nice. Let's put this business of choosing off until the others are here, though I think I'll finish up with the one over the dining-room."

She wasn't quite convinced.

"What about Eilys?"

"Oh, Eilys can have the one that's left. That's only fair."

She scowled at me affectionately.

"I'm glad you're mean and selfish enough to go as far as that. I suspect perfect angels." She led the way downstairs. "Very soon we must go to München to choose the carpets, curtains, and new furniture. You're all going to have the best of everything. I don't care what I spend, I shall enjoy it."

"You're frighteningly generous, Ida."

"No I'm not. I've got loads of money." She said it naturally and quite inoffensively. "I'll tell you what, you and I and Gladys will go. We can stay a night or two in München and hear some concerts, and we'll shop like mad. What terrific fun! I wonder if Gordon would find time to go with us? We must have an escort, it's impossible to go to München without a man, and Jarzy isn't sophisticated enough, and nothing would make Onkel skip that school of his. Would you like it?"

"Very much. But excuse me, Ida, who did you say Gordon was?"

"Gordon? Oh, I must have told you." She stood still in the hall. "He's my lawyer. English. So good-looking—oh, you wait!"

"I'm not much for handsome men. They always know it." I was trying to provoke her.

"Not Gordon. He isn't at all vain."

She whisked us both out of the house, and said suddenly, "Let's go on to Dorfen. We might as well make an afternoon of it, and we can have coffee and cakes at the new Swiss place. They say it's fabulous, all their ingredients flown in for the pastrycooks. I hope there's enough petrol. Jarzy will grumble at me, but what's a ration for but to gamble with?"

We drove towards town and Ida pointed out all the interesting bits.

"You can't think how it's changed," she said. "Believe me, when we came here thirty years ago the men used to wear *lederhosen* and the women *dirndls* with frilly petticoats. Now the only people who wear those are the tourists and they look absolutely ghastly. They've got the wrong sort of knees and waists. Look, that's the church, and the old Post Hotel—it's fifteenth century, I believe—with a beer garden where we used to go when we were younger and dance to the fiddles and concertinas. We're just coming to the station . . . and the *platz*—you can park there, on that side."

She led me across the road to a quaint restaurant.

"We must have a table in the window. We might see somebody exciting go by."

"Are there any exciting people here?"

Her eyes widened with shocked reproach.

"But Delia! There are always exciting people everywhere. When you don't think people are exciting any more you are finished. And if you don't expect something wonderful to happen it never will. Goodness, I always take it for granted that everybody I don't know is a spy or a film star."

We found the right table and Ida called the waiter.

"The pastries here," she told me, "will astound you."

"Everything here astounds me. Including the way they've got over the war."

Ida nodded. "They lost it, dahling, and the losers always come off best, don't they?"

She had placed me sitting sideways where I could see both room and window, while she herself sat facing the window with her back to the room. About three tables away, and behind Ida, two men were sitting. One of them I couldn't help noticing, nobody could. His looks were so strikingly handsome, so outstanding that he seemed almost more than life-size. I took in the magnificent build, the wide flat shoulders, the finely set head of dark hair just greying at the temples, the classic features and strong chin, the storm-grey eyes, the grace and power of the gesticulating hands. He had a face full of controlled energy, and the sort of personality that makes its impact from any distance. You could have put him in a corner of the room with his face to the wall, and he would still have pulled anybody's eyes.

I dragged mine away, and a minute later had to look again. Annoyed with myself, I stabbed at my pastry. Ida was chattering away, giving a tabloid biography of somebody who had just passed in the street.

I was going to have to look again. *I wouldn't!* Ida put down her empty cup.

"We'd better go," I said. "Jarzy will think we're joy riding on his precious petrol."

"There isn't any hurry."

"It's past five o'clock," I pointed out.

"All right—where's my bag? I'd have liked another of the ones with the nuts."

"It'll only make you fat—like me," I said.

She called the waiter and paid our bill, and as she did so the handsome man and his companion rose too. I saw them out of the corner of my eye coming in our direction, and the next minute they were beside us and Ida was exclaiming with delight.

"Well! Gordon! Don't tell me you've been there behind me all the time. Why ever didn't you come over and join us?"

"I'm with a client—I must catch him up."

His voice was as good as his looks, deep and dark and significant.

"Not for a minute, you mustn't." Ida was a flutter of smiles. "Look, this is Delia. She's here, and I adore her."

He smiled at me with flattering interest.

"I hope you're going to like Dorfen?"

"I like it very much. I think it's magic."

"It's a lively little town. Ida will see you miss nothing."

His dark grey suit was perfect, like his snowy linen and long blue silk tie. I felt slightly stunned.

We all walked out into the street.

"We've been to see the new house, Gordon," said Ida, fluttering her lashes. "Delia likes it. I've been thinking that she and I and Gladys ought to go to München to do the shopping. Could you come with us? Oh dahling, do! I won't be seen in München without a man, and you're so personable in case we meet any Grand Duchesses."

"When do you plan to go?"

"Any time that suits you. But while our enthusiasm's at boiling point, please."

He looked at me and crinkled his eyes.

"Did you ever know Ida when her enthusiasm went off the boil?"

"I've only known her since yesterday," I said, "but I can't imagine her tepid."

"You'll be worse than tepid yourself, you'll be frozen!" cried Ida, tapping him smartly on the arm. "Look at you! Walking about in this weather without a coat."

"I hardly ever wear one."

"Then you ought to. You're not a boy."

"Dear Ida, so flattering. Pricking the bubbles of a man's illusions. Up to this minute I thought I looked twenty-two. But

I think I can manage to go to München with you if you'll leave it for a few days. I'd love to meet some Grand Duchesses, preferably with legal difficulties."

Ida's eyes shone.

"All Grand Duchesses have legal difficulties. Oh, this is working out just as I want it. Now why don't you come home with us and have dinner?"

"I'd love to," he explained patiently, "but I told you, I'm in the middle of a business appointment. My client is discreetly waiting for me over there, and in about three seconds from now he'll take his business elsewhere. Where's your car?"

"Parked on the *platz*."

"I'll take you to it."

"Oh no, you'll not, if you're going to be so mean and not come to dinner. Good-bye, dahling, and I'll be ringing you about München."

"Good-bye, Ida." He gave me a warm and charming smile. "Good-bye, Miss—er—"

Ida and I walked to the car. The air, crisp and dry, was blue now with dusk. Lights flashed out everywhere.

"There!" said Ida. "Wasn't that lucky walking into him? Didn't I tell you he was gorgeous? And so magnetic. I'd give anything to be twenty years younger and marry him."

"Don't tell me that any male so spectacular isn't married already," I said lightly.

"Well, not at the moment. Of course he may have shed one or two wives along the road in his time, but that's neither here nor there. I don't see how any woman could meet him without falling madly in love with him. Have you fallen madly in love with him?"

"I never know when you're joking," I said, engaging bottom gear and slowly driving away.

"I never joke about love, it's too important. The awful thing is, you never get too old for it. Nobody young like you could understand that. You feel twenty-five inside when a gorgeous man smiles at you, and then you look in the glass and see that you're practically ninety."

"Oh Ida, you couldn't ever look old!"

"It's sweet of you to say it, dahling, but I have my dark moments."

"Well, cheer up now, or I'll tell Mr. Whatever-his-name-is that you went off the boil directly he left us."

She gurgled with laughter.

"Oh, you are funny! And he is Mr. Portmeed, but of course you'll call him Gordon like everybody else."

(Shall I? I thought. Shall I really?)

As we drove up to the garage Gladys came out of the house to meet us, slightly hysterical.

"Ida dearest, where have you been? You've been away so long I was worried to death. I expected you back for tea, I was getting frantic."

"Don't be silly," said Ida calmly, stalking into the house. "Delia was driving and she's terribly capable, and we went to town and had coffee and cakes at the Swiss place, and Gordon was in there. I asked him to come back to dinner but he had a client."

"Thank goodness for that." Gladys sounded edgy. "I should need about five hours' notice, everything has to be perfect for His Highness."

"He's going to München with us to buy the furniture."

"Oh really?"

"Delia and I will rush up and change. What's for dinner?"

"Chicken pie and Queen's pudding," said Gladys, whose taste in cookery was rigidly British.

"I'll only take a minute," I cried, "and then I'll come down and help you."

"That would be kind of you."

Ida tripped upstairs singing at the top of her voice,

> "There was a girl called Gladys,
> Her cooking skill was high,
> She made a rubber pudding,
> And a pterodactyl pie"

to the tune of *A-Hunting We Will Go*.

I felt an unreal sense of exhilaration as I pulled off my suit, sprang into a dress, and ran downstairs to help Gladys. I thought she might be feeling a little sore that I should be taken out for a treat while she stayed at home and did the work, but she was so pleasant to me that she obviously had no such idea.

Her only comment on the trip to Munich was, "Why does she have to drag *him* into it? She could have taken Jarzy."

For my part, I could understand why Ida preferred Mr. Portmeed for her escort, but I said nothing.

At supper Ida announced cheerfully and without warning, "We went round the new house and Delia has chosen her room."

My forehead flamed. I kept my head down so as not to see those looks of polite disfavour. (There she goes, pushing herself in, the snake.)

"I made her," said Ida. "And she chose the worst room. That shows how noble she is."

My head shot up. "Ida, really!" I said, outraged.

My hunted look met the calm and friendly eyes of Onkel. They twinkled.

"It was not the worst room," I choked. "There is no worst room. They are all lovely rooms."

"Not to be upset, Delia," said Onkel. "If Ida says you are noble, then you are noble. We do not argue with Ida. She call us what she like, and we sit down under."

They all smiled at me encouragingly.

"Thank you, Onkel," I said. "But I will not be called noble when I am simply being fair, and Ida knows—and oh, this is ridiculous!"

I looked round the table. They were all smiling. They all knew Ida better than I did, and it was the kind of house where nobody minded anything. Suddenly I felt happy, as if the evening was suffused with gaiety.

"Come, Delia," said Onkel, "you and I will choose the music, and sing."

He led me to the drawing-room.

"I can't call you Onkel," I said. "It sounds so silly. Please tell me what I shall call you?"

He looked delighted.

"If you could call me Franz?"

"Of course. That's much better."

"No one has called me Franz since my family, so long ago. I have missed it. Thank you many times."

He began to bundle music on to the piano rack.

"Look, you will have to play this . . . and this . . . and this."

6

Two days later Ida came running from the telephone.

"That was Gordon. He's going with us to München from Wednesday till Friday. And he wants you to have dinner with him tonight. He's calling for you."

"You mean you and me?"

"No, you silly girl. Just you."

"But whatever for?"

She rolled her eyes up. "He wants to get to know you! You can't get to know anybody except in a *tête-à-tête*."

"Well, it's kind of Mr. Portmeed, but—"

"And don't call him Mr. Portmeed like a typist in an office. You'll never get anywhere like that."

"Where am I supposed to get?"

Her eyes widened like saucers. "Have you no *ideas*? Really, Delia! He's irresistible. And I hope he takes to you, truly I do. If I can't have him myself I'd as soon you had him as anybody."

"Aren't you going a bit far?" I said. "I've only known him for three minutes."

"*Only* three minutes!" She tossed her head. "I would say two minutes is enough to know if a man's interested in you, and he obviously is, so go along and get dressed and mind you do me credit. He's taking you to the Magda, and it's very chic."

"Why? When is he coming?"

"In half an hour."

"Oh Ida!"

I stood in front of the long glass in my room, looking at myself critically. What I needed for this charmer was an off-the-shoulder black velvet with an eye-catching brooch slapped on a bit too low. And what this charmer was going to get was my slate-blue with the restrained neckline, which was all I possessed in the way of a dinner dress.

I put it on, and gave some assistance to my week-old hair-do.

Ida came in carrying a tray of pots and bottles.

"Oh dear," she said, "I don't like your dress, but nothing of mine would fit you."

"It's a good little dress," I said sarcastically. "And it's so exactly Me."

"All right, dahling, it'll have to do." She put down her tray and examined the contents with a pointed finger. "But the last thing you must look is subdued. A stronger lipstick, now, and just a little something to dramatize the eyes. Just a flick, but oh, the difference."

"I refuse," I said, "to look like a garnished salmon laid out on a dish."

She looked keenly disappointed.

"I could make you look irresistible."

"That wouldn't do," I said. "Mr. Portmeed is already irresistible. You told me so. It wouldn't do to have two irresistible people at one table. It would give the waiter shingles."

There were actually tears of pleading in her eyes.

"Please, please, please, let me. Just the merest flick, dahling."

I burst out laughing.

"Go on, then. Do your worst. I couldn't care less."

I looked at myself in the glass when she had finished. It wasn't me. It was a glamorous stranger with defiant eyes. I smiled weakly, and the Thing showed me two rows of white teeth in a film star mouth.

"I'm doing this for you, Ida," I said. "Not for any man."

The man arrived at half past seven in his car. We had a drink in the hall, and Ida chattered madly while I hardly said a word. Obstinately I thought he might as well be warned from the first that he had a dumb cluck on his hands.

In the car, going to town, we exchanged polite nothings. Was I settling down? Did I find the life a great change? How was I reacting to Ida's rather amusing set-up? She had told him that I had always lived very quietly in the country.

Fury filled my breast. Why does everyone hate to be accused of having lived quietly?

I gave him an imaginary picture of wildly exciting war experiences, bombs whistling down on First Aid Posts—the lot, and hinted that if Ida hadn't sent for me I should by now have been on my way to a job in Malaya.

He seemed impressed, and I found some meretricious courage. He was so handsome, so sophisticated, and yet so anxious to please, and sitting opposite to him in a luxurious restaurant, with a rosy lamp on the table and the band playing Viennese waltzes, I gave up fighting at last and let myself be dazzled.

Why not? This was new, this was intoxicating fun.

The wine waiter came to our table and Gordon asked me what I wanted. I knew as much about wines as a baby.

"You choose," I said. "Men always know so much better. I'd like to try something new."

It was the right approach. He smiled and gave the order.

"It was wonderful of you to come out here," he said. "You're going to be so good for Ida. I might have known she'd pick herself the right goddaughter."

"I was only eight weeks old when she took me on," I said. "It was a gamble."

"But Ida's instincts are infallible."

We finished the *hors-d'oeuvres* and he offered me his cigarette case.

"Oh no, thank you."

"Don't you have the habit of smoking between courses? Perhaps you're wise."

I was just going to say that I didn't smoke at all, but hated to appear naïve. I took a cigarette and he leaned across with his lighter poised. His finger lightly brushed my cheek, a nuance of a brush, and his face came near. It smelled of very good shaving lotion.

We arrived at the duck, done American style with orange and pineapple slices.

"So you've seen the new house," he said. "Ida has really gone to town on it, she doesn't care what she spends. I'm sure you're going to enjoy living there."

"Living? But I haven't even decided how long I'm going to stay."

"Oh?" He looked taken back. "I understood you were likely to make your home here. You're happy, aren't you?"

"Very. But I haven't made any decision about the future."

"But of course you must stay. You'll like it better and better. And it isn't nearly as far from civilization as Malaya."

I had forgotten about that imaginary job in Malaya. I mustn't go and trip up.

"Ida is too kind to me," I said. "She's quite startlingly generous."

"Ida is a very rich woman."

I put out a few spikes.

"What has that to do with it?"

"Don't be embarrassed." His deep grey eyes, his smiling mouth, were fabulous. "I'm her lawyer. I know all about her affairs."

"I'm not interested," I said almost curtly. "Either I like her for herself or I don't. As it happens I do, but if I thought there was anything mercenary about our relationship I'd be off home tomorrow. I mean that, Mr. Portmeed."

His look was warm and intimate.

"You don't have to convince me. And I wish you'd call me Gordon."

"If you like."

"I assure you, I'm practically one of the family. You can't keep up this 'mister' business, and I shall certainly call you Delia. It's one of my favourite names. Oh, you're going to have a busy time. You'll be so involved in all this removing, and chasing round with Ida here and there, that you won't have time to think about anything else."

I put down my knife and fork.

"I shall, you know. I have things planned for myself. As soon as

I get my breath I'm going to work at the refugee camp in this town."

He looked amazed.

"You are? Well, it's a deplorable mess out there. Whatever attracts you?"

"It isn't a question of attraction. I suppose I can do some good?"

He pushed out his lower lip and studied me.

"Are you by any chance a do-gooder?"

"A born one," I said coldly.

He looked down at his fingers, flexing and releasing them.

"There must have been unfortunate people in England for you to tackle without taking on the human waste of Europe."

"I don't look at it that way," I said. "The refugees need me more. They're in a mess because they're the victims of other people's beastliness, not through any fault of their own."

"True," he said. "But don't get the idea they're angels. They swear, they fight, and they drink like drains."

"So would you," I retorted, "if you'd gone through the same horrors and had as little future as they have."

"Could be." He gave me a quizzical look. "Aren't you serious! Another cigarette—yes? And your glass is empty."

I felt squashed, and angry with myself as though I had been talking like a schoolmarm.

"You started it," I said.

"I did not!"

We both burst out laughing.

"This is beyond me," he said. "Come on, let's dance."

I hadn't even noticed that the band had changed over to swing music and several couples were on the floor. Gordon linked his arm in mine as we rose, and every nerve in me pinged like a plucked guitar string.

He drew me on to the limited square of the dance floor. I was apprehensive because I wasn't much of a dancer, my experience having been confined to small country hops, remarkable mostly for the dearth of men under sixty.

With Gordon's arm firmly round me and his cheek an inch from mine I soon realized that this was something new in my life. He danced perfectly, steered me adroitly, and I hadn't the slightest fear of tripping.

In other ways I had already tripped. I felt a langourous warmth and dizziness, breathlessness and a dry mouth, and a general tingling which was foreign to me.

The music stopped and we went back to our table.

"Thank you, Gordon," I said. "That was lovely."

There! I'd called him by his name quite naturally. My mother would have had a stroke at the way I was doing this all over the place. Jarzy. Franz. Gordon. In her world, except in rare circumstances, you didn't call a man by his Christian name unless you'd known him from infancy or were practically engaged to him.

I was conscious that there wasn't a woman in the room who hadn't taken a look at my partner. Not only one look but several, sideways, under discreet eyelashes. And enviously! He seemed unaware of this, or perhaps he was so used to it that he was bored by all this glancing.

I was madly happy about everything except my dress. Mentally I tore it off and stuffed it into some handy incinerator. Some day I would have a dress like those other women, or die.

Gordon didn't seem to be looking at my dress. He talked amusingly about films, politics, personalities, skiing. He told a wildly funny story about a waiter and a dachshund. I couldn't look anywhere but at his marvellous face. We laughed a good deal, and my heart did happy somersaults.

Then we danced again, almost continuously. I told myself that he couldn't really be enjoying it, but if he wasn't he put on a good imitation. The floor got more crowded, the air hotter, the music livelier. Much of the time, pressed close, we tapped feet and hardly moved. I shut my eyes and thought, Let this last!

At half past eleven I said I must go.

(Always leave before he wants you to. Where in the past had I picked up that bit of worldly lore?).

"Must you really? The evening's gone like a flash."

"Really I must."

He drove me home. The car was narrow and his arm touched

mine all the way. He talked with cheerful insouciance, local legends, local gossip. I must—he said—go to Austria when the spring came, it was so beautiful.

When we got home it was past midnight.

"I'd ask you in," I said, "but I expect they've all gone to bed."

He looked disappointed. Perhaps I should have asked him in in any case. Perhaps I appeared gauche.

"Thank you for a most lovely evening, Gordon. It was marvellous."

"Thank you, Delia. I've enjoyed it tremendously."

He got into the car. I let myself into the house with the key Ida had given me. To my surprise Gladys came out of the drawing-room, very Pekinese in her cheongsam dressing-gown.

"I thought you might like a cup of coffee," she said. "Shall I make you one?"

"I'd love one." I was taken back by her offer. "But I could have made it myself. You shouldn't have waited up, Gladys."

"I don't mind. And Ida wants you to go in and say good night. She never settles down till about two. Come and get warm by the fire, I shan't be a minute."

I sat on the fender bench and held my hands to the red glow. I wasn't cold. Shivering slightly, but warm at the same time. Reliving every minute of the fabulous evening, every word he'd said, wishing my own conversation could have been clever and more provocative.

Gladys came back with a large cup of coffee. I sipped it gratefully.

"Well? Have a good time?"

(Was there a touch of astringency in her tone?)

"Lovely," I said guardedly.

"So you got on swimmingly with His Highness. I thought you would."

That was downright caustic, there was no mistake about it.

"Do you mean Mr. Portmeed?"

"Who else? There's only one—thank God."

"He couldn't have been pleasanter," I said. "We had dinner at the Magda. He brought me home. You don't seem to like him."

"I detest him."

"That's candid," I said lightly. "But why? He was awfully nice to me."

"He would be—to you."

"But what's the matter with him?"

She made a face. "He's slimy."

"Oh no! Not the least bit. I was prepared for him to be conceited and he wasn't even that. You can't really have anything against him."

"Not anything you could put into words. It's just how I feel."

A lame excuse for detesting anybody, I thought, and said, "Ida likes him a lot."

"Pah!"

"Oh, let's not talk about the poor man."

It was easy to see he had never invited her out. I was no beauty myself, and in ten years' time I might be on the shelf, making coffee for other girls coming back from dancing with fascinating men.

I gave Gladys the warmest smile I could summon up.

"It was sweet of you to stop up and make the coffee. Now I'm going to slip in and see Ida. Good night."

I found Ida sitting up in bed wearing a marabout wrap of vivid pink and reading a Colette novel.

She popped up like a jack-in-the-box when she saw me and her eyes danced.

"There you are at last! I've never stopped thinking about you all evening. Did you have a divine time? Tell me, tell me!"

I sat on the edge of the bed.

"I had a wonderful time, he treated me like a queen, we danced and ate and talked—oh, so glamorous!—and none of it was in the least real."

"What on earth do you mean, none of it was real?" Her eyes widened into indignant triangles.

"Well, he knew and I knew and you know that he only took me out to please you. It was a social duty and he carried it off with brilliance, dignity, wit, and aplomb."

"What the dickens is aplomb?"

"It's a quality that diplomats have. Look, I must get to bed, I'm dropping. By the way, I hated my dress."

Ida plucked a bit of my skirt between her finger and thumb, and screwed up her nose.

"It's horrid. I'll buy you a beauty."

"You can help me to choose one. I'll buy it myself."

She bounced in the bed. "I wish you wouldn't be so disgustingly independent."

I got up. "Night-night, Ida dear. I'm terribly tired."

"*Tired!*" She gave a small shriek. "You're not getting away with that. I want to know everything. What did you and Gordon talk about?"

I pretended to think.

"Oh—refugees."

"*What!*" she screamed. "No, oh no, I won't believe it, I can't bear it. A wonderful man and soft lights and wine and dancing and you talk about—oh, not even you, Delia, you couldn't. You're teasing me, dahling, and you know perfectly well what I'm dying to know. Did he make a pass at you?"

"Certainly not."

"He didn't? Oh Delia, what were you thinking of not to—"

"He's got beautiful manners," I said.

She beat her fist on the satin bedcover and gave a low moan.

"That's the end—the last straw. You'd every chance in the world, and all he shows you is his beautiful manners. When I was your age—"

I began to laugh. "What did you expect him to do? Hurl me on a divan?"

"At least that would have meant something."

"Good night, Ida." I kissed her cheek. "Thank you for arranging such fun for me. I really enjoyed myself."

"Good night," she grumbled.

Safe in my own room at last I stared at my reflected face in the glass. The make-up was still flattering, but the look in my eyes disturbed me. Eyes that peered half eager and half afraid down the slippery slope of infatuation. It was mad. Surely I had the strength of mind not to give way to it.

I would not think of him. The eyes in the glass hardened. Common sense had won. I slept without even a dream.

It was Sunday morning, brilliantly fine, rime on the hard earth. I woke early, felt wonderful, poked my stove, sat up in bed and wrote to my mother and sister. How to translate this world into terms of theirs? It was almost impossible.

This is a beautiful place. Ida is charming. I am so happy here. Trivialities like these didn't begin to touch the fringe of my present state, but they were all I could use—and all they would understand without alarm.

I filled my letter with diluted pleasure and reassurance, comforting affection, but no enchantment.

Jarzy, Franz and I drove to church in Dorfen, all three companionably in the front seat of the car. Ida had said that her cough always came on in the quiet bits, and Gladys that the world was in such a mess it had put her off religion completely.

"You think it strange that I do?" said Franz. "I go because I like it. I am of a universal faith."

Gladys said that was more than she could take in.

In the car we talked music all the way, and I was the one who knew the least. Jarzy had learned to sing in a choir school at Warsaw, Franz in the old days had never missed a Bayreuth festival. They were both good company, Jarzy effervescent, Franz knowledgeable, perceptive, and with a shrewd wit. Hard to realize that a week ago I hadn't known they existed, and here we were today, friends, gaily arguing, bantering, singing snatches of this and that.

A bell was ringing in the steeple of the small, white church. Inside the seats were of pine, stiff-backed. There were more people than I'd expected and the minister was young and eloquent. At the end he came and spoke to me by name, answering my look of surprise with, "You have come to stay with Frau von Mester. I have heard of you from the American lady at the refugee camp."

"Mrs. Nixon? She wrote to me. I'm hoping to go and help her there soon."

"She is looking forward to that very much. And I hope I shall see you there myself. I go two or three times a week."

I walked on and joined the men. Jarzy decided that we should go home another way. It was midday and the winter sun was as high as he could climb and as dazzling as he could shine. The north wind had polished the outlines of the hills and put a burnish on the dark green woods, deepened the purple shadows and made the far-off snow crowns brilliantly white. Every stretch of water that we passed was sapphire blue, every pine-tree with its formal shape stood out sharply and was rimmed with light.

"Look!" I kept saying. "Oh look . . . look."

"Wait till spring comes," said Franz, "then it will be something to see."

Everybody, I thought, is taking it for granted that I will still be here when spring comes.

7

IDA, Gladys, and I left for Munich by train. Gordon had gone on the day before. All through the journey one half of me was looking forward to the excitement and fun of what I should see in Munich while the other half hugged a defiant core of joy that I was going to see Gordon again.

The hotel was big and splendid, full of business men, tourists, and American officers, and Ida in her lavish way had booked us rooms with private baths.

Gordon joined us at lunch, looking in every way the perfect escort. As he smiled at me I felt a vibration. I began to read the menu as if my life depended on it.

He was business-like.

"Now, Ida, if you're planning to spend a lot of money, I do ask you to think. That's all—just consider."

She made her eyes large and provocative.

"Do you mean all my tins and coppers and mines and things are sagging, or softening, or easing, or whatever it is they do?"

"Well, no—but—"

"Then what are you bothering about?" She gave a triumphant crow. "I've come to enjoy myself, and I'm going to spend everything I've planned to spend. Don't you be such a wet blanket, Gordon."

"I only want to remind you that you're buying luxury goods at highly inflated prices. Black market prices, in fact."

"All right. So I am," she said complacently.

"And I'm speaking to you as your lawyer."

"Then don't, dahling. Speak to me as my loving friend."

She beamed at me, then turned down the corners of her mouth, and said, "I don't know why we brought him. He's going to spoil all our fun."

"I don't know why we've brought him either," said Gladys. "Jarzy would have been much nicer."

Gordon pretended to be mortified.

"Do I get up and go?"

Ida put her hand on his. "Don't be silly, dahling. Eat your trout, it's delicious. We're going shopping this afternoon."

"For furnishings?"

"No, for clothes. You're going to choose us each a dress for the concert tonight. I won't have you sitting with us and looking at every woman's dress but ours."

He crinkled his eyes.

"I never notice what women have on if I like the women."

Ida rapped his fingers with the end of her fork.

"That's what all men say, and it isn't true."

We drove to a dignified house in a quiet square. In a velvety salon with brocaded walls there were no dresses to be seen, only gilt chairs, and a willowy, blonde vendeuse with a queenly manner. It was not the kind of place where I had ever thought to shop.

"We wish to see dresses suitable for the concert tonight," said Ida. "For all three. My friend is critical and extremely wealthy. He is only interested in the best."

Gordon set his lips and glared, but Ida couldn't have cared less. She was having a good time.

Dresses were paraded on slender models of outstanding grace and beauty. I didn't see myself in any of them, my heart sank.

"Give your mind to it, Gordon!" Ida cried. "Don't just sit there, you're not trying. Exclaim a bit, can't you."

"All right," he said lazily. "We'll have the grey brocade for you, with the blue roses. It's wickedly eye-catching. I don't know what Delia wants, she'll have to give me an idea."

"None of them would fit me by miles," I said despondently.

The vendeuse chipped in. "For the *gnädige Fräulein* any dress will require the merest hint of an alteration. It can be done in an hour."

"Hurray," said Gordon. "Then I go for the red one. It's your dress, Delia."

"Heavens! Me in red?"

"It's subtle," he said. "You'll look perfect in it."

"Gordon is always right," said Ida. "Have it taken to the fitting room. Now for Gladys."

Gordon looked bored with the game. Gladys scowled.

"The blue and black is charming," he said dutifully.

"I hate it," said Gladys.

"Perhaps you'd rather choose for yourself."

"I would," said Gladys. "I'll have the green one."

I felt a bit bored with Gladys and her pointless dislike of Gordon.

We were fitted, and left the salon. The dresses were to be delivered shortly to the hotel. The murmuring over so many thousands of marks had made me nervous.

"Go and get your hair cut, or have a drink, or something, dahling," Ida told Gordon. "I'm going to get the girls some lingerie."

We went to a store and she loaded us with French chiffon undies, to say nothing of cosmetics, and came out into the street again to find that Gordon had bought us each a bottle of scent.

"I hope they're all the same," said Ida, tearing off the wrapper.

"As if I'd have my women in a smell-fight!"

In our beautiful dresses, wafted on a cloud of Arpège, we went to the Bach concert. I sat between Gladys and Ida with Gordon beyond Ida at the end of the row. I was glad it was that way, it gave me a chance to take in the magnificent music. I knew I had never in my life looked so good as in that red dress, the cut and colour had an enchanted quality. Ida too looked exquisite and years younger than her age, with those flamboyant roses standing out on the demure grey. Gladys's green didn't suit her, but that was her own fault.

Knowing that many women's eyes were on Gordon, Ida flirted with him to the top of her bent, enjoying herself hugely. He, I had to admit, took it admirably, playing it her way but never overdoing it.

All next day we spent on heavy shopping for the new house. It was strenuous. Normally consumer goods were in short supply, but Ida knew where to go. Carpets, curtains, furniture were chosen. Gordon advised, I put in my oar when I felt I could give intelligent help, Gladys's principle was to select the cheaper article of two, Ida's was, when in doubt buy both. At the end of the day she was the freshest of us all.

There would be some delay in delivery, she was told.

"Well, don't delay too long," she retorted with spirit, "or I'll be sitting up to my knees in flood water."

Throughout dinner, when the rest of us were too tired to talk, she chattered with unabated enthusiasm, recapitulating every purchase. The furnishing for our individual rooms, was I satisfied? Was Gladys satisfied? Would Jarzy and Franz like what we had chosen for them?

We went to the opera where an Italian company was doing *Tosca*. I sat next to Gordon this time, and it was fatal to concentration. I tried desperately to take in the superb music, but his shoulder was just too close to mine, brushing it occasionally, making me dizzy—and exasperated.

Back in the hotel we sat in the hall and ordered coffee.

"I'm dropping," said Gladys. "Aren't you, Delia?"

I nodded. "It's been so thrilling. All day."

Even Ida admitted that there were limits to what the human frame could stand.

A man known to Gordon came and spoke to him, and they went off together to the American bar.

"Come, girls, bed," said Ida. "I feel thirty this minute, but I shall feel ninety tomorrow, curse it."

We collected coats and bags and went up in the lift. Before we reached our floor I discovered that I had left my chiffon scarf downstairs. The others got off, and I went down again. The scarf was where I had dropped it, and as I picked it up Gordon came out of the bar alone.

"Don't say you're packing up the evening! Have the others gone to bed?"

"Yes. I came back for my scarf. I'm just going."

"Oh no—please. You haven't had your last drink, and I'm going to keep you company. What shall it be?"

Weak-willed, I sat down. He called a waiter and gave the order, whisky for him, a glass of sherry for me.

"This will wash away the taste of the hotel coffee which to me seems heavily *ersatz*." He sat down comfortably and gave me a long, relaxed smile, sipping his drink lazily. "That's what we needed, Delia. There's an awful lot of love in *Tosca*."

"Is drink the antidote to love?"

"It's the consequence, isn't it?"

"Are you being cynical? I suppose all lawyers must be, after seeing the worst side of people so much."

"What worst side?"

"Well—greed, vindictiveness, deceit, quarelling."

"Oh, but those things are often very funny. Human weaknesses are the most amusing things in the world—like tragedy in the theatre. You think your heart is being wrung, but actually you're being entertained."

"I suppose that's true." I put down my glass. "But a profession that deals in nothing but human weaknesses could be wearing."

He shrugged.

"My profession is a stepping stone."

"To what?"

"Oh, I'm ambitious. A law practice in Dorfen isn't any great shakes."

"If you were in England you could become a K.C. And then a judge. You'd look awfully well as a judge. Or in robes at a Coronation."

He laughed aloud.

"I haven't the right qualities. Nor the capital. And I'm not in

England, and I don't see myself in the law for ever, and I think you're trying to take the mickey out of me. You practically ignored me all the time at the opera house."

My heart gave a thump.

"I ignored you! I was listening to the opera. What did you expect me to do—chatter?"

"That's a prevarication. What have I done wrong?"

His impact on me was gale force ten. I got up.

"I'm sorry if I was dull. I must have been flattened out by all that shopping. I'd better go to bed. Good night."

His eyes were quizzical and his lips firm.

"Oh no. You've got your coat. Put it on, and we'll take a walk round the town. München is fun after dark, and there's a moon coming up."

"It's much too cold—and too late."

"I'll see you're not cold," he said meaningfully.

I shied away like a nervous pony. Already Ida would be popping along to my room, wondering why I hadn't come in.

"Ida will be waiting for me."

He stood up. "Delia, come here!" He looked tall, peremptory, magnificent. It was like being issued an order by Augustus Caesar. My knees shook.

"Do you think Ida is going to read you a lecture for going out with me? Be your age!"

"I am being my age. It's past midnight."

"Are you frightened of me, or something?"

"I'm not frightened of anything or anybody."

"Then put your coat on when I tell you, and don't argue."

We walked along a lighted street and into an even brighter lighted street buzzing with bars and pavement cafés. There seemed to be more people about than in the middle of the day. It was gay, exciting, carefree, un-English.

The boughs of the plane trees made black shadows dance across the pavements under the white arc lights, voices were dancing too and strains of music. Gordon took my arm and led me to a table. Behind us a concertina band was playing the latest musical comedy hits.

"What are you going to have?"

"A Schnapps," I said wildly.

"What on earth for?"

"They always do in books."

He said to the waiter, "Two beers."

We sat watching the people go by. The moonlight stood no chance with the street lights, but the sky above was like clear polished steel flooded with silver radiance. It was a perfect night.

A man came along and started talking to Gordon, who introduced him to me as Otto Something-or-other and asked him to sit down and join us. He and Gordon talked so fast in German that I couldn't follow. Then two more people turned up, called Mignon and Paul. They knew Otto, so they stayed. Then an American called Burt arrived with a girl called Frieda. Frieda took an interest in me and asked me if I'd been to hear Gersib play, and I said no, we'd been to *Tosca*, and she said, "*Mein Gott!*" and lost interest.

Everybody jabbered at the tops of their voices, and Paul and Mignon kissed between sentences. At last we all got up and moved along to another pavement café, and lost Mignon and Paul, and collected Pepin and Harry and Leni and Yacob and George.

Leni, who spoke English, asked me was it true that Englishwomen had given their wedding rings and the gold out of their teeth to build a gold statue of Winston Churchill for the nation, and if so, what had he done to make the English throw him over as soon as the war ended?

I said I couldn't possibly begin to explain British politics, nobody could, and Otto said it was well known that England was nothing but the mouth of Eisenhower.

Then we went to another café kept by a friend of Yacob's, and by then we had lost some people and gained some more, but they were all the same, talking about Art (the fundamental thing), the Russians (power politics), the French (existentialism), the Berlin blockade, the American way of life, having no future, the atom bomb, and where do the Jews go from here? Leni, who had taken a great fancy to me, asked me how long Gordon had been my lover, and I said he wasn't, and she said why did I deny what was obvious? Gordon caught the exchange, and winked at me. I felt delirious.

We finished up at a night club full of deafening jazz amid blonde German girls, business men, tourists, Latin types, and students, and I only danced once with Gordon—Leni appropriated him and wouldn't let go—and the rest of the time I was crushed up against the Americans, Burt and Harry and George, who told me I was a girl that a guy could tell his troubles to, and anyway, the English-speaking people ought to rule the world because nobody else had a clue.

"Are we going home?" I said to Gordon at three a.m.

"Might be an idea," he admitted.

George said, why not all go round to his apartment where he had the newest American records that you couldn't buy yet in Yew-rup, and in the midst of the confusion—everybody preparing to go with George—Gordon and I escaped at last.

In the streets most of the garish lights were out now, and the moon, silver-green, was triumphant. It was magical.

"Smell anything?" I said.

"Such as—?"

"Fresh air. It's heavenly."

My feet hurt in their new shoes and I limped. Gordon took my arm. It was blinding bliss.

"Let's catch a taxi."

In the taxi he put his arm round me, and a minute later he kissed me. It was over too quickly to take in, and wasn't the thrill it might have been. I had a feeling that he felt he had to.

He sat back. I yawned.

"Wasn't it fun?" I said.

"You enjoyed it?"

"I certainly did. All those crazy types."

He laughed. "They certainly are."

At the hotel the yawning night porter took us up in the lift.

"Thank you so much, Gordon," I said. "It was all the greatest fun and something new to me."

"You see! I was right to make you go." He stooped his handsome head and kissed the back of my hand, and then, rather more warmly than in the taxi, my cheek. "Good night, Delia, sleep well."

The moonlight fell across my pillow, but I had no romantic

daydreams. A man like that behaved gallantly to every woman he took out. Automatically. Scores of them. Look how he'd carried on with that Leni!—dancing cheek to cheek.

Ida barged into my room at nine o'clock next morning when I was dead to the world. Painfully I became conscious.

"Where did you get to last night?" She cried with cheerful eagerness. "Don't tell me! I can guess. Gordon took you to a night club."

"As a matter of fact he did. You'd gone to bed, and—"

She flopped down on my bed.

"Don't apologize, dahling. I'm glad you went. And I wouldn't have gone if he'd asked me. At my age a woman can look nothing but a hag at one o'clock in the morning among a lot of blooming young girls. What was it like?"

"We picked up a lot of bohemian-intellectuals. They were amusing and slightly mad and set on keeping it up all night. We just came home."

"Let's all have our coffee in here," said Ida, snatching the telephone to give the order. "I'll go and fetch Gladys."

"So I hear you were off on the bummel with Gordon last night?" said Gladys, coming in.

"Yes, it was a positive orgy," I said lightly.

She gave me a look of pitying scorn.

"Rather you than me."

Ida threw a roll at her. "You're a very wicked girl not to like dahling Gordon."

I felt light-hearted and carefree, stretching and curling my toes in the beautiful bed, lapped in comfort and luxury. I felt a rich happy warmth spreading through me, I felt alive. I thought, this is all very demoralizing, but it's wonderful and I love it. I loved Ida for her vivid living, I loved Gladys for her reliable ways and lack of resentment, I loved Franz and Jarzy waiting patiently for us at home. And Gordon—whew!

I threw back the bedclothes.

"I simply must get up."

"Aren't you going to tell us any more about last night?" said Ida in a voice bleak with disappointment.

"There isn't anything to tell, honestly."

We left for home in the afternoon, and just before we left there occurred one of those trivial, foolish little incidents which can upset one's emotional stability, and which a minute either way could have avoided.

I was sitting in the hall of the hotel waiting for Ida and Gladys to come down. Gordon had gone into the writing room to send off a note.

Standing near me was a tourist, an Englishwoman, waiting for her husband. He came out of the writing room and joined her.

He said, "Do you remember that solicitor fellow who once acted for your sister? Afterwards he got seven years for embezzlement and came out after five, and disappeared? What was his name?"

They began to walk away.

The wife said, "Oh I know who you mean. Let me see, what *was* his name? It'll come—wait—"

Her voice was fading.

"Well, I just—" he began.

They were out of earshot.

It was nothing at all, that tantalizing bit of talk, but what was the man going to say? What was the bit I missed? "Well, I just—" what?

Nothing at all. A dozen remarks could have fitted. I felt fidgety and on edge.

The porter appeared carrying our luggage and followed by Gladys and Ida, and at almost the same moment Gordon came out of the writing room and joined us.

"Are you all ready?"

"No, I'm not!" Ida looked wildly round her. "I haven't got my little green bag. Where is it? I—"

"It's here, dear, I've got it," said Gladys.

("Well, I just—well, I just—well, I just—" *What was the matter with me?*)

"The taxi should be outside by now," said Gordon.

("Well, I just saw the fellow himself in the writing room"—oh no!)

I must have gone white. Ida said, "Is anything the matter, dahling?"

I bit my lip. "Of course not."

We piled into the taxi. At the station Gordon, looking weary as indeed we all probably did, bought us magazines for the journey. Ida got *Die Kunst und das Schöne Heim*, a sort of equivalent of the British *Ideal Home*, Gladys had a popular illustrated called *Quick*, and mine was *Panthéon*, an art review. I opened it in the train and spent the journey looking at one picture and not really seeing it. Gordon was completely hidden behind his *Sud-deutsche Zeitung*.

He left us at Dorfen, where Jarzy had brought the car to meet us. Ida greeted and kissed him with tremendous warmth as though she hadn't seen him for months.

"Have you and Onkel been all right? Have you had enough to eat?"

"We have been fine and we eat like the horse. You have had a good time?"

"Wonderful!"

We got into the car. Ida said to me, "It's heaven to be going home, isn't it? You've no idea how I've worried about this boy. The awful time he went through in the war, *that* did him no good. And so young! The young are not tough, they can't stand exposure. They catch tuberculosis."

Jarzy turned a sunny face, throwing back his fair forelock.

"Why do you worry, dear Ida? Me, I do not catch tuberculosis. I live to be one hundred, same as you do."

"And then there's Onkel," went on Ida regardless. "Every time he coughs I have heart failure. I mean, twenty months in a boot cupboard in a Berlin cellar before they caught him, and heaven knows what trash he lived on. Think of going to Auschwitz on an empty stomach! Gladys and I were at least well lined. Nobody appreciates how I worry about those boys."

"But we all do," said Gladys. "You're like a mother to them."

Ida was furious.

"Don't be insulting. Anybody would think I looked eighty."

"Ida darling!" Gladys was nearly in tears. "I didn't mean—"

Jarzy made a forceful attempt at diversion.

"You have not tell me yet what you do in München."

Ida was caught. "Oh, haven't I? But it was stupendous. We had such a time, shopping, a concert, the opera, gorgeous food at the hotel."

"We practically bought up the whole of München," said Gladys. "You wait till you see the things for the new house."

"And what did you do, Dahlia?" He beamed at me. "Did you like it?"

"Gordon took her to a night club last night," Ida butted in, "and I don't know what happened, but she's been as glum as a morgue all day."

"Perhaps it was what didn't happen," said Gladys.

I made a face at her. "Wouldn't you like to know?"

We were home at last, and as we drew up at the door it flew open, and Franz came charging down the steps, joy shining out from his face, and welcomed us back with every sign of delight.

Home! Home! It was wonderful to feel wanted, to revel in the comfort of the blazing hall fire, to run upstairs to my own room and then down again to the bright dining-room where everybody was chattering at once, so happy and intimate.

Franz had cooked us a delicious supper, and even while we ate it we couldn't stop talking. Gladys had cut off snippings of everything we had bought, and she spread the swatches all over the table regardless of whose food they fell into.

Ida ran on, "The blue and cream is for your room, Onkel, I do hope you like it, if you don't you can have the green, or if Jarzy wants the green—where is the green? Oh, it's in the salad, fish it out, Delia—you could have this beige with the bit of red in it. And there are rugs to go with everything. The turquoise is for Delia—not that one, that's for the hall curtains—and Jarzy, don't snatch!"

She insisted on getting up a bottle of champagne to celebrate, and as we sat over our glasses and cigarettes everybody kept breaking into song.

That was the moment when I suddenly felt that I belonged. This was home, where I wanted to be, with these four people so oddly assorted and brought together in drama and tragedy such as I had never known, yet holding out hands to make me one of the family. It was a warm and beautiful feeling.

Gladys and I cleared away and washed up. We felt that the men had done enough while we were lolling in luxury at München.

"Gladys," I said, "I feel so at home. It does make me happy. It's generous of you all to have accepted me."

"But why not?" She smiled kindly. "We like you."

"I think you're all wonderful. It's terrible of me, but I feel I never want to go back."

She nodded. "I understand because I feel the same. I've got a married sister in England who still writes and offers me a home, but I haven't been in England since before the war and I've lost the feeling for going. Of course Onkel and Jarzy haven't any home but this. The Nazis wiped out their people."

"One can hardly bear to think of such tragedy."

She shook out her drying cloth and hung it up.

"Delia—"

"Yes?"

"There's something I've got to say to you. You won't like it, but it's for your good. Don't make a fool of yourself over Gordon Portmeed. I can see it coming on. He's nine foot tall and no good, and you're heading for trouble."

A shock of rage made me shake.

"I'm sure you mean well, Gladys." I controlled my voice. "But you go too far."

"I'll say nothing else," she said. "But I like you, so I've warned you. I know one gets nothing but abuse for telling the truth."

I went to the drawing-room, biting back my anger.

"At last!" cried Ida, bustling round the piano. "Onkel wants to try some *lieder*, and when Gladys comes we'll get out all the gayest things we can find."

I pretended to fan myself. "You're never going to sing tonight! We're all tired."

She glared at me. "I'm not tired. I want to sing and sing and sing, because we're all at home again. That's reason for singing, isn't it?"

I played and played. I thought the most beautiful sounds I had ever heard were the laughter and singing in the softened light. I forgot that it was possible to be tired.

Up in my room at last, nearly midnight, I was quiet and alone for the first time in three days.

I put on a dressing-gown and suddenly the peace was broken by those voices again.

("What was his name? It'll come to me—wait—"

"Well, I just—")

Whirling round, I went to Ida's room. She hadn't begun to undress.

"I shouldn't get so excited," she said ruefully. "Now I'll never sleep. But it's all been such fun."

I sat on the bed.

"I do want to thank you, Ida, for giving me such a lovely time, for the beautiful dress, and everything. You've been too kind and it was all wonderful."

She patted my hand. "Don't you thank me. I was the one who had the pleasure. A miserable lonely old time I should have had without you and Gladys and Gordon."

As I hoped, she had brought his name into it.

"How long have you known Gordon?" I asked casually.

She laughed. "I feel as if I'd always known him, but it's actually about two years."

"Where did you meet him?"

She twiddled a curl and stuck a hairpin through it.

"Honestly, dahling, I hardly remember. I think it was at somebody's house, but I don't remember whose. He's a very good lawyer, so knowledgeable and helpful and up-to-date. My husband's old lawyer who had charge of my affairs was a stuffy old mole, if ever there was one—*and* intransigent. So I ditched him and took Gordon on instead, and it's been heaven."

I began to help her to pin up her curls, and went on in as careless a tone as I could muster, "What did Gordon do before you knew him? Where was he during the war? In one of the services?"

She slid her eyes round to me suspiciously.

"Why do you want to know? Why didn't you ask him yourself? You spent half last night with him. What *did* you talk about?"

"Sorry," I said with a disarming grin. "It doesn't matter in the least."

She shook out her nightdress and dropped it on the bed.

"Actually he did tell me," she said. "He wasn't in the fighting services. I gathered he was in one of those frightfully hushy things that you don't talk about even when it's over. You must ask him yourself. I'm sure he'll tell you."

"Yes, of course." I kissed her. "Good night, Ida darling, and I do hope you'll sleep well."

"I shan't," she grumbled. "I'm convinced all that furnishing brocade will turn out to be the wrong shade."

"Read a book," I said, "and forget it."

"All right," she agreed. "Open the cupboard and find me something spicy and wicked. That'll relax me."

I couldn't sleep either. In the early hours of the morning I sat up with determination and said, "I will not think of that damned splinter of conversation again."

Then I lay down and was promptly asleep.

PART II

I

THE refugee camp was an old Luftwaffe barracks two miles out from town. The bleak, damp, crumbling place had been roughly sliced up into small compartments for families, and big bunk-lined dormitories which were living- as well as sleeping-rooms for hundreds. There were concrete passages like rabbit runs with here and there a tap and a sink.

This crowded place was unspeakably depressing. The first thing that hit you was the noise, the second was the smell. The smell of misery. There seemed to be two kinds of refugees, those who stayed sunk in apathetic silence, and those who made a ceaseless din. This human din was probably some kind of release. People tramped around with heavy tread, banged about, quarrelled, poured out expletives in five languages, for no apparent reason. Then there was the echoing din of feet in stony passages, running taps, clanking utensils, weeping small children and shouting older ones, for it takes more than sordid surroundings to suppress a child's exuberance.

These were the people who had tramped, drenched and famished, across Europe from a homeland that no longer existed for them, and the unclaimed leftovers of the concentration camps.

The administration was housed in a big green-painted office with filing cabinets full of forms. There were forms for everything and everybody. Every scrap of humanity had its own file to say who it was and where it came from, its reasons for existing, its qualifications if any, and the disabilities which might condemn it never to be a person in its own right again.

There were medical forms, and dossiers, and those special forms which every day were tearfully filled in by people who clung to the hope of getting out, finding a job, going to a reception country. Cheerfully earnest young students of various nationalities coped with this department in their vacation time.

The woman who greeted me when I first arrived was a high-powered American called Nora Nixon.

"They call me the Camp Counsellor," she explained, "but the last commodity you can sell here is counsel. People only want one thing—to get out quick." She gripped and held my hand. "My, but I'm glad to see you. I've been looking forward to this minute ever since the British Red Cross told me you were coming to help out. Try not to die on me inside a week! Some do. But you don't look that kind."

"I feel pretty inadequate," I said, "but I'll do my best."

I soon found out that she was a superhuman character, working all the hours there were, holding in her hands all the rough, taut, fraying threads of the organization; prescient, tough, tender, understanding, bracing, astringent. She was a sergeant-major, a guard dog, a ferret, an electronic computor, a feather pillow. She saw people as individuals with names, while the rest of her helpers only had time to take them in as a mass of distressed humanity.

"Snap out of that attitude," she told me. "Don't look at this crowd as pathetic flotsam or you'll do them no good. Every one of them was Somebody once. If you respect their right to a past you're on the way to giving them the right to a future."

"But they all need everything at once. They all talk at once. You want to do something for everybody—at once. It's too huge. And what on earth can *I* do?"

"What we all do." Her smile was calm and dry. "Keep chaos at bay. *They* believe that *we* can."

"Thank goodness," I said, "there are some gay ones."

She spread her hands. "They're the ones who know they'll get out. But if anybody's likely to be the death of me, it's the gay ones."

Knowing I was a Red Cross nurse—and assuming wrongly that I was as experienced in practice as in theory—they made me the doctor's assistant. I accompanied him on what was optimistically called his morning round but which, since practically everybody in the camp was suffering from something, went on all day.

Some you took to, some you couldn't bear, the surly ones, the grumblers, the spivs. But you treated them all alike.

Some stood out. You got to know them, you wanted to be friends. Among these, for me, were the Todors.

The Todors were a Roumanian family, political refugees from the Reds. The men of the family had been wiped out, all but Madame Todor's father who was eighty-four and her nephew Max. These two with Madame and her niece Isold had walked from Bucharest with what they could carry, on a hopeless journey that took weeks, and had ended up at Dorfen camp.

Max had been lucky enough to get a job in town as a grocery roundsman. Isold, twenty years old and as thin as a rail, a T.B. suspect, was "good with children" and kept busy by Nora Nixon. Madame Todor herself was the family pivot, the kingpin—or should it be queenpin?—sitting in their bare little cell of a room surrounded by a few household treasures, as poised as she had sat in her own drawing-room, with only a tightening of the lips as the din surged louder in the clanging passage outside.

This family was still civilized, still urbane, after being pushed about the ditches of Europe.

On most of my four days a week, when I went off duty, I would spend half an hour with them.

"Miss is here!" was the cry. "We will have coffee, Isold."

They all spoke good English, and French. Madame with her jolly wide mouth, her dead-leaf hair carefully netted, her great beaky nose, her jumble of garments made somehow impressive by the black lace stole draped round her shoulders, her flashing eyes and instinctive panache, would have been a personality anywhere.

She excused herself for having dabbed at her eyes in my presence. "I have been have my once-a-week cry," she said with dignity. "It is wholesome a little to cry sometimes. One must not always be cheerful, it strains too much ze tempers of ze family. More zan once a week to cry is not good for ze eyes and one can never get a new pair."

"I hope you weren't crying about anything special, Madame Todor?"

"But no. It is a habit. Ah, here comes Isold."

The girl put her kettle on the small iron stove.

"I had to wait for the tap. Everybody always wants it at once. I hope it won't take an hour to boil." Rashly she thrust in the last of the wood. "Max must go out and get us more when he comes."

Coffee, adulterated stuff as it was, was precious to the final drop, but I had to accept a cup, one of the two beautiful china cups which Madame had brought out of Roumania.

"Think of it!" Isold's tone was scoffing. "She carried those two cups wrapped in paper under her coat all the way. For eleven weeks. She never put them down for fear she broke them. Cups!"

"And what did you save that you loved?" I demanded.

"Me? Nothing! I tell you, this old woman, my aunt, compelled me to carry a bundle of family things, the lace tablecloth of her mother, rather than a blanket which would have been some good."

Madame gave her niece a look.

"Most important is to be civilized. Pappa, here is your cup of coffee. Drink, zen you can go lie in your bunk and have ze little nap."

"In zat den!" The old man humoured himself with a good grumble. He had told me how he hated having to sleep in the crowded dormitory, but their room was barely big enough for the narrow bed in which Madame slept.

"And I tell you I do not go to ze bed when a lady calls." He glowered at his daughter. "I wish I could offer Miss a cigarette out of my silver box."

"But you haven't got your silver box," said Madame briskly. "And you haven't got cigarettes unless Max bring you some when he come."

"Why haven't I got my silver box? Anybody would sink I have forgot how to behave."

"We all have," said Isold.

"You do not speak to ze grandfazzer like zat!" Madame rapped out.

Isold shrugged. I had already noticed how often those narrow, sharp shoulders went up. It seemed an awful thing that for a girl only a few years younger than I was life could evoke only one comment, a shrug half apathetic and half cynical.

Madame had noticed it too.

"And do not show to me ze shoulder-bones any more. Me, I do

not show ze shoulder-bones, and you are young and I am fifty-eight."

"Do those children make you very tired, Isold?" I asked her.

"Not more than usual. I'm always tired. What is there here to make you alive?"

"I'll ask the doctor to see you tomorrow."

"Thank you, that I don't want." She added, "I want clothes, and to dance, and to work in a job for good money."

I knew there wasn't a hope of her getting a job, she was too delicate. Nobody was going to take a chance on Isold, no individual, no nation.

Max, whom they adored as the last of the Todors and their present link with the outer world, was good to his family. He spent all his spare time with them, when many young men would have taken care to keep well away from the gloomy camp. But he came, and never empty-handed—a few cigarettes, a little cheap coffee, some tinned goods that were sub-quality and sold to him for a mark or two.

I found out that he had actually been given the golden chance of which everybody dreamed, to go to Australia on the quota—and had refused it. It was a tremendous sacrifice, but Max found it unthinkable to break up the family.

"He is right," Madame told me. "We are ze Todors, all zat is left of zem, and if we separate zere is no more family ever, so Max he stay. Soon he must marry and have children, so still zere is more of us and still togezzer."

Marry who? I thought. Marry on what? Live where?

He came in before I left, and greeted me with clicked heels and splendid politeness. For the rest, he had rather effeminate good looks and an air of Thank goodness, there's another day over. But I couldn't forget what he had done for his family in turning down a furture for himself.

"Good evening, Aunt Tati—good evening, Uncle Jan. I hope you're both well. I know you've just eaten."

"It was ragout of mutton," said the old man. "Nearly always it is."

"You don't need to tell me it was ragout of something. To judge by the smell, the mutton has been walking up and down the passages all day and paying a long visit to every corner. As for the insects in this place, they seem to be a great deal hungrier and eat a great deal more than the Christians."

"Zere are no insects here," said Madame. "Take you what is left of ze cold coffee I keep for you, and do not talk so clever."

"No, keep the coffee and warm it up tonight. Look—" Max produced a very small bottle of wine with a flourish. "For you, my dear aunt."

"Where did you get zat?"

"Don't ask questions." He sat down on the bed and put up his legs. "Drink it, roll it round your tongue, old dear, and go off into a lovely rosy dream for once."

He took an instrument from his pocket and briskly flicked out the cork.

"Hold out your cups—come along."

While the old man, Isold, and Madame sipped, he gave me a faint smile and said, "I have been to school in England for two years, would you believe it?"

"Yes, I would. You speak so fluently. Haven't you any school friends in England who could help?"

He shook his head with a wry grimace.

"Schoolboy friendships, what are they?"

"I do not like zis wine," said Madame. "It taste of potato. I hope you did not steal it."

"If you want to know," said Max, "it isn't potato—just old stock. The grocer let me have it for one mark. It had been knocked about and the seal was broken. Chuck it away if you think it's going to poison you."

"I shall drink it," said the old man. "Me, I drink anysing."

"Pappa, you will poison yourself. You will be dead drunk like zose silly old White Russians who always roll about in ze passage. Zey brew zeir stuff somewheres. So proud zey are in zeir dirty fur coats."

I thought, if I asked Ida she would give me a small bottle of champagne to buck them all up. And yet it seemed silly to think about luxuries like champagne when what they really needed was good food, clean air, and hope.

Isold downed her wine, and said defiantly, "Marusha, that Hungarian girl, has got a job. She goes every day to an American lady to look after her children. Lucky her! It is a warm house and she has a lovely lunch. Mrs. Tallent has given her a pair of beautiful shoes so she doesn't have to slop through the streets with brown paper in her shoes. I wish it was me."

"Wish, wish wish!" Madame made immense gestures with both hands. "I wish only little zings. I wish ze people next door do not quarrel so and scream. He wants to get zeir children sent to Sweden and she won't let zem go. Zey quarrel about zis late at night and we cannot sleep."

"Perhaps if the children went," I said, "the parents could go later."

"Pooh!" said Isold. "The father has only one leg and one usable hand. He isn't any good. He was in a forced labour camp. He's no use to Sweden, you can't blame Sweden."

"Eizer you have to be hard and let ze strong ones go, and break ze family for ever," explained Madame, "or you stay all togezzer and be poor and brave and do not boo-hoo about it. I do not boo-hoo. And you ozzers will not boo-hoo in front of ze gracious Miss who come so kindly to visit us when she get nossing from it."

"Me, I have hope," said the old man. "Max, he is out in ze world. Perhaps he marry a rich girl and zen we all have a house again, and I will live to see ze family rise."

Max gave him a look of indulgent scorn.

"You're living a hundred years ago, old dear. What rich girl would marry the grocer's man? And what rich girl wants to marry *all* the Todors?"

"And why should he not live one hundred years ago if he want to?" Madame cried. "It is his little pleasure, very small. I am old too and I know. Where do you expect us to live—in ze future zat isn't? It is all right for you and Isold, you are young."

"Who'd be young!" Isold shrugged. "To hear you, anybody would think it was gorgeous."

"It's no joke being young," said Max, "when you've neither money, girls, wine, or dancing."

The old man glared at him. "And what makes you sink zat when you are old you do not want money and girls and wine and dancing, eh—eh?"

"Me, I am ashamed of you both," said Madame. "You lost your dignity on ze way here."

Isold giggled, and we all had a good, heart-lifting laugh. Then came the racy stories. Madame Todor had a fund of them, recollected from the old days. She was a born raconteur, with the gift of enhancing detail and exaggerating in just the right place, and she could go on for ever.

I had to tear myself away.

At home they regarded my work at the camp with a kind of amused condescension, all but Franz who couldn't bear to see anybody teased.

"I don't want to hear any more about those Todors," said Ida. "You obviously like them a lot better than you like us. I'm surprised you bother to come home."

I was a little surprised by her apparent indifference to distress near her own doorstep.

"Ida, do you have to talk like that? You understand perfectly, or you should. A family like that, to be living in squalor, after all they've gone through—"

She patted my arm.

"Dahling Delia, I just don't want to see you turn into a do-gooder. They are such bores. And I cannot think that anything so dreadful has happened to anybody that something dreadfuller hasn't happened to somebody else."

Was I a do-gooder? Was I a bore?

I shut up like a clam about the camp, and went steadily on with my four days a week. Though I hadn't much money I started taking something for the Todors on most days, even if it was only a pot of jam or a cake that I'd made. Their passionate gratitude worried me. Just as I didn't want the people at home to think me a bore, I didn't want the Todors to look upon me as a ministering angel. It was all embarrassing.

Nora Nixon had comments too. She who never missed the tiniest detail couldn't fail to notice or hear about my small gifts.

"Another present for the Todors? Please don't spoil them, Delia. Spoilt people get uppish, and God knows I can't cope with any more uppish ones in this place. It's the uppish ones who bombard me from morning till night, expecting favours."

"Don't you think they deserve a little?" I retorted. "Wasn't it fine of them to stick together, when Max could have gone to Australia? Particularly fine of Max, though they put no pressure on him to stay."

"Max was a fool not to go. There's such a thing as being unrealistic. The family can't keep together much longer anyway, whatever they think. The old man will have to be moved into a Home for the aged, and Madame Todor is unemployable and will be shoved on from camp to camp."

"But that's appalling."

She gave me a bleak, weary look.

"See, Delia—this is life. This is Europe 1949. It's one hell of a mess, and in sorting it out you can't make exceptions. It's the old business of the greatest good of the greatest number. Max has got a job, at least, so he's also got a chance of some day being in a position to do something for the others if he wants to."

"Some day! They may all be dead."

"Pity! But that's it. Isold might get a job if we can stop her looking such a T.B. type. Also she's no earthly good at housework or I could get her a daily domestic job in town."

"She's never done any housework. She—"

"I know, I know! These upper-class ones. I'm not unsympathetic, but they won't realize their position."

"If Max went to Australia would he be in a position to send for the others?"

"It's unlikely. And Australia naturally wouldn't take the useless ones."

"Useless! What a ghastly word!"

"I wouldn't use it to anybody but you, but you want the truth, don't you?"

I tried to see it from the practical angle. I tried not to go soft over the Todors when there were others, right at my shoulder, who were just as sadly placed.

Meanwhile I hadn't seen Gordon since we were at Munich, he had been away. Half of me was glad of it, and half of me longing for him to come back. Yet I couldn't help feeling that there must be plenty of enjoyments preferable to and more peaceful than thinking about a man. I was for ever pushing him out of my mind. I didn't want him there. It was like living in a small house and stuffing half of it with waste paper. And as for seeing all things through the medium of one unrequited feeling, that was degrading.

I walked home one evening to find him sitting there.

"Hullo, Delia." He stood up and took my hand. Shaken, I could think of nothing to say. I wished that he wouldn't look at me as though I were the one person he'd been longing to see, when that was just part of the charm he could turn on for anybody.

"Let me get out of my uniform," I said. "It smells of disinfectant, and worse."

His eyes ran over me, lazily observant.

"Certainly you'd look nicer without it. And you've gone thinner, haven't you? What have you been doing to yourself?"

"Nothing," I said. "And I hope I am thinner. Now don't *you* start!"

"It's that camp she goes to," said Gladys. "She works like a slave. She's probably incubating enteric for all we know."

"Shut up!" I snapped, goaded to irritability. "You might have ended up in a place like that yourself, then you could have felt more kindly about people who try to help."

"Meaning, I suppose, if I wasn't living on Ida?"

"I didn't mean anything of the kind."

"Now stop that!" shrieked Ida. "Delia, go and put on your nicest dress and drown yourself in scent. Isn't it heavenly to have Gordon back again? Now you'll be at the piano all evening, because we're going to sing all the ones we hadn't a deep enough bass for."

"Oh, let me off," cried Gordon. "Please, Ida. I came here to relax."

"Well, you can't. Don't be so lazy. You ignore us for two whole weeks and then want to loll about and be amused."

He laughed, and passed round cigarettes.

"Jarzy is out, so we can't sing without a tenor."

"Jarzy has gone to the gymnasium with a friend, but he promised to be back by nine. Then we shall start singing, and if Jarzy prefers trapezes and things to his dinner that's his affair. Oh, and Delia, I've had a letter, and they're going to let the water in a month from Saturday. We're going to be wildly busy packing and removing, so *that's* going to put paid to your camp."

I bit my lip. Gordon gave me an inscrutable look. Feeling hunted, I flew upstairs. Why should I dress up for him? I dragged out my modest blue, climbed into it, and went down without even a squirt of scent.

There was champagne for dinner, roast ducklings, one of Ida's choicest sweets. She was delighted that Gordon was there, only the best would do for him.

After that came a merry evening, hours of music. Certainly he laid himself out to please Ida, singing tirelessly, making jokes.

I played and played, terribly conscious of him. While Ida, Gladys, Franz, and Jarzy sang a quartette, he stood beside me and turned pages, his shoulder sometimes brushing mine as he leaned over. I felt his eyes on me, I looked up and there was a small, intimate smile flicking up the corners of his lips, and saying, "Listen to them carolling away . . . and here are we two apart, in a little corner of our own."

It was intoxicating. I wasn't any longer resisting or reasoning. I played on mechanically, and to me the words of every song were Gordon, Gordon, Gordon.

2

"ZE one I tell you about was Cousin Willi," said Madame Todor. "He was so debonair, so beautiful he dress, and ze women loved him, zough he was a dreadful wicked old sing—not so old, perhaps fifty. Well, we had dined, and what a dinner! We ate about eight courses, all delicious, and Pappa bring up ze Tokay. Zen we play bridge, and my husband Karel and I play against Willi and zis woman—zis Madame somesing. Oh, she is so stiff, so formal, it is terrible. Like in England zey say ze damp blanket. She say, 'Before we play I make it clear, zis—I do not drink, I do not play for money, and I do not allow anybody—but nobody!—to swear in my presence.' And Willi he just look at her and he say, 'Well, Madame What-you-call, all I hope is zat your bridge is not so good as your morals.' And Karel and I, we pretend to wipe our noses so we do not even show we laugh, but inside we are nearly sick wiz not laughing."

She brought out a greyish rag and wiped her eyes, laughing again at the recollection.

Handkerchiefs! I thought. I must try and get her some, they're expensive, but I can manage one or two next time.

"I could listen to your stories for ever," I told her, "but I've got to go. Did you say the others were well?"

Two horizontal lines deepened between her brows.

"Fair—fair. Isold goes outside to cough so I will not hear, but I know. She will not go to ze doctor, she is afraid what he tell her. And Pappa he has start drinking wiz zose horrible old White Russians. I shall stop him if I have to chain him."

"I'll mention it tactfully to Mrs. Nixon," I said, covering her hand with mine. "She has a good new helper now, an English boy—Mr. Gerald. He takes a lot off her hands. Don't you worry."

She bent down suddenly and kissed my hand.

"I do not know how I should be if it was not for you, dear Miss. You are so true, so faissful, my friend. I am all gratitude."

"Oh please! I care so much for you all."

She was huddled as close as she could get to the small stove, which since the wood in it was damp gave out the minimum of heat. It was a raw day. Madame Todor was wearing all she'd got, which was hardly adequate. Her cold fingers repaired the torn buttonholes on the old man's coat, taking tiny fine stitches.

"I wish I hadn't to go," I said, "but I'm on duty now. Oh, and

I've brought you a pack of cards—English, you'll find them a bit different, but you'll get used to them—"

She gave a cry of delight.

"Wonderful! Oh, I am luckee—luckee! Now I shall tell everybody ze fortune. I shall be in business, zey all come."

"Good." I beamed at her. 'Tell them they're going to England and America, and they'll have homes and all the things they want. Give them hope, it's bound to do them good."

She nodded. "So! I tell zem somesing pretty. In Roumania I do zat for all my friends."

"And tell Isold she must see the doctor, and not to be so stubborn."

"What is stubborn?"

"What Isold is."

"I know."

Isold oughtn't to be coughing over those little children, I thought as I hurried along the ringing passage, hugging myself against the raw, penetrating damp. I spent four hours with the doctor. Bad feet, bad eyes, bad ears, every little injury turning septic. Trying not to feel beaten by the crushing enormity of the job.

I caught the bus home, and as I walked up the drive a taxi passed me and pulled up at the door.

A girl stepped out, in a cream coat trimmed with mink and a small hat of matching fur. She was lovely, striking, unexpected.

"Hallo," she said, staring at my uniform. "Is anybody ill here?"

"No, I just live here," I said.

Her looks broke every rule of classical beauty, but I had never seen anything so alluring. Her hair was a black satin bell, curling up from her shoulders. Her eyes, small, wide apart, darkly lashed, were like chippings of sapphire. Her lightly tanned, heart-shaped face was too high at the cheekbones, too pointed at the chin, too wide of mouth. And having realized all this in a flash, there was still her smile and her vibrant grace and animation, and the terrific impact she made.

She flashed me a friendly glance.

"I believe you must be the other one."

"The other what?"

"Ida's goddaughter."

"Oh, you're Eilys Mallins."

"Weren't you expecting me?"

"Not today. We—"

"But I sent a tel—oh, lord!" She snapped her fingers. "I meant to and never did. Is it terribly inconvenient?"

"Of course not. They'll all be thrilled. Come along in."

The front door opened and Jarzy appeared, astonished.

"Hallo, Jarzy!" Eilys cried. "Remember me?"

"But of course. How lovely that you have come."

"Help the man to get my stuff off the taxi, will you my sweet? It took him hours to get it on."

We swept into the house, and Ida hearing the voices came running in her scarlet housecoat with a sugar basin in her hand.

"Eilys! But, dahling, what a stupendous surprise!"

"Not meant to be. I forgot to send the telegram."

"And is that all you've got to say when you burst in like a bomb?"

"Oh, but I have messed things up. You don't want me."

Ida recovered, hurled the sugar basin on the floor, and embraced Eilys.

"My dahling, you're terribly welcome. We're all delighted. How beautiful you look—such chic!—what a treat. It's much nicer that you've come as a surprise. Delia will take you straight up to your room while I think about supper."

"Which room?" I said. "I can't think."

Ida stroked Eilys's mink collar.

"My pet, you don't mind going under the tiles, do you? The attics are sweet, and you'll feel like Mimi."

"I don't mind going anywhere," Eilys said, "so long as the water doesn't actually come in."

"Oh, but it will. The water *is* coming in, and we've got to move in two weeks."

"Is she raving?" Eilys looked at me.

"They're going to flood the valley to make a reservoir," I explained. "We have another house to go to."

"I see. Never a dull moment in the country." She spun round and called to Jarzy, "Angel, are you going to bring all that luggage up to my sordid attic where I'm going to be like Mimi, and I don't care if you'll be my Rudolph."

"I come quick!" Jarzy shouted, trying to collect five suitcases, two hat boxes, and a wardrobe trunk.

I took Eilys upstairs, and said, "You don't have to go up aloft. There's a room on the first floor. It only needs hot bottles, and I'll light the stove and fetch clean towels."

I opened the door.

"Lovely," said Eilys, whipping out a gold cigarette case and lighter. "Have one?"

"Thanks," I said. I had been smoking a lot since Gordon started me off. "Now Ida's got another excuse for a celebration."

"You don't have to tell me anything about Ida." She dropped her coat on the bed. "I spent a night here a year ago. Still the same comic set-up, I imagine. How do you like it here?"

"Very much indeed."

"That's something. I hope I shall! My father thought it might be a strain. He says it's obvious why we are here—you and I—so that Ida can find out if we're worth leaving her money to."

"That's something I'd hate to consider," I said. "I'm not very good at worldly arithmetic."

She pulled off her hat and shook out her hair. She wore a beautifully tailored dress of cream cloth, and pearl and gold jewellery.

"Tell me, why the fancy uniform?"

"I do Red Cross work at the refugee camp."

"Oh? That must be very depressing."

"You're kept too busy to feel depressed."

"I hope you're not going to do it all the time." She made an enchanting grimace at me. "You and I have got to back each other up. I hope you'll like me."

"I think you're lovely," I said with complete candour.

"I like you too. We'll get along madly well. You're called Delia, aren't you?"

Jarzy came staggering in.

"Suitcases. The rest to come. You must have brought five hundred dresses, Eilys."

"Oh darling, you're being so sweet and noble about it!" Her

look was full of warmth and contrition. "Never mind the luggage, just tell me how you are. I've been longing to see you ever since I knew I was coming. Tell me, did you ever finish that divine poem you were writing when I was here?"

"You couldn't remember that!" Jarzy looked at her in fascinated wonder.

"I never forget anything about my friends."

He went a little pale. "I did not finish it. There was no inspiration after you go."

I went off to find clean towels for Eilys's room. What a charmer! She had the same art that Gordon possessed, of making you feel you were the only person who mattered.

Downstairs Ida was letting herself go over the supper, another excuse for a celebration. Chickens fried in butter, a special salad, zabaglione—nobody must do this but Ida, shrieking with panic lest she spoil it—and champagne.

Down came the charmer at last, with her arm through the enchanted Jarzy's, laughing and gay to meet everybody.

"Gladys *darling*! Still looking after them all?"

Wrapped in a warm, scented embrace, Gladys looked embarrassed.

"Oh yes, I'm just the family dumb cluck."

"You're certainly not! You're terribly, terribly clever and they couldn't get along for five minutes without you . . . Oh *Onkel*!" A switch of the heavenly smile, the radiant eyes, "You're looking so much younger and better than you did last year. It must be happiness that does things to you."

Franz kissed her hand. "And happier still now that you have come," he said gallantly.

We sat down to our Lucullan meal.

Eilys put her hands to her cheeks. "Ida, you've never done all this rich food for me?"

"Why not?"

"My figure."

I thought she had nothing to worry about, trying to look impersonally and without envy at the delicate poise of her head, the slender neck, the small high bosom, the fluid grace of her body and long slim legs.

"Who looks at the figure," demanded Jarzy, "when the face is so gloriful?"

"Practically everybody, darling. If I had to choose one or the other, I'd rather have the face of a gorilla and an ooh-ooh figure, wouldn't you, Delia?"

"Nature never offered me any choices," I said. "She made me up out of leftovers."

"Very attractive leftovers." Eilys sparkled at me. "Don't you think so, Onkel?"

"I think Delia is also beautiful," he said gallantly, "and I don't like skeleton women. No men do. Women like to be thin only to impress other women."

"So there!" said Ida. "Open the champagne, Jarzy . . . How is your poor father, Eilys?"

"I'm afraid he's quite ill." She looked sad. "It's such a shame. Daddy always loved life, and now he's tied down by this wretched heart."

"Did you leave him at Cannes?"

"Oh no, I wouldn't have done that. Didn't I tell you? He's gone to a clinic at Lausanne and I'm afraid he's going to be there for a long time. I'm just a roofless ruin, Ida, and I'm afraid you've got me on your hands."

"Lovely! Now the family's complete."

"Thank you, darling, I'm going to love it here." She took the glass that Jarzy offered and smiled at me through the dancing bubbles. "Deel and I are going to stick together, aren't we, Deel? Closer than twins—and God help anybody who comes between us!"

"The only thing that's wrong with you," said Ida, propping her elbows as her hands cradled the glass, "is that you sing like a hen. I remember from last time."

"Is that a crime?"

"It is in this house," I said.

"Gladys, you must give her a few lessons." Ida jumped up enthusiastically. "Take her in the drawing-room now and try her for pitch while Delia makes the coffee. The boys can wash up."

"Poor, poor Gladys!" Eilys began to carol a popular song, giving it every raucous distortion her voice was capable of. We all laughed crazily. It was the beginning of a hilarious evening.

So she's here! I thought. Nothing now to conjecture about her. She's arrived, and she's not only going to fit in, she's going to be a riot.

You didn't have to try to like Eilys, you couldn't help yourself. There she was, a girl who had everything to charm and please, who lived all the time in clover and made no more account of it than if it was mouldy hay.

3

ON Saturday afternoon, the weather wintry, grey, and repellent outside, I sat on the floor in front of blazing logs and darned Franz's green sweater with not quite matching wool, wondering if a complete contrast—scarlet or purple—wouldn't have been more fetching.

Ida had taken Eilys over to see the new house, with Gladys and Jarzy.

Franz smoked his pipe, full length on the sofa beside me.

"I'm thinking it is nearly too good," he said. "A lot of happy people is nice to be among."

"I don't see why it's too good," I said. "You don't think Fate has it in for us, or anything? It's all very cosy and I love it." I held up the half darned hole and made a face through it. "This isn't going to look very smart when I've done."

"I wear it to walk in the mountains only."

"Now I wish I'd put a gayer colour in!" I dropped the sweater. "I hope Eilys likes the new house. She couldn't have chosen a drearier day to see it."

"I think Eilys would like anything," he said. "She is that kind of person. So sunny."

"Yes, and wasn't she amusing last night, doing those imitations?

I was terrified that Gladys would realize she was being taken off."

"But it was not a cruel imitation, it was funny. I think Gladys knew and she laughed as much as anybody." He slapped his cushion. "I love lazing here and talking to you, but I ought to be doing some work."

"You work awfully hard. Is there any reward in teaching?"

"But of course." He sat up. "These boys after the war, they are different from the ones before. They have not recovered yet, and I help them not to be always the defeated. They will be needed for the world some day, for a free world."

"I think you're rather wonderful, Franz."

He chuckled. "Oh no, I'm not. Ida is wonderful and Eilys is wonderful. It wouldn't do to have us all wonderful in one house."

"Now you're cheering me up to endure being ordinary. One thing I've lost since I came here is the sense of ever feeling lonely."

"Me also." He sounded pleased. "Shall I drag myself up and put on a nice record for us?"

The others came streaming in for tea, hot cakes and cherry jam, exclaiming how frozen they were, and how Franz and I looked too cosy for words what with the big fire and the dance music, and what had we been getting up to?—this from Ida.

"I think the new house is heaven," said Eilys, dropping her furs on the floor and snatching a hot cake. "I can't wait to get there and leave this one to the eels."

"I'm a bit torn," Ida said. "After all, I've lived in this one for the best part of my life. I ought to be sick with nostalgia."

"But you're not. I saw your eyes shining when you were deciding where you'd put the furniture. We may as well start packing up at once."

"The carpets and curtains haven't come yet," said Gladys, taking everything literally.

"Why bother about a little thing like that?" Eilys kicked off her shoes and held her feet to the fire. "Let's go in and picnic till the stuff arrives. I don't mind bare boards. I'm all for spontaneity."

"It is not summer," said Jarzy.

"Well, it would be silly enough to be fun. Doing silly things is usually the most satisfying in the end."

"Whoops!" said Ida, waving her tea cup and splashing everybody. "Let's get on with the packing."

"I have little to pack," said Jarzy.

"Me also," said Franz.

Ida shrieked. "Listen to those layabouts! I've got loads to pack."

"Darling, you need not do a thing," said Gladys. "I'll do it all for you."

"What have I done to deserve you?" Ida lay back in her chair. "Jarzy, take off that awful record that Delia in some moment of insanity chose, and put on something soothing or I shall explode."

Eilys caught my hand.

"Come up with me while I change."

We went up to her room, and I sat on the bed while she pulled off her suit and rummaged among her racks of dresses for the one she wanted.

"I feel a bit low," she said. "I've been thinking about our apartment at Cannes. We'll never go back there. I had a letter this morning, and the doctors say that Daddy won't get better."

"I'm terribly sorry, Eilys."

"So you'll have me here a long time, whether you want me or not."

"That's going to please everybody."

"Deel, you are sweet. Zip up my back, please . . . Did you know," she went on, choosing a necklace from her brimming box, "that Mike is going to study law when we get to the new house?"

"Who is Mike?"

She laughed. "Jarzy, of course. I always call my men Mike, it's my favourite name."

"I didn't know about him studying law."

"It's one of Ida's ideas. With somebody called Gordon. Who on earth is he? Ida's one of those maddening people who talk to you about their friends by their Christian names, as if you knew."

"Gordon's her lawyer," I said. "In Dorfen. English. You'll be meeting him."

"What's he like?"

"Very handsome."

"Any fun?"

I felt as though I were carrying a toppling armload of bricks.

"Oh, just your type. You'll get on like wildfire."

"That's quite enough for me. I hate the sound of him." She brushed out her hair and sprayed scent. "Listen, Deel. Do you think we could get Mike and Onkel to take us to the pictures tonight? There's a sizzling film in town."

"I don't see why not."

"I'm ready now. I'll go down and ask them while you change."

I had just got my dress on when she came bursting into my room. For the first time, I saw her looking furious.

"This is the limit!" Her blue eyes fairly blazed.

"What's the matter? Have they turned you down?"

"Not likely. They want to go. But what do you think? Ida takes it for granted that she's coming too! And Gladys! My God! So far as I'm concerned the whole thing's off."

She was quite enraged.

"But, Eilys," I said, "the whole family always does move in a body."

"Why on earth—? *Why?* We four could have had fun, but do we have to trail the old woman along with us?"

"Ida—an old woman?"

"Well, isn't she?" She snatched at a cigarette and lighted it.

"I never thought of her like that. She certainly doesn't think of herself that way."

"Then it's time she did. She's nearly seventy, and she ought to be glad of a nice evening knitting over the fire, with Gladys fawning on her and holding the wool. It irritates me, the way she pretends to be our age."

"It's your point of view," I said, "and it does give me a surprise. She's never struck me like that."

She calmed down a little, but still glowered, blowing out fierce smoke rings.

"The outing's off. I'm not going."

"Eilys, don't act like five years old."

"I'm not being childish, I've just lost interest. I shall tell them I've changed my mind. Damn Ida! . . . Now you're shocked to the core, aren't you?"

"Nothing shocks me," I said coolly, though actually I was considerably rattled. "But in this house it's one for all, and all for one. And Ida is adorable."

She gave a small exasperated yelp.

"Come on down, if you're ready, and let's forget it."

I couldn't quite forget it, because it was the first note of disharmony I had heard and it was bound to spoil the music, if only for one evening. Perhaps I was always too easily satisfied, perhaps Eilys had a right to feel and express dissatisfaction.

By now Ida was full of the idea of packing. Nothing could stop her, and we all had to help her. Alone, any of us could have packed all we possessed in half an hour, even Eilys—who hadn't opened the greater part of her luggage—but Ida had to face the accumulation of more than thirty years.

On the subject of the furniture she had quite made up her mind. She knew what she was taking and what she was abandoning to the waters.

I felt strongly about this and spoke a bit rashly.

"All this good furniture, it seems awful to leave it to be destroyed. Please, Ida, couldn't it go to the camp? It would be so valuable."

"No, it couldn't!"

I tried to swallow a lump of resentment.

"My furniture isn't going to be worn out by anybody," Ida said hotly. "It's like giving away your old dog or horse. It's done its life-work and it's going to have a peaceful end. I think that's romantic."

"I agree with Ida," said Jarzy. "The old furniture goes with the house. They belong together always."

"Thank you, dahling," said Ida. "You're the only one with a shred of understanding."

"I understand too," said Gladys, terrified to appear for one instant out of line with Ida. "I think it's a beautiful idea, to let it lie peacefully under the soft green water for ever."

"I can see I'm howled down," I said, "so I'll get out of the argument."

Eilys, sprawling in a big chair, gave me a wicked look.

"Surely you're not giving up, Deel? Can't you come back with a rocket?"

Ida glared at her.

"There'll be no rockets here. It's my furniture. My husband and I bought most of it together, and the rest came from his family home. Anything I want to take I shall take, and a few heirlooms I shall take, but nobody tells me what I take and do not take, is that clear?"

"Couldn't be clearer," said Eilys.

Ida, checked in mid-air, gave her a doubtful glance. There was a second of tension, and somebody changed the subject. I went upstairs to pack china of which there was a great quantity in a store-room. Ida valued it all and wanted to take it.

While I was busy I heard footsteps on the attic stairs, and when somebody came in, thinking it was Jarzy, I said with my back turned, "There's a broken teapot here, Jarzy. Could you run down with it to Ida, and ask her if she wants it repaired, or shall I scrap it?"

"It isn't Jarzy. It's me."

An electric shock went through me. The teapot cracked down on the floor and the little lid rolled away into a corner.

"Gordon! I didn't know you were coming."

"I hadn't anything special to do so I thought I'd see how you were getting along. Ida's got a trunkful of her husband's old papers. She wanted me to glance through them in case they were significant but they might as well be destroyed. Now what are you doing so energetically?"

He went down on his knees beside me.

"Don't you spoil that perfect suit," I said.

"Oh, let me help!"

"I don't suppose you've ever packed china in your life."

"Anything for a new sensation."

"Well, go down and get yourself introduced to Eilys. She's a new sensation."

He gave me a flashing smile.

"It's already been done. She's quite a beauty, isn't she? Gives you a shock."

"From a man's point of view," I said, "the shock can't be a painful one."

He picked up a saucer, and copying me, wrapped it in a piece of newspaper and popped it in the crate.

"How do you get along with her? Does she fit in?"

"Very much so. You can't help liking her. And she isn't a bit conscious about her looks. I suppose when you're the kind of girl who gets so much admiration it finally fails to excite you."

"You and she have got something in common," he said. "You're going to be very rich women one day. Ida hasn't made any secret about the disposition of her estate."

I wished he hadn't said such a thing. I sat back on my heels.

"That's something I'm not interested in, Gordon, and I hate to hear it referred to. I'm very fond of Ida, and I've never been so happy in my life as I am here, and then people talk about me coming into her money as if they ignored the fact that when I do Ida will be dead. It's horrible. Don't you start that!"

He looked reproved and understanding.

"Oh, but you're taking it too seriously. Delia, I do realize how you feel about it, of course I do. Ida's going to live for a long time yet, so please don't be touchy when I point out that it can't be so dreadful for you and Eilys to know that some day when you're middle-aged women you might be glad to come into a fortune. Ida doesn't feel embarrassed about it, so I don't see why you need to. And I'm her executor."

My hand went up to my cheek.

"What do you mean, a fortune?"

"Ida's estate must be worth a quarter of a million sterling."

"No!"

"Yes."

"But what about Gladys and the two men?"

"Don't worry. They'll be well provided for."

I grabbed a cup and wrapped it energetically.

"I don't want to talk about it," I said. "I won't think about it. It's absolutely awful for you and me to be sitting up here talking about her money. Never mention it to me again."

Suddenly he touched my cheek, lightly with two fingers. My heart bounced all over my chest.

"All right, I won't. It worries you, and that's the last thing I'd ever want to do, Delia. But you mustn't ever worry your head about anything Ida chooses to do. She's always done exactly as she likes, and devil take it, she always will."

"You're telling me!" I spread my hands. "She's going to drown all this nice hand-painted Bavarian furniture because she thinks it's too old-fashioned for the new house, and she thinks it would be happier left to the waters than being worn out by strangers—can you believe it? There's a cupboard painted with Alpine scenes that I'm going to insist on taking for my own room, even if it doesn't match the new furniture she's bought me. Ida's so sentimental and yet so tough at the same time, she baffles me sometimes."

"She baffles us all. You ought to know that by now."

He lighted two cigarettes and put one between my lips. The intimacy of the action startled me.

"You look pretty tired to me," he said. "Relax a bit. And I wish you'd stop flogging yourself at that camp. They're not worth it."

"I think they are."

"And I think they're not."

"I love going," I said doggedly.

He got up and dusted his knees.

"Shall I carry these things downstairs for you, if they're ready?"

"I wish you would. Thank you very much."

When I had finished I went down. In the hall Gordon and Jarzy were chattering nineteen to the dozen in German, as they always did when they were together to increase their fluency.

In the kitchen, among the neglected packing-cases, Eilys, with a spotted handkerchief tied under her chin, was doing her impression of Gracie Fields, voice, eyes, mouth, and all. Gladys and Franz were the audience, rocking with laughter.

"Here!" I said. "Who's working? Only me?"

"I shall now," said Eilys, "give you my celebrated impression of Gladys singing Mimi."

It was wickedly funny, but I didn't think Gladys appreciated it and I daren't laugh too much.

"I'm dropping," I said. "I'm going up to change."

A few minutes later Eilys followed me, with two cups of coffee on a tray. She planted it on the bed and spooned sugar into the cups.

"Ida's weeping over some amber velvet curtains. They're no use to her, but she can't bear to part from them. I said—just being funny—why not make them into an evening cloak? There was a Dior picture in the paper she could copy. She fairly jumped at the idea and started hacking them up. Deel, she does get on my nerves sometimes."

I said nothing, but pulled out a clean blouse and a pleated skirt. Eilys slowly stirred her cup.

"Go on. Tell me you wonder why I stay when I feel like that."

"I wasn't even thinking it."

She handed me my coffee and I began to sip it.

"You see, Deel, I stay because it suits me to. Now Daddy's ill I haven't anywhere else to go. My parents were divorced when I was eleven, and the court divided me between them until I was fourteen and then I could choose for myself. I chose Daddy, he's more my sort. Profligate, irrepressible, giddy, and unreliable."

"I haven't noticed you were any of those things."

She lay back on the bed and threw her arms wide.

"You should meet my mother. She's intense, she breeds dogs in Suffolk and has you up at the crack of dawn to exercise them. There's no life down there, just a hard bed, simple food, and work for the sake of work—oh, not Me at all. I couldn't!"

"It sounds as if it would be a strain."

"I only tried it once. It nearly killed me." She sat up abruptly. "By the way, you never told me about Gordon, the glamour boy."

"I did tell you."

"Then I wasn't listening. He's got everything, hasn't he? Side-face, he'd wake the flame in a female zombie. But not in me. I know that type so well. All ego, and takes it for granted you're just waiting to fall. Within five minutes of being introduced he said he'd call for me with his car and take me out to dinner. I just said no, thank you. It rocked him."

It rocked me too.

"You mean you aren't going?"

"Why should I? I don't want to."

"But, Eilys, you ought to go really. He's Ida's executor. He only wanted to get to know you. It was a sort of courtesy invitation."

She put her head back and gave a little yelp of laughter.

"He'll get to know me in my time, not his."

"Oh!" I said, dropping my hairbrush.

"What's the matter?"

"Only—well, he invited me out almost at first sight, like he did you, and I went. Did that look naïve?"

"Not a bit, if you wanted to go. It was up to you. But with me I just felt he was asking to be slapped down, so I did it. He was so sure he'd made a kill."

I sat down on the dressing-stool.

"Eilys, I don't know much about men. Do you?"

She threw out her hands. "I suppose there's nothing I don't know—since I was fourteen. And I learnt the hard way. In a man's world. Our set was pretty rakish. There's nothing you need to know, Deel, except to treat them casual, take all you can get out of them, and brush them off."

"That sounds awfully cynical and hard-boiled."

"Well, men are hard-boiled enough where we're concerned. They haven't any noble, chivalrous feelings, believe me, whatever the pretty stories say. It's themselves they're out to do good to, not you—mind you, I'm not blaming them, I'm just telling you in case you have the wrong idea. Whatever a man gives you, does for you, he expects to be paid for it because he's doing it from some dark, veiled motive of his own, not to make things nice for you. Remember that. Now I've got you scared."

"Oh no."

"Yes, I have. You think I'm not very nice. You're so right. Niceness is an atmosphere they try to surround the young with. I think that's a mistake, it doesn't prepare them for life. Holy boots! Now we're talking about life. What started all this?"

"Me, knowing nothing about men."

She gave me the warmest smile.

"Don't you ever worry. If you ever get in a jam come and tell me. I'll put you right."

"Now you're terrifying me," I said, laughing.

She, I thought, was putting on a pose. All that disillusion, sophistication, over-statement.

"Eilys, you're a tonic," I said. "And I might as well tell you that I've been madly envious of you because life has given you so much, beauty and wit and gaiety and the gift of making everybody fall for you on sight."

She jumped off the bed.

"Life's going to give me a whole lot more yet. And you too, Deel. You'll see! You haven't learnt to take your chances properly. Snap into it, and grab everything, girl. It's the only way. Listen, I'm going to be reasonable. Do you really think I ought to go out with this Gordon creature?"

"I think Ida would like you to, and it looks frightfully rude of you not to."

"Does it?" She thought that over. "All right then, I'll go. Not tonight because it would look as if I was climbing down and that's a thing I never do. But next time he asks me. I'll try and bear it. I know—I'll talk to him earnestly and endlessly about the ballet. I'll choke him to death with culture."

I spluttered with laughing.

"Come on, we'd better go down."

Was it childish of me, I wondered, to be so happy because Eilys hadn't taken to Gordon?

4

FROM that evening she and I were the closest of friends, and I only had one secret from her, the one I would have died of shame for her to discover. We did everything together, it was obvious to all that we were a pair. Gay, glamorous, and uninhibited, she made every day more exciting for me, and I woke each morning with a happy feeling of fun and sparkle to be shared with my friend. Ida was delighted that we got along so well. The five of us together made a compact and completely contented group. Ida's tight little family.

Working at top speed and nearly giving off electric crackles, Gladys made up an evening cloak from the amber velvet curtain, and found an old green satin dress to cut up for the lining. Ida was thrilled; joy bubbled out of her. She who bought herself model dresses was over the moon about this piece of make-do.

She came to my room to show it off, and very striking it looked. It was more than vivid, it was positively rowdy.

"Don't you think it has kicks?" She twirled on her high-heeled shoes. "Next time I go anywhere I'll wear it. When we get settled in the new house we'll give a party—I know lots of people —and we'll be asked back. What a lovely time we're going to have!"

"You're the one person who could wear it," I said. "You look sensational, Ida."

"Oh Delia, you are sweet." She seized my hand and held it against her cheek. From anybody else it would have been affected, but from Ida it was somehow right and touching. "You're one of the nicest people I ever knew."

I laughed it off. "We're all rather nice, aren't we?"

"I know, I know. Oh, we're so lucky! I think we're the luckiest, happiest family in the world . . . I say! I can hardly bear to take this gorgeous garment off. I could trail around all day in it. Do tell Gladys how beautifully she's made it, it'll buck her up."

"Of course I will."

Gradually we got the stuff that was to be saved from the old house into the new one, unpacked, arranged. We had picnic meals when there wasn't time to cook. Franz was at school all day, and Jarzy now a pupil with Gordon, so we four women coped with the job in hand.

And the last day came, the last breakfast.

"Don't you two men forget," said Ida, "that tonight you don't come home here, you come to Tom-na-hurich."

"What?" screamed Gladys.

"When I was a little girl," said Ida dreamily, "I went to stay in the highlands of Scotland at a house called Tom-na-hurich. It means the hill of the fairies. I said that if ever I had a house of my own, that's what I'd call it. And this is my first chance, my first very own house. So you'd better practise saying it."

"The postman had better practise saying it," said Gladys. "And do you think you'll get away with that with the tradespeople?"

"It will break every jaw in Dorfen," said Franz.

"Don't be silly," said Ida. "It's nothing to most German words."

"I shall call it Schloss Tommy," said Eilys.

Ida glared and we all shrieked. She seemed on top of the world today, and it was I who, going up to the bedroom which I had only occupied for two months, felt the queerest pang at the thought that in a matter of hours this room would be swirling in water and trailing weed. I looked out of the window for the last time, down the valley, misty with the waking green of spring, all to be drowned under the cold flood. Nobody would see it again, and nobody but me with my old-fashioned sentimentality seemed to care.

Gordon was coming to fetch us in his car in the afternoon, for he had to be in court in the morning. We ate a sandwich lunch and sat in the denuded drawing-room on the old sofa and chairs which weren't going with us. It gave me a positively morbid feeling to touch the worn covers.

"Doesn't this room look huge with the piano out?" said Ida. "But the piano looks splendid in the new drawing-room. We'll have the most wonderful sing tonight, think of it."

"I'm thinking," said Eilys dryly. "I'm the one that can't sing, can't play. I'll be reading a good book with my fingers in my ears."

"Oh, but you mustn't be sad about that, dahling. When we're settled Delia shall teach you to play a little bit, it will save you from being bored, and Gladys can start your singing lessons. You've got terrific vocal chords if only they were controlled."

"That'll be madly gay," said Eilys.

"Oh look!" cried Gladys at the window.

Passing the bottom of the drive went a flat horse-drawn lorry piled with miscellaneous household goods. It was driven by a young man, and next to him sat an old, bent, dejected figure. I recognized the old man I had talked to in the valley, the one who dreaded having to leave his home.

"It's old Seibler," cried Ida. "He's left his cottage for good. He's the last, they're all gone now."

"All but us," said Gladys. "We'll be the last."

"Oh God!" wailed Ida, and burst into tears.

Such tears. I had never seen anybody cry so whole-heartedly, so lavishly, but whatever Ida did she did on the grand scale. Now she was crying, and it would be the weep of the century. Nothing restrained about it. All her previous calm was spent and gone. She was a poor old woman being turned out of her home, and sobbing with abandon, she was getting every ounce out of the situation.

Gladys flew to her, clasped her, sobbed with her, but nothing could comfort Ida. She shuddered with despair as she clung to Gladys, they wailed in concert.

"Oh Gladys, do stop it and take her upstairs," I said. "You're making her worse."

"I won't go upstairs!" howled Ida. "How can I! My beautiful drowned bedroom. It's come to me all of a sudden. I've realized."

"Ida, please."

"Don't be so heartless," murmured Gladys with streaming eyes. "Don't you see we're in agony?"

"But Gordon will be here at any minute. You must do something to your faces."

I got them into the kitchen. I bathed Ida's swollen face and drenched her sorrow in half a bottle of hock left on the window-sill. Gladys dabbed her own red-rimmed eyes.

I powdered Ida lavishly out of my compact.

"You don't want Gordon to see you like this. You look about eighty," I said bracingly.

That did it. Ida made a miraculous recovery.

"Give me my bag. Let me get at myself. Gladys, don't stand there drooling, you silly girl."

I flew back to the drawing-room. On the sofa Eilys was rocking with sardonic laughter.

"What a comedy act that was!"

"Rather grim comedy," I said. "I don't think Ida realized until just now, then it hit her between the eyes."

"Don't you believe it, Deel. It was pure exhibitionism. If she'd only be her age!"

"I'll admit she did rather overdo it."

"Overdo it? It was sheer ham."

"That's a bit unkind. You can't judge the depth of other people's feelings."

Suddenly I heard the crunch of Gordon's car on the drive. He came in, cool, immaculate, in superbly good form.

"What? You two girls the only ones ready to go?"

"We were all ready a few minutes ago," Eilys explained, "but now Ida's doing nostalgic swoons in the kitchen and Gladys is bellowing in sympathy."

He quirked his lips. "Can I do anything to help?"

"I wouldn't try. How did you get on this morning? I should think you are quite something in a divorce court."

He pulled a face. "Actually defendant's counsel tore me in strips, and my client wasn't a bit pleased with me. You see how honest I am with you."

"How sad. Was she young and beautiful and rich?"

"There wasn't a she. My client was the husband and he hadn't a leg to stand on. . . . By the way, Delia, I've ordered a splendid cold supper to be sent round for you all from the Kutzner Hotel. Then you won't have to bother about anything, and perhaps you'd all like to go out somewhere tonight."

"Not a hope," said Eilys. "Ida says we're to have a lovely sing."

He gave a small yelp.

"What's the matter with Delia? She's looking dim."

"Sorry," I said. "Perhaps I'm nostalgic too. After all, nobody will ever sit in this room again."

"Oh, but you must reduce it all to absurdity. After all, you might say at lunch, 'Nobody will ever eat this hamburger again'. Who's going to fetch Ida?"

But Ida came out of the kitchen in a sudden rush, followed by Gladys, still sniffing, and made straight for the car crying, "I won't look back. Not one look back will I give."

None of us looked back. We left the charming green valley behind.

Gordon kept up a stream of spirited talk all the way to the new house, and Ida opened the door with her key, and we were in. There it was with its lovely shining floors, the piney smell, the big newly-furnished rooms, log fires—Franz had seen to those, flowers everywhere—Jarzy's contribution, and a welcoming air that swept away every lingering bit of regret. We ranged all over it, too excited to take our things off. It felt like home already.

"It's wonderful . . . it's wonderful."

The men came home to Gordon's sumptuous supper, waiter and maid laid on, and afterwards Ida made a ceremony of opening the piano in the new drawing-room, the music came out, and I sat down to play.

"I haven't unpacked," said Eilys. "I haven't even got a book to read."

"Well, just sit and think," said Ida unhelpfully.

"Perhaps Eilys will come out with me," said Gordon. "We might find some kind of entertainment."

"Oh yes, do go with Gordon, dahling," Ida cried.

Eilys looked at me and rolled her eyes. I giggled. Off they went.

Next morning she came down late.

"You can blame Gordon," she said. "He would go dancing. I danced like a wet log—didn't feel like it—but he kept me out till two."

"At the Magda?"

"Heavens, no. At a night club called the Püpchen. It was lethal."

"It's extremely kind of Gordon," said Ida severely, "to take an interest in you two girls."

"I've done my duty," said Eilys. "Who's coming to see the flood waters pour in? Round about midnight. Mike's going to take me. Onkel doesn't want to go. How about you, Deel?"

"I don't think I want to," I said. "It's a bit macabre."

"It'll be worth seeing."

"Not for me." Ida gave a dramatic shudder. "I've got past liking the spectacular. And it'll be cold up there."

"You don't know what you're missing. We're taking a midnight feast."

On being told that he and Eilys were going to see the flooding of the valley alone, Jarzy looked so radiantly happy that I was anxious for him. He could never hide his feelings about Eilys.

Ida had noticed it too. She came and sat on my bed while I was arranging my things in the new room.

"It would be nice," she said, playing with my sewing box, "if Eilys took to Jarzy. I'd love to keep you two girls in the family."

"It's a thought," I said lightly. "Who have you picked for me?"

"Gordon, of course."

I gritted my teeth and began to scrabble in my bag.

"You're the only one I'd give him up to," Ida went on. "I adore him. You must encourage him, dahling, he's terribly shy."

"I hadn't noticed it." I started laying things out on my dressing-table. "And it's awfully bad policy to fling people at each other's heads. It never comes off."

She looked disappointed.

"Don't you fancy him, dahling?"

"I think he's terrific, but—oh Ida, you are the most maddening, absurd—"

"As long as you're fond of me—"

I said with real feeling. "Ida, I simply love you. You know that."

"You won't go back to England, will you?"

"I'm so happy here," I said, "that I'll never, never want to."

5

EILYS and Jarzy brought back a description of the valley flooding worthy of the slickest commentator. They had been sitting high on the moonlit hillside when the engineers opened the dam and the green cliff of water began to crumble and gush and turn into a torrent that swept on with deafening noise. It was sensational. They stayed for hours, in fact they only came home for breakfast.

"And did you—I mean, actually—see *It* happen?" breathed Gladys, horror-struck. "The house? I should have died."

"We did not see it get as far as the house," Jarzy confessed. "It was too dark to see much at all. Eilys has what-you-call lay it on thick."

"Oh Mike, you've let me down. There was one huge lake when it came light this morning, but if you want the truth the water was only creeping round the house. The valley will take days to fill up. So we didn't have the fun of watching it gurgle down the chimneys, Gladys."

"Now you're going to upset Ida."

"Not a bit," said Ida briskly. "All that's finished. When the lake is nice and full I'll go and have a look at it myself."

Eilys spread cherry jam on a fresh roll.

"This is heaven. Being out all night seems to suit me. I don't know when I last got any sleep, what with Gordon's night club, and then a nice cold mountain top with Jarzy."

Jarzy's soul was in his eyes for all to see. I felt sorry for him.

Eilys went off to her bath, and with her wonderful hair brushed out on her shoulders, and wearing a pale blue housecoat, she came to watch me dust my room.

She walked up and down, smoking, restless.

"Can't you settle?" I said.

"Deel," she said, "I'm bored to tears. Two nights running, all that burning masculinity, it was exhausting."

"Did you have to rouse it?" I flipped the duster at her. "I'd have thought that staggering round a crowded floor, clasped to a man you can't bear, was a real passion damper, and as for sitting on a wet hill at midnight watching a lot of water crawling down a valley—"

"Men don't notice surroundings." She knocked off her ash. "They've only one fixation in their minds. I tell you, the only one of our three I respect is Onkel, because he's never made a pass at me."

"Give him a chance!" I said sarcastically. "He's got heaps of hidden charm."

She threw herself face downwards across the bed.

"I'm going to give up selfish pleasures and go in for good works."

"You do just that."

"Oh, I mean it."

"What sort of good works?"

"Well—I thought I might go with you to that camp, you seem to get a kick out of it. I could do something, it would be a change for me, God knows."

I slapped down the duster.

"Oh no, you don't! You've got to have a better reason than that to do welfare work. It's a job, not five minutes' fun. It's work, not flapping your eyelashes."

She rolled over and gazed at me.

"But I'm dead serious—honestly, Deel. Do you think I'm not capable of doing something useful?"

"Of course you're capable of anything. Do you really mean this?"

"Of course I do. Please take me, next time you go."

"They're desperate for helpers." I thought for a minute. "Come if you like, but it isn't pretty."

"When are you going there again?"

"Tomorrow."

She put her head on one side, and bit her finger.

"Gordon said he'd call tomorrow and take us both for a drive, so I think it would be a good thing if we weren't here, don't you? It would shake him."

"So that's why you want to go to the camp, to be clever and dodge Gordon!"

"Not a bit. Really."

"You didn't tell me he was coming."

"I didn't have the chance before, and I don't think it's important."

"All right," I said. "We'll go to the camp."

I hoped I was doing right. Eilys was incalculable, but with all her flippancy she had brains and ability, and I knew that as a worker she would get a welcome.

I was right. She started off by charming everybody, and Nora Nixon was delighted.

"What can you do, Eilys? Anything special, or a bit of everything?"

"I'll try anything once." Eilys's smile was like the sunrise. "I'm frightfully willing. But strictly non-medical, please. No blood."

Nora laughed. "Could you sort these cards—new arrivals? Make a note of names, ages, nationalities, diseases if any."

"I'd love to. I can even spell."

"Don't take any notice of the din in this room. You'll get used to it, everybody wanting attention at once. If you get stuck, ask Gerald."

She sat down at the desk and I went off to join the doctor. When I got back three hours later she was still at it.

"Come with me," I said. "I want to introduce you to some friends of mine."

On the way to the Todors' room I gave Eilys a sketch of their history. Madame flung out her hands and grasped mine, excited almost past words.

"Miss! Miss Delia! What a long, long time! We sought you had us quite forgotten."

"We've been moving house," I said. "This is my friend, Eilys Mallins. She's going to help here."

I was getting used to seeing The Look on people's faces the first time Eilys was sprung upon them.

Madame clasped her hand.

"Anozzer beautiful young lady—so good, so generous! Oh, zis is wonnerful. Please to sit down." She raised her voice. "Pappa! Look! Two angels have come to see us. Get you up off zat chair and welcome zem to our home.'"

The old man, more dilapidated than when I saw him last, pulled himself up with obvious pain. He bent his creaking back, lifted Eilys's hand, and brushed his lips across it.

"You are gracious, Miss. I hope you are well?"

I could see that Eilys was moved by his pathetic courtliness. Madame stood by beaming, achieving tremendous dignity in spite of the saggy corpulence which comes from a diet of stodge.

"Shall we not sit down?" she said. "Our guests will take ze chairs, Pappa, and you and I will sit on ze bed."

"Bed?" cried Eilys. "But you need two easy chairs. Why haven't they got easy chairs, Deel?"

Madame's smile was ineffably gracious.

"In our own home we had ze easy chairs. Now we just remember zem, and use ze imaginations, isn't it? Be seated, and when Isold come in she can make us coffee."

"And I've brought a cake," I said. "I made it yesterday—look."

"It is ze best I ever see," said Madame, inspecting my undistinguished offering.

"But you've got to have easy chairs!" Eilys broke out. "You can't relax on those horrible things. Surely it's only a matter of asking, Deel? This whole place looks disgraceful. It's scandalous. If nobody makes a fuss nothing ever gets done. It's like an orphanage I went to in Villemont, no playroom for the children, I made an awful row and got them to put in a playroom, and I ordered little pink rompers—gosh, but I put the fear of God into them."

I caught her eye and shook my head. I had already warned her about this sort of thing, and also about keeping the conversation away from life in the camp and the contrasts outside of it. But Eilys was unquenchable. She had taken to the Todors, and she was off!

"We ought to have brought a bottle of wine to go with the cake, Deel. Remind me next time."

"Wine?" The old man's eyes popped with delight. "Zen we play we are in a beautiful restaurant."

With a smile of glowing sweetness Eilys carried him a slice of cake.

"I'll bet you've known plenty of gay restaurants."

Suddenly he looked years younger as his furrowed face twinkled at her.

"Do you know—but you'd never believe—now listen to this—" He chuckled, whispering to her, catching her nods and the flash of her eyes, going on and on with his little story, quite captivated by her vivid interest.

Madame Todor threw up her hands.

"But look at Pappa, how he is took wiz your beautiful friend."

Eilys was saying, "There are lovely restaurants in Dorfen, you know, but I mustn't talk about them because I am told you only like to talk about miserable things—"

"Now where on earz did she get zat idea?" cried Madame Todor, obviously dying to be in on what promised to be a really entertaining conversation. But the old man wasn't going to be manoeuvred out of star role.

"Ah, Dorfen. I have too little money to go on ze bus even if my legs were good, which zey are not, but Max once took me to a beer garden—it was before Christmas and ze guitars were playing carols. It made me magnificent feeling, I drank and sang and drank and sang. And ze lights in ze streets! Well, zis old fool pretended he was at home in Bucharest, and I said to Max, 'Fetch ze car, it's only just round ze corner, my boy, and we'll go to ze ballet and perhaps a little supper after.' And I acted I had on my white tie and my opera cloak and my order ribbon—old fool. But it made me feel so good. And we laugh all ze way home on ze bus, Max and I . . . home, did I say? I am worse mad zan ever, you see."

Madame couldn't be out of this.

"Miss Ei-liss, tell me, are zere good shops in Dorfen? Tell me about ze fashions, ze china, ze linens. Tell me, like it was in a book. And is zere music—concerts?"

"But of course there are French fashions—fabulous things. And everything to attract the Americans and get their dollars, like it is all over Europe now. The prices are frightful but you can't resist. People are bringing out their stored-up pre-war things. I saw some Meissen china—"

She made it sound like an Arabian Nights' entertainment, exaggerated, colourful. Wines, music, jewellery, cars. Nobody could hope to stop her, and to tell the truth she had her audience enthralled. The two old people drank it in with glittering eyes, and when Eilys embarked on a wildly comic account of the night club she had been to with Gordon they shook with laughter.

Madame wiped her flushed face.

"How long since we laugh like zat, Pappa? Zis young lady she is like Mam'zelle Julie Orloche from Paris, from ze *Folies Bergère*, who stay with us once. She make us scream too—so nottee, so chic. But zis one is more beautiful."

"Oh no," Eilys cried. "My face comes out of a box."

"Mine is horrible." Madame grimaced. "Like old, old shoe. I have no cream to put on it all zese monzz."

"No foundation cream? But what kind do you use? I'll bring you a big jar next time I come. Do you like the French ones, or—"

"Ze Coty—ze Lancôme. Oh, it would be wonderful. But you are too kind."

It hadn't occurred to me that a woman of nearly sixty, a refugee who had lost all, could worry about her face when she hadn't even a cloth to put over her stained table. Ought I to have thought?

The door opened and Isold and Max walked in. They greeted me, and catching sight of Eilys stood rooted. Madame made the introductions. Max bowed over Eilys's hand, his eyes captivated; Isold was staring at her dress, her shoes. I had suggested she should wear a dark, simple dress, but this was a Balmain model in fine blue wool, a real work of art, and her shoes were crocodile pumps.

"Come now, Isold," cried Madame. "Fetch water and make us some coffee. Miss Delia has brought us a cake, and Miss Ei-liss has cheered us up so, we laughed like I cannot remember."

Eilys had already taken in the fact that Max was a personable young man. She looked at him under her lashes.

"I'd love some coffee. This is quite a party."

"I shouldn't expect too much from the coffee, Mam'zelle. It isn't what you or I would call coffee."

"Oh, please call me Eilys. I'm going to call you Max. It's a name I adore."

"Excuse me staring at your dress," Isold said. "It's heavenly. Could I touch the sleeve to feel the cloth?"

"Good gracious, yes. Do you like it? It's quite an old one. Would you like to have it? You're thinner than I am, but it's a bit tight for me. I'm sure it would fit you. I can't very well take it off here and go home in nothing, but I'll bring it for you next time I come."

Starry-eyed, the colour flooded Isold's sallow cheeks.

"You can't mean it! Oh!"

"Look, Pappa." Madame nudged the old man. "Zis angel, now she take ze clothes off her back for Isold. I see I shall have to make zat coffee, Isold is in a swoon."

"I'll make it," I said. I hadn't been in the picture at all for half an hour, they could well spare me.

I went out to the tap in the passage, waiting my turn in a queue of women, and came back to find the junkshop assortment of cups and mugs ready on the table. I put the kettle on the stove and Madame tipped the coffee tin over a jug.

"Is that all?" said Max. "It won't taste of anything."

"But that is the end."

"Write it down, Deel," cried Eilys. "Some of Ida's best coffee next time we come. Let's console ourselves while that kettle's boiling. I give it about half an hour."

Out came her gold cigarette case and was handed round. Everybody eagerly seized the cigarettes. It was like suddenly being round the Christmas tree.

"But how awful not to have enough cigarettes! Write it down, Deel. I know I'll forget something. And now—" She turned her lustrous gaze on Madame Todor, "—you were going to tell me about Roumania. I've heard Bucharest used to be very glamorous—"

It was like putting a needle on a long-playing record. There was no stopping Madame. The time flew, the saga went on—vivid, impassioned—the others interrupted.

"Zis house zat Pappa bought, it was near the art school where Max was studying, and much too big, but—"

"It was not too big—"

"Isold was to have her coming-out party zere—"

"And Max's student friends—"

"So many guests. No house can be too big when zere are so many friends. Zis coming-out party for Isold—"

"But nobody wants to hear about the coming-out party that Isold never had. It was the war, everything was the war—we're all sick of it—"

"Please, please have another cigarette, Max—never mind if it's the last. I have more at home."

The kettle boiled. At least the pale-coloured brew was hot, if horrible.

I prised Eilys away at last in a buzz of farewells, laughing excited faces, tears even.

We pushed our way through the rowdy, smelly passages, stepping over small children, avoiding at least two free fights. We were outside at last.

Eilys opened her mouth in a wide gasp.

"Get it! It's fresh air. The smell in there nearly finished me off. Wet wool, disinfectant, babies, and stew. Do they ever eat anything but stew? I shouldn't think so from the way it clings."

"There are plenty of people outside this camp who live on stew too," I told her. "You might realize that there are only two ways of eating in this country, the way we eat and the other. The way we eat costs the earth. Ida has the money and doesn't mind spending it, so we get chicken and steak and butter and cream and imported coffee."

"Black market?"

"I'm afraid so."

"Well, I'm all for it."

We walked across to the car which Ida had lent us for the afternoon, and Eilys said, "You might as well drive straight into town."

"What for?"

"Because I want to get Isold a good lipstick, and face cream for the old woman, and cigarettes for Max, and a few bottles of rich old tawny for Pappa."

"You can't do that."

"Holy mackerel! Who's going to stop me?"

I felt mean, she had been such a riot in there, but I couldn't let it go on.

"Eilys, think. If you're going to be any help in this camp you've got to be impartial and do what you can for everybody, not shower luxuries on one family."

She gave me a belligerent blue stare.

"I thought the Todors were special friends of yours."

"In a way they are. But I mustn't let myself spoil them or let you either. They're awfully attractive and appealing in their miserable condition while many aren't, but they're only one family among scores. You never went in the big room. That would have shaken you. About two hundred people just sitting on benches or huddled in their bunks because they're too despairing to have any interest in life. Every one of them is a real person needing everything.

Eilys, we can't have favourites and show it. We can't buy wine and lipsticks for one or two when others haven't got coats or shoes. And I wish you hadn't talked about easy chairs. Don't you see it?"

"No, I don't." She climbed into the car. "If I come here to help I'll do it my own way. You can be a little Saint Popsy to your heart's content, but don't you tell me what not to do!"

I started the car.

"You'll make Nora Nixon's job a lot harder."

"And who the hell is she? The commissar with the knout? Don't make me laugh. And don't be such a prig, Deel."

Was I? Prig was such a hateful word. Was I right, or was Eilys, spilling out her gaiety and profligate generosity? I felt miserable.

"Eilys, I don't approve and I'm not going to drive you to town."

"All right, don't. I'm losing interest anyway."

"Please don't take it like that."

It was our first clash of opinion. We hardly spoke all the way home. And hardly was Eilys in the house when she was begging Ida for coffee and saying that she intended to raid the larder. Ida argued, and it ended up in a fine old shouting match.

"That girl," cried Ida, stamping into the hall, "has no respect for me."

I couldn't help laughing.

"She's not used to being crossed. I think she always has her own way."

"Not with me, she doesn't! And I'm not going to feed half Europe. And it's all your fault, Delia, for letting her loose in that disgusting camp. They get plenty to eat there, I know they do because I've enquired—I'm not callous, and if it interests you I've given them quite a lot of money. But they're not sharing my coffee, my wine, my *pâté de foie gras*. You're bad enough, I won't stand two of you at it."

"But I agree! Ida, honestly I don't want her to do this kind of thing."

"Then stop her. You started it. And take that uniform off. You look like a policewoman. What you girls need is men—not howling peasants."

6

THE next evening Franz asked me if I would like to go with him on the bus to see the new lake, a pleasanter way of describing the flooded valley. Jarzy hadn't come home that evening, Ida was reading a new novel, and Eilys was writing to her father. Gladys looked as if she would have liked an invitation to join us, but we rather guiltily avoided asking her.

Franz was always good company. We laughed a lot on the bus as we talked about the day.

The old road through the valley didn't exist any more. The bus put us down at the beginning of the hill road which was now being developed. The workmen had left. We wandered for a while and then found ourselves on the verge of a vast calm lake of water like grey silk shot with turquoise.

"Oh, look! I can't believe it."

The winding road was beautiful, a new landscape. We kept on exclaiming. At last we stopped at the edge of the water. There was hardly a ripple on that soft grey-blue surface, only a silvery sheen from the reflected sky. The bank on which we stood was reproduced down there in detail, an upside-down enchanting loveliness of larches and silver birches, and all round our feet were the plumy bright green shoots of young bracken. It was impossible to realize that in this lake our valley and our house lay buried.

"Franz, it's beautiful. I thought I should feel a pang, but I don't."

"Neither do I. It's so pretty, as if Nature had made it and not man. I love a lake. There was one not far from my home."

I thought of his family, lost in the horrible maw of Jewish persecution, and I knew he was thinking of them too.

"It is true," he said, "that beautiful things last for ever, and the ugly things hurt less and less until they go quite away from you. It was meant that I should live and have friends and work, and I am happy and grateful. I owe everything to Ida."

"She owes a lot to you. She and Gladys came out of Auschwitz with a man to look after them. Didn't that mean something?"

He laughed. "When did Ida need her spirits keeping up? She only accepted my arm that day because she had a big, bad foot tied up in rags. She hated not being able to come out what she called under her own steam."

"That's like Ida. I can imagine it."

It was one of those soft spring evenings which tell you that it will be summer soon because April feels like June. The evening light turned gold, brightening the tops of the larches and the pale heights of far-off mountains. I could have stayed for hours, but we had to leave because the bus was due.

"I hope this lake doesn't get too popular," I said as we took our seats. "I hope they won't encircle it with beer gardens and bathing places and boat jetties for the tourists."

"I do not think they will. There are other lakes nearer to Dorfen, and tourists like things close to hand."

"I hope you're right, and that they won't run coach tours out here."

We walked up to the house, and at the door stood Gordon's car. My throat went dry. I almost wished he hadn't been there, to spoil with emotional tumult this peaceful evening I was enjoying.

He came out of the house.

"Delia! I'm so glad you're back early. I'm going to take you for a drive."

"But Franz and I—"

"Franz has had his turn. Now it's mine."

"That's sensible," said Franz, abandoning me.

"But don't any of the others want to go too?"

"They're all busy. Don't make difficulties."

We drove away.

"And now," said Gordon, "you can tell me what you mean by going off with another man when you should have waited for me?"

I took myself firmly in hand.

"Franz and I went to see the new lake."

"Oh? And you're just going there again, with me. You may find it quite different."

"It's beautiful."

"Good. We'll appreciate it together."

"But it's going to be dusk soon," I said feebly.

"What's the matter with the dusk?"

Travelling in Gordon's car was a very different thing from the country bus. In no time we had arrived at the lakeside, and Gordon, looking round, exclaimed, "I say, this is something. A new landscape. Let's explore."

We left the car and walked on to the place where Franz and I had been an hour before. Gordon was carrying a rug which he spread on the bank.

"Sit down. This is marvellous. Here—light cigarettes for us while I unpack the knapsack."

I wondered what it was he had been carrying. He brought out a bottle of hock and two tall green Venetian glasses.

"I'm a great believer in pampering all the senses at once."

He poured the wine, and I sipped mine. It was delicious and went well with the heavenly evening and the beauty of the lake. A rug isn't very big, his shoulder touched mine.

"A good effort on the part of the water board, Delia, and so pleasantly deserted. Let's make the most of this spot, before lines of tourist coaches come here to park. It won't be this year, thank God. They've got to make a motor road first."

"Franz thinks they won't want to come out here. They've got the Ammsee at Dorfen."

"Let's hope Franz is right. Well, this is your second *tête-à-tete* this evening. How did the first one go?"

"Why should I tell you?"

He gave me an intrigued, almost ardent look.

"Where were you yesterday? I called to take you girls out."

"We were both at the camp. Eilys wanted to go."

"Oh yes, Ida told me. How did Eilys make out? I don't see her as a lady bountiful."

I knocked off my ash.

"We don't want lady bountifuls. We want conscientious workers."

"Sounds dreary. I bet Eilys shook them with her looks."

My pang of jealousy was childish, and yet I couldn't help thinking, here's the time and the place and the loved one all together, and he has to talk about Eilys! Then I saw the funny side of it and began to laugh.

"She was a riot. She offered the dress off her back to a Roumanian girl, and with all that destitution round her the thing that worried her was that an old woman hadn't got any face cream."

He fairly shouted, startling the silence.

"So she's going to fit them all up with cosmetics, no doubt."

"She's already started."

(Eilys, Eilys. Always Eilys. What was the matter with me, that I wasn't able to steer a conversation the way I wanted it?)

Gordon lay back full length, holding up his glass to the late sun and squinting through the golden liquid.

"This is wonderful. A sort of Rhiengold effect. Come on, do a sort of Rhine maiden effect on me and help me to relax. Phew, I've had quite a day. Ruddy awful, irascible client this afternoon, I dread him coming—can't get rid of him."

"What do Rhine maidens do?"

"Sing, or murmur poetry or something."

For the life of me I couldn't think of a line, I who had by heart reams and reams of the Oxford Book of English Verse. And the first time I needed a bit of it the whole lot fled. Hopelessly inadequate!

I plucked bits of grass and made a pattern on the rug.

"What's the matter now?" he said. "What's your problem?"

I had to break out with the thing that was on my mind.

"I've had a letter from my mother. She's strained her back and my sister isn't well. They'd like me to go back. I suppose I ought to think about it."

He sat straight up, showing startling interest.

"Go back? I never heard of such a thing." His tone was masterful. "Of course you can't go back. They can manage perfectly well."

"How do you know they can manage?"

"Of course they can manage! They're only trying to get hooks into you."

"Gordon, really!"

"Well, aren't they?"

I picked up an old splayed-out fir cone and flicked it into the water.

"I don't know how you got the idea, but—"

"I'm not completely unperceptive."

"Gordon, the first time I went out with you I told you I hadn't lived a sheltered life. It was a lie. Everything I told you that evening, about going to Malaya, about my wildly exciting adventures in the war, was a lie."

I gulped out this frightful confession. He simply laughed and said, "Well, what of it? It made a good story."

"Oh, you are marvellous to take it like that. Listen, I've done nothing—absolutely nothing. My mother has run my life for me."

He made a gentle exclamation and took my hand. The scenery suddenly dazzled in front of my eyes and jigged about.

"My sweet, too-angelic Delia. That's all over now, can't you realize it? You've got a life here. You're enjoying yourself."

"Too much," I muttered.

"What do you mean, too much? Nobody can enjoy themselves too much."

"The way I was brought up they can," I said drily. "If you're really enjoying yourself you've got to stop because it's the red light. You're damaging your character. Oh, why on earth can't I be like Eilys—throw everything off, make fun of everything?"

(There! Eilys again, and I'd done it myself this time. I deserved all I got.)

"Like Eilys!" he said. "You! For Pete's sake, what's got into you? Why do you have to underrate yourself? Don't you realize that everybody here likes you as you are—including me? Listen, Ida needs you. I need you. We all need you. Just forget all that nonsense. You're staying. Would you like *me* to write to your family for you? I'm good at stiff letters."

"Heavens, no," I said. "I can do that myself, if I have to."

"You have to."

It was a moment of which any woman might have taken advantage. Not me. I wasn't up to the job. I sat staring across the darkening lake, and he naturally took it as a check and let go my hand. A chilly wind began to blow. Then came an interruption which completely put an end to the situation.

"Look!" I said. "What's that—over there—it looks like a big fish—it couldn't be—"

We both stared at the broken lake surface, the ripples, a dark moving shape.

"It's somebody swimming."

"So it is."

It was a man. He came to the bank near us and pulled himself out. He wore swimming trunks and flippers on his feet, and pulled off a goggle mask.

"It's Jarzy," said Gordon.

He saw us and waved, picking up a towel from the bank fifty yards away.

Five minutes later he joined us, wearing shorts and sweater and carrying his swimming things.

"Now what are you two doing here?"

"What are you doing yourself?"

He grinned, flicking back his wet hair.

"I had a wonderful swim, the best yet. What do you think? I swam in and out of the chimneys of our old house. They are only a metre or so down. I stayed under a long time. What a lovely evening! Oh, I am as hungry as four wolves. I hope there is a bus soon."

"The last one probably left ages ago," Gordon said. "Delia and I came to see the scenery, but it'll soon be dark. You're lucky, Jarzy, I've got my car. Let's go."

I sat beside Gordon in the car and Jarzy in the back leaned over between us and hummed the latest hit-song.

"I've got to get back to town," Gordon said, putting us down at the gate. "Give my love to Ida."

"She'll be disappointed if you don't come in."

He gave a wink and a smile. "She'll get over it."

Jarzy grabbed my hand and we ran up the drive. The hall door was open and we could see the glow of the logs inside. Devouring his supper, Jarzy described his adventure.

"Between the chimneys!" Gladys exclaimed. "Could you have swum right into the house?"

"I think I could. We left all the shutters back—do you remember? —and the windows open. But I do not try such a thing, there is no point and I am tired by then."

"It was daring of you," said Franz.

Ida sat listening with wide eyes, and suddenly two tears appeared and ran like little diamond drops on to her cheeks.

"Darling, darling!" cried Gladys in alarm. "What is it? What is the matter?"

"Oh, I am such a fool." Ida swept the tears away and blew her nose. "But hearing you talk about the house I couldn't help remembering my china cat, the one that you and Jarzy brought me from the fair the day that Delia came. I did love him and I meant to keep him for ever, but I forgot him and left him behind in the drawer of my bedroom chest. I've missed him so, and I'm a damned old fool to talk about it."

"Darling, you're not. You're all heart, that's what you are."

"Let's shut up about it," said Ida.

"I do wish I had got him out. I wish I had known," said Jarzy.

Ida gave a small scream.

"Oh no, you don't! You can forget what I said, my angel boy. No dangerous pranks for you. And what was Delia doing in all this, I'd like to know, running backwards and forwards all the evening with men, and sitting on the bank waiting for Jarzy to appear?"

I giggled.

"If you must know, Gordon took me to have a look at the new lake. He wouldn't come in, he sent you his love."

"But you'd already seen the lake with Onkel."

"All right. I saw it again."

"Twice in one evening! What goings on!"

"It just happened like that."

"How madly romantic!" said Eilys, wrinkling up her nose.

"Now don't you start." I jumped up. "It's my turn to clear away, and then we'll bring you all some coffee."

Gladys offered to make the coffee.

"It beats me," she said when the others were gone, "how you could leave Onkel and go off with that hollow mountebank."

The expression was so funny I nearly laughed in her face. "If you mean Gordon, I think he'll survive you calling him names."

"You're very light-hearted about it, aren't you?"

"Look, Gladys, we all know you don't like Gordon. Let's leave it at that, shall we?"

She set out the coffee cups with studied care.

"I've only said it for your own good. He'll let you down. That sort of man only exists to let women down."

"I should worry!" I put brown sugar on the tray. "And there's nothing to let me down from. And seeing that Ida thinks so much of Gordon, that ought to be good enough."

"Ida trusts too many people. I hope I'm not here to see the day he lets *her* down."

"I'd say there was nobody better able to look after herself than Ida."

(I was to remember those very words when the time came.)

Eilys's sparkling face came round the door.

"No coffee for Jarzy and me. We're going into town to sit under the lilacs and smooch to an accordion band."

"The lilacs aren't out yet," said Gladys.

"Use your imagination, honeybunch."

"I am," said Gladys.

"Good-bye!" cried Jarzy, peeping over Eilys's shoulder. He looked as though he had swallowed a sunset and had a pocketful of stars.

7

I GOT nothing out of my evening by the lake with two successive swains but a bad cold. Any other girl, I felt, would have seized the chance for a bit of jolly haymaking, but not me. I just didn't seem to have the talent.

For the next few days I crept round with a sore throat, trying to smother my discomfort, while Ida went on at me, "You caught that cold at the camp. It's probably some loathsome virus. You'd better see the doctor."

"It's only a cold," I said. "I got it sitting by the lake. I hadn't a warm enough coat on and the wind turned cold."

Ida made her eyes enormous.

"When I was your age and went out with attractive men, the last thing I felt was cold."

"I dare say. But I don't need a doctor, I'll be perfectly well to-morrow."

I spent some time composing a letter to my mother, making convincing excuses for not going home. Early habits being strong, I felt guilty, but I couldn't bear the thought of going. Was I being selfish, avoiding my duty? Was I for the first time exercising a legitimate right to live my own life?

Or was I making a plain fool of myself over a man?

Aided by a regiment of remedies forced upon me by Gladys, my cold faded away. I hadn't been to the camp for a week.

Eilys had been. She told me so.

"Mrs. N. thinks I'm a good worker. She doesn't approve of me and I don't think she likes me, but I'm indispensable in that office. And I simply adore the Todors."

"I suppose you bought that foundation cream?"

"Yes, I did. And a few other things. And Isold looks marvellous in my dress. I gave her some shoes, too. She takes my size. She won't be ashamed to go into town now."

I went myself next day, without Eilys. She had a hair appointment and was lunching in town.

After a hard day's work I found a few minutes to drop in on the Todors at six o'clock.

When I went into their room I blinked, thinking for a minute that I was in the wrong place. The first thing I saw was a blue velvet tablecloth, and the family sitting in blue, plump upholstered chairs.

"Oh, it is Miss Delia. Come in, come in. You have been so long, we sought you forget us. But we were oll right, Miss Ei-liss come, and look what she do for us! Look—and look!"

It didn't require much looking for. Madame Todor wore a rose-coloured cardigan and the old man a jaunty yellow woollen waistcoat. Isold in matched lipstick and rouge was lovely. There was a fluffy blue rug beside the bed. On the shelf were china cups and saucers.

"And look . . ."

In the cupboard were colourful tins containing coffee, sugar, tea, and a whole flock of grocery packets.

"And look . . ."

In the drawers were handkerchiefs, stockings, underwear.

"Here also . . ."

A blue footstool and the old man's feet upon it in thick, cosy slippers.

"Zat angel, Miss Ei-liss, I cannot tell you. All zis and more, just from ze kind heart. She have no need to, and we have no words to sank. We are dumb—dumb. It is a dream, we all cry, Pappa and me and Isold too. Wine for Pappa because she say it do him good, and many, many cigarettes for Max."

In my bag I had brought a little coffee and a few biscuits. Now it seemed they were scarcely worth offering. Eilys had certainly been spending money, a packet of it considering what prices were in Dorfen, but doubtless her father made her a generous allowance.

I was stunned. There didn't seem much I could say. I told them how glad I was to see them so comfortable, and left soon after, explaining that I had had a heavy day.

In Nora Nixon's room, she went straight to the point without wrapping it up.

"I suggest that you have a showdown with your rich friend Miss Mallins. She's been spending a fortune on the Todors. I couldn't send the stuff back, but I'm furious. Can't she see that in a place like this you can't single out one family and load them with privilege? It's shocking for general morale, and bad for the Todors too. Everybody here knows what they've got. Now they're all screaming at me to find them a rich patroness like 'Miss'. My life's a misery."

"I'm sorry, Nora," I said. "I knew nothing about this. It's given me a shock too. But I haven't any control over Eilys. I haven't known her long. She's just a fellow-guest with me at our godmother's."

"Apparently she has more money than sense. She isn't at all the kind of helper we want. I'm sorry about that, because her work in the office could be valuable."

"I'll try to speak to her," I said. "I feel about it as you do. If she had all that money to spend she could have spread it more fairly."

"Fairly!" Nora Nixon snorted. "China cups and lambskin rugs and cosmetics and wine, when there are people out there without soles to their shoes, and we're short of medicines and bandages. Get tough with Miss Mallins! Tell her I will not have luxuries brought into this place when we haven't even necessities, and I will not have the Todors spoiled. If she has so much money, what about a few blankets for my old people, sleeping under coats and sacks?"

She was boiling. I felt utterly depressed.

"Do you mean you want me to tell her she isn't to come any more?"

"I'd hate to be as drastic as that. God knows we need every pair of hands. But can't she just be sensible from now on? Is she very wealthy?"

"Oh, I don't think so. Her father probably gives her plenty of spending money, and does she love spending!"

Back at home I gloomed, chin-deep in my bath, wondering when I should feel strong enough to tackle Eilys, but I had hardly got back to my room when she burst in, wearing a new hat.

"Do you like it, Deel? Or not so much? Just say heaven or hell, that's sufficient."

"Then it's hell, the way I happen to be feeling."

I dragged tight the sash of my dressing-gown and brushed my hair savagely.

"What on earth's the matter? You ought to have come with me shopping. I had a lovely lunch and saw a whizzing film."

I told her exactly what was the matter, warming up as I went on. I told her everything that Mrs. Nixon had said.

As I had expected she flared up like a bonfire.

"I never heard such a fuss about nothing. If Mrs. N. tries to take away those presents I'll have her blood."

"She wouldn't do that, but can't you see how unfair it is to make pets of one family in a camp that is seething with misery, when other people haven't enough for decent living?"

"Oh, I see what you mean. I'm not stupid. But what I won't see is that anybody has a right to criticize anything I do."

"Mrs. Nixon has a right to ask you not to go there any more."

"Then she'll be a damn fool to throw away a good office worker. Come off it, Deel. I made the Todors as happy as larks and I made myself happy too. I loved buying that stuff."

"It made my little contribution look sick," I said, slapping down my brush. "I took a screw of coffee and a packet of biscuits, and Madame already had tinfuls of both on her shelves—thanks to sweet little angel Eilys."

Strangely enough, that hit the mark. Eilys went pale. She seized my hand.

"Oh Deel, what have I done! I never saw it that way. On my honour I never meant to be so mean to you. Please forgive me—please! I'd let myself be carved up before I'd hurt your feelings. I am a beast. I hadn't an idea in my mind beyond giving the Todors a thrill, and if I do anything at all I have to do it in a big way."

"It's all right," I said awkwardly. "Let's forget it. It was childish of me to mention it."

"No, it wasn't, you were quite right." She thought for a minute. "I owe you something. Would it please you if I sent round a couple of dozen blankets for the camp?"

I stared. "A couple of dozen! At the price they are? Can you afford it?"

"I guess so. It won't come to as much as I'd have spent on clothes if I'd been summering at Cannes."

"Mrs. N. will be over the moon."

"I don't care if she lands there and drowns in a crater. I'm doing this for you, Deel. And now is the squalid affair settled? Because I'm more than bored with it."

I left it that way. I had already found out that in any argument Eilys would finish on top, simply by taking the wind out of your sails.

At the camp her sins were forgiven with the arrival not only of blankets but babies' baths, children's shoes, and crates of first-aid accessories from the chemist. Eilys had had her orgy of spending, and was on the way to making Miss Mallins everybody's pet.

I had to swallow the fact that with the Todors she was queen and I her handmaid. She was the golden girl, and I just a nice unobtrusive friend. She kept the old ones happy in a whirl of gay chatter, coffee, wine, and cigarette smoke. She took a particular interest in Isold, bought her a swimsuit, and carried her off for afternoons at the Ammsee, Dorfen's gay lakeside resort. It did them all a world of good, but—perhaps unnecessarily morbid—I wondered where all this was going to end.

One unfortunate thing was that Max had been captivated. Eilys could no more help adding another attractive male to her collection than she could help breathing, but Max, realizing his position, had only become more morose and cynical.

The old man was her slave. She played up to him, with games of gin rummy which she saw that he won, and risqué stories to make him chuckle.

I never discussed the matter of indulging the Todors with her again. She worked enthusiastically in the office, and was complimented by everybody on her knack of dealing with parents who demanded places for their children in the quota countries.

8

It was June and a beautiful Bavarian summer, all gold and green and flowery. Ida put long wicker chairs on the balcony and we spent our free hours out there, lazing, reading, chattering, and listening to records.

It was the happiest time I ever spent in my life. I hadn't a care. Eilys didn't like things so quiet. She went into town a good deal, and from the way she talked seemed to have found a few kindred spirits there. There were casual references to a Karl and a Dwight and a Robin.

We came to breakfast one morning to see a white china cat with bright blue eyes sitting on Ida's plate.

She gasped. "Oh Jarzy, did you get this? You bought me another cat just like Sigismund. How clever of you, dahling."

"He is Sigismund." Jarzy nonchalantly spread jam on a roll.

"But of course. I'll pretend he is."

"But he is!" Jarzy tried to sound casual, but a triumphant snort broke through. "I got him last night."

"You did what?"

Gladys shrieked, "That's why you came back for your swimming things. You've been in the lake—in the house! Was it very hard?"

"Not very." Jarzy grinned. "I have tried before and did not tell you because I could not do it. But last night I get in. It is like being in a tank, all dark green, but I have my big torch and I am very quick. I am lucky too. I find the chest, it is fallen against the bed. I think the drawers will be swelled and I cannot open, but you have left them a little open, Ida, and I put my hand in and he is there! I grab Sigismund and I am swimming out. Lucky the lake is low because of the dry weather, and in a minute I am up and bursting for air, and it is all right. I laugh and shout and wave him in the air."

With a cry of rapture Ida leaned over to kiss him on both cheeks. "My hero! Dahling, it was adorable of you and I'll never forget it. You oughtn't to have done it, but you did it for me. I'm sure it was dreadfully dangerous."

"Dangerous? What rot," said Jarzy modestly.

"Of course it was dangerous," said Franz. "You could have been trapped down there."

"I had to be quick, that was all."

Ida was wildly excited.

"This is Sigismund's Day! We'll have a party. Gladys, go and ring up the Swiss place and tell them to send round their best pastries and a thrilling cake, and we'll get some people to come in this afternoon and drink Jarzy's health."

"I will not be here," he said. "I will be at work."

"Oh no, you won't. I'm going to ring Gordon and tell him he's responsible for getting you here in time for the party. What's a silly old law office in comparison with a celebration like this? Delia, go and ring all the people in my book—it's on my desk—and tell them to come at four o'clock. Eilys, you will rub up the silver and find all the pastry forks, half of them aren't unpacked yet. Onkel, you can let your class off early today because it's important for you to come home. Where shall we have the party? In the drawing-room or outside? Both, I think. All over the place. And if people want to sing and bang their glasses, all the better."

Eilys made a face at me. Ida's wholesale enthusiasms always irritated her. But we both went off to do as we were told.

About a dozen people turned up in the afternoon. On the top of a big white iced cake, to everybody's surprise, stood the china cat, and Ida's story lost nothing in the telling.

Jarzy was white with embarrassment.

"I tell you, this hero, this fabulous boy, risked his life just to get my cat for me. If I'd known he was contemplating such a thing I'd have been paralysed. I'd never have mentioned that I'd left the creature behind. So terribly dangerous. Plunging down into those ghastly black depths, fighting for his last breath—"

"Ida, will you stop! It is not like that at all. It is nothing. It is easy, I have luck, that is all."

"Don't you think it was dangerous, Gordon?"

"Of course it was," Gordon said. "The only reason he brought it off was that the lake happened to be low. If there had been another twenty feet of water over the house, as there will be when they release it from the dam, he could have found the walls crumbling down on him. He'd have been trapped!"

"Aren't you an old crow!" Eilys mocked him, slipping her arm through Jarzy's. "All you old safety-firsts seeing the danger, and the gay boys like Jarzy just plunging in and doing the job."

Gordon looked annoyed and ignored her pointedly. Several people agreed with him that Jarzy had really risked his life.

"So, dahling, you'll swear to me never, never to attempt such a thing again," cried Ida, rapping Jarzy's hand. "Especially when Gordon says it's going to be really perilous when they let more water in. I know you love me, without having to risk your life to show me."

"And all for a china cat," said Eilys. "While you were down there, Mike, there was my gold clock. As a clock it's probably ruined, but my father gave it to me and I was rather fond of it, and with Ida rushing us off on the last day I went and left it on my bedside table."

"Was it valuable?" somebody asked.

"It certainly was to me. I was sentimental about it."

"Don't you dare!" screamed Ida, turning on Eilys. "Don't you talk about gold clocks. Jarzy's done enough."

"I know he has. I'm not suggesting anything."

"I should hope not."

"I've forgotten it already. And aren't we going to drink a toast to Mike?"

"Oh no, please!" implored Jarzy.

"But what are we here for?" Ida whirled round. "Onkel, open the magnum . . . Now, everybody, fill up glasses . . . This is to wonderful, wonderful Jarzy who made our day!"

"Oh heaven!" said Jarzy. "I do wish I am out of this."

When the glasses were empty, Ida cried, "Delia, put some records on. Something gay because we feel madly happy. Let's dance."

"You will dance with me," said Franz, taking my hand. He was an easy though unadventurous dancer and we got along well.

"Isn't this funny and crazy?" I said. "Just like Ida."

"But she fills life with sunshine. Who else would have everybody dancing and drinking wine and laughing on an ordinary afternoon? It is a simple way to be happy. We are all friends. It is rejoicing about the little things that is the best fun in life."

"You're right, Franz. That's the secret of our life here, why we're so contented."

Gladys, a smiling Pekinese, drifted by in the arms of Mr. Lawson-Compton, the British Consul. Eilys was dancing with Jarzy—cheek to cheek, of course—and Gordon, looking rather aloof, had Ida for his partner.

When we changed over he came to me.

"Shall we dance? Or do you, like me, think it's a bit much on a hot June afternoon? We wouldn't stand it for anybody but Ida. Can't we slink out to the garden?"

"You'll do nothing of the kind," cried Ida, suddenly appearing. She had a genius for missing nothing. "What do you think you are—cripples? Now get along and dance."

It was a slow fox-trot. We hardly needed to move.

"Eilys is a bit fed up with me," he said as we shuffled gently. "I told her I didn't admire her choice of a new young man."

"You would be popular! I suppose she told you to mind your own business. But who's her new young man?"

"Hasn't she been out a lot in the evenings lately?"

"That's nothing new. I don't ask her where she goes, she wouldn't care for that."

"She's running round with a refugee from the camp. A rather wilted young Roumanian grandee who drives a grocery van in town. I hear they have dinner at various popular spots, and dance, and Eilys pays. I thought you might be interested to know. I told her it was hardly the thing. Ida wouldn't like it."

"The man is called Max Todor," I said. "I know his people in the camp, a very nice family. I'm more concerned for him than I am for Eilys—he's a fool to get involved with her—but he'll have to look out for himself. I'm certainly not going to tackle Eilys if that's what you mean. She'd flay me."

"I wasn't suggesting it." He scowled, and then laughed it off. His arm tightened round me and I was conscious of nothing else. Am I too easy? I thought. Am I always there when he wants me? How can I pretend to be subtle and elusive when I'm naturally the opposite of those things?

If I were a more intriguing person, perhaps he wouldn't talk about Eilys every time he came near me. He was irritated by her and she disliked him, and yet it was obvious that he was more keyed up when he was with her than with me. Or was it just her beauty, the thing that captivates men and means so little really?

Gordon pressed my hand as the music stopped.

"There! I've got to tear myself away now. I have an appointment."

"I expect there'll soon be another party."

"Nothing surer, if Ida has her way."

He was gone, and the rest of the afternoon meant little to me.

Eilys came up to me a few days later.

"I've got a tremendous idea. I want to tell you about it, Deel."

Eilys without ideas could be pretty devastating, but Eilys with ideas . . . I began to hedge.

"What kind of idea?"

"I can't tell you here. Let's go for a walk, or we'll have Ida crashing in. There's no privacy in this house."

We strolled along the winding lane, in the dusty, golden warmth of the afternoon. You couldn't walk anywhere in that locality without being struck by the loveliness of it, the winelike sunshine, the tangy air, the fields of oats and barley swaying silver-green, and the great distances of mountain and woodland under the summer sky.

"It's about the Todors—"

"Oh!" I exclaimed.

"Why 'oh'?"

"Nothing. Go on."

"Something's got to be done for them. Max gave up going to Australia so that they wouldn't be broken up, but it isn't going to do much good, seeing they're stuck in the camp and may never get out. They've simply got to get out."

"I think so too. But—"

"Max says they may push the old man into a home, and Madame into another one, and heaven knows what Isold will do. Well, it isn't going to happen. I'll see it doesn't. So this is my idea. When I leave here I shall go and live in Switzerland with Daddy, and I'll take the Todors with me. Pretty good, yes?"

"I may be ignorant," I said, "but I don't get this. Take them with you—how?"

"All they need is to be sponsored. For somebody like Daddy to make himself responsible for them, financially and all that."

"Are you sure?"

"Of course I'm sure. Daddy will arrange it. He only has to pull the strings, and nobody's better at it."

"But what makes you think he'll agree to?"

"Because he does every single thing I want him to, always."

"But won't it cost the earth? And won't you have to keep them?"

She snapped her fingers.

"That doesn't amount to much. Listen. When Daddy leaves the clinic I shall take a big chalet and get a nurse and maids. The old Todors can live there, and Madame can run the house. I shall send Isold to a model training school, and Daddy can arrange for Max to go into the hotel business. He'd be marvellous at that, he has just the manner for a hotelier. He and Isold would soon be earning plenty of money, and then they could make a home for the old ones. Believe me, it's all perfectly simple."

"I'm still half a mile behind you," I said, "but it sounds marvellous."

"I'm glad you agree it's a good plan. I know it is. Daddy will love having a home in Switzerland, he'll get better in no time when I tell him what I've arranged for him. I'll write tonight. We've got lots of friends round about Geneva who'll help us—influential people. The only sort of friends worth having anyway." She swung her hair and her eyes were like sapphires. "The Todors will go mad when I tell them. I just want to see their faces."

"Wouldn't it be better not to tell them until things are a bit more—well, fixed?" I felt the need for some caution.

"But they are fixed!"

"You're absolutely certain?"

"Oh, don't be so cagey, Deel. Of course I'm certain. I've been making bigger things than this happen all my life. I shall tell Daddy to ask some of his friends to look out for a chalet. He won't need any pressing to do that. He's aching to get out of that dreary clinic, only he thinks I want to go back to Cannes, and he has to be near his doctors."

"Will it be soon?" I asked.

She looked doubtful "Not as soon as I'd like it to. There's the chalet to find, and it has to be got ready and staff engaged and our furniture sent from Cannes. I think I'll be here till September, only I can't bear not to tell the Todors now and give them something to look forward to. Actually I did speak to Mrs. Nixon about it."

"You did?"

"Yes. She said if the right people took it up it would go through. So what are you worrying about?"

"I'm not," I gasped. "I'm thrilled."

"We'll go tomorrow and tell the Todors. I can't wait."

"Do you want me to come too?"

"Of course. It'll be gorgeous fun."

I was too hot and excited to walk any more. I flopped down on the wide grass verge which was sprayed all over with wild flowers, speedwell, orchis, buttercups, primulas, every kind of little flower in exquisite shades. Eilys lay down beside me looking like part of an alpine meadow herself, in a wide-skirted white dress with bright confetti dots. I looked at her and thought, here was a person with everything, grace and glossy loveliness and gaiety, and the confidence that must come from having the power to make all one's dreams come true. Lucky, lucky Eilys.

"What does it feel like to be a fairy godmother, Eilys?"

"I wouldn't know." She picked a deep purple orchis and brushed it along her cheek. "And I don't like that word. It reminds me of Our Mutual, and a little of her goes a long way with me. I couldn't really stay long in this set-up."

I was surprised. "You mean—here, with Ida? I never was so happy in my life."

"It may suit you. It doesn't suit me."

"But the freedom—"

She gave a scornful shout. "Freedom? When we're all completely under Ida's thumb and she has to know everything we're doing at every minute? Every time I go out on my own she and I have a skirmish, did you know that? You try flying your own flag and see what happens. Of course Ida has the right gang around her in you and Onkel and Mike and Gladys, all docility and flattery."

"Aren't you being a bit disloyal after all she's given you?"

"Given me?" She sat up and waved the orchis in my face. "She's given me damn all. I've given her four months of my company, but she knows I see through her and that's why she doesn't think much of me."

"But she thinks an awful lot of you!"

"Oh sure, sure!" She dropped her eyelids mockingly. "In

your cosy little world everybody loves everybody, don't they, Deel? Just like Peter Pan."

I picked a primula and threw it at her, and it bounced off her chin.

I reached round me where I sat and began to collect a posy of the beautiful flowers to take home for my room. A young farmer leading a horse along the lane stared at Eilys without reserve or inhibition—a long dazed stare, as if he couldn't decide whether she was a local fairy or just a dream.

9

It was like having a ticking bomb in the car next morning when we set off to the camp. Before I had time to park properly Eilys was out, and when I got inside there was no sign of her. I guessed she had gone straight to the Todors without waiting for me, but it was her big plan, her stupendous surprise. No wonder she couldn't wait—not Eilys!

"Isn't Miss Mallins coming in this morning?" Gerald asked as I went into the office. "We had a rush lot in last night. There's piles to do."

"She came with me," I explained. "I expect she'll be along in a few minutes. She wanted to see the Todors."

"The Todors? She would!"

Half an hour later I found time to slip along myself. As I thought, the glad news had been broken.

Madame was still choking between tears and laughter.

"Zere, zere! I felt it, Miss Delia, zat it would all come right some day. Ze very first time we see Miss Ei-liss I know she is an angel sent to us. She take us out of zis bad place, out of our troubles. In Swizzerland we have our new home,—all togezzer, ze Todors—and Miss Ei-liss look after us. So good, so good." She took my hand between both of hers. "You know zis heavenly sing zat have happen?"

"Yes, I know. I'm so glad for you, I can't tell you what I feel. Eilys is going to be a real friend to you all."

"Oh, don't lay it on, Deel," Eilys cried, fanning herself dramatically with one hand. "It doesn't seem any great thing to me. It's the obvious thing to do. Madame and 'Mr. Pappa' can live with us until Max and Isold make enough money to provide a home of their own, and that shouldn't be long. My father will find a hotel for Max to manage—he'll be marvellous at that. And there's heaps of money in modelling if you've got the right face and figure and manner, and Isold has. She only wants training."

Isold was standing in the middle of the floor, her expression both dazed and exalted, her hands so tightly clasped that it must have hurt.

"Me, a model. Me!"

"There's nothing to it," Eilys said. "I know a woman in Lausanne—actually she's an old flame of my father's—"

"Ole vlame—what is zat?" Madame interrupted.

"I mean, she and my father were once lovers and they're still very great friends. She'd do anything for him, or me. She'll start your training, and then we'll send you to a model school and get you into a good fashion house. I've got lots of contacts there. You'll be terrific, Isold."

"But all zis is going to cost so much money!"

"Not really. From your point of view it's an investment, and Isold can pay us back for the model training if she wants to, when she gets rich. And if you're worrying, Madame, you're going to earn all you get by running my house for me. I'm sure you'll be much better at it than I could be."

"When does all zis happen?" the old man broke in. "I hope I live so long. Now I start to pray zat I live. It is a change, because so long I pray zat I die."

Eilys gave him her sunny smile and patted his shoulder.

"Not long to wait. Only till the autumn. I've written to my father already, and he has friends who will find us a chalet. It might be even earlier than September. I wish we could go at once—it can't be too soon for me—but we can't."

"And Miss Delia, will she be coming too?" asked Isold, looking so pretty and radiant that I hardly recognized her.

"She's only got to say. You think it over, Deel."

"I hate to cast a shadow on the party," I said, "but what I'm thinking is that it's ten o'clock in the morning and they need you badly in the office, Eilys, if you can tear yourself away." I added, to Madame Todor, "Do you think you can keep all this a secret until nearer the time?"

"Oh yes, don't go shouting it about," Eilys said, "or I'll never get any peace. The whole camp will be wanting me to take them away, I'd better go to the office now or I'll be unpopular."

I stayed behind for a minute or two.

"Tell me it is true," said Madame, working her shaking fingers. "I do not dream, no? It is so sudden—so hard to believe."

"But that's Eilys!" I said. "She can do anything she wants to do, and she's fond of you all, and why shouldn't wonderful, unbelievable things happen sometimes? We can get into a way of expecting nothing but disappointments, as though there weren't any miracles. But there are, and this is yours. I'm so happy about it, I could shout."

"The luck had to come to us some day, Aunt Tati," Isold cried. "And now it's come—it's come. Wait till we tell Max!"

"And zat cough of yours, it will be cured in Swizzerland. I sink you cough only because you are so unhappy."

"I'm going to work and work, Miss Delia." She was breathless with excitement. "I'm going to make a lot of money, and pay Eilys back, and help to buy a house for us. And Max will be wonderful in an hotel. He knows how things should be done. He has such style."

Madame clasped her temples.

"Oh stop! My head he go round and round. Zis is too much. I will make some strong coffee, Pappa, and when we are alone, you and I, we will lie down a little or we burst. And first we will pray zat we live, and we shall sank God."

On the way home Eilys said to me, "Don't breathe a word of my plans to Ida."

"She'd be interested."

"No, she wouldn't. She'd interfere. She'd try and put a spoke in it. She can't bear anybody else to have ideas."

"All right. If you say so."

I was depressed. It isn't pleasant to feel that two people you care a lot about are getting across one another, and it was only too obvious by now that Ida and Eilys didn't hit it off. If Ida was a bit of an exhibitionist, so was Eilys, and two such vibrant personalities in one house are bound to clash. It was such a pity. Everything in our home was ideal except for this slight sense of "atmosphere".

It worked both ways. Ida and I were lazing on the balcony one day when she said suddenly. "Do you know anything about some good-for-nothing Roumanian that Eilys is running about with?"

I stalled for time. Surely Gordon couldn't have been so mean as to talk!

"Eilys likes fun," I said. "She knows a lot of people. I don't ask her who she goes out with."

"And she doesn't tell you everything! Amy Lockwood told me she'd seen them together lots of times, at the Magda, and bathing at the Ammsee. And this fellow actually delivers Amy's groceries!"

I gave a wobbly laugh that tried to be nonchalant.

"I won't have it," said Ida. "Anybody who's my guest must behave. If there's any scandal I'll send her home."

I was frightened. I felt sure she would tackle Eilys, and the ensuing battle would shake the roof down. The last thing I wanted was for Eilys to walk out in a fury.

But nothing happened. Had Ida decided to leave well alone? Perhaps she too dreaded an open row.

When the storm did break, like all storms it was unexpected and out of a clear blue sky.

"I'm stifling," Eilys cried one day at lunch. "Let's go out, Deel. Let's have a picnic."

"That's a good idea," I said. "We'll take a tea basket down by the lake."

"Lovely!" cried Ida, clapping her hands. "We'll go in the car."

Eilys's brows went down, and her lower lip came up over the top one. I felt horrified and helpless. It was Gladys who came to the rescue.

"You can't go, Ida darling. You said you had to go into town to get some stockings, and call at the nursing home to see Mrs. Wallace, and I'm going with you."

"Oh, so I did. I'd forgotten. And the bus goes at two, we'll have to hurry, Gladys."

Eilys's face cleared like magic. She followed me to my room.

"What an escape! With those two out of the way we'll have a heavenly afternoon by ourselves. Don't let's go out after all, it's too hot. Let's laze in the drawing-room where it's cool."

"Anything's all right to me," I said. I was so relieved at not having to face a situation.

We changed into cool dresses and spread ourselves luxuriously in the drawing-room. It was beautifully quiet and comfortable, the glass doors into the conservatory standing open and a soft, flower-scented breeze blowing through. Eilys produced chocolates, cigarettes, and new fashion magazines.

"Isn't this divine? I don't know when I've felt so lazy. Let's get Onkel and Mike to take us out somewhere tonight. Meanwhile we'll just relax, and have drinks with ice in them at about four."

She studied some pictures from the dress collections, and then said suddenly, "Ida got me on the raw this morning. Some tatty pal of hers told her that I've been seen about with Max Todor, and she went for me like a Victorian aunt. I'm not standing for that sort of thing."

"Laugh it off," I said, more coolly than I felt. "And throw me the *Harper's* if you've done with it."

Her face went tense.

"Ida's a bit much to laugh off. Trying to be girlish with me, and minding my morals at the same time. I was livid. I detest people who create situations they've no intention of developing. She pretends to be bohemian and unconventional, but the act doesn't belong to her period, and when anybody behaves in a way that's free and modern she starts to steam at the cracks. I can stand old women if they behave like old women, but her sort—no, *sir*!"

"Oh, shut up, Eilys," I said uncomfortably.

She threw her magazine on the floor with an angry slap.

"She should worry about my morals! I bet she was tearing up the tramlines when she was my age—"

"I thought we came in here to relax?"

"—and would be still if she got the chance. That's what I call indecent."

"Do you mind!" I picked up the magazine she had dropped and prepared to read it. "I'm awfully fond of Ida and it's obvious to everybody by now that you're not. It's a pity because she's the kindest person on earth, and you're only here for a short time, so try not to spoil the pattern. I adore you, Eilys—you know I do—but you can be beastly irritating. One thing I will say, I don't think much of you for running an affair with Max while you're a guest here. Dorfen's a small place, and people do talk, and it's bad manners towards your hostess. When you get to Switzerland it's your own business. Now can we stop talking about Ida, and read?"

Eilys gave a clear derisive laugh.

"I don't want to talk about her. She's not worth getting worked up over, the silly old tomtit."

I gave a startled jerk as a chair scraped back, out in the conservatory. There was a rustle. My heart stopped. Ida stood between the glass doors.

"That's quite enough, thank you, Eilys. The old tomtit happens to be here."

I went stiff with horror. Apparently undisturbed, Eilys tapped the ash off her cigarette.

"Oh dear!" she said softly. "How very, very stagey." She looked straight at Ida. "You're supposed to be in town."

"It was too hot," Ida said. "Gladys kindly offered to go for me. Perhaps it was as well I stayed. It's been so interesting—so very interesting—to hear what Eilys Mallins thinks about me. And that tone of yours was a revelation. I may be a tomtit in my old age, dear, but you will certainly be a snake."

Eilys looked calm and scornful.

"Did anybody ever tell you about listening to other people's conversations?"

"It was naughty of me to do so, but I was so fascinated." Ida's voice was silky. "And I told myself that it was a pity if I couldn't bear the truth about how someone else sees me—perhaps how the world sees me. Perhaps I may learn my lesson. Perhaps I may do something about it. Perhaps I ought to be grateful to you, Eilys. I'm not quite sure yet."

Eilys got up.

"Let's call it off. You win."

Ida raised one hand.

"Oh, please don't attempt to apologize."

"I wasn't."

"But I do agree! It would be ridiculous. You meant every word you said, but you wouldn't have said it if you'd dreamed I was there. One sentence you used stands out. You said I was given to creating situations which I had no intention of developing. There's one situation I've created which I certainly have no intention of developing. You are still my goddaughter, Eilys, but no longer my heiress. Is that a fair *quid pro quo*, do you think?"

"Absolutely fair," said Eilys. "And now I'd better go and pack."

I felt wretched. Ida came right into the room and sat down on the end of the sofa.

"Oh no, please. You can't possibly leave. Think of your father. He'd have to know why you'd left me in a hurry, and it would upset him terribly. He's too ill for a shock like that, so for his sake you'll have to stay. I've too much regard for him to worry him about such a nasty little affair."

"But—"

"No, Eilys. I'm sure you'll see it. This silly business between you and me is now closed, and we'll try and continue to be civilized and to use our common sense for the rest of the time you're here."

Eilys clenched her fingers, turned them up and looked at the whitened knuckles.

"I'll have to think about it."

"Do that. I'm sure you'll agree with me. You must try to learn to think in a more adult way. And also to have some consideration for other people."

"Quite!" said Eilys. "And now perhaps you'll excuse me?"

"But of course. Why not sit in your room until supper time?"

Ida was at her most dignified, but when the door had closed

behind Eilys she looked at me almost impishly, and said, "I carried that off rather well, didn't I? The young aren't all that clever. Get me a long drink, dahling."

I ran to the kitchen and fetched her a glass of fruit juice with a big lump of ice in it. She was sitting with her feet up on the sofa. She swallowed the drink thirstily.

"That was nice. I needed it. Home life in the raw, what?"

"It was horrible." I couldn't hold back a shudder. "I hope you and Eilys will forget all about it now. It was one of those stupid things that ought to be forgotten because it should never have happened. Eilys talks extravagantly—for effect—and doesn't mean one tenth of what she says, and you really ought to have shown yourself as soon as you heard us talking. Can't you cancel it all out?"

Ida's eyes hardened.

"She meant it all right! I'm glad I heard her. Now I know exactly where we stand, and for the rest of her visit we'll remain on polite terms. I sent for you two to come here because I wanted to know you better—and heaven knows I do! It worked. Tomorrow I shall see Gordon and rearrange my affairs."

I lit a cigarette to break the tension I felt.

"Ida, you're still feeling hot about this. You need time to cool down—and you will cool down. You'll see things differently. Don't do anything in a hurry."

"Do what in a hurry?"

"What you—hinted."

"I didn't hint," she said with deliberation. "I said it straight out, and I meant it . . . give me a cigarette . . . thanks . . . I told her that she'll get nothing in my will—and nothing is what she'll have. It would be unthinkable after what's happened, and that isn't revenge, it's common sense. I can find better uses for my money than leaving it to somebody who thinks so poorly of me. I'm not in the least hot, Delia, I'm perfectly controlled. This isn't a situation that's going to alter its significance tomorrow—or next week—or ever. It's final and decisive."

"But Eilys knows she was talking nonsense. I'm sure she's ashamed of it, Ida, but naturally she won't show it."

"Why naturally?"

"Because she's high-spirited and sensitive and terribly proud. She'd never beg your pardon for something she knows is unpardonable."

"Oh, she's sorry, I dare say, in her way. But that gets her nowhere."

"Please, Ida," I said, "please think it over before you make things final. It seems such a drastic thing to cut her out of your will for one silly, childish mistake."

"It wasn't a childish mistake. There's nothing childish about that girl. I began disliking her long before this afternoon, and now I dislike her more. She's selfish and irresponsible. You fitted into the family beautifully, she's been the wrong sort from the start. She doesn't do her share in the house—she hardly does a thing. She's always out. She treats my home like an hotel. Everything with her begins and ends with Eilys Mallins." She blew out a cloud of smoke and went on, "I know she didn't have a good upbringing—estranged parents, and then the divorce, and the usual circus of staying with either parent in turn and being played off against the other. In these days that's considered an excuse for becoming a delinquent. It's utterly false, a sign of messed-up values. At twenty-four a woman ought to have taken stock of her own character. If she hasn't she's no good. Am I right?"

"I like Eilys so much," I said unhappily. "We're friends. There's so much more in her than you see, Ida. She's got an awful lot of kindness and generosity and a genuine desire to see everybody happy. When she irritates me I just tell her so, and she doesn't resent it. I feel terrible about this."

Ida looked at me tenderly.

"Dahling, I don't think you're the best judge of people. You could be let down. That's why I want to surround you only with the kind of people who'll never let you down. Trust me! I've had the experience of life, and I know. And, damn it all!—" she gave a crow, "my will's my own business!"

"I wasn't trying to interfere. I have to say what I feel. And I'll never stop being fond of Eilys."

"And you think this is all so stagey? Of course it is. Life follows the theatre more closely than the theatre follows life, and it can be more corny than the theatre would dare to be. This is one of the corny bits. Rich old godmother overhears what she isn't supposed to hear and cuts goddaughter out of will. But it's happened, Delia, and I've no intention of breaking the dramatic tradition just because it's a hackneyed one."

"But could you please not go to Gordon right away?" I pleaded. "Not tomorrow! You can't be as calm as you say, and it's awful to discuss a thing like this in an emotional state. If only you'd promise me that you'd wait a day or two—"

She thought it over.

"All right. Just to please you I'll let tomorrow go by. But it won't make any difference. Dahling, do you think you could bear to go and make us some tea?"

10

As I went upstairs a little later, Eilys came out of her room and followed me into mine. She looked quite beautiful, in fresh make-up, and more serene that I could have looked in her position.

"Well?" she said. "I bet you've been pleading for me on your little knees with your little hands folded, and cutting damn little ice. Right?"

"Oh, Eilys," I said, "I'm so upset about it."

"Then don't be. I'm not. Nobody's going to crack the whip at me on the strength of a miserable legacy I shan't see till I'm fifty and past caring."

"But you must be upset!"

"Frankly, Deel, I couldn't care less." She started rearranging the bowl of flowers on my bedside table. "It'll all blow over in a day or two, you'll see. As for clearing out of here, I'd rather have liked to make the grand gesture and go, but she's right, it would be inconvenient. Daddy would have to know why I'd left—I wouldn't put it past her to write and tell him—and it might make him worse."

"Eilys, about the will—I tried—I do hope she'll think it over and change her mind. She promised me she wouldn't go to Gordon for a day or two."

She gave a snort of laughter.

"Don't *bother* about it, Deel. I wouldn't take her money now if she offered it to me on a meat dish."

"That's just bravado. You must mind—"

"Look! If she wants to be melodramatic, let her. I'm not playing it her way. I'm not going to fawn on a woman I despise, for money or anything else. No, I'm concerned with the present, and it doesn't suit me to leave here just now, not until I've got a new home fixed. I've nowhere to go. Daddy is old-fashioned and wouldn't hear of me living in an hotel by myself, and I can't think of anybody I'd care to stay with. Daddy would insist on me going to Mother, and I told you about that, twelve hours a day in gumboots and everything smelling of dog. So I shall have to stop here, but oh—" She flung herself backwards across the bed, arms outflung. "I haven't put my foot in it with such a clonk since the school garden party when a woman asked me how I liked the new headmistress, and I said, 'My God, what a zombie!' and it turned out that they were sisters. I was fifteen. Pity I'm not fifteen now. You can get away with murder when you're fifteen . . . well, well, well. I didn't go to that school again. Go and fetch me something long and wet and icy, Deel, in a nice green glass, and I'll try and behave at supper."

Everything appeared normal at supper. The others couldn't have noticed anything, and afterwards Eilys went off with Jarzy to the cinema. I was the one who worried. I lay awake half the night. Eilys must not lose that legacy, I thought. It was unfair that she should, for a moment's stupid behaviour, miss something that would make all the difference to her future. If her father was not going to live very long she would need what people call "prospects", however flippant and careless an act she put on about it now. It was no use telling myself that Eilys Mallins' future was no concern of mine. I just had to worry about my friend because I was made like that.

In the early hours of the morning I decided that I must see

Gordon before Ida did, and I must do it at once before I had time to think it over and falter.

At breakfast I asked Ida if I might borrow the car to go into town and get my hair done. I could also take Jarzy in to the office. I felt like a conspirator and hated it.

On the way in Jarzy was very gay. He and Eilys had had a wonderful evening. Instead of going to the pictures they had found a new *weingarten*—marvellous atmosphere, lanterns in the trees, and a guitar band—and hadn't got back till two a.m. At two a.m. I had been worrying myself stiff about Eily's future. I still was.

"Listen, Jarzy," I said, "I want to see Gordon for a few minutes privately. When's the most convenient time, do you think?"

"About ten, I should think. I do not know if he has to go to court this morning."

"Would you find out? I won't keep him more than ten minutes."

"What time is your hair?"

"I haven't made an appointment," I said. "I can see to that later. Tell Gordon I'll come to his office at ten, and if it isn't convenient, not to worry."

"I think it will be okay."

"And, Jarzy, please don't mention this at home tonight, will you? It's nothing at all, but—"

He made his eyes round and gave me a comical stare.

"I will be the grave!"

I was in town before nine, and having nothing to do I parked the car and sat in the pretty little square surrounded by attractive shops and chestnut trees in bloom, watching the clean cloths being spread on café tables, and the first customers coming in by bus, and the late business men panting to their offices.

At ten I was at Gordon's office and found him expecting me.

He got up from his desk as the girl secretary showed me in. "Delia! What a charming surprise to start my day. Why didn't you let me know yesterday that you were coming?"

"I didn't know myself."

"Lisl, bring in some coffee . . ." He made a fuss of me, drawing up a chair. "Do sit down. I wish I had a prettier office to entertain you in. It's horribly functional. I could at least have got some flowers."

"But, Gordon, I'm not going to keep you a minute—"

"But this is a special occasion! A visit from you—now relax! I'd take you out for coffee, but I have a client in half an hour."

"I shan't stay anything like that long."

"Cigarette?" He passed me the box, flicked on his lighter, and brushed my fingers with his as I lit up. I started to wobble. He gave me a deep, exciting smile.

"Now what is it?"

"Gordon, I had to come. It's rather serious and unpleasant. Ida and Eilys have had a row—to tell the truth she started it—and she's going to cut her out of her will. She mustn't do that."

He crinkled his lustrous dark grey eyes at me.

"Now that's a speech you wouldn't get away with in court. All those 'shes' and 'hers'. Try again slowly. What happened to whom?"

I told him the story. He listened, lower lip thrust forward, tapping lightly with a pencil.

"Eilys has gone too far," he said when I finished. "Is she crazy?"

"No, just terribly impulsive and idiotic in some ways. The whole thing was horrible and unnecessary. She does talk wildly and I know she didn't mean what she said, but she and Ida have been getting on one another's nerves lately, and this was the climax. Ida's coming to see you, probably tomorrow. About her will. I had to get here first. Gordon, you must try to stop her doing what she intends to do—I mean, cutting Eilys right out. It isn't fair. Eilys is going to need that money some day, though she's being high-handed about it now. Ida won't try to understand her. Eilys is so lovely really, such a good friend, sweet and generous—"

A look flickered across his intent face. It nettled me with its suggestion of amused incredulity.

"Well, she is!" I said. "And I know her better than anybody else does."

He leaned over and covered my hand with his. I was furious with the way mine quivered.

"You do worry about other people, don't you?"

"I know I do. Especially when I'm fond of the people involved. What's wrong with that? I've pleaded with Ida, but she's turned very hard over this. I thought if I didn't see you she'd come in here and tell you what she wanted done, and you'd do it without question. Then it would be so final. Gordon, please talk to her when she comes. Get her to tell you exactly what happened, and then reason with her. Try to play it down."

"Reason? With Ida!"

"But you're the one person who can. You can do *anything* with Ida."

"That isn't true, you know."

"But I think you can. Even if you got her to leave Eilys less it wouldn't be so bad. But to cut her right out!"

At that point the coffee arrived and Gordon poured it.

"I'm glad you came and prepared me. I understand the situation and I'll play it carefully. I don't want to see Eilys cut out any more than you do. It seems a bit drastic, for a few insults. I mean, the young always insult their elders, don't they? I don't think there's a chap living who hasn't called his father a mean old devil behind his back. But let anyone else say it and the son would knock hell out of him. The great thing is for you not to worry any more. Promise?"

"Oh yes, I promise," I said. "I know it's going to be all right now you're handling it. What a relief!"

"Don't count on me too much. Ida can be really tough. I shall do my best."

I drank my coffee thankfully.

"Another cigarette?"

"No, thanks. I've kept you long enough." I got up. "I'm going to do my shopping now."

"Well, buy yourself a new hat and listen to the band in the gardens. They're from Berlin and quite marvellous. I wish I could go with you."

(Oh Gordon, I do wish you could!)

I walked out feeling much happier, went to the hairdresser's, and drove home.

Three, four, five days went by and nothing was said, nothing happened. Ida went to town, but whether to see Gordon I never knew. He didn't come, he didn't ring. I began to hope that she had changed her mind and dropped the whole thing.

Then one evening Gordon appeared. Ida had invited him to supper, and it was a lovely summer evening. We all sat on the balcony and sniffed the scent of grass and roses.

"Gordon," I said, in the middle of a lull in the chatter, "I wish you'd take me for a walk along the lane. I'm tired of sitting still."

Everybody looked at me as if I'd thrown a hand grenade.

Franz was astonished, Gladys glowered.

"Don't be so forward," Ida cried, pretending to slap my hand. "Snatching my man from under my nose!"

Gordon was already on his feet.

"There's nothing I'd like better," he said gallantly. "Come along, Delia, we'll make up some poetry."

"That's a new name for it," Eilys drawled. "Blow your whistle, Deel, if the man gets rough."

We walked off into the enchanted countryside. The softened colours of field and tree, hill and sky, the scents, the winelike air were most beautiful. We took a path through a birch plantation, between the slender silver trunks, under the filigree of gold-green leaves.

"Well!" said Gordon, laughing. "That was out of character for you, Delia. They all think it's a plot. What do we do now—make passionate love? They'll expect us to come back looking guilty."

My face flamed.

"Did I sound awful? I had to talk to you. Whatever will they think of me?"

"Heavens, don't take it seriously!" He took my arm and pressed it. "What do you want to talk about?"

"I've been waiting all this time to know what happened—if anything. Ida hasn't said a word. I began to hope that she hadn't been to you."

He dropped my arm.

"I'm sorry about this. I swear I tried my hardest. Ida came to see me two days ago. I said all I could, but it was like bashing against the face of a quarry. She was really determined, and I'm afraid what you feared has happened."

"Oh no! She's disinherited Eilys?"

"I can't put it more explicitly," he said. "I can't discuss a client's will, obviously. But you'll have to try and forget it. Nothing can be done now, unless she has a change of heart later. Now don't let this worry you."

"But it's spoilt everything. We were so happy before. I suppose everything was too perfect to last."

He gave me a sweet, encouraging smile.

"Life never stays perfect for long. We mustn't expect it to. Now do put all this out of your mind. Ida isn't going to die tomorrow, and if ever I see signs of her relenting towards Eilys I'll be only too ready to encourage it." He gave an amused laugh. "I don't know what the family picture us doing at this minute, but they'd be surprised if they knew what we were talking about."

I'm not surprised, I thought unhappily. This is all that Gordon and I ever do talk about—Eilys. A beautiful evening in romantic surroundings, and for all I'm capable of making out of it I might as well be walking with my grandfather.

What did a woman do to get a man going that way? A mere nuance of a look, a droop of the eyelashes was all that Eilys needed. But if Eilys had been in my place now Gordon wouldn't have been joking about making love, he'd have been hard at it.

He looked at his watch.

"Pleasant as this is," he said, "I think we'd better be turning back unless we want to be unpopular. I promised Ida I'd sing, and you'll have to play."

"To hell with it!" I broke out, trying to sound like Eilys. "I always have to play."

He gave me a bright, approving look.

"I'm all for rebellion as a general principle, but I don't think this is quite the time for it, with Ida in a mood for beheading goddaughters. And I don't want her to take her business away from me! Come in, let's face it."

We walked back faster than we had come. When we were almost in sight of the windows of the house he suddenly slid his arm through mine and clasped my fingers.

"Let's give them something to gossip about. Can you manage to look guilty?"

"Let's pretend we've had a row," I said, slipping away from him, and running up the steps. "Let's scowl at each other."

Nobody saw us arrive. They had already settled down to their music, all but Eilys who as usual had disappeared. The scores were laid out on the piano and I began to play. We had a merry evening. Gordon was charming, flattering and gallant to Ida, extremely pleasant to Gladys, talking knowledgeably to Franz, ragging Jarzy. Once or twice he smiled at me, a smile that seemed specially for me when the others weren't noticing.

The windows stood wide open to the garden, to the violet dusk and the flickering summer stars coming out in the soft evening. The music stole out among the roses.

I thought, I won't let anything spoil this, neither the business of the will or anything. Perhaps it will all come right in the end.

II

THE Todors had plenty to talk about now. It was too much to expect them to keep their wonderful prospects a secret. The camp officials were pleased at their tremendous luck, and other poor creatures who had been in the place for ages and didn't have a hope of anything better shared Madame's cups of coffee and made jealous or generous comments, according to their nature.

"Me, I look forward to cooking my beautiful cooking for Ei-liss," said Madame Todor. "I shall make ze delicious *soufflé* I make at home when we give ze dinner party."

"It sounds dreamy," Eilys said. "Really I can hardly wait." She passed round a box of French chocolate liqueurs. "A friend sent me these from Monte Carlo. They're fabulous."

"So we did have zem at home," said Madame, hovering over her choice.

"And so you do have them again . . . Deel? . . . Try two at a time

—it's sheer luxury—and let's hope Mrs. N. doesn't burst in or she'll say I'm up to my usual debauchery."

I couldn't help thinking she would not be so gay if she knew that Ida had carried out her threat, that she really was disinherited.

Max, who had dropped in after his work was done for the day, accepted a chocolate, his hot brown eyes burning as they followed Eilys's every movement. The fever was on him, that was plain to see. She had collected him, and the fact showed through his usual detached politeness. It made me uncomfortable.

The weather just then was intensely hot and humid, and the camp was airless. Isold looked far from well, unhealthily pale and coughing painfully. To her this summer was one to be lived through because of the escape that autumn would bring her. Eilys seemed very fond of her, and she worshipped Eilys, who occasionally took her on life-saving excursions into town to sit under the trees and eat ices and talk about her modelling career. This somehow made up for the sleepless nights in the crowded women's dormitory and the doctor's medicines that did no good.

"Have you heard from any more agents?" I asked.

"I'm not bothering with agents any more. Daddy's friends are looking out for a house. The main thing is that Daddy is so pleased with the scheme, and he's ready to pay. After all, he'll be getting out of that clinic into his own home."

"And for us anysing—but anysing—is right," said Madame. "A little shed in your garden it is heaven, so we can breaze."

"You can't be looking forward to it more than I am." Eilys furrowed her brow. "I want to get you out of here, out of this disgusting hole. And myself too."

"You see I am still alive," the old man said, his shaking hands dropped between his knees. "I stay alive till September, God wills it."

We left and got into the car outside.

"Phew!" said Eilys, pushing back her hair. "My clothes are sticking to me and these cushions feel like hot wet sponges. What a revolting place this is!"

"It's only the weather," I said. "It'll change."

"I wasn't thinking of the weather. Oh Deel, I'm so bored."

"Bored? But you're always out. You've got friends. Jarzy took you to a party last night."

"But there's nothing here for me. It's a waste of time. I could scream, it's so dreary. Oh, it's all right for you. You like a quiet life. You go all ecstatic about polishing the floor and strumming on the piano—you're nearly as bad as Gladys. It isn't my kind of life at all."

"You'll be having a heat-stroke," I said. "Stop thinking about your silly little boredoms and think about those poor things stifling in the camp. I can hardly bear it."

She gave me an indignant look. "I'm doing something about it, aren't I?"

"Yes, you are. I spoke without thinking, and I'm sorry."

It was fresher when we got into the country, there was even a faint breeze stealing down from the hills.

But no peace at home. Gasping for baths and clean clothes, we found tumult, confusion, and Ida's voice calling.

"What on earth's the matter?" I said.

Ida was half-way up the stairs.

"Oh girls, you'll never guess. It's *wunderbar*. Gordon phoned. He has to go to Austria for a few days, to Gustaaf—wherever that is—and he's asked me to go with him. We're starting tonight, and I haven't even time to get my hair done. I'm thrilled! It's years since a man asked me to go away with him."

"She's delirious," said Gladys, coming out of the kitchen with her arms piled with freshly-ironed lingerie. "She's incapable of packing, she's too excited. She doesn't know what she wants to take. I keep putting things in and she pulls them out again. Can you help, Delia?"

"I pity you!" said Eilys, making a sympathetic face at me and dashing for her room.

"What fun for you, Ida." I thought for a minute. "What are you going to travel in?"

"My pale blue linen. But the problem is, how many evening dresses?"

"Will you need any? What kind of a place is it?"

"How should I know, dahling? One can't be caught out. It may be terribly smart and chic, full of international society."

"Put in one evening dress, Gladys," I suggested, "and please, Ida, could I have just ten minutes for a bath, then I'll—"

"One evening dress! But how can I possibly decide *which* one?"

"The one you bought in München."

"But Gordon will think I have nothing else. I must take my pink too, and the black tulle."

Gladys moaned. "And she wants her jewellery!"

"Of course I want my jewellery. I can't let Gordon down, looking like a pauper with a few strings of beads."

I gave up all hope of my bath and change, and followed Gladys into the bedroom where most of Ida's wardrobe was scattered over the bed and chairs. We folded and packed, and took out again, and repacked.

"Really, Ida, you could go round the world in this collection."

"But how can I know what I need? And it'll all go in the car."

"You're over-excited," said Gladys, sounding like a nanny. "You'll pay for it if you're not careful. Mind you come back all in one piece, and don't overdo things. You're not eighteen."

"That's exactly how old I feel."

"I don't know how you can!" Gladys stuffed in a box of stockings. "That man!"

Ida burst out laughing.

"You look lovely," I said, as she pinned a diamond brooch on her suit. "Your light cream coat will be enough."

"Oh, but I must have my black one too."

"Why not the fur one?" I asked sarcastically.

"Don't!" implored Gladys, flinging a dark look at me. "Or she'll take it."

"All complete," I said, panting over the fasteners of the third suitcase. "Gordon will faint when he sees this lot."

"He will not," Ida yelled. "Gordon is used to travelling in the grand style."

"He'll need to be!"

I rushed to my room, and tore downstairs ten minutes later to find that Franz had prepared supper.

"Oh, Franz, how thoughtful of you."

"It is self-defence. Jarzy and I are hungry."

"Aren't we all? And yet it's too hot to eat."

Gladys burst in. "No supper for Ida. Gordon said they'd stop on the way and have dinner and stay the night. Have you got a bromide, Delia? I must give her something to calm her down."

"Don't talk such nonsense." Ida appeared, cool, poised, pretty. "I'm all ready, and I'm going to enjoy myself. And this minute I'm going to sit down and have some salad and a glass of wine. Pour it for me, Onkel."

Gordon arrived five minutes later.

"Is she ready? Or is that too much to hope for?"

"She's ready," I said. "Anybody would think you were taking her to Monte Carlo. We've had more trouble over her evening dresses than—"

"Evening dresses! But Gustaaf is the quietest place, right off the social track. I'm only going to see an old English banker who can't leave his bed. Ida seems to be expecting too much, I hope she won't be disappointed."

"Never with you, my dahling," cried Ida, swimming out of the dining-room in a mist of heady scent. "Gladys, where's my crocodile bag? I'd rather have it than this one."

"Gordon says you won't need any evening dresses. Gustaaf is a very quiet place. That means we can take the big case out."

"But are you sure? Better leave it in."

"You only need what you stand up in," said Gordon. "My God, where are we supposed to put all that luggage? We ought to be off."

"As if I'd go away with a man in what I stand up in!"

"Phew!" Gordon made a grimace. "Three big suitcases, a hat box, two small bags, and I don't know how many coats. I've got a briefcase containing all my papers, a brush, a shaver, and a pair of pyjamas."

"Do you always elope so light?" Eilys mocked.

"But I'm ready," said Ida, making a round to kiss us all. "Good-bye . . . good-bye . . . be careful while I'm away. Don't let them do anything they shouldn't, Onkel. And water all the indoor plants."

"How long do you expect to be away—months?"

She sprang into the car, settled herself serenely, and waved a ringed hand on which the bracelets jingled. She looked as pretty as a picture and as happy as a child setting off to the circus.

"If Mrs. Compton rings up, tell her where I've gone, and I can't go to her thing on Thursday."

"We shall get away soon!" said Gordon. "Any more messages?"

"Good-bye . . . Good-bye. . . ."

"Now be careful!" shouted Gladys. "Take the greatest care, darling. I mean, *really*—"

The car slid away, with Ida waving until she was out of sight.

"Sensational!" said Eilys, her lip twisting derisively. "Let's hope she gets a taste for travelling and pops off to Italy for a month."

"That might not suit Gordon," I suggested.

"I didn't mean with Gordon." She caught my hand. "Let's go and finish our supper in perfect peace. Isn't freedom wonderful? We'll have a lovely time while it lasts."

Gladys was weepy over her food.

"It's the first time we've been separated. She'll be lost without me. I hope he'll look after her. I shan't sleep till she gets back. It's so horribly quiet in the house."

"Quiet like when a pneumatic drill stops." Ignoring Gladys's outraged look, Eilys's eyes flashed with delight. "Can't you two men take Deel and me into town? We could go to that place with the hunting horns on the wall and the swoony music and come back about breakfast time."

"Don't mind me," said Gladys. "I've got a frightful headache and I'm going to bed."

"You do," said Eilys. "And Deel will bring up your breakfast the minute we get in, won't you, Deel?"

"I will not," I said. "But I'll see that you do. I'm not going out."

"Nor I," said Franz, smiling with almost laughable relief. "I stay in with you, Delia."

Jarzy was pale with joy at the thought of having Eilys all to himself. Being in the mood she gave him all she'd got with her beautiful eyes. I felt a little sad and angry. Jarzy was too nice a boy to be just another of Eilys's scalps. But how they fell!—the brave young men of any nationality, it seemed. It was the older ones, Franz and Gordon, who were somehow inoculated against glossy hair and a heart-shaped face and the look in those sapphire eyes.

Eilys and Jarzy went off, Gladys retired to bed and I followed her to get some eau-de-Cologne and make a bit of a fuss of her, for Ida's sake, and because she did so much for us, and because it couldn't be much fun to be the odd one out.

When I went down again Franz had carried coffee to the balcony, and there we settled down with the radio playing softly behind us, smelling the cool of the evening, the verbenas and the tobacco plants and the stocks that Jarzy had planted, and talking idly and cosily.

"This is the nicest evening I have spent for a long time," he said with simple candour. "When you have somebody you like to talk to, and nobody to interrupt, and the house is empty behind you, and there is only the soft air and music."

Then he told me diffidently about the book he was planning to write.

"A novel?" I asked interestedly.

"Now do I look as if I could write a novel?"

"I think you do."

"You are going to be so disappointed, Delia. It is a history book but somehow different. A comparative history book, to show how the same thing has happened again and again through the ages, with the same results, only nobody troubles to take warning from history, so we have the same disasters, the same kind of wars and enmities and blunders. Perhaps the boys who read my history book will grow up to alter all that. But I have the nerve, seeing it already published!"

"I think you've got something there, Franz," I said. "Nothing you write could fail to get published because you're clever and interesting, and the boys at your school will read it out of curiosity if nothing else, and that's a start. I think it will be fascinating. I suppose you will write it in German? I'd love to translate it into English for you. You might get an English publisher."

"You would? But that would be wonderful. I hope Ida won't think me unsociable, to sit in my room working at night."

"I shall tell her you're engaged on a work of genius."

He crinkled his eyes in fun. "So long as she doesn't expect me to read her what I've done at breakfast!"

"Will there be any money in it?"

"I cannot think so. Who on earth will buy it?"

"Everybody!" I cried. "It's going to be a marvellous book."

We sat in the dusk, looking at the sky like a great shimmering plate of dark blue with crystalline rim, and waiting for the moon to rise.

"I wonder where Ida is now?" I said. "I bet she's dragged Gordon to a concert if there's one within miles."

"I can picture them," said Franz, "arriving at some *Gasthof* in the country, and Ida changing into her best dress and her jewellery while poor Gordon paces the dining-room, weak with hunger. Will she *never* come down? And when she does come, she will get everybody singing and it will be so late, and Gordon will be wondering if she will ever be ready for an early start in the morning."

"And talking of early starts, hadn't we better pull ourselves together and go in? It's not far off midnight."

"But look, the moon is coming! It makes you wish some evenings could last for ever."

During the next two days Eilys took no advantage of the freedom she had promised herself once Ida was gone. She mooched round the house, picked up magazines and put them down, and changed her nail varnish three times a day.

I was irritated with her.

"What's the matter with you? Didn't you say it was going to be all jam and joy with Ida away?"

She shrugged. "I'm bored. There's nothing to do."

"What a pity!"

"I hate practically everything. Let's get the car out, and go to one of those big vulgar tourist hotels, and see what we can pick up."

"I'd be a dead loss to you."

"I think I'll go into town for lunch."

"Do that," I said. "Buy yourself a smile if they sell them anywhere in Dorfen."

She began to laugh. "Oh, Deel, am I so revolting? I'm only in a mood."

Crazy! Inconsistent, if anybody ever was. She went off to town and bought us all presents, fluffy slippers for Gladys and me and ties for the men, and peaches and grapes for supper.

We had a picture postcard from Ida next morning. She was having a wonderful time and hoped we were managing without her.

"It feels as if she'd been gone for weeks," said Gladys, "let alone three days. We must arrange something special for when she comes back."

Excited by the idea and by having something out of the ordinary to do, she went into town and staggered back with a sheaf of expensive flowers, a new gramophone record which she knew Ida wanted, and an iced cake.

"But we do not even know when Ida comes," said Jarzy. "All the flowers may be dead and all the cake eaten. If they get anywhere near Salzburg and there is music, poor Gordon, she will never let him come back."

12

It was about ten o'clock on the evening of the fourth day, and we were all in the drawing-room with the window wide open to try and raise a breeze.

The telephone rang.

I don't know if I am alone in feeling that the very ring of the telephone can tell you whether the news it brings is good or bad. On the face of it this is absurd, the ring is consistent, a telephone bell with an unvarying sound, but I have always had this peculiar idea.

This was the wrong sort of ring. A shiver started in my middle.

"I will go," said Jarzy, getting up.

My fingers tightened on the edges of the book I was reading.

Nobody else took any notice. Gladys was sitting at the little pie-crust table re-stringing some beads of Ida's, Eilys was mending a chiffon slip, Franz was copying notes out of a text-book.

So when after several minutes Jarzy came back I was the only one who was looking for him and saw what I half expected to see and dreaded, a stark white face.

He came no further than the doorway, and in a few seconds they all became aware of the tenseness and looked up.

"What's the matter?" That was Franz.

"The telephone. It is Gordon. There is—there has been a—a bad accident."

"Jarzy, what's happened?" I gasped out.

"I can hardly hear what Gordon say—he is so—so—"

Gladys's shriek hacked off his hesitant words.

"It's Ida! She's hurt! Oh my God—tell me!"

Jarzy came into the room.

"Yes, it is Ida. She—she is dead."

Gladys gave a grinding wail which went on and on. She flung her hands across her face, and all the beads went rolling and popping across the polished floor. For a few seconds that was the only sound in the unreal silence.

"Was it a car accident?" said Franz. "Where was Gordon speaking from?"

Jarzy sat down suddenly on the nearest chair.

"Gordon is at Gustaaf. He is coming back tomorrow. No, it is not a car accident. They are in the mountains and Ida is picking flowers—and she falls—fell down a cliff. I can hardly tell what Gordon is saying, he is so shocked."

"How awful—how awful," I said.

Gladys broke into hysterical sobs.

"I knew something terrible would happen! I knew I should never have let her go. I can't bear it! I wish I was dead too. Oh, not Ida—not Ida—oh God!"

"Get her upstairs," said Franz quietly.

I went to Gladys and took her by the arm.

"Come with me, Gladys—please come upstairs. I'll look after you."

She resisted at first, but after a minute or two she let me take her away, crying wildly and pouring out a flood of broken words. She had gone all to pieces. I took her to her room, got her into bed. Then I brought her a couple of sleeping tablets, crushed them up and made her swallow them.

"Try and keep still. I'll come back soon . . . Gladys, please stop making so much noise. It's just as awful for us."

"It isn't—it isn't. Nobody cared for her like I did."

"Try to be quiet."

"Don't leave me!"

"I'll just go to the others, and then come back."

When I went down nobody had moved. In a stunned sort of way Eilys got up and poured drinks.

"How's Gladys?" said Franz.

"Pretty hopeless. I've given her some tablets."

"None of us can believe it," Jarzy said.

Silently, Eilys handed us each a glass. We drank the whisky automatically.

"When did you say Gordon was coming back?"

"Tomorrow. He'll come straight here. He said something about an inquest. It's terrible for him."

"I think we should go upstairs," said Franz. "We can't talk. Let's leave it all till tomorrow."

It had been too shattering, we couldn't take it in. I looked in at Gladys. The tablets had worked and she was asleep, in a contorted position and whimpering as she lay.

The following hours I can't remember, except that somehow the night passed and when daylight came and the birds were chirping in the sunny garden I thought I must have had a nightmare. I went down. The men had made coffee, but we couldn't eat, and there was nothing to talk about, so we avoided talk of any kind.

Franz and Jarzy stayed at home. Two policemen arrived to bring us the official news of the accident, but they had no details. A reporter came hot on their heels, but Franz made short work of him. Gladys stayed huddled in bed and refused even the tea I took to her. We had to wait all day in that state of suspense—

waiting, waiting for Gordon, and not knowing when he'd come.

But he arrived in the evening and walked straight in. He looked haggard, severe, his eyes and mouth were drawn. His clothes looked as if they hadn't been off for forty-eight hours.

"Sit down, Gordon," I said. "Don't feel you have to talk yet."

"Yes, take it easy," said Jarzy.

He looked at us all under taut brows.

"I came straight here. I suppose you don't know anything yet? I've got to tell you."

"What you need is a drink," said Eilys. "Wait till I get you one—"

"No, please." He held up his hand to stop her. "I'd rather get this over and go straight back to my place. I haven't eaten or had my clothes off. The inquest was this morning. It was all straightforward."

"None of us can believe it," said Franz. "We are all stunned."

"Yes—well—it is unbelievable."

The door opened and Gladys walked in. She looked ghastly. Gordon stared at her blotched face.

"So *you've* come," she said harshly. "What happened?"

"That's what I'm going to tell you."

"Gordon, do sit down," I said.

"I'd rather stand. It won't take long and I'm not staying. The bare facts are these. It was our last afternoon, latish, about six. We thought we'd go for a drive, to have a look at the new mountain road they're building at Effenstahl. It spirals up to a great height, and it isn't finished yet, they haven't linked it up with the down road through Klum, there's no through way, you come to a dead end."

With one finger he eased his collar. A silly bit of my brain thought, how incredible to see Gordon with a crooked tie.

"Nobody's using that road," he went on, "except for sightseeing. It was desolate up there, we didn't even see another car. Ida was enjoying it all. You know—pepped up and singing—at her gayest. All of a sudden we passed a great clump of gentians in bloom, over the side of the road, on the slope. She told me to stop. She said she wanted to take some roots home. I said something like,

'They'll never grow, and isn't it illegal to take out gentian roots?' But she said she must have some. You know what she was like when she wanted anything."

His voice was gritty. Jarzy said, "You *must* have a drink." Eilys tipped whisky into a glass and added soda.

"Thanks," said Gordon. He sipped a little and put down the glass.

"Hadn't you better get on with the story?" said Gladys in a grating tone.

"Gladys!" said Franz sharply.

"I'm going on . . . I stopped the car about thirty metres past the flowers. I'd barely come to a stop when Ida had the door open and was out. I said, 'Don't you try to get them, it may be slippery. Wait for me. I've got to park the car in a safer place.' I ran the car on a little way, into the side of the road, and braked. By the time I got out and looked back Ida was already at the flowers. I yelled to her, 'Be careful!' She gave me a cheeky wave. She was over the side of the road, on the slope. I started to run. In a second I saw her slip and stagger. She may have turned her foot, she had on those high heels. I saw her sliding. My God, how I ran! She tried to grab at something, but there was nothing to hold. I was a yard from her—only a yard—when she went over the drop. Her hands were full of the gentians she'd clutched. She screamed to me. And then she was gone. I was grasping wildly at nothing. It had all happened in a minute. I stepped over the side, the turf was as slippery as glass. I lay down and edged to the drop and looked over. I couldn't see anything for the overhang, but it was all of eighty feet down. I rushed to the car, reversed it and raced down to the nearest chalet. They had a telephone. They fetched out a rescue outfit from Gustaaf. It was about an hour later that they found her. She must have been killed outright."

He picked up his glass and drained it, put it down.

"There isn't any more to tell. If there are any questions you want to ask, please do." He gave a hard sigh of relief that the telling was over, and covered his eyes.

"I don't think there are any questions," said Franz. "You have made it very clear how the terrible thing happened. It needn't have happened. That's why it's so dreadful. We can see what you've gone through."

"Ida was like that," said Jarzy. "We never thought it would kill her, being like that."

"When are they bringing her home?" Gladys burst out.

"Tomorrow."

Gladys crushed her handkerchief to her mouth and rushed from the room.

"Thank God, she's gone," said Gordon wearily. "There are some things one can't stand." He moved towards the door. "If you'll excuse me I'll get along. I need to get myself straightened out and I'm sure you do too."

"None of us can take it in, Gordon," I said.

"I can't myself. I'll come round tomorrow early. We'll have to make arrangements for the funeral."

I went out to the car with him. I wanted to say the right thing. Nothing came to me.

I said lamely, "I'm so sorry this had to happen to you, Gordon."

He gave a slight nod.

"We all understand how you must feel."

"You've all taken it very well—except that damned woman. She's no right to give you a bad time."

"Gladys? She's rather emotional. You know how she worshipped Ida. We can't be hard on her."

He put his hand for a minute on my arm. He seemed abstracted, far away, and no wonder. There didn't seem to be anything else to say.

He got into the car.

"Don't take this too hard, Delia. You're the one who might. There's a lot of tragedy in the world. The others are perhaps more hardened to it than you."

He drove off.

When I got back into the hall they were all standing about just as I had left them.

Nobody spoke for a minute. Then Jarzy said in a despairing burst, "Gentians! She had to die for a handful of gentians!"

13

HUMILIATION for me. I was sick, with one of those dizzy headaches that leave you squint-eyed. I had to stay in my room. Just when I was needed I was no help to anybody.

Eilys was sweet, running upstairs to me with tea, soda, tablets from Gladys, sympathy and general comment.

"The phone keeps on ringing. People haven't any sense. I ignore it—let it ring. And the flowers that come! They reek. All in such damned bad taste too."

"How is Gladys?"

"Working like a cab horse, cooking for the men."

"I feel so ashamed not to be helping."

"What on earth for? Thank God the funeral's tomorrow and then we can start living again. This is going to make a difference, isn't it, Deel?"

"I haven't begun to think about that yet."

They had brought Ida home, she was lying in her own room. I didn't even see her.

I tried to write to my mother to tell her what had happened, but the pen jigged across the paper.

I struggled up for the funeral, shaky but under control. The church was packed, I had no idea Ida had so many friends, and curiosity had brought scores of acquaintances. The tragedy had made a sensation in the town. We were bombarded with questions, condolences, all very trying.

In the car going home I thought, this is the end—the end of our almost idyllic happiness, the break-up of the home that Ida made for the people she loved. Perhaps it was too good to last. What next? What was going to happen to Gladys and Franz and Jarzy? Eilys would be off to Switzerland, and I back home, back to the old life, and this interlude would be just a dream fading painfully. And I would never see Gordon again. I was wretched. The others sat in silence. Probably they too were thinking bleakly of the future.

Gordon came next day. He wanted to see the others, so I left them in the hall and went up to my room.

Some time later he knocked at my door.

"Can I come in?"

"Oh Gordon, do. I'm only tidying." I pushed out a chair. "Do sit down. I thought it was the others you wanted to see."

"I did. But you're the important one. I've got to get on with this business of telling you about Ida's will."

"Oh." I sat down on the window seat some distance away from him. "Need you? I mean, now? It all seems so harsh and cold-blooded."

"It's necessary and it won't take long." He gave me a heartening look. "It's all very simple."

"I'm sorry," I said, "but nothing seems very simple to me now."

"What are you worrying about? . . . First of all, Ida was a very practical person at heart. She never foresaw such a thing as her sudden death, but she did make provision for any emergency. She put her affairs completely in order only a few weeks ago. And she has left this house to you."

"To me! This house!" It was something I had never dreamed of. I was stunned.

"Yes, to you. There's a condition. That you make a home here for the others—the family, as Ida called them—for as long as they want or need it."

"You mean—to stay here? Oh Gordon, I'd taken it for granted I'd have to go away. I was miserable. I can't get my thoughts turned round quickly enough."

"But of course you'll stay. And do as Ida wished, won't you? There's no question about it."

"There's nothing I'd like so much. But to *own* the house! Why me? The others have a greater right to it than I have. I don't know what they'll think. I haven't any right at all."

"They know already," he said, "and they're satisfied. Ida would have found it hard to know which one of them to leave it to, and she knew she could trust you. They may not all want to stay—they haven't had much time to think about it yet. But you needn't worry about them. Gladys, Franz, and Jarzy are all well provided for. And you yourself get—roughly—a million marks."

"A—*what did you say, Gordon*?"

"In sterling, about eighty thousand pounds."

I stared at him. I pressed the back of my hand against my mouth. The huge amount didn't seem real to me who in my whole life had never owned eighty thousand pence all at one time.

"Did Ida have so much money?"

"That's only the beginning of it. There are some minor bequests which I take care of. The residue of the estate goes to build and endow a school of music here in Dorfen."

"The residue? You said that Franz and the others were provided for. But what about Eilys?"

He lifted his shoulders and held out one empty hand.

"Eilys isn't mentioned in the will. Don't say anything, please! It was Ida's own business. She wanted it like that and she got it like that. You know what happened, and I couldn't do a thing. The money that goes to the school of music is the portion that Eilys would have had."

"I see." I fiddled with my fingers. "It's all right telling me not to say anything, but it is terribly unfair, now isn't it? It's awful. I mean for Eilys to get nothing—absolutely nothing at all."

"Eilys knows," he said. "She seemed quite unmoved."

"Unmoved! What did you expect her to do—scream? As if she'd show anybody that she minded! Whatever face she puts on she must feel it. Oh, poor Eilys!"

"Look," he said patiently, "let's not talk about Eilys. I've told you the part that affects you, and you needn't be bothered with any more details. I can let you have some money immediately for current expenses, and the rest will be settled quite quickly. You'll have control of your capital. It's carefully and soundly invested—we can go into all that later on."

"Thank you, Gordon." I added, "I hope Ida remembered you for all you've done."

"She did." He gave an ironic smile. "I've been able to settle a few of my creditors, thank goodness."

"Creditors?"

"Oh, I'm very extravagant. Even lawyers have vices. My apartment is dearer than I can afford, I like the best of everything, and I don't make overmuch money." He got up. "Now you're going to settle down and get over this upset, aren't you? The others will help you. You'll all brace each other up. There's no question of you not staying, is there?"

"I want to stay very much—and now I have the house—and the family—but oh Gordon, to live here without Ida!"

He took my hand and held it between both his.

"We won't ever think or talk about the past. You're going to be very happy. That's all that matters."

He kissed my cheek, more warmly than conventionally.

"I must go. Good-bye. But remember I'm always here to help."

When he was gone I began to feel nervous about going downstairs to the others. What if they should resent my having the house? They would be quite justified, but I couldn't bear any coolness from them, and if any was apparent I would even ask Gordon if it was possible for me to make over the house to them. I wasn't well up in the subject of wills and legacies, I didn't know whether one was able to refuse a bequest.

But when I did go down I knew they were glad to see me, and Jarzy said with a smile, "So you are to be our landlady, Dahlia."

It sounded so sweet and funny that I broke out with, "Oh, I do hope you're all going to stay. Please, please do. Let's make as much of a home of it as we can. Forget it belongs to me, it belongs to all of us equally."

"Bless you for that, Delia," said Franz. "There's nothing I want more than to stay."

Gladys hesitated for a minute and then said, "I'll stay too if you put it like that, Delia. At first I thought I couldn't—not with Ida's things all around, and the memories, and feeling that any minute she'll come into the room—and knowing that none of us will ever want to sing again. But now—well, I couldn't live anywhere else."

"*C'est ça!*" Eilys spoke briskly from the window seat. "And now the tender words are spoken and everybody has said and done the right thing by everybody else, can't we, for God's sake, cheer up a bit? So far as I'm concerned, Deel, you know I'd like to stay till the autumn because it isn't convenient to go anywhere else. And being cut out of the will, I think the least you can offer me is free board and lodging."

"That's wonderful," I said. "You're the most welcome guest, Eilys. And I do agree we ought to put this awful thing behind us and brighten up."

"I suppose you'll be playing the piano any minute now!" said Gladys.

I ignored the acid remark. Poor Gladys. I knew she was more hurt than any of us.

The next day I wrote to my mother and told her what had happened, and also that I had decided to make my permanent home in the house that was now mine. I suggested that if she and Ursula wished to come and share it I would welcome them.

She replied as I thought she would, with the conventional expressions of shock, grief, resignation. Neither she nor Ursula would consider for a moment giving up their home for mine. They could not think of anything worse than living on the Continent, and they believed I would soon tire of it too. Perhaps later on, if they felt equal to it, they might come and pay me a visit.

Then came a paragraph which made me laugh out loud.

" . . . I hope, Delia dear, that now you have come into all this money you will be very, very careful about fortune-hunters. I know what these foreigners can be like, so smooth and completely unscrupulous. I could tell you stories—"

My heart was suddenly light, and I felt a mad, unreasonable happiness surrounding me, and was ashamed that I could feel so at this time.

Life began to go smoothly again for us all, except for Gladys. She was frankly a bit of a headache, and I wondered how long she intended to keep up her attitude of silent, almost sullen gloom. She worked all day in the house with a dogged persistence which in itself was irritating to see. She never went out, and spent her leisure time in her room. She was like a cold shadow about the place.

I had to speak to her at last.

"Gladys, there's no point in you working like this. It isn't necessary and we all hate seeing you do it."

She set her lips. "I like it this way. It's all I have left."

"You won't be doing it any more," I said. "I've been lucky enough to find two good maids."

She flamed up.

"You'd no business to do that without telling me! They'll spoil everything. We've always had the place to ourselves."

"They're coming tomorrow," I said firmly. "It will be more comfortable for all of us."

"And what am I supposed to do—nothing?"

"You can enjoy your leisure."

"Enjoy!" She gave me a look of bitterest reproach. "What do you think I'm made of?"

The cook and maid, two pleasant, homely girls, arrived and the house began to run efficiently. But Gladys, released from duty, grim and silent, brooded upstairs in her room and hardly spoke to us.

"What the hell is the matter with her?" Jarzy demanded. "If she goes on like this she had better get out. I cannot stick."

"Can't you order her to either snap out of it or leave?" Eilys asked me.

"How can I? She's simply unhappy and shocked. We've got to be patient with her. It would be barbarous to turn her out. We ought to treat her like a sick person. She'll get over it in time."

"Delia is right to be kind," said Franz.

"Oh, Delia is always right to you. It's us who have to put up with Gladys."

I invited Gordon to dinner. We hadn't seen him for ten days. I was glad to see that he was his old self again, the strained look gone. Confident, vital, and fascinating, he was *my* guest in *my* house and it was thrilling.

We had a special dinner, the best of everything, candles on the table. We all began to feel relaxed. Gladys alone didn't come down, I had hardly expected her to.

Eilys, appearing in a cocktail dress, a satin coat over her arm, announced that she would snatch a bite and fly.

"Where to?" asked Gordon with a kind of tactless irony.

She widened her eyes.

"What insolence! But I'll tell you no lie. I'm going out with Max. I'm in the mood for Max."

He made a scornful exclamation, and she flung a few insults at him and left in a whirl of brocade skirts.

"She only does it to make you rise, Gordon," I said. "Why do you let her?"

We took our coffee into the drawing-room, and afterwards Franz and Jarzy both went out.

"Well? How is it going?" asked Gordon when we were alone.

"Beautifully," I said. "We're very happy here. I think of Ida with such loving gratitude."

"That's how it should be."

"Gladys doesn't seem to be able to get over it."

"Oh, damn Gladys! What does she matter?"

"One has to be sorry for her."

"But she can't be allowed to spoil things for you. She could have made an effort to come down to dinner, for your sake." He scowled. "Perhaps it was because I'm here. I know she hates me like hell."

I gave him a quizzical look. "You've never exactly exerted your winning charm on her, have you?"

"Pooh!" He went on, "It's a lovely night. Would you like a walk?"

I fetched a light coat, and we went out into the twilight, along the lane, across the field path and up the hill. We hardly talked. He took my hand as we walked. The soft air smelt of wine-presses and warm grass. We climbed to the pine wood, and nothing besides ourselves seemed to be moving except a flight of rooks trailing like a dark scarf across the silvery sky with one shimmering star.

"What a magic night!" I couldn't help saying. "It's as if we were quite alone in the world."

"I could wish we were."

We were at the stile which divided the steep meadow from the wood. I leapt nimbly on to the rail, and suddenly he put both hands on my waist and checked me.

"Don't be in such a hurry. Can't you keep still and give the magic you talked about a chance?"

My heart bumped into my throat. I began to babble.

"It is a lovely night, and such a beautiful part of the world. So old and romantic. And to think the Hitler legend had to start here!"

He shouted with laughter, and shook me.

"You would have to spoil it. What a thing to say!"

I began to laugh helplessly.

"Listen to me," he said, suddenly serious. "You were talking about something you called my winning charm. I'd like to make it clear that I'm saving all of that for one person, though I doubt if she'll value it. Will you, Delia?"

He forced my eyes to meet his, and at the look in his I lost my breath.

"You know!" he said. "Come on, darling, face it—have I got a bit of a chance?"

I couldn't speak. I was struck dumb, bewitched, incredulous. This couldn't really be happening.

Slowly, triumphantly, he pulled me down into his arms and locked me tight. His cool cheek pressed against mine, and the streak of silver at his temple glinted across my dazzled eyes.

"Say it!" he said. "Say you love me. You do, you know."

I felt as if I was going to suffocate. Or faint. Or do something equally idiotic.

"I absolutely adore you!" I muttered.

"Then escape me never. Don't you ever try to get away. Don't you ever try!"

A million thrills ran through me. He put me a little way away from him and held me there, his hands cupping my face.

"Darling, darling Delia, I never meant it to happen like this. I didn't even mean to say it tonight. I was going to do it much later on, with a proper measure of deliberation, the right approach, and a few well-chosen words. You must blame the magic of a summer night. But barring my indecent haste—I love you, and that's all that matters. I've loved you from that evening we danced at the Magda and you were different from anybody I'd ever met before. Why should I have to wait to tell you this? I do believe you've loved me a long time too."

"I've given myself away a hundred times," I said helplessly.

He gave a small shout, half laughter and half triumph. "This, believe it or not, is a proposal of marriage. You'd better say yes, my sweet, and then we'll get down to details."

"Yes," I gasped. "But it isn't real. It's a dream."

He pulled me close and kissed me full on the mouth. Everything blacked out. The next thing I knew I was sitting on the grass, supported by his shoulder.

"Well!" he said with a comical, ardent stare. "You've paid me quite a compliment. That's the first time a girl's passed out under my kisses."

"I feel a fool," I said weakly. "I can't even do my first real love scene properly."

"Real love scene! I haven't started yet."

I thought, this isn't me. This isn't happening. It was like when he told me about the money, and I had rationalized that by never even thinking about it. But this! I could never, never think about anything else.

The sky faded to pewter and then to dark, dark blue pricked by glittering stars. The pines were jetty silhouettes and a pale mist rose on the grass.

"Happier about it now?" he said at last.

"I'm past being happy. I think I'm drunk with joy."

"Me too."

We walked down the hill in the dark, but for me the night was shot through with fire and wonder and rapture. There are no words to describe this but the banal clichés of love. It seems a pity.

"Darling, we'd better fix the wedding," he said. "People may think it's a bit sudden after the tragedy, but we were in love long before that. I don't see what we have to wait for, and the registry is next door to my office."

"The what!" I said explosively. "No cold-blooded hole-in-the-corner for me. I'm going to have a real wedding in church."

"Don't you think under the circumstances it ought to be quiet?"

"It can be quiet in church. Darling, I want a proper wedding. I wonder what the family will say?"

"Do you mind what they say?"

"Mind! They'll be delighted. But I don't think we'll tell them at once. Let's allow it to leak out gradually." I went on, "Oh Gordon, wouldn't Ida have been thrilled about this? Perhaps she can even see us now."

"Perhaps she could even see us an hour ago," he said meaningfully. "She must have wanted to pitch in! Other people's intimate moments were just Ida's cup of tea."

My cheeks flamed, cooled, burned again as we went up the steps of the house into the lighted hall. I rummaged in the pocket of my linen coat and unearthed a powder compact.

"That's right," he said laughing. "Take the guilty look off your face."

"You look a bit rumpled yourself, darling. Is that bindweed on your collar?"

He seized my compact, and screwing up one eye peered into the small glass.

"Good lord, look at me!" He smoothed his hair with his hands, straightened his tie. "I'll just look in to say good night to the boys and then make a quick getaway. Slip into town tomorrow and meet me for lunch—yes?"

I slept wonderfully, and woke early, and knew that it was true.

14

It was beyond human nature to carry such a flame inside me and not reveal it. Within twenty-four hours I realized that everybody in the house must have noticed there was something different about me, and be puzzled by it. I felt I was walking with a maudlin grin on my face, even talking to myself. You can't live in a rainbow bubble of joy without showing it. Twenty times a day I rushed upstairs to look at the ring Gordon had bought me, longing to wear it. I had hated to take it off, once he had put it on my finger, and why should I?

Why could I not wear it? I put it on and went to Eilys's room while she was changing for supper.

"Notice anything about me?" I said casually.

"Only that you've been drunk for a couple of days." She sprayed scent on her shoulders. "So what? I could probably guess if I tried, but you tell me."

"Gordon and I are engaged."

She didn't even start. I might have said, "I've bought a new hat."

"My, my!" she said. "Congratulations!"

"Aren't you surprised?"

"Darling Deel, nothing on this earth surprises me. What did you expect me to do—shriek? When did this happen?"

"The night he came to dinner and you went out. Thursday, wasn't it?"

"Was it really?" She pulled a wide-skirted dress over her head. "Well, if you're happy, Deel, I'm very glad because you deserve to be. Would you zip up my back? . . . So you're going to marry Gordon. Let me give you a word of well-meant advice. Gordon's the masterful type. Don't you ever be the little woman. Keep your end up. I know these dynamic men!"

"I think I'll manage," I said gaily. "It's been hopeless trying to keep it dark. Look—my ring."

"Gorgeous!" she said. "That must have set him back a bit. Have you fixed the wedding yet?"

"Gordon wants it to be soon."

"I'm sure he does. Where are you going to live? Are you bringing him here? It might be a bit crowded."

I bit my thumb. "I never thought of that. It's going to be a problem."

"Not really." She clipped on her gold ear-rings. "I shall be getting out soon, for one. It wouldn't be a bad idea if I married Mike. I know he wants me to, and that would be another one off your hands. By the way, have you told anybody else?"

"Not yet. You're the first. I thought I might screw myself up to it this evening."

"Inspired idea! Get some champagne up, and we'll make a thing of it before supper."

Her gaiety and co-operation were just what I needed.

"Come and help me," I said.

We manoeuvred the others into the drawing-room where we usually had a glass of sherry before supper. I even got Gladys to come down. On the side table stood a bottle of champagne with glasses standing round it.

"What is that for?" said Jarzy. "What in goodness do we celebrate now?"

"Just you wait," I said. "Open it, Franz."

"Slosh it out, Onkel," said Eilys. "Let joy be unconfined."

"But why—"

"You'll know in a minute. Ready, Deel?"

The filled glasses were standing on the tray. I went hot and cold.

"This is it," I said, my voice wobbling. "I'm going to get married—to Gordon. It may not really be a surprise to you, I've been behaving crazy for two days, so I think it's time I told you. Eilys thought you might like to drink our health."

"Whoops!" shouted Eilys, reaching for a glass.

Jarzy shouted too. "But hurray! What do they say?—bless the bride."

Franz said warmly, "It is a surprise, but I wish you so much happiness, Delia."

I smiled with tears in my eyes.

Gladys hadn't spoken. I looked at her. Her face was distorted, terrible, and suddenly it blazed and she stood up.

"You fool!" She flung at me. "You stupid, wicked little fool."

There was a stunned silence.

"Gladys—" I began helplessly.

Her voice bit like acid.

"Can't you even see it? You—heiress! Could anybody be such a gullible fool? He had to have that money somehow—it was either you or Eilys—and with Eilys cut out it left just you. The slimy fortune-hunter!"

"How dare you!" I shouted, boiling over with rage.

Franz stepped to my side. "Stop that, Gladys. Stop it, I tell you."

She took no notice. She had more to say.

"He planned my darling Ida's murder. So clever! Quite undetectable. He knew it looked better to get rid of Ida first, before capturing you, than to propose to you and *then* push Ida over a cliff. He was sure of you before he did that filthy deed, you've been making eyes at him ever since you came here. And I've watched you since—all of you—while he got away with it. Yes, he's got away with it—you blind fools! And all you can think of, Delia, is bouncing into that murderer's bed."

I went mad with fury. I snatched up the first thing that came, my brimming glass, and hurled it at her. It missed, but the liquid sprayed out and trickled down her face.

Jarzy rushed at her.

"Come!" he yelled. "Out of the room with you!"

"In a minute," said Gladys, wiping her face with her hand. "I shall be leaving this house for good. You all think I've gone mad, don't you? I'm not mad, I'm the only one who's sane—who's been sane all along. It's you who won't look at the truth because it's hideous. For my murdered darling's sake I've said what I had to say, and I can't do more."

"Wait!" said Eilys suddenly. "Gladys, have you got any proof for what you've just said?"

"Proof! If I'd had proof do you think I wouldn't have used it? I've no evidence, even. Nothing. Nothing at all. I just know."

My legs gave way, I sagged into a chair.

"You have made a terrible accusation against Gordon," said Franz. "And you have no evidence. You said so. That is a wicked thing."

"I've told you, *I know*."

"How do you know?" said Eilys. "Come on, tell us. This is interesting."

Gladys's burnt-out eyes turned to her.

"I can't tell you or anybody else. How I know is by something inside me that never tells me wrong. Like I knew that Ida and I weren't going to die in Auschwitz. I was right then, I'm right now. I know! And I've done my duty by telling you. Perhaps you won't be so pleased with yourselves now."

There was an ice-hard conviction about her that made me

shudder, and a dreadful dignity as she began to walk to the door.

Passing me, she stopped.

"This isn't spite," she said. "I always liked you, Delia. You've been very kind to me. If you make a hell for yourself now it isn't because I didn't warn you."

She walked out of the door, leaving it open. Eilys slammed it.

"Boy!" she said. "Wasn't that drama? The old bitch ought to be locked up."

I shut my eyes. Sickness surged into my throat. Franz held a glass to my lips.

"I'm all right," I said.

"Delia, you must not take any notice. Poor Gladys, she has gone mad. Forget it all—you must."

"I should think so," said Eilys. "Laugh it off. She was raving!"

I took a long breath. "She'll have to go away. I couldn't have her here after this, could I?"

"I should think not!" said Jarzy. "She goes. I ring a hotel at Dorfen now and take her in the car."

"But I can't turn her out tonight." I put my hand to my head. "She has all her things to pack. She'd better go tomorrow morning."

"Jarzy and I shall see to it," said Franz, full of concern. "And Eilys is right. We must forget what she said. I wish you hadn't had to hear such stuff."

I got up. "I'm all right, but I'm going upstairs. I'll probably feel as you do tomorrow. The main thing I want to say is that I rely on you all never to let Gordon know what has happened. He must think that Gladys left because she didn't want to stay."

"Of course, Delia."

The men took Gladys away in the car early next morning. I made myself see her, trying hard to pity her, poor thing. I even said as kindly as I could that I hoped she had somewhere to go, and she replied that her sister in England would be glad to have her. I then said good-bye calmly and formally, and without looking me in the face she too said good-bye, and went out to the car and out of my life for ever.

My chief concern was that in the evening I was to dine at the Magda with Gordon to meet some friends of his, and I had to pull myself together and put on an act. The abominable scene with Gladys had kept me walking the floor all night, and I was as jumpy as a cat.

The forced normality with which I behaved that evening must have stuck out almost worse than hysteria, and soon I could see I had Gordon worried and that the impression I was making on his friends was poor, which didn't help me.

"By the way, Gladys has left us," I said casually as we danced. "She's gone to make her home with her sister in England."

"Really? A bit sudden, wasn't it?"

"She'd never really settled."

"That's true . . . and what's the matter with you tonight?"

"Bit of a headache," I said lamely. "Starting a cold, or something."

"Well, make an effort, darling. You're not yourself at all."

I brightened up deliberately, but it couldn't have been a success because as we were leaving Gordon said, "While I run you home you can tell me just what did happen."

"How do you mean?"

We got into the car.

"Something's put you out," he said. "I think you had trouble with Gladys."

"Trouble? With Gladys? What on earth makes you think such a thing?"

"Because she did leave rather abruptly. There was no question of her leaving two days ago, then this morning at the office Jarzy told me she'd gone, and he sounded cagey about it too. I've an idea there was a row. Not that it matters, but why can't I be told?"

I gave a casual shrug. "You know Gladys has been difficult ever since Ida died. She was so devoted to Ida. She did turn a little huffy, so we weren't sorry when she decided to leave."

"Huffy about what?"

"Oh Gordon!" I burst out, exasperated. "About nothing at all."

"It it was nothing, why can't you tell me what happened?"

"If you really want to know," I extemporised, "we were playing the piano and singing, and she took exception to it, and there was a bit of a ding-dong, and she packed and left."

"And why on earth couldn't you have told me that in the first place?"

"Because I didn't think it was worth bothering about."

"Then why did you make a mystery of it?"

"I did not make a mystery of it!"

"And why did you tell me a completely different story from the one Jarzy told me? That Gladys had had a letter to say that her sister was ill and needed her. No mention of a row about playing the piano. There's something odd. You've been on edge all evening."

"I'm not in the witness box."

"And a good thing for you you're not," he said, frowning, "because either you or Jarzy is lying—in fact both of you, I think. So what are you hiding? I'm going to find out if it's the last thing I do."

"Darling, I don't know you when you're like this," I said. "I told you I've a headache, and you go and build up a situation just to upset me. What's the matter with you?"

"Sheer curiosity," he said stubbornly. "Call it my professional training. Let the dog see the rabbit and he'll not be called off. Let's analyse this situation you say I've built up out of nothing. There's a mystery about Gladys's departure. You and Jarzy are both frightened to tell me the truth, so you tell me different stories, and they're both lies. What do I assume? That Gladys's leaving had something to do with me, and I must be shielded from knowing it."

"Of course not! How could it?"

"Just a little too vehement, my darling. So it has to do with me! There was a row, involving me. Could it be due to the fact that you announced our engagement? Jarzy congratulated me very warmly this morning, so you did announce it, and Jarzy was pleased, and presumably Gladys wasn't. Why not?"

I gritted my teeth. "Gordon! For heaven's sake—"

"Come on. Let's have it all."

"I shan't tell you!" I said desperately.

"Don't worry. I'll find out."

"All right, then. If you must know, Gladys was very rude to me.

She was in love with you herself, and she went off the handle when I told her we were engaged."

He slid a look at me.

"That's the feeblest lie of the lot. Gladys hated me like rat-poison. And why in heaven's name, if that's all that happened, didn't you tell me and we'd both have had a laugh over it? Oh no, my sweet, nobody tells me lies and gets away with it."

"Have it your own way," I said, nearly choking.

He stopped the car and put his arms round me.

"Come along, Delia—out with it!"

"If you don't stop this third degree," I said, "I shall get out of the car and walk home. I mean it."

He started the car and drove me home, and we hardly spoke another word.

I was tired enough to sleep for a week, and I couldn't sleep at all. I tried to persuade myself that by the next time I met him Gordon would have dropped the matter.

But was that all I needed, for Gordon to stop asking questions? Could anything ever be the same again?

Those horrible words of Gladys's kept dinging in my ears . . . "If you make a hell for yourself now, it isn't because I didn't warn you."

A hell for myself? Already I could feel the ice of it closing round me, and it was worse than I could have dreamed.

Next day brought a sheaf of roses from Gordon and a loverlike note to say that he hoped I was feeling more myself. Eilys, who always came down late, appeared as I was putting the roses in water.

"Roses! Nobody sends me roses. I don't seem to get the right sort of men. Have a good time last night? You look a bit below."

"I behaved like a wet hen," I said.

"More fool you. You really *are*, Deel!"

"I can't help it. Gordon knows there's something up, and he says he won't rest till he finds out."

"Boy!" She studied a chipped nail. "He's perceptive, isn't he? And I don't think he'll let go till he knows all—not Gordon."

"But he mustn't know! And he can't know if none of us tell him."

"Don't you kid yourself." She went on reflectively, "I think you'll have to tell him in the end. He's asked for it, and he might as well know. You'll have no fun while that's on your mind."

"Eilys! How could I tell him a ghastly thing like that?"

"So bad? What does it boil down to? That Gladys blew her top, went mad, and accused him of murdering Ida. She might have accused me, or anybody. She hated pretty well all the world, did Gladys. I'll tell Gordon if it'll help you."

"You certainly will not!"

I walked up and down the room in a brain-storm.

"You do take things to heart," Eilys said mockingly. "Everything's a tragedy to you. Gordon will probably take it in his stride."

"*Take it in*—a frightful accusation like that? He might even think that we—that I—" The words stuck in my throat.

"Thought there might be something in it?" said Eilys coolly. "Well, do you?"

I gasped at the outrage.

Eilys lighted a cigarette. "Gladys sounded pretty convincing, I must say. It's a story that could hang together."

"You're not telling me that anyone would dream that Gordon was capable of—"

"I wouldn't put it past him," she said, flicking her lighter.

I made some sort of raw sound.

"Look, Deel" she said kindly, "I hate to see you in this state. I'm fond of you. You're the only one of your sort I know in this wicked world—except perhaps Onkel. He's innocent too, and Mike's dead honest, if not entirely stainless. But all the rest of us are bad lots at heart, and your darling Gordon's no angel, so the sooner you realize that you're not engaged to the hero of a library novel the better. Gordon's short of money and in debt, and he's had one or two sticky passages. I know all about it, he told me, recognizing a kindred spirit no doubt. Don't you ever compliment yourself on being the kind of woman that men hide their worst side from. It's noble but unrewarding. And don't start tormenting yourself that he's marrying you for your money—my God, Gladys had some pretty ideas!—though he'll be glad to get a rich wife, and that's a fact."

"You're very outspoken," I said. "But I think you mean to be kind."

"Of course I mean to be kind. I'm taking the bloom off your innocence, and that's the act of a friend."

"You said that terrible thing," I persisted. "You said, 'I wouldn't put it past him.' What did you mean?"

Her eyes sparked. "I mean that I know more about human nature than you do. That's all."

"But that's no answer. It's too much and too little. Do you realize you're talking about murder? Gladys accused Gordon of *murder*. It isn't anything to be shrugged off. It's hideous. And now you—"

She made a face and spread her hands.

"I must be more careful if everything I say to you is going to be analysed word by word."

"You said, Eilys—or you inferred—that Gordon was capable of having murdered Ida. You couldn't say a thing like that and mean nothing."

She looked exasperated. "What of it? Anybody is capable of pushing somebody over a cliff to do themselves a bit of good."

"You couldn't mean anything so cynically immoral."

"That I wouldn't know about." She stretched a long leg and let the shoe dangle from her toe. "I'm not well up in morals—you are. But just be realistic. Mind you, I'm not coming down to cases, but say that a man's got his eye on an heiress who won't come into anything so long as an old woman goes on living, and a chance suddenly offers itself out of the blue, and what a chance! No possibility of a witness, and only a bit of nerve needed to carry it off afterwards. Let's be squalid-minded and admit that the only one who wouldn't be tempted is Little Lord Fauntleroy . . . Now, Deel, don't be upstage about this. You started it. I didn't want to discuss it, but you made me. If you've any sense you'll forget the whole thing from now on, *and* that damn silly Gladys. If it was me involved I wouldn't give it another thought. To go back to the beginning, if you can't make yourself tell Gordon what Gladys said, then let me, and put an end to all this dreary stuff. Gordon's not a sensitive plant. He can take it."

"Tell him if you want to," I said. "I'm past caring."

"That's no way to talk," she retorted. "Give the man a chance to clear himself."

"That's what I want to do."

"Of course you do. And Gordon's a great talker, he'll soon have you calmed down. Drag it all into the open, I say, and then bury it."

PART III

I

"BEFORE we talk about getting married," said Gordon, "we've got to have one thing clear. Do you believe what Gladys said, that I murdered Ida?"

His jaw jutted, his eyes pierced mine.

"How can you even ask me a thing like that, Gordon?"

He held me at arms' length and his grip hurt my shoulders.

"You hadn't the guts to tell me about it yourself. You got Eilys to do it."

"I did not. She insisted on telling you and in the end I gave in to her. I never wanted you to know."

"Very right of Eilys. And quite wrong of you. But when I put a simple question to you, you don't answer it."

"I'll answer you now. *No*, *no*, NO. And it makes me sick that you should even have to ask me. I was trying to shield you from it. I couldn't bear you to know about that scene with Gladys. Of course she was insane."

"I'm glad you realize it. And you don't have to shield me from anything. I can take whatever comes along—except mysteries. I can't stand mysteries. What with you and Jarzy both telling me vapid little lies—ah well, it's over now. Don't look so shocked, darling. Gladys is out of our lives for ever. What could have made you so worked up?"

"The very thought of that accusation. It was so foul and filthy."

At long last he smiled. "You've never been used to people with foul and filthy minds, my sweet. In my job I come across them all the time. It's a bad old world, and you haven't learned to be tough. Nothing shocks me, not even to know that Gladys Jones had a mind like a sewer. I know her sort—you don't. So you let yourself be impressed."

"You're as bad as Eilys. Just because I wasn't capable of laughing such a horrible thing off you say I was impressed—as if that was abnormal! Who wouldn't be impressed to hear the man she loved described as a murderer? I think it was natural of me. I've had a dreadful time, and it was all for your sake, Gordon."

He clasped me tight and put his cheek against mine. Back it came, the old thrill and rapture.

"My, my! Aren't you sensitive? Harden up, Delia my love—you'll need to if you're going to live with me. All the trouble over now?"

"Yes, if you say so."

"Quite sure?"

"Yes."

"No nasty little bits of Gladys hanging round and popping out of the drains?"

"Oh darling, don't joke about it. It was hell."

"I know. One I *could* murder is that woman. Never mind, she's gone and she isn't worth remembering."

I gave a sigh that shook me all over.

"Let me go, Gordon. I can't get at my hanky."

"Are you crying?" His tone was full of gentle derision.

"Indeed I'm not. I never cry. But I've put lipstick on your beautiful expensive tie."

"Not to worry. I've got another."

He drew me down into a big chair.

"Well, now the All Clear's gone we can breathe again. Darling, let's settle things and we'll both feel better. Let's get married soon—next week?"

"Oh, not so soon."

"But why ever not?"

I was angry with myself, but it wasn't any use. There was still a struggle of some sort going on inside me.

"I just can't tell you why. I suppose because of the awful mood I've been in. Because of all I've been through in the last few days and what it's done to me. I want to get my happiness and peace back."

"And how long will that take you?" he said, not too pleased.

"Not long, I hope. I want to have a divine sense of peace on my wedding day. So don't rush me, darling. Please don't."

"But I thought all the trouble was over?"

"It is. But I'm not really straight with myself. You can't expect the boiling sea to calm down in five minutes."

Held so close against him, I felt him stiffen.

"I suppose you'll have to take your time. But, Delia, don't let it be long. Believe me, the best way for you to get straight with yourself is to marry me and come away for a honeymoon in Switzerland. You'll find it quite a cure."

"It sounds heavenly," I said. "But please understand."

"I expect I'll have to let you have it your way."

I suppose that should have been enough. But something was happening to me and I was helpless against it. It was as if Gladys had sown in my brain some deadly seed which was now putting down roots and forcing upwards an evil shoot. It was poison, paralysing stuff, mind-destroying.

I struggled to be reasonable, logical, to beat the thing down. But for me there started up a voice in the night.

Could he be marrying you for your money?

I won't believe that.

What has a girl like you got to attract a man like him?

He loves me.

You believe that?

Certainly I do.

And you don't even think for one minute that he is after the money?

No, I don't.

That doesn't sound completely decisive. Say—perhaps just a little bit?

I won't listen to such a suggestion!

Oh, be honest. You can't help wondering, can you? . . . He's in a great hurry to marry you, isn't he? Have you asked yourself why?

Why shouldn't he be?

So you're frightened to give an answer to anything. Do you believe there's a shred of truth in Gladys's accusation?

Of course not!

Don't you? Hasn't it ever entered your mind that there *might be*?

NO!

Yes, it has, or you wouldn't be shouting like that.

I won't admit any such thing.

What's stopping you from marrying him, then?

I only want to be—

You want to be what—sure?

Oh, stop it—stop it!

I fought hard to free myself from this profitless and daunting nightly inquisition. I saw Gordon three or four times a week, and every time he begged for an early wedding, persisting until his very persistence built up in me an illogical refusal. Not yet . . . not yet.

And the night inquisition became more sinister.

He's over-persistent, isn't he? . . . He wants to make sure of that money of yours, doesn't he? . . . He knew when Ida was still alive that you were her heiress—didn't he? . . . And didn't he know as well that you weren't worth anything to him so long as Ida lived?

I walked the floor. I took tablets, anything to stifle that hateful voice.

If only Eilys hadn't made that dreadful remark—"I wouldn't put it past him." What did she really mean?

Questions. Questions. Nails hammered into my head and heart.

I knew so little about Gordon, nothing at all, in fact. Ida had known very little about him either, she took everybody on trust.

So I began the profitless task of trying to delve into my lover's past, like turning over a garden with a teaspoon.

"Darling, it seems absurd, but I don't know a thing about you. I don't know where you come from or whether you've got a family, or where you spent all the years up to now—not anything at all."

He cocked a surprised eyebrow.

"It all seems irrelevant to me. Don't you like me as I am now?"

"I only want to know those things. Any woman would."

He made a face.

"It's all very ordinary. I don't know what you expect. I was born in India, and my father wasn't even a pukka sahib, he was office manager for a timber exporter. When I was nine we went back to England and I went to school. My grandfather stumped up to put me through Cambridge where I studied law. Then I went into practice—lots of hard, dry work. Served with S.O.E. in the war. Afterwards, came out here. What a saga! Are you any the wiser?"

"At least I know something now. What made you settle in Germany?"

"The lord knows.. At least, I was out here with the law commission after the war, and I just stayed."

"Where are your family now?"

"Parents dead. One sister, in Canada when last heard of. We don't write. Now, darling, please don't ask me where all my aunts, uncles, and cousins are, because I don't even know if I've got any. I'm sure you know every one of yours and send them cards at Christmas. I'm not family-minded and I'm not interested in the past. Anything wrong with that?"

We were driving out to a village that was famous for its *Gasthof*, with iced hock laid on.

"Don't you mock my quiet upbringing!" I said.

"I wouldn't for the world. I only want to show you that mine's nothing to make a song about."

"But, Gordon, tell me some of the things that happened to you. It's all important to me."

"Important! I've got my war stories, if you like, though anything drearier to have to listen to I can't imagine."

"I didn't mean war stories," I persisted. "When people become friends, let alone lovers, they have to get to know each other, and there's no better way than telling things that they remember. Were you ambitious when you were young? Did you want to be a lawyer, or were you pushed into it by your parents? Did you ever have any exciting clients—cases? Did you—oh, don't be cagey!"

(Oh God! Why did I have to think about that couple in the hotel in Munich?)

He took one hand off the wheel and laid it on my knee.

"Cagey! I like that. You must have come across some extraordinarily articulate men. I can't think of one thing in my professional life that sticks out enough to interest a cow."

"But it says in the magazines that men simply love to talk about their work. You know—get a man to tell you about his job and you've won his heart."

"Not this man, my sweet. Too dull."

"But nothing's dull to me that happened to you. Every

little thing that ever happened to you is You, don't you see?"

He stopped the car and took me by the shoulders.

"My dear girl, I can think of much more interesting things to do which are also Me. This, for instance—"

Under his violent, almost hurtful lovemaking I went limp, beyond will or reasoning.

At the inn we sat in a bower under the high tents of the chestnuts, alone with the evening sunlight and the wine and the tang of garden scents.

"Delia, no more nonsense, I do beg you," he said. "Let's get married. You'll enjoy it, I promise you."

(But would it drown that midnight voice?)

"Not yet, Gordon. We've only been engaged three weeks."

"I'm sick of this 'not yet' business." He sounded irritable. "You've never given me a valid reason—never—and you owe me one. I'm not made of pig-iron."

"Have you ever thought," I said, improvising quickly, "about Franz and Jarzy? They haven't even had time yet to get used to the new conditions, and me owning the house that was their home. If I get married now they'll feel they have to clear out, and they haven't got anywhere to go. I can't do it to them—anyway, not yet."

I glanced at him. His face was expressionless.

"And Eilys too," I went on. "She hasn't anywhere to go until autumn, so I oughtn't to make things inconvenient for her after telling her she could stay with me as long as she liked."

"Is that all?" he said. "If it's just the others you're worrying about, why make a hoodoo of it? Why didn't you say so at the beginning? I can solve the problem. Franz and Jarzy can move into my flat in town, and my Frau Betz will look after them like a mother. They'd enjoy it. And as for Eilys, there's no reason why she shouldn't stay on as our guest until autumn. The house is big enough. She can even have her own rooms if she's sensitive about intruding on us." His voice tautened. "Oh no, Delia, it won't wash. You're the most ineffective liar on earth. You should take a few lessons. Now when I lie it's one hundred per cent convincing, like a lie ought to be."

"You make me wonder," I said, "how often you've lied to me."

He shrugged. "If I say, 'Never to my knowledge', you'll think

I'm at it again. But don't let's side-track. I've caught you out in every untruth you've tried to wish on me about this marriage of ours. All I'm asking for is the true reason you're putting me off. I'll consider anything sensible in the way of a reason, but you won't give me one."

"I can't think of one," I said, stupidly stubborn. "I just don't want to get married yet."

"Liar!" he said with one hand on my throat and his lips an inch from mine. "You're dying to go to bed with me. Deny that if you can!"

"I'll deny anything," I choked out.

His mouth came down on mine savagely, and then he drew back and looked straight into my eyes.

"You mean you're squeamish about going to bed with Ida's murderer."

I gave one gasp.

"That's it, isn't it? You think that damned bitch Gladys had something. You think I murdered Ida to get you and your fortune, don't you?"

"I do not!"

"Yes, you do. You're lying every minute, everything you say is a lie. Now I've brought it out into the light you're trying to kid yourself that your silly little qualms don't exist. When Eilys told me what Gladys had so kindly said about me, my first thought was, could Delia possibly believe that? And I told myself, not on your life—not Delia. But I was wrong. You did believe it. Now we're in a pretty state—aren't we?—for a pair of engaged people. What I'll accept from you is this—that you tell me now you don't believe I murdered Ida, and we'll be married next week, and forget the damned thing for ever. Can you do that?"

"I don't believe it, Gordon," I said. "I swear I don't believe it." All my doubts melted into limbo, all my silly midnight arguments were abandoned. "But I'm not going to commit myself to a wedding date yet. It's all too close."

"For God's sake! What's too close?"

"I know what I feel," I said. "And if you push me I shall have to end our engagement."

Instantly his manner changed. It was amazing. I had no idea I held such a weapon.

"Darling, you'd never do that."

"I shall, if you drive me to it."

He cupped my face in his magnetic hands.

"I believe you would. You're no coward, and I like your spirit. All right, I'll have to wait. But if you love me, don't make it too long."

His marvellous eyes were so pleading that I nearly threw away my victory, but steeled up in time.

"I'm glad we've come to an understanding," I said. "When I feel I'm ready to marry you I'll tell you. I promise."

"And we're still tightly engaged?"

"Of course."

"Then let's behave as if we were."

Happiness seeped through on the tide of his kisses. It was easy to let everything slide on that glamorous languor of love.

That night I slept without brain-racking or bad dreams. From then on, the atmosphere of the house became pleasanter, more relaxed for us all.

Franz's school holidays began, and he liked to take the bus to the lake and walk on the hills, far from the tourists who now crowded the district and its popular spots. The only person Franz ever saw, he told me, was the old man, old Siebler, who had never got over his enforced removal and liked to go back and gaze at the watery spot where his cottage lay drowned, with all its memories of a lifetime spent there.

One afternoon I went out with Franz. Tired at last of walking, we sat down and scanned the mountain scene, blue and shadow-swept under the towering clouds.

"I've been thinking, Delia," he said, "about you and Gordon."

"Oh?" I was wary.

"I did wonder—I mean, now that you're engaged you will want to marry soon. I hope you will not be considering Jarzy and me, that we shall have to leave your house? You are so kind, it might be on your mind."

"But you're quite wrong," I said. "I mean—"

"You will not hurt our feelings at all," he went on. "It is natural for you and Gordon to want your home to yourselves. Jarzy and I have already talked about it, and we would be very happy to share an apartment together in town. We should be perfectly—what do you say?—okay. Please believe that."

"Oh Franz, of course. It's sweet of you to be so thoughtful, but there's no need. We're not getting married yet, in any case."

"And you're sure that has nothing to do with me and Jarzy?"

"Nothing at all. Honestly."

"But Gordon thought it did have."

"Has Gordon talked to you about it?"

"To Jarzy. About you worrying that we have nowhere to go when you marry."

"That's quite a misunderstanding."

I suddenly wished with all my heart that I could pour out my problem to Franz, for I had nobody to confide in—Eilys was too cynical—and he would be the one person who might understand all my undefined feelings, my lack of decision, my self-questioning. And he could be trusted.

"I'm not happy, Franz," I broke out. "I'm worried."

He looked at me with anxious surprise.

"Unhappy! But you have everything to make you happy."

"That's what it looks like. I'm in love with Gordon, and I can't make myself marry him. It sounds idiotic. Gordon can't understand me, and I suppose he's justified. Everybody would think me a blazing fool."

Franz thought for a while.

"It is to do with what Gladys said that night."

"How could you know that?"

"Because I put myself in your place and I know how I would also feel. A little bit of her poison sticks?"

"Oh Franz, it does stick. And I hate myself for letting it."

"How can you help that? But it will go if you don't encourage it to stay."

"It isn't so easy," I said sadly. "I'm waiting for it to go. I've no right to discuss Gordon with you or with anybody, but this is getting me down, to be so alone with my huge, awful thoughts."

He looked at me gently.

"Such ideas must be all gone before you marry him, Delia. You couldn't marry him and then brood and wonder."

"Tell me I'm wrong," I pleaded, "to have such thoughts at all."

"You want me to have cold logic about this?"

"Of course I do."

"Then I think you are right to consider."

I was startled. "You mean, *you* think Gordon could be—capable—of—"

He held up his hand. "I did not say such a thing. What I mean is that any man could do anything. I have in my life seen such cruelty, such treachery and evil. My brother's own best friend did sell him to the Nazis. I have now lost faith in any man's outward appearances. I have only faith in God, and in someone like you who I know is true and without wickedness. So I say that if you doubt it is because your heart tells you to take care. You cannot go against that."

"You do understand, Franz, that I absolutely loathe myself for even remembering what Gladys said?"

"But who could help remembering? None of us can help."

"Have you thought about it too?"

"I have thought about it. I have even pictured how it could have happened."

My finger nails clawed at the turf where I sat.

"How it could have been—planned, even? " I said.

"We're going too far," he said. "Like it says in Shakespeare, 'that way madness lies'. We will not woo madness. I say it is a great pity and bad luck for Gordon that he did not have friends in the car that day for witnesses. That was very unfortunate for Gordon and I am sorry."

"Do you think," I asked, "that other people besides us have wondered?"

"Come," he said getting up. "Enough of this. It is wrong to discuss because evil creeps in. We never intended to talk so, and in spite of ourselves we have talked evil. So an innocent man could suffer. It is a poisonous thing, suspicion, because the minute you look at it it begins to grow, and then the shoot is a tree." He took my hands and pulled me to my feet. "You must pray, Delia, for such thoughts to be wiped away. That is faith, isn't it? Have you prayed?"

"No. I was afraid to."

"Then you will. And I shall too, for you and Gordon."

"Oh Franz, I feel so much better," I said. "I shall put myself in Gordon's place and realize how ghastly this must be for him. Thank you for all you've said. It was right to bring things into the light. You won't mention this to anybody else?"

"Need you ask? Never."

"Has Jarzy ever—?"

"No, no. He is always strong for Gordon."

"Yes," I said. "Jarzy doesn't fail Gordon. It is left for me to do that. I feel a worm."

"Then we will walk home," he said cheerfully, "and talk about what is nice."

2

ONE afternoon a woman named Mrs. Schiller called and introduced herself as an English friend of Ida's who lived in an hotel in Neisbaden. I had never come across her, and this was explained by the fact that she had been in Switzerland for several months.

She was a woman of seventy or more, with a face like a child's elephant, dumpy, full-cheeked and snouted. Her pebbly grey eyes, quick and hard, took in every detail of the room. And of me.

"Do sit down, Mrs. Schiller," I said. "You'll have some tea?"

"That's very very kind of you." She had a soft little confiding voice which disarmed you.

I rang the bell for Sigrid.

"So you are dear Ida's goddaughter? I've heard of you."

The words, "The one who came into the money," could not have been more clearly spoken if she had actually articulated them.

"Can I offer you a cigarette?"

"Not just now, my dear. I felt I had to come. That appalling tragedy! I only heard about it after I got back. It was the talk of our hotel, in fact it still is. Ida was so well known."

"It was a terrible thing," I said, "but having happened it seems a pity that people should make a topic of it."

She looked at me with a slightly less amiable expression.

"I'm glad you are able to accept it in such a strong-minded way, Miss—er. Of course you hadn't known her long. Those of us who had were devoted to her."

"I was myself," I said tersely.

Sigrid came in with the tea. I poured out, and handed my guest a cup.

"Ah yes," she said with a sigh, staring at the white-and-gold china. "Ida's. How well I remember those happy tea-parties."

"Yes, it's all very sad." I hoped she wouldn't stay long if this was to be the motif of the visit. "But we have to go on living and it isn't right to mourn for ever. Ida wouldn't have wanted us to."

"And now the house and all these things are yours."

"Yes . . . Did I give you sugar?"

"Thank you . . . So you're settling down here?"

"We're doing our best to. We feel that this is home."

"Ah . . . well, at least you'll not be short of money. Ida was a rich woman, poor darling."

"It isn't a subject I care to discuss."

She nodded, pushing out her underlip.

"I always think that inheriting money must be a very sad thing. Especially from someone like Ida who was in the full prime of life. Such a vibrant, popular woman. I don't think I could ever get used to seeing her things about after she was gone. I couldn't ever think of them as mine."

I swallowed hard. It was necessary to be polite to this old thing, because she had been Ida's friend and this was allegedly a visit of condolence.

"How long have you lived at Neisbaden?" I asked, to divert her.

"Oh, ever since I was married, and that's forty years. My husband was German, an ear specialist. During the war I went to my daughter in Zürich, the one I've just been staying with. But I love Neisbaden, all my friends are there. And so many of Ida's too. I've known Ida for twenty-five years, that's what makes it so terrible to me."

"Do have some cherry cake," I said. "My cook makes it. It's really good."

"No, thank you. I never touch it. Just the tea." She went on, "There's something I feel compelled to ask you, Miss—er—?"

"My name is Delia."

"Thank you, dear. This is what I must ask you—what did you think about that accident?"

She had caught me right off guard.

"How do you mean?"

The little grey eyes bored into mine. "I might as well say just what I mean—what's on my mind, and I'm not the only one by a long way. That accident was suggestive. Oh, I'm not putting anything into words, I'm much too prudent to do that, but it's well known that Ida thought too much of that lawyer. What a pity she went off with him like that, just the two of them!"

"Mrs. Schiller, I would rather not—"

She went straight on, "You know, do you, that he appeared here suddenly after the war? Nobody knew anything about him. And Ida, if you please, must confide her affairs to him, taking the man on trust. That was Ida all over. Oh, I warned her, believe me, about mystery men and rich lonely women. But she never could resist a handsome man. People say this fellow was a bit too sure of himself. There *was* something—"

I interrupted her fiercely and fell bang into her trap.

"Mrs. Schiller, I ought to tell you before you say any more that I am engaged to Mr. Portmeed."

"Ah." The pebbly eyes glinted, the full little lips sucked in. "So it's true. I couldn't believe it, but I have it from you yourself."

"Perhaps," I said, struggling to sound calm, "you'd like to talk about something else—before you go?"

She looked injured, or pretended to.

"I never thought to be turned out of Ida's house by Ida's goddaughter."

"You must know that wasn't my intention. But I don't like this conversation."

"No? I thought it would have concerned you, that people are talking."

"Talking?" Now she was out-playing me again, but I had to know. She kept me on the hook, peering at me shrewdly.

"You seem a nice girl. I think you must be rather innocent."

"Innocent of what?"

"Oh, my dear child, you don't know how people's tongues wag in a place like this. It's only right you should learn, for your own sake. And for the sake of Ida's memory."

(Don't relish it so, you old spider!)

"Do go on." My voice was firm but I was shaking inside.

"Well now. It's the look of the thing, you being her heiress. Everybody knows how rich she was."

I wasn't going to let her have it all her own way.

"You needn't be tactful, Mrs. Schiller. You're trying to tell me that the cheap gossips have decided I'm easy game for a fortune-hunter. It's what I'd have expected of them, and it couldn't worry me less."

"Not only that." She made little chopping movements with her hand. "That's just the beginning. People are really awful."

"Awful?"

"It's that accident." She made "accident" sound like an obscene word. "You can't stop people having nasty thoughts. And rumour spreads so. I'm very careful myself, you can be had up for slander. But when it's all over the place already—"

My heart thudded. "What is?"

"I feel I have to tell you, if you really don't know already." She lowered her voice, it hissed slightly like a very old cistern. "This is what is being said. That it was a very odd accident. Improbable. And there's no way to prove or disprove a *thing*. And it's just too profitable for somebody we won't name. Mind you, I don't want you to think for one minute that I associate myself with this talk, but you know what human nature is."

I held on to myself.

"If you mean what I think you mean, Mrs. Schiller, I suggest you name the person you're talking about, and that if you've any accusation to bring you put it into plain language. As you said, there's such a thing as taking action against malicious scandal. If you don't care to be honest, I'd be obliged if you'll leave my house."

Her cheeks turned slowly purple.

"I don't know if you can afford to talk like that, my dear. Some naughty people have even wondered if—well, if you know more about the whole business than you'd care to tell."

"Get out of here, you filthy old hag!"

Both of us shot round to the doorway where Eilys was standing.

"I've been listening," she said. "You slug!"

"Don't, Eilys," I said. "She'll have a stroke."

My visitor, her cheeks livid and mottled, was breathing in noisy snorts.

Eilys set her teeth. "We don't want her fat corpse on our hands. Come on, you—out! Your chauffeur's waiting."

Mrs. Schiller stumbled out of the drawing-room, a chair crashed in her wake. She was gone. Outside, the car started up.

"I wish you hadn't gone for her," I said. "Now she's off to tell the tale round the neighbourhood."

"Not she." Eilys was calm. "She'd never dare to say she was chucked out, she'd lose face. Who is the old beast, anyway?"

"A friend of Ida's. You heard her tell about that ghastly gossip? Eilys, I'm desperate."

"What for?" She slid down on the sofa and relaxed. "Don't you give a damn what people say. If you're satisfied, to hell with everybody else. And all gossip strangles itself to death in the end. . . . Is that tea drinkable?"

"Hardly."

"Sigrid can make me some more. I took Isold out to lunch, and then we both had hair-dos, and I sent her home with an armful of carnations for the old lady and some roses for Mrs. N.'s desk. Tactful touch, that. It may stop her badgering me to buy shoes for Hungarian kids."

"I'll make you some tea," I said. "Sigrid has the ironing."

"Why on earth should you make my tea?"

"It'll calm me down."

When I came back with the fresh pot, Eilys said, "I hope you're not going to let this business eat you. I know you."

"How can I help it? Gordon's my man."

"H'm." Eilys picked over the cakes. "Do you want him or don't you? I've wondered lately. If you want him, marry him, and stop acting like Lady Windermere's Fan."

"It isn't as easy as that. These accusations—"

Her eyes gave a spirited flash.

"What of it? If I wanted a man I'd have him whatever he'd done."

"That could be madness on the grand scale."

"That could be love! Love's always on the grand scale if it's anything at all." She hooked one arm behind her head. "It's flattering if a man will do murder to get you."

"What a revolting, tasteless thing to say. And I won't have you talking as if Gordon was guilty!"

She looked thoughtful. "Whether he is or not I couldn't say. Nobody will ever know. There's no evidence so they couldn't make anything stick. It's up to you now. You know whether you want Gordon or not, and if you do, don't keep him dangling. It's unfair."

I beat my fists together till it hurt.

"Eilys, I'm nearly out of my mind at the mere suspicion that Gordon could have done this terrible thing, and you talk as if he did it and it couldn't matter less!"

"I never said he did it." She licked cake icing off her fingers. "And I certainly don't suggest that he planned it. But if he suddenly found himself with Ida on the top of an eighty-foot drop, miles from anywhere and anybody, and it occurred to him what one little push could fetch him—a rich wife and security—well, he's only human. Aren't we all? If he did plan it, then he's a cooler character than I thought, that's all."

"Oh, that's devilish!"

"There you go again." She lay back and lighted a cigarette. "Words out of a corny play. This is life, whether you like the look of it or not. All men are wicked, Deel. Any man is capable of anything—I've told you that before. I'd never trust the best of them, but heavens! how they can fascinate the soul out of you. That's where we women are at a disadvantage. We know they're bad lots, but we'll have them at any price once we've fallen for them. Gordon's no better and no worse than others, but he's so alluring that his women fall harder. And that's apt to make a man ruthless, if you see what I mean."

"No, I don't see what you mean. It's utterly immoral and I won't accept it."

"Well, you'd better accept the fact that your young man has just turned in at the gate," said Eilys, looking over her shoulder.

My eyes flew to the window in time to see Gordon's car draw up at the door. I was ready to rush upstairs, but the hall door was open and he came straight in.

"Hullo, girls."

"Hullo, Gordon," I said in a flat voice. "Would you like some tea, or can I get you a drink?"

"Something cold, please."

Shakily I mixed him a drink. He stood with his back to the hearth, sipping gratefully, and looking superb in his dark, well-cut suit and perfect linen, with his broad shoulders, long graceful body, magnificent head, air of aplomb.

"How pleasant to feel cool," he said. "It was stifling in town. What's the matter with you two girls? Eilys looks as if she'd stepped in something, and Delia's breathing is coming in jerks. Been rowing each other? Couldn't be."

I bit the inside of my cheek, the pain made my eyes water.

"You might as well know," Eilys said coolly. "Deel has had a visitor, a venomous hag from Neisbaden who says she's a friend of Ida's."

"Mrs. Schiller? I know that one."

"Apparently Neisbaden is nattering about Ida's decease. Saying it all came awfully conveniently for you, Gordon."

"But it did, didn't it?" he said without emotion. "You can't blame the gossips. It's a juicy murder-mystery right out of the paper-backs. The old woman with the money, the goddaughter with prospects, and the wicked attorney who can catch the lot if the old woman passes out. Ha!"

They both saw me fold up and flop into a chair.

"There goes Deel," said Eilys. "She can't take it, Gordon. You and I are too crude in our realism. I sent the Schiller woman packing, and Deel and I have been arguing ever since whether you did it or not."

"We have not!" I said sharply. "Gordon, I—"

He lighted a cigarette. "I'd love to have been here and heard you. Reach any decision?"

"Naturally not," said Eilys. "Nobody ever can. You're as safe as houses, if you did do it."

"That's nice to know." He blew out smoke. "If it's any interest to you, I didn't, but I don't expect anybody to believe me. It would be too much to ask of human nature, on top of such an intriguing set-up. I thought there was a scandal brewing! It's hit me already, I've been losing business. But I've known so many scandals, and they all die out when they've been chewed to rags, as this one will. I'll survive. Meanwhile Delia won't marry me because she still has a lingering doubt. I'm prepared to wait if I must, but you might put in a word for me, Eilys. She might listen to you."

"Oh no, she won't. She thinks I'm evil-minded."

"And for why? Were you so evil-minded as to tell her you thought I did it?"

"Not in so many words. I told her you could have."

"That was friendly of you."

"I also told her that even if you did there was nothing to fuss about if she wanted you. Didn't I, Deel?"

"Dear, dear!" he said. "Generous if hard-boiled. The murderer would like another drink if he may."

"I can't stand this kind of talk!" I broke out. "I can't and I won't."

Instantly Gordon was all concern.

"Of course you can't, darling, and you shan't. Eilys, go away—you're an outrage. Leave Delia to me, I want to reassure her."

When she was gone he pulled me into his arms.

"My poor darling, that was hell for you. But you must not be so vulnerable. Get yourself a tough hide like Eilys—or like me, if it comes to that. Did you think this scandal was going to leave me pale and droopy, the noble innocent all distraught? People are saying nasty things—yes. I've been unlucky in that if Ida had to die like that we didn't have a witness. But once the sensation has faded away—and it will—we'll get married and be happy ever after. I promise you. You must not worry so. Leave everything to me."

I began to wonder if perhaps he was right. Maybe other people, unlike myself, were brought up in a world where this kind of trouble happened and blew over. Were all my values out of date? Or just wrong-headed?

Under the caresses of his practised hands I surrendered to the daze of infatuation and every sense was blurred. Then the recollection of those sickening conversations broke through.

I sat up and pushed myself away from him.

"What's the matter?" he said, not pleased.

"Oh Gordon, leave me alone!"

"That's a sweet thing to say! I'm doing my best."

"It's all been too much for me today. I must be alone to think."

"Being alone and thinking doesn't seem to do you any good."

"I know it doesn't," I said wretchedly.

"If we got married it would at least show the world that you believe in me. It would be a gesture. That is, of course, if you *do* believe in me."

"Please don't put it like that," I said. "You put me in an awful position."

"I can't see it. Either you believe in me or you don't."

"But I do—I do."

"Oh, my God!" He jumped up, his face taut and hard-boned. "You don't know what you do think. You're impossible to deal with."

His anger crushed what hope I had left.

"Perhaps," I said, "it would be better to call our engagement off until I can come round to your way of thinking."

His eyes froze.

"This is great!" he said scathingly. "Just great. Real trust and affection in every sense. I suppose you realize what you've just said. You throw me over—there's a new sensation for the neighbourhood. What is the obvious conclusion that people come to? Do I have to tell you, or are you capable of working it out for yourself?"

"I spoke without thinking," I said. "Of course people would

take it as meaning that I doubted you myself and that would be bad for you. You know I didn't mean such a thing. We'll go on as we are. I only want to do the best thing for you."

"Thank you for that. Am I invited to stay for supper?"

"Of course. I'll go and see to it. The boys will be in soon."

But for me the midnight questioning again, bitter and grim.

Isn't he overdoing his eagerness to marry you? . . . Could he be anxious to grab what he's risked so much for?

Do you really believe in him with a clear, shining belief? . . . If you did, wouldn't you marry him tomorrow?

Did he really kill Ida, and does everybody know it except you?

3

To keep me from thinking, to fill my time, I was putting in hours a day at the camp. Eilys, in one of her calmer phases, also came often, doing her office work, everyone's little ray of sunshine, and cosseting the Todors who existed in a dream of Switzerland . . . "It won't be long now—not long now."

Madame Todor told me, "When Pappa is weak and the pain in his back is bad, he say, 'No matter, I will have a real bed next winter.' And now Isold is so happy, her cough he nearly go."

Now the Todors were taken care of, and I had the new thrill of spending my own money, I was able to help many others in the camp and remove some of the more obvious hardships.

I sometimes found myself envying my friend Eilys, not so much for her attraction and power to charm, but for her easy acceptance of life, her debonair temperament, her way of manipulating every circumstance to her advantage. The things she planned would always come right for her, frustration and defeat would never exist for Eilys. Most of the seemingly outrageous things she said were said for effect. Always easy-going, good-natured, gay and stimulating—

how lucky I was to have such a friend. I began to rely on her. She was my refuge from myself.

At home things were steady. Nobody ever mentioned Ida now, it was as if all that had been tidied away into the past. Gordon came —not too frequently—and actually I was very rarely alone with him. He was like one of the family.

Even the gossip, a nine days' wonder, seemed to be fading out. It hadn't enough to feed on. We heard no more of Mrs. Schiller.

Letters from my mother were rather trying.

". . . You tell us very little, dear, about your engagement. And have you still no plans for the wedding? Of course it must be here. What about invitations? Who is to give you away? And bridesmaids? Please answer my questions! I have hopes that you will settle down in England, not far from us . . ."

Each time I wrote I had the dicey job of putting her off without suggesting that anything was wrong.

One morning Eilys got a letter from Lausanne. It was from her father's doctor, to say that the invalid had had a heart attack and it would be advisable for her to come and visit him.

She went off at once, and the house seemed dreary without her vital personality.

"Isn't it dull without Eilys?" I said to Jarzy one evening as we were watering the flower boxes along the balcony. "Where's all the gaiety gone? Surely we can do better than this by ourselves."

"If I get the car out, would you like to go to the lake?"

"I'd love to."

We found a deserted spot where we could sit and look across the shimmering water to the rose-gold ranges dreaming in the evening sun.

"Doesn't the water look deep!" I said.

"Yes, it's very deep now. Our old house must be far down below."

I leaned forward and cupped my hands round my face.

"Do you remember when you dived down for Ida's china cat? How pleased she was. I don't suppose you could do that now they've let the rest of the water in."

"It would be dangerous to try. But not impossible, I think. I often do dive and swim here, you know."

I sat up, and said, "Don't you ever try anything dangerous, for heaven's sake!"

He gave a scornful laugh. "I'm not a funk. Why do women always say, do not do the dangerous? Men are most happy when they do the dangerous."

"I know you're not a funk, but there's no need to be foolhardy."

"What on earth is Fool Hardy?"

I laughed. "Is that a new word for you? It just means reckless."

He stretched himself full length and began to pick the wild pansies growing in the tufted grass.

"Dahlia—"

"Yes?"

"Can I say something to you that means a lot to me?"

"Of course, Jarzy."

He seemed to have difficulty in going on. I half guessed what was coming.

"Do you think—oh, to hell! I suppose you know that I love Eilys. Can everybody see that?"

"I guessed it."

"I love her more than ever, and soon she intends to go away. Do you think I should tell her? Could I possibly have a chance?"

"That's something I couldn't say." I frowned, wondering what was the right answer. "Nobody knows what Eilys's deeper feelings are, she doesn't show them. She's always so casual on the surface, and though I'm with her so much I haven't a clue to what goes on inside her. I do know that she likes you very much. How deep it goes I couldn't guess."

He made a pattern on my shoe with the little flowers.

"But tell me honestly, should I ask her?"

"Yes, Jarzy, I should if I were you. Take her out one evening, and ask her. But choose your time. If she comes back worried about her father, that isn't the time to bring it up."

He sat up abruptly. "I can't think that she could care about me."

"Oh, don't be so humble. All people in love have that feeling. You two are ideally suited, you're gay and good-looking and companionable and like the same things. I'm sure Eilys isn't so sophisticated as she sometimes sounds. She could be lonely, and if anything happens to her father she will be. Has she told you about the house she's going to buy in Switzerland?"

"Yes, she has. And the Roumanians who go there too." He began to laugh. "She will have a Pole also in the bunch if she marries me. What a lovely mix-up family in her chalet! And I can afford to marry, I have money that Ida leaves me—not rich, but quite enough—and I hope some day I shall practise law." He gave a desperate sigh. "Nothing will be worth anything to me if she turn me down flat."

"Pester her!" I said. "Don't take no for an answer. She likes dominating men, so sweep her off her feet. That's my advice to you, and it's good."

He brightened up. "You've made me feel hopeful, Dahlia. I shall go right for her, I shall not take No. And soon you will be rid of the family that is push on you, and you will have your house to yourself, for just you and Gordon. There is Onkel, but he can go and live in an apartment and come to stay with us in his holidays."

The evening was beautiful, full of soft light and gentle sounds, and suddenly my heart felt happier than it had for a long time. Jarzy must have seen a smile on my face, because he said suddenly, "I suppose you are going to marry Gordon soon?"

"Why should you be anxious about that?"

"Because Gordon is my best friend."

I thought for a minute. "We shall probably get married in the autumn, after the rest of you are settled."

He pushed the hair off his forehead.

"I'm glad. I know how you did feel though I say nothing."

"You did? Jarzy, sometimes I feel like a snake."

He nodded. "And me, I sometimes think like a snake."

"How do you mean?"

"Well—we talk free now. I have thought how that—you know what I mean?—could have been done if anyone was wicked—and Gordon is not. Gordon likes money, I know. But never, never would Gordon do what they say. He could not, it is not possible. You are lucky that he loves you Dahlia, and you love him, and if Eilys and I are one well-matched couple, so are you and Gordon another. It was sad for Ida to die, but she would be happy to know that four people she love had made two nice pairs."

We talked until it was dark and the stars came out over the hill-tops, and somehow the trouble in my mind seemed to melt away as the last late-flying birds melted into the dusk. I began to see how patient Gordon had been with me, and under such provocation too. I had behaved melodramatically from first to last and I was ashamed of myself.

I couldn't wait to get home and ring Gordon up. It was half past ten and there was every chance that he'd be in his flat.

"Darling," I said when I heard his voice, "don't be surprised. This is Delia. I've been the most awful fool. Jarzy made me see it, and I had to tell you at once without waiting till tomorrow, even."

"What have you done now?" He sounded terrified.

I laughed aloud. "You may well ask. I deserve that. What I mean to say is that I've been absolutely criminal to behave to you as I have, and to talk so crazily. You've been so patient. Darling, please, please forgive me. You've always been right, from the very first."

Relief was surging in his voice as he replied. "This sounds too good to be true. You can't be actually suggesting that you'll marry me, can you?"

"That's the idea," I said.

"When?"

"Let's make it September—definitely. That's less than two months away. And there's a prospect that the others may be settled by then. Can we meet and talk it over?"

"With all my heart! Lunch tomorrow?"

"I'd love to. I'll come round to your place at one. Gordon, you haven't said you'll forgive me—or is that too much to expect?"

"My sweet, there's nothing to forgive." He sounded delighted. "You were justified in being obstinate, I suppose, but oh, the relief of knowing it's all over! Here's a passionate kiss for you—get it?"

It was wonderful happiness, and so was our next meeting.

Eilys returned at the end of the week, but her news wasn't good. The doctors gave her father a few weeks at most to live.

"Ought you to have stayed longer at Lausanne?" I asked.

"It wouldn't do any good. Daddy is unconscious half the time, he didn't seem to know whether I was there or not."

She looked weary and crumpled after her journey, slumping back on the sofa, her slender white shoes dropping from her heels.

I brought her some tea and she revived.

"Were you able to do anything about your new chalet, like you hoped?"

"Oh yes. At least, I went to two agents. There are some nice places for sale round the lake, only I hadn't time to go and view them. But I sent some friends, and I really think I shall let them decide for me. It will save bother. Lord, I've never felt so shot up in my life! How has everything been here?"

"One important thing has happened," I said. "Gordon and I are going to get married in September. I've come to my senses."

She gave me a long considering look.

"That's something." She pushed back the damp hair from her temples. "What caused the change of heart?"

"Jarzy showed me what a fool I've been."

"Trust Mike! He's very sound."

"So everything's all right," I said.

She dragged herself up. "Get me something long, wet, and icy, darling. That place was like Dante's Inferno."

"Let's hope it'll be a long time before you have to travel again," I said.

4

It was a very short time.

Eilys's father collapsed and died a few days later. The unexpected telegram came in the middle of the morning, and she tore it open and exclaimed, "Oh, Daddy is dead."

"Oh Eilys—how sad. You'll have to go, won't you?"

"I'm afraid so. It'll be just for a few days, over the funeral."

Her eyes suddenly ran over with tears. "Poor Daddy. I can't realize it. I haven't anybody now."

"You've got us," I said. "You know we'll do anything for you. Shall I pack you a case? I know just what you'll need, so you can sit down and have a drink while I see to things. It's been a shock for you."

"My knees feel funny. I never expected it, Deel, not so soon."

I packed some clothes for her, and she came upstairs and changed out of her sun frock into a dark linen travelling suit, while I rang up Munich airport and managed to get her a seat on the Geneva plane. Then I got the car out and drove her over.

In the evening I told Gordon what had happened.

"I'm worried for Eilys," I said. "I don't know what her father's financial position was, but most of his income may die with him for all we know. He was only about fifty, he may not have made much provision for the future. I can't help wondering how Eilys is going to be left. He always gave her a generous allowance, but it's going to be a different thing when she has to support herself, and she'd be much too proud to let anybody know if it wasn't easy."

"I don't think you need worry," he said drily. "Eilys will get by."

I was very surprised. "Gordon, you sounded almost callous—as if you couldn't care less. I know you don't like Eilys much—"

"I don't 'like' her at all, I never have 'liked' her, and I don't care for the word 'like'."

"But need you sound so irascible about it?"

His face relaxed.

"My dear, I didn't mean that. But the way you take everybody's cares on your shoulders is ridiculous—you even invent troubles that may never exist. I can't think that Eilys will be poverty-stricken, and with her looks and talents she can get somebody to look after her any minute she wants to. She'll take herself off to Switzerland now, and catch herself a stinking-rich old husband, and wallow in luxury, and become a wealthy widow—then at it again."

"She certainly won't!" I said, full of indignation. "Not if I can help it. And I'll take good care she's never driven to do such a thing. I'm much too fond of her. And if you can keep it dark, Gordon,

Jarzy is very much in love with her and wants to marry her, and I hope she'll accept him."

Gordon looked thunderstruck.

"Jarzy!"

"What's so surprising? Haven't you noticed it?"

"No. . . . He hasn't a chance."

"What makes you think not?"

"Well—it's fantastic. Eilys is gunning for bigger game."

"I wish you wouldn't reduce everything to materialism. Eilys isn't like that a bit, I know her better than you do."

He shrugged and gave a short laugh.

"So? Then let's swap materialism for romance for a while, shall we?"

He lighted two cigarettes, took one from between his lips and slipped it between mine.

"Say thank you, darling."

"Thank you, darling."

"Not like that—like this."

His cheek against my hair, we lazed on the balcony swing-seat, watching the moon come up like a huge golden melon. We had the house to ourselves.

"It won't be long," he said exultantly, "before this is ours—ours alone, like tonight, but all the time. Everybody gone but us. Just you and me. Now tell me if you dare that you don't long for that too?"

"You know I do, but at the risk of rousing your fury, Gordon, I'm not satisfied yet about Eilys. We didn't talk it out. You must listen to this—to please me. I've never been happy about what Ida did to her, and I've felt shocking about having eighty thousand pounds while she who had an equal right got nothing at all."

"I don't see what you can do about that," he said idly.

"I do! I'm going to ask her to accept half of mine, and then I'll feel a darned sight happier."

"You're going to—WHAT!"

"I knew it would shake you, but you'll get used to the idea and feel like I do that it's only fair. You and I don't need all that money. And what you said about a rich old man walking off with Eilys has recoiled on your own head, She shan't be put in such a position. I shall insist on her having the money."

"She won't take it."

"I think she will. She's realistic. I mean, if I had a shilling and she had nothing she'd take sixpence, so why not forty thousand out of eighty thousand? It's exactly the same thing."

He took a hard breath.

"I won't say what I think of your traumatic reasoning, but I certainly won't have anything to do with such a plan."

"You won't have to," I said calmly. "I'll see to it all."

"I'm Ida's executor. And your financial manager."

"I don't care. You don't frighten me, the money's mine, and I can go to another lawyer, can't I?"

He put his arm tightly round me.

"My sweet, you cannot do a thing like this, take it from me. You've got a better heart than you have a head. There isn't another person on earth who would entertain such an idea as to give away half their capital—snap! just like that—on an impulse. You'd be sorry later."

I shook my head. "I've made up my mind, and you can't stop me from offering it. There may be a maggot in my brain, but I won't be happy until I've made this offer to Eilys. If she does refuse it, as you think she will—"

He looked gloomy. "She'll take it all right. She's very likely hard up, and she's the sort who'll do anything for money—like me."

"Don't say things like that, Gordon. You don't mean it, but I hate it."

"You just can't bear anything ugly, can you?" he said, his tone exasperated. "You're a great one for truth, and yet truth itself is usually ugly."

"That isn't what I've found."

"You've found—or learned—a lot of odd things, and you'll have to spend a long time with me unlearning them."

"I'll enjoy it."

"You won't enjoy it so much if you're going to begin our life together with the mad act of throwing half your capital away," he said ironically. "You really must let yourself be guided by me. It's what I'm for."

"Goodness!" I said. "I'll never get engaged to a lawyer again."

"That isn't funny."

"It isn't meant to be. I'm awfully sorry you feel about it as you do, because I hate to go against you, and I'd hoped you'd see it my way."

"I wish to God Eilys had never come here," he said moodily, slapping a bit of imaginary dust off his trouser leg as if it were Eilys herself.

I patiently ignored this outburst and went on, "Darling, I love you even when you infuriate me. But don't you see, even forty thousand, which is what we'll have left, is terrific? It's a fortune—far more than we need. I'd really rather have it than eighty thousand, which frightens me a bit."

"That remark," he said, "is carrying unsophistication to extremes. I can't really think you're so ingenuous, Delia. If you are, you certainly want looking after. I hope you're going to let me handle your finances after we're married?"

"Of course," I said. "Provided I can always lay my hands on a thousand or so if I want to, and no questions asked."

"A thousand! What for?"

"I might see a fur coat I fancied."

"You mean you might want to hand it over to one of your lay-abouts at the refugee camp. who tells you he was a count in his own country and misses his Tokay and cigars. Really, you frighten me."

"I'm not as bad as that," I said, running a conciliatory finger along the back of his hand. "And to come back to where we were when I got diverted, though I loathe having to do something you dislike, I am definitely going to offer this half share to Eilys because it's only decent to do so."

"And doesn't it occur to you that it's ethically wrong to use Ida's money for a purpose of which Ida would have heartily disapproved?"

I was slightly staggered. "I'll think that one out, Gordon, but I don't think it will make any difference. I'm the living one, and I've got the money, and I must do what I think is right with it."

He said no more. My heart sank. Was Gordon really thinking of my interests, or was I less desirable to him with forty thousand pounds instead of eighty? Was it worth all he'd gone through, to get—oh no . . . Oh God, no . . . not that again!

Eilys came back at the end of the week, looking washed out and limp. I rushed her upstairs, got her changed into a white silk dressing-gown and fluffy mules, put her on the divan, and brought her tea, eau-de-Cologne, and a lot of fussing.

"Hey, lay off, Deel," she said. "This is undeserved. I'm not suffering from grief, it's night clubs. Daddy wouldn't have wanted me to gloom around and the friends I was staying with took me out every night. The funeral was frightful and I felt as low as a clod. There was a wreath from Mummy, only it said, 'From Colonel and Mrs. Walter Brasker' and I couldn't for the life of me think who those characters were. I never thought of Mummy as Mrs. Brasker, and he's a crummy old creep. Then I had to interview dreary lawyers, and you know what that does to you. I was nearly howling."

She let me rub her wrists and temples with frozen cologne, and said, "That's heaven . . . Darling, I decided I couldn't ever live in Lausanne, it's so noisy and towny."

"You don't have to, do you?"

"I saw the most divine chalet up in the hills at Mognay, just what I'd like. It's vacant from September. I've a good mind to clinch it, but honestly, I'm too tired to write just yet."

"Don't think about that now."

Her lips gave a petulant twist. "I'll have to think about it some time."

I was anxious. "Eilys, I do hope your father's death isn't going to make a great difference to you financially?"

"Difference? . . . oh, money. I never think about that, it's such a bore."

That remark, from my point of view, didn't settle anything. Eilys looked so beautiful, so sweet and wan, that I was full of pity for her. It wasn't much fun when you had always been cared for and indulged to be flung on the world to make out for yourself, and probably at a lower standard of living than you'd been brought up to.

During the next few days she seemed to recover her spirits, and I decided it was time for me to tackle this money question. and in

Gordon's presence. I wanted him to be in on it, to hear exactly what was said so that there shouldn't be any misunderstanding or argument later on.

Franz had gone to Stuttgart for a day or two, so I chose an evening when Jarzy would be out with friends and rang Gordon to ask him round for supper.

"Two lone women," I explained. "It feels gruesome."

"What about the two lone women coming out with me? I've discovered a charming place about ten miles away where the food is exceptional and they don't encourage the tourists. I could call for you both at seven."

"Gordon's taking us out to supper," I told Eilys.

She raised one eyebrow.

"Don't be so self-sacrificing, darling. You know I'll be *de trop*."

"Don't be silly. We want you. You can sparkle for us."

The evening was misty and warm, the restaurant when we came to it a slumbrous, medieval place with a singing stream beside it. We ate in the garden, under a trellis thick with clematis, and all the hues of day were dying into twilight as little coloured lights came on.

As we sipped our Niersteiner I said, "Eilys, I want to speak to you about something, and I want you to take me very, very seriously."

Her eyes shot wide open. She looked from me to Gordon and back at me again.

"What have I done now?"

"Delia's got a bee in her bonnet," Gordon said with an unsmiling glance. "She has to let it out. Listen to the buzz."

"It isn't a bee," I said, "it's common sense. Please listen to me. Eilys, I think it's possible that your father's death has altered your financial circumstances."

She looked wary. "What if it has?"

"Has it, Eilys?"

"Sure it has. Why?"

"Just that—you remember after Ida's death how Gordon told me that I'd been left a huge sum of money while you got nothing? I protested against the unfairness of it."

"Oh, that old row with Ida. I brought it on myself, didn't I? You don't have to bother about that, Deel."

"But I am bothering," I said crisply. "It may have been all right when your father was alive, but it isn't all right now. I feel a lot of responsibility. I've told Gordon and he knows I mean it. I can't enjoy my money while you go short, and I'm asking you to accept half of it—share and share alike—as it ought to have been from the beginning."

I hadn't expected to see her so amazed. She was dumbfounded, looking with a baffled expression from me to Gordon and back to me.

"I insist," I said. "You're to have forty thousand pounds and then I'll sleep happy. I'll be well off. I haven't got luxurious tastes. Please don't argue, just take it."

Eilys suddenly put down her glass.

"I'm not going to argue. It's the most generous gesture anybody's made to me in my whole life. You're a friend, Deel. I admire you from the depths of my squalid soul. But you're keeping your money! I don't want it and I don't need it—take it from me I don't, it's the truth. Thanks for the offer, but I'm perfectly all right for money."

"You're just saying that."

"I am not just saying that. If I wanted the money I'd grab it like lightning. I wouldn't have any finer feelings. You know me! I tell you, I don't need it, not any of it."

"What am I to believe, Gordon?"

He flicked one hand up and let it fall.

"I'd be inclined to believe the girl. But perhaps as we're in confidential conference she wouldn't mind giving us some details. What is your financial position, Eilys? Did your father leave you anything?"

"Yes, he did," she said tersely.

"How much?"

"Gordon, don't be rude," I said.

He gave a short bark. "Let's talk straight, for pity's sake. Eilys evidently isn't going to beg her bread and butter or sell herself for gold, which is what you've got on your mind. She has, Eilys. She thinks you're doomed to drift from tycoon to tycoon till you shrivel up in the ashes of lucrative passion."

"Holy boots!" Eilys gave a snigger. "Here's the truth, then. My father was a rich man with a lot of sound business interests, though he never shouted about it. Even Ida didn't know how rich he was. Nor I, if it comes to that. He died worth half a million sterling, and after his executors have settled up and paid off a few bequests I get the lot. Should be enough to get me by, yes?"

If I was astonished, Gordon was stunned. Taken for a minute off his guard his face went white, his mouth a bitten-in line. Then that look was gone, I might have imagined it.

"You made me say it." Eilys spread her hands at me. "If there's one thing I loathe it's talking about money. I rely on you two never to mention this to anybody for my sake. A rich girl has no friends, only hangers-on, and I've no wish to be stung. In the autumn I'll be moving out of your lives, and the fewer people who know my affairs after that the better. See?"

"Of course," I said.

She got up. "Can't we go to the cinema, or something? It's pointless sitting here the whole evening."

5

EILYS and Jarzy suddenly became very friendly. They started going out together every night, dancing, swimming, lazing at an outdoor restaurant. They both seemed extremely gay, and Eilys had bought several new dresses, gorgeous ones. She bought one for me too, and made me accept it. When I took it back to the shop for a slight alteration I learned that it had cost seven hundred marks.

This radiant mood had to mean something. I wasn't surprised therefore when her announcement came. Gordon and I were in the garden puffing smoke at the midges one evening when she sauntered out of the house and joined us.

"Could you bear some sensational news?—Mike and I are that good old-fashioned thing, betrothed."

"Oh, that's wonderful! That's just what I hoped for." I really could not have been more delighted. Everything was turning out perfectly.

"Bless you, Deel," said Eilys. "Mike told me he'd breathed his dreams to you and you'd encouraged him. No comment from Gordon?"

"Are you thinking what you're doing?" said Gordon with pulled-down brows and a definite edge on his voice.

"Listen to him!" Eilys said derisively. "He thinks Mike is getting a bad deal. But I know when I'm loved for myself alone, and that means a lot to a girl like me. I know where I am with Mike."

"Does Mike know where he is with you?"

She shook her hair, and shot him a spiked look.

"That's a bit uncalled for. I'm doing you and Deel a lot of good. Aren't you grateful? Mike and I get married, we're off your hands. Now you've only got to get Onkel fixed up with a bit of cosy Teutonic *amour*—or should I say *liebestraum*?—and you have the place to yourselves in romántic solitude. You'd better come inside and drink our health."

She went into the house and Gordon shoved his fists down into his pockets.

"Darling, aren't you pleased about it?" I said.

"I'm wondering what Eilys is up to."

"*Up to!*"

"Oh, forget it."

I was irritated. "You've never even said yet that you were glad we shan't have to struggle along on only a measly forty thousand pounds."

His eyes widened. "Now don't you start being sarcastic! That would be the last straw."

"Oh, come in, darling." I slid my arm through his. "Let's make things nice for them. I think it's a lovely thing to have happened."

He let his face break into a smile, and we went inside to find Franz opening a bottle of wine.

Jarzy rushed at me and gave me a smacking kiss.

"So I did pull it off! I am engaged to the most beautiful girl in the world, but if I say the most wonderful Gordon will knock me down, because of course he thinks that you are."

"Congratulations, precious!" I said, hugging him. "I couldn't be more happy. I don't know which is the luckiest, you or Eilys."

"Look at her, she is unfaithful to me already," said Jarzy, grinning. "She is kissing Onkel."

"Poor Onkel," said Eilys, "I wish he had a wild romance on his hands, then we'd all feel like the last act of a musical comedy."

"Spare me!" said Franz. "And don't spill the wine . . . Now! To Jarzy and to Eilys, all happiness."

We drained our glasses and slapped them down.

"What do you think?" said Eilys, hugging Jarzy's arm. "This poppet of mine says he wishes I hadn't a *pfennig* in the world so that he could work his fingers to the bone for me."

Jarzy went scarlet.

"Don't make him blush so," said Franz. "Have you no reserve?"

"Not a shred."

"Get on with the celebrations," said Gordon with a rather forced smile. "I have to go home and stew over the affairs of a most unpleasant client. Mind you land sober at the office tomorrow, Jarzy."

"That may be difficult."

Eilys and Jarzy behaved like the traditional engaged pair, very young, very demonstrative. This was unlike Eilys and I sensed she was doing it to impress, but whom she thought she was impressing I couldn't imagine. Perhaps it pleased her, now that her affairs were settling down into a normal pattern, to play it unsophisticated. Certainly the two of them had no eyes for anybody else, and I have never seen a man more bemused with love than Jarzy, enchanted by his incredible luck in getting the girl he thought was unattainable.

"All the time I want to do things for her," he said to me in a burst of confidence. "Yet there is nothing I can do. If only I could do something big, something exciting, to show her—it would be wonderful, Dahlia."

"You don't need to," I said. "She's perfectly happy."

"But there ought to be something I can do."

"Who do you think you are—Sir Lancelot?"

"Of him I never heard."

"Oh, he was one of the knights of old. They had to do feats to impress their women, but that's out of date now."

I was amused by the disenchanted way in which Gordon surveyed the public ardour of the lovers.

"You do glower at them," I said, baiting him. "They're only young and uninhibited. They probably get a kick out of showing their feelings."

"It would be a good thing," he said, "if Eilys were to get the tails of her romances disentangled. I hear that the grocery man, the one who calls himself Roumanian upper-crust—"

"He is Roumanian upper-crust."

"Whatever he is, I've been told that he's under the impression that he's going to marry Eilys."

I was a bit staggered.

"That's ridiculous. People here seem to say anything. She's going to set him up in the hotel business in Switzerland, that's all."

"He evidently thinks the other goes with it. Anyway, he's given up his job as being beneath his prospects, and spends his time sitting over steins at pavement cafés and smoking the cigarettes she keeps him supplied with. You'd better find out what it adds up to."

"I don't see how I can interfere."

But curiosity got the better of me.

I said to Eilys, "How's Max these days? Gordon heard he'd given up his job."

"I told him to," she said calmly. "It seemed pointless to go on driving a van when he's going to be an hotel manager. He isn't very popular with the camp people, because they think he's idling, but I say he's perfectly right to give himself a holiday. It won't be long before we go. Gordon—" she went on scathingly, "seems to hear everything. Any more snippets?"

"Only that Max seems to think he's going to marry you."

She gave a little shout.

"Then he can think again! I don't know where he even got the idea, unless—oh! The ring."

"What ring?"

"We-ee-ll—when we were out at the Ammsee one day, Max produced a ring that had belonged to his mother—an antique, baroque-type thing with a barbaric-looking ruby in it—and said he would like me to have it, and I thought it would hurt his feelings if I didn't take it, so I did. Don't tell me that was some old Roumanian betrothal custom! I must straighten this out. Actually I don't know where on earth I've put the ring. I don't remember seeing it since."

"Have you told Max that you're engaged to Jarzy?"

"I haven't actually told him." She flared up suddenly. "Why the hell should I make a thing of it? And will you tell your interfering fiancé that I am carefully and competently looking after the Todors' interests—and my own—and Mike's—and I don't need any help from him. No help at all."

"Oh dear!" I said. "Why must you and Gordon be continually at war?"

"I do *not* know. And I do *not* care. Does it matter?"

"It'll be a good thing," I said, "when we're all married and settled. Then perhaps there'll be nothing to argue about, and you and Jarzy will come and stay with us."

"Sure we'll come," she said ironically. "Oh, sure! We'll bring the children, and I'm certain that little Eilys and little Gordon will be ghouls, and little Deel and little Mike will be angels."

"When are you going to get married, Eilys?"

"I'll tell you one thing," she said. "Mike and I will be getting off from here in two weeks."

"Two weeks! As soon as that?"

"What are we waiting for? There's nothing to stop me going tomorrow, but Mike won't walk out on Gordon without giving reasonable notice. With all respect to you, Deel, and not being ungrateful for your really generous hospitality, I'm bored to screaming with this place. We'll go to Geneva and stay at an hotel and get married when we feel like it. Everything will be easy when I'm actually over there. I bet you I have a house inside a week, and ready to move in a week after that, and I'll send for the Todors, and everything will work like a charm."

"I would like to be at your wedding!" I said.

She rolled up her eyes.

"Don't be sentimental. I loathe weddings and I haven't the smallest wish to be at yours."

When I told Gordon that evening what Eilys had said he wasn't amused.

"Going to marry when Eilys feels like it, are they? Perhaps by September she won't even feel like it at all."

"But they're going off in two weeks."

"Two weeks!" he exclaimed. "But—that's fantastic."

"Why fantastic? There's nothing to keep Eilys here now."

"But two weeks! Look, it's the limit, Jarzy walking out of my office at a flick of the finger after I've put in so much work on him." He looked upset and almost angry.

"But, Gordon, you know he's going, so what's the difference of a week or so? Darling, you have been a bit prickly lately, I think you're working too hard. As soon as we're married we'll go off for a really long holiday. Choose where you want to go—anywhere. I've been nowhere, so any place will be a thrill to me. Sicily? North Africa? Greece? Think of the Isles of Greece in September!"

"I'm thinking," he said, unsmiling. "And it'll be for a fortnight. That's all I can afford."

"You can't be as pressed with work as that."

"I'm not talking about time, I'm talking about money."

"Money! We've got eighty thousand pounds. Let's blue the lot on our honeymoon and then it'll be off our minds for good."

He looked at me as if he wasn't sure whether I was joking or just being madly irresponsible.

"A man doesn't let his wife pay for the honeymoon."

"Well, *our* money is paying for *our* honeymoon. What else is the wretched stuff for? If I thought it would ever come between us I'd give the lot away."

That did nothing to move the frown from his face. I asked myself if I was really beginning to harden up. When he prepared to leave, and held me close and loverlike, I even found myself wondering, Do his kisses mean "I love you", or "I'm getting what I want"?

"You're not really annoyed about Eilys and Jarzy going off, are you, Gordon? Really, it makes things easier for us."

"Of course. Let them go. We'll be better off without them."

I felt relieved and happy.

"One thing has just occurred to me. After they're gone Franz and I will be here alone. Is that madly compromising?"

He laughed. "I shouldn't think so. I can't see him making passes. If he does, just tell me."

"I only wondered if you'd want us to get married sooner."

"I don't think so, darling." He ruffled my hair "I've got work and commitments over the next few weeks. Let's stick to September, shall we?"

At last, I thought, everything is turning out beautifully.

6

"WHERE'S Mike?" asked Eilys, coming down one morning to her usual late breakfast. "He must have been frightfully late in last night. I didn't even see him, or hear him."

"Neither did I. But he told us he wasn't coming home for supper."

"Didn't you hear him at all?"

"No, I didn't."

"What time did he go off this morning?"

"I haven't seen him this morning. He must have gone before I came down myself. Ask Sigrid."

"Herr Jarzy?" said Sigrid, fetching Eilys her coffee. "But he has not been here at all today. He has not slept in his bed."

"Not slept?—" Eilys stared. "He's been out all night? But why? He never mentioned that. Ring Gordon's office, Deel, and ask Mike from me what he's been playing at."

I rang the office.

"Herr Jarzy," said Gordon's secretary, "has not come in yet."

"Not arrived at the office? Will you please ask him to ring Miss Mallins as soon as he gets there?"

It was an hour before the telephone rang. Eilys seized it.

"Really, Mike, what do you think you're up to?—oh, it's you, Gordon . . . Not in yet! . . . Well, where is he? . . . You tell me!

He hasn't been home all night . . . I don't know, I haven't the slightest idea . . ."

She put down the receiver and said to me, "Gordon says he left the office at the usual time last night. All Mike said was that he had something important to attend to. And he hasn't shown up this morning, and it's nearly twelve o'clock."

"What can we do about it?"

She was obviously annoyed, but spoke casually. "Not a thing. I suppose he'll walk in when he's ready to. He may have gone to München and sent me a telegram which hasn't been delivered. You know what the local office is!"

"But if he'd been going to München he'd have told you. He only said he'd be late home last night, didn't he? And why should he go to München?"

"How should I know?" She flipped the newspaper she was holding on to the floor in one exasperated gesture. "Let's not make a thing of it. There's sure to be a simple explanation. I'm going into town to get my hair done, and I'll find somebody to have lunch with. If Mike rings up, tell him I'm furious."

Franz was more concerned than any of us. He set off for the post office to see if by any chance there was an undelivered telegram, but there was none.

I rang Gordon.

"What, no news?" he said. "I can't understand it. Why didn't he tell Eilys where he was going?"

"That's the mystery of it. It makes me frightened that there's been an accident. What can we do?"

"I'll ring the hospitals. If you don't hear anything from me it's because I can't find out. I'll come round this evening, but I'm sure he'll have turned up by then. How is Eilys taking it?"

"She seems more annoyed than worried. She's gone to town, to the hairdresser's."

"Well, don't you worry either!"

The day was long. At about five Eilys came surging up the drive.

"Where is he? What's the explanation?"

I had to tell her there was no news.

Gordon arrived later. "Nothing from the hospitals. I've rung several of Jarzy's friends, but nobody seems to know anything of what he intended to do last night."

"Ought we to tell the police?" I said.

He considered. "I think we should allow more time for a natural explanation. He's only been gone twenty-four hours, and they'll tell us not to bother before tomorrow. If we haven't heard anything then I'll call them."

"I take a poor view of that," said Eilys. "German police sniggering at me because my young man's run out on me."

"Couldn't face marrying you?" said Gordon.

"That's what they'd think, isn't it?"

"Seems the obvious explanation."

I told them not to joke about it, they laughed at me.

Next morning we rang the police, and after that we had no peace when they took over.

They inspected Jarzy's room. What clothes was he wearing when last seen? Was anything missing from his room?

"Yes!" said Franz suddenly. "He's taken his swimming things. They've gone, his mask and flippers."

"But if he was just going swimming, why didn't he tell us? And why did he tell Gordon he had something important to do?"

They asked where did Jarzy usually swim, and we told him, in the new lake.

Two whole days went by. By now we were all thoroughly on edge. I had a feeling of complete despair, of being at the mercy of fate.

"Just as everything was going so well," I said to Gordon, "this had to happen."

"But nothing has actually happened." He gave me a steadying look. "Even now there could be a simple explanation. What are you getting so worked up about?"

"I'm worked up," I said, "because I've got a feeling that Jarzy had planned to do something dangerous, and that was why he didn't tell us where he was going. We'd have stopped him."

"Dangerous? Why should he do anything dangerous?"

"Oh, don't ask me. I don't even know what I mean."

The police search was now in full action. We could only wait.

It was Eilys's attitude that puzzled me most. She seemed to be more irritated than distressed, more mystified than anxious. She stormed about the house, spent hours flat on her bed playing the wireless and dropping cigarette ends to the floor, finally throwing her swimsuit into the new car she had just bought herself, with, "I'm going to pick up Isold. No point in hanging about here."

It was Franz who in the end brought the bad news. I was alone in the hall when he came in. His face looked just like Jarzy's face had looked the night he came from the telephone to tell us about Ida.

"I'm afraid it's all over, Delia," he said. "They've found him."

"Found him! Is he—all right?"

He lifted both hands and dropped them. His face was blank.

"Not dead—not Jarzy! Oh—"

He nodded. "The divers found him. He'd been trapped in the ruins of our old house in the lake."

"In the ruins?"

"The tremendous weight of water had brought most of the roof down. Jarzy was in the room that used to belong to Eilys. He had in his hand a gold clock."

I stared at him, shattered by recollection.

"That was Eilys's clock. Oh Franz, do you remember, when he brought back Ida's cat, and we had a party, and Eilys said she'd left behind in her room a gold clock that she valued—that her father had given her?"

"I do remember. So he was trying to get it back for her. What a mad thing to do. What made him?"

"He told me once—" I had to catch my voice, the gay memory of Jarzy was too close, "—that he wanted to do something special for her. Something great. I laughed at him. I never dreamed he meant anything like that. It never entered my head, I'd completely forgotten about that gold clock."

"Sit down." He took my hand and put me in a chair, pushing cushions behind me. "I shall get you some brandy."

When he came back with the two glasses, I asked, "Does Gordon know?"

"I think the police rang him up. Where is Eilys?"

"She said she was going out with Isold. She took her car, they may be at the Ammsee. Oh Franz, could you ring Gordon and ask him to try to find her? She won't know anything."

"Yes, I'll do that."

Gordon brought Eilys home about an hour later. She was shocked, and had a look on her face of almost resentful bewilderment as though she couldn't believe anything like this could happen to her.

"I don't understand it, Deel. Why didn't he tell me?" She began to cry, helplessly like a child cries, the clear drops running down her face unchecked.

"Take her upstairs," Gordon told me. "Get her to bed if you can."

Eilys allowed herself to be put to bed and fussed. She looked pathetic, and completely at a loss.

"I suppose it was heroic of him—but so mad. It isn't real at all, it's like something that happens in a film."

"Life sometimes is," I said unhappily, bringing her a ribbon to tie back her hair.

She sat up suddenly. "Deel, you don't think I knew about this, do you? Nobody could think I ever asked him to go, could they?"

"Of course not!"

"Because I swear I didn't, I wouldn't have dreamed of such a thing. We were all talking at that party of Ida's, and it just slipped out—I mean, about my clock. I didn't mean anything. I've never given it a thought from that day to this. You can tell the police that's the truth."

"I'm quite sure they'll never ask."

"You know that if I'd had the slightest idea of what was in his mind I'd have stopped him. I didn't want him to do crazy things for me! He just threw his life away. I wish he'd never found the damned clock, then nobody would have guessed what he went into the house for. Now I shall remember it all my life, it'll haunt me."

I held her hand tightly, a little taken back that her distress seemed more for her own situation than for the cutting off of Jarzy's life.

"No, Eilys. You'll get over it, even if you can't believe that now."

"As long as nobody thinks it was my fault. I bet Gordon does! He hardly said a word in the car."

"I'm going to ring the doctor," I said, "and ask him to give you something to make you sleep."

The doctor kept Eilys in bed for a couple of days. She got up in time for the inquest, when the incident of the gold clock had to be explained. Everything was straightforward and there was little comment.

But our spirits were utterly crushed. This second disaster which had come down on us was the worse of the two, we simply couldn't accept it. Jarzy had been so young, so vital. We missed him every minute of the day.

Nor were we allowed any privacy. One reads in the newspapers about sensational things that happen in other families without thinking what it feels like to be at the receiving end. Now it was our turn—for the second time.

The romantic tragedy of the young man, his girl, and the gold clock was too good a story. The press hadn't been on to anything so satisfying for months, and not only the local papers but the national ones, and those of other countries, ate it up. It went round the world, to a public avid for drama. Reporters were continually on our doorstep, the telephone never stopped ringing. It nearly drove us mad.

Then came the curious ones, the gapers, the sensation-hounds. They stood outside in the road and stared at the house. They came up the drive and tried to look into the rooms. Through open windows you could hear them talking with noisy excitement . . . "It was the old lady's house . . . the one who fell down a cliff in Austria not long ago . . . she left a fortune—you remember? . . . now this young man! . . . must be an unlucky house . . . they say . . . they say . . . they say . . ."

The only way for us to live was behind drawn blinds. We appealed to the police to drive the people away, but more came. Coach tours were organized to disgorge mobs of morbid sightseers along the lake-side—"scene of the fatality". It was unbearable.

We stopped looking at the newspapers for they were plastered with photographs of Jarzy, dug up from heaven knows where. A picture of him with his R.A.F. squadron "Taken in England in 1942". His brief life story was a gift—"refugee from Poland . . . career as a pilot . . . prisoner of war." This brought Ida into it, and her tragedy was raked up in detail.

The funeral was an ordeal. The church was packed and hundreds milled about outside, waiting for us to come out and face the newsreel cameras. Eilys was their main objective, I thought she was going to be pulled to pieces. People tried to touch her, to snatch her scarf or glove as a souvenir.

Gordon came to the rescue, seized her and me, and beat a way for us to the car. Staring, yammering faces were pressed against the windows. Gordon dabbed gloomily at an angry scratch on his cheek.

Eilys shuddered, rubbing a wrenched wrist.

"A man asked me if I'd do a deal for the film rights of the story—can you imagine? Another wanted my exclusive story for a British Sunday newspaper—any price I cared to name. How foul can people get? Then they said could they come and photograph the clock? I told them it was ruined anyway, and I'd thrown it into the garbage can, and by now it's been carted off, thank God, to where I'll never see it again. Let them print that if they want to!"

It all had to die down in the end, but it seemed to take a long time. And there were now two locked rooms in my house, two rooms of memories into which nobody ever went or wanted to go any more.

Eilys's period of shock had been intense, but the reaction came quickly. Soon she was dashing about again.

Her plans for leaving were, of course, all postponed.

"Can you put up with me a bit longer, Deel? Because I think it would be a good thing if I gave up the idea of going to an hotel and got my chalet direct so that I could go straight to it. As soon as that's done I'll leave, but I've scarcely had time to think."

"Eilys, you know I'm glad to have you as long as you want to stay."

"That's so sweet of you."

She went off to town and came back with an expensive American handbag, for me. It was typical of her, no use protesting.

Madame Todor, when next I went to see her, was full of the tragic story.

"Zat poor, poor young man. He love Ei-liss so much he die for her. Zat is love! It is like in ze opera, ze ballet, so gallant, so beautiful. But any man would die for Ei-liss, I am sure our Max would. He adore her. He give her ze Todor family betrothal ring and she take it. She have it still."

"Yes . . . well . . . I—" I was acutely embarrassed.

"When we all go to Swizzerland quite soon now, who knows? Ei-liss, so young and so lovely, she cannot be alone for long wizzout any lover. We are pack, we are ready now to go, and Pappa is so glad he is still alive zat he cry for joy when ze time is nearly come."

"I'm more glad than ever now," I said, "that she is taking you. It's an interest for her when otherwise everything would have felt so empty, and she'll be happy in your company."

"You will not like her to go, you are such friends."

"In a way I shall miss her terribly, but I'm going to get married myself quite soon."

I was a bit concerned about the Max situation, but that was one for Eilys to work out. Perhaps he would be a success, perhaps she might marry him in the end, Without being unkind, I couldn't help feeling that her affections were elastic enough, and I knew that in the last day or two she had been out with Max.

"But I've lost that stupid ring," she told me with a grimace. "I can't find it anywhere. I'll have to stall if he asks me about it. I wish people wouldn't thrust their family heirlooms on me."

"You've got to find it," I said. "Advertise for it—anything. It probably means an awful lot to the Todors."

"But I can't even remember when I last saw it. I probably dropped it at the Ammsee. I'll have to tell Max I put it in a safe deposit."

There seemed to be little comfort or pleasure in my house these days. The atmosphere was oppressive, the natural gaiety vanished. It was hard to settle down to either work or recreation with this awareness that only Franz, Eilys, and I were left out of six. And the ghost of Jarzy's laughing presence was there all the time.

I wasn't seeing very much of Gordon either, not enough to keep my spirits up, and when he did come he seemed to have lost his vitality. He was strained, abstracted. But weren't we all?

"I told you I was having a busy time just now," he said. "Do you want me to take you out to dinner?"

"If it's somewhere quiet."

"Why quiet?"

"I don't seem ready for gaiety. After all we've—"

He cut me off, a little petulant. "I know, I know. 'After all we've gone through.' Trust you for a cliché. You are a bit morbid, darling."

"I only wish I could throw it off. I wish I could put it right behind me like Eilys can, but I keep wondering—"

He interrupted, "I'm sure you do. Next cliché coming up—'I keep wondering who's going to be the next'!"

"I wasn't going to say anything of the kind!" I was furious.

Suddenly he smiled. When he turned on the charm like that nobody on earth could resist him.

"I'm sorry. Delia, Delia, you do let me take rises out of you. My sweet, I've told you before, as you go through life you've got to leave everything behind you, especially the bad bits. Don't ever give them a thought. Don't let them get claws into you. Of course we'll go somewhere quiet if you'd rather. But remember about going on living."

"The house feels so miserable."

"To hell with the house. Get rid of it, if you like."

"Ida's house? Oh no."

"Then shut up about it. Make it come alive—you must."

"I'll try. And, Gordon, we'll go wherever you like tonight. You choose."

"Well, put some glamour on and we'll go to the Magda. It'll do you good."

I felt happier, and smiled up into his eyes.

"Eilys goes there, so I don't see why I shouldn't."

7

Two weeks went by. Gordon was away for a few days on business, Eilys always seemed to be out, and I felt lonely.

Was it morbidity that took me to the lake shore, or just the hope that there was still some peace and beauty left there?

I drove along in the car one evening, parked it, and walked beside the rippling water, silky, innocent, and so deep. So it must have looked when Jarzy reached it on that last evening, alone, keyed up with excitement because of what he was planning to do for Eilys.

I wouldn't think like that! I wouldn't let myself. Gordon was quite right. This had been a favourite haunt of mine and I wasn't going to have it ruined for me, or get myself into a state of mind when I could never come here again. Jarzy had deliberately and cheerfully put his life into hazard, and every man is free to bring about his own disaster.

The sky was clouded over now, but pale sunlight seeping under the edges of the pall began to lay frail patterns of gold across the water. There wasn't a sound except the soft sucking of wavelets at the brink.

Suddenly I saw a bent figure sitting beside a tree. It was old Siebler. I hadn't seen him for weeks.

He looked up and gave me a nod of recognition.

"Good evening, Herr Siebler."

"*Gnädige Fräulein.*"

"You're like me," I said. "You like coming to this peaceful place alone."

"I come all the time. Every day. I stay all day—all night sometimes. It's the only place I care for. It's where I belong."

"Your house was here, wasn't it?"

He nodded shakily. "You understand, *Fräulein*. It is good to hear that. Nobody else understands."

I sat down beside him.

"Don't you think my German has improved a great deal?"

"You speak very well." He jerked a thumb over his shoulder. "I have a place there, among the larches. Nobody knows, nobody can see me. I have blankets and some food, and some wood to carve. That's where I stay nearly all the time."

"So long as the weather is warm?"

"Well, yes. I'm eighty-two and the winter's coming. I shall still come here and wear my old guide's coat, sheepskin you know. What matters, young *Fräulein*, is not being cold but being in a place you loved a long time ago, where your real life was."

"I can understand that too. I think I could stay here for a long time, just looking at the lovely view. Suppose I build myself a little hut beside your hide-out?"

"You have a good house of your own."

"It has sad memories."

"Ah, yes—yes." He narrowed his eyes, peering across the pearly water where the last of the gold had already disappeared. His eyes were the colour of the cloud above, rather large and protruding in the square mahogany-brown face with its shaggy brows and drooping white moustaches.

He picked up an empty pipe and pushed it into the corner of his mouth as though he felt comfortable with it there.

"That poor young fellow," he said. "That was a bad business. This was where he came to swim. I often saw him, but he never knew I was here, just a few yards away, among the bushes. He used to dive in off that very stone—that one. This business of the clock for his girl, that was a tale, wasn't it?"

"You read about it in the paper?"

"Oh yes. A mad thing to do with the house fathoms deep. These daring young fellows, they always do things once too often, like when I was young, jumping from rock to rock in the Glaspenberg. Very dangerous. But he didn't really want to do it, that young fellow."

"How do you mean, he didn't want—"

"The young Polish fellow, the one I'm talking about. He didn't want to go in. He wouldn't have gone if it hadn't been for the other one egging him on."

My heart thudded a warning. I couldn't quite take in what the old man was saying.

"Are you talking about the evening he was drowned? Do you mean he—that there was someone else with him—that he wasn't here alone?"

He turned his heavy gaze on me.

"That's what I'm telling you. I could hear every word they said. The young man said he didn't think he'd risk it, but the other one said he'd never forgive himself if he was a coward and didn't try. 'Go on,' he said, 'it's not like you to be a funk.' That made the young chap hot. 'I'm no funk,' he said. 'Well, have a damn good try,' said the other, very urgent, telling him how much this girl would love him if he got this clock for her. That was the first time I'd heard mention of any clock. I listened and watched them. I didn't like it. I had a feeling that this other chap was too keen, that he didn't mean well. You can feel these things, you know. But it wasn't my business. 'Come on, have a nip before you go,' said this chap. 'It'll keep you warm and give you guts.' And he brought out a flask, and the young chap drank. Afterwards I wondered if there'd been something in that drink—you know—one of these fancy drugs. You can feel evil like a cold draught of wind, can't you? It felt wrong to me."

I was listening to him avidly, hardly able to grasp all he was saying. It was like being suddenly brought into the dark of a cinema half-way through the film, and trying to guess who the characters are and what the action is about.

"Wait a minute," I said. "You're saying there was another man with Jarzy who made him go into the water. Is that right?"

"That's what I've told you."

"And Jarzy didn't want to go! This other man made him go against his better judgment? And you got an impression that he didn't mean well to Jarzy?"

"I've told you the truth. I saw it all and I didn't like it. There was something bad going on. Suppose there had been something in that drink, it would make sure he never came up again."

His face blurred before my eyes, the trees began to jig about.

"Who was the other man? What was he like?"

"Now how should I know who he was? He was an older chap, tall, dark. Would you happen to know him?"

"No, oh no."

"Well, he knew that young fellow would never come back alive. He knew all right. I've seen such bad things in my time, I can't be deceived."

"Why didn't you show yourself?"

He gave a contemptuous bark.

"Me interfere? I'm too old. I don't want to get mixed up in anything. Other people have got to look after themselves, like I did in my time. I only told you about it because the Polish young man came from your house and I thought you might be interested. Perhaps you are, perhaps you're not. If you don't know the other fellow it's neither here nor there, is it?"

"But there was an inquest. Didn't you feel you should—"

"No, I didn't," he snapped out irritably. "I couldn't stand having anybody badgering me with questions. It hurts my head. My head gets funny sometimes, dizzy, you know. No, I'd never let myself in for anything like that. What would be the point of it? They can't bring the young fellow back, so talking gets nowhere in the end. And don't you let on that I told you, *Fräulein*, it wouldn't do any good. They'd say, 'That old fool Siebler, he sees things that aren't there.' I don't argue at my age, but I've got as good a mind as anybody."

"Please tell me some more," I begged. "This older man, how was he dressed?"

"Dressed? How should he be dressed? He had clothes on, I didn't look at his clothes."

"Did they speak German?—but of course they did or you wouldn't have understood them. But did this other man speak German like a German or like a foreigner?"

"Poles are foreigners, aren't they?"

"Oh, they were both Poles?"

"How should I know if they were both Poles?"

His face flushed darkly and he put his hand to his head. "There you are, my head's going funny. I won't answer any more questions."

"I'm sorry," I said. "I'm going now."

I drove some kind of co-operation into my shaky legs and got up. His thick white eyebrows lowered snakily at me.

"Don't you go saying anything to those nosy newspapers."

"Of course not."

I ran all the way to the car. You can drive a car automatically and remember nothing of the journey when at last you arrive at your own garage. I walked round the side of the house and caught giddily at the rail of the balcony.

Eilys was just inside the open hall door.

"What's the matter?" she said. "Anything wrong?"

"I drove a bit fast."

"Silly of you."

I went up to my room, shut the door, and sank down on the bed.

Why had I ever gone to the lakeside? What devil had driven me there on this peaceful evening? Yet would I have chosen not to go, to be ignorant of this new terrifying thing?

The man, the older man who had taunted Jarzy into making his last dive, who had offered the flask . . . old Siebler couldn't have made up a thing like that.

Why, if all was innocent, hadn't this man come forward to tell that he was with Jarzy? All those days when Jarzy was missing, this man had known. This man hadn't wanted to be mixed up in it. This man had wanted Jarzy to die.

But why, why, why?

Why would anybody in the world want Jarzy out of the way? Everybody liked him—everybody.

The supper gong rang. It occurred to me that I should have to pull myself together and go downstairs. If I didn't they would be coming up to see what was the matter. I mustn't draw attention to myself.

I made up my face and went down in a kind of daze, talked trivialities during the meal. Then I sat in the hall with a book in my hand and never read a word. Eilys was writing letters, Franz was reading. At ten the tray of drinks came in, and after that I was able to go to bed without it looking odd.

Then began the long, long night. I made up wild fantasies. No stories, however sensational, could be impossible in these days. A foreign agent? An enemy from the war years?

Nothing really made sense. And there were still two days to be got through before Gordon came back.

On edge as I was, every unaccustomed sound in the house made me want to scream. In the middle of the next afternoon I heard shrieks of laughter and the clinking of glasses from the drawing-room. I went in.

Eilys was there with two people, all yakking their heads off.

"Hullo, Deel," she cried gaily. "Look who I found in town! Some old friends from Antibes—Lucien and Maggy."

The man was very smooth, with patent leather hair, arty beard and moustache, and Côte d'Azur clothes. The girl was a platinum blonde, all gestures, jewellery, and miles of leg.

"What are you drinking, Deel?" the man asked affably, picking up the name. "Any friend of Eilys is a friend of mine."

"Shut up, you clot," said Eilys. "Deel's my hostess. It's her whisky."

Maggy shrieked. "That was a clanger you dropped, boy!"

"I don't want anything," I said ungraciously. "I only wondered what all the row was about. Make yourselves at home."

I went out quickly. The noise went on for what seemed hours, they were playing poker. At last they left.

Strung up, I snapped at Eilys, "I'm not very taken with your friends."

She took it without resentment.

"They weren't very taken with you." She began to laugh. "Come off it, Deel. You're not nice company these days. I know it's all very dreadful about Jarzy, but it happened three weeks ago and I can't sob for ever. You might give me a break. They even let Mary Queen of Scots take her corsets off when her husband died."

"I'm sorry I snapped," I said, "but those people were so rowdy."

"At least they were gay. They did me good." Eilys looked out of the window at drizzling rain. "When did you say Gordon was coming back?"

"Day after tomorrow."

"Perhaps he'll brighten you up."

My hands were pulling at each other, and I held them down.

"Eilys—"

"What?"

"You know a lot of the crowd that Jarzy knew. Can you think of any tall, dark man, older than he was?"

She looked puzzled.

"Only Gordon."

It was the name that was trembling to be said and must not be spoken.

"Do think. Somebody else."

"Jarzy knew a lot of people in town. I can't think of anybody in particular like you describe. Tall, dark, older? Why do you want to know?"

"It doesn't really matter."

She gave me a keen look.

"Are you all right? The way you've been behaving the last day or two—it's no business of mine, but perhaps you're feeling it's time I left. You're right, it is! It'll give you a chance to settle down, and I ought to have gone before. I'll pack and get myself off to Geneva."

A twinge of dismay shot through me. I realized coldly that I couldn't possibly let Eilys go. Not yet! If Eilys went, I'd be up against stark reality in the matter of my marriage to Gordon, and terribly alone. Alone with this new dread, this unspeakable situation.

"Oh, don't go yet," I cried too sharply. "I want you here."

"Why?"

I went a little hysterical. "Eilys, don't go. Please, please don't go!"

She widened her eyes and let out a whistle.

"If you feel like that about it, I needn't go. But you're not yourself, Deel, and that's a fact. Good lord, look at your hands shaking! If I do stay, you'll have to snap out of that fit of nerves or you'll give me the creeps."

I pulled myself together.

"I'm very sorry. It won't happen again. I just don't want you to go."

She spread her hands, made a face.

"Then let's make Onkel take us to the cinema. I want to see that silly film at the Blue."

8

GORDON walked in unexpectedly in the late afternoon of the next day while I was ironing a wide-skirted dress for Eilys and she stood watching me.

I gave him one brief glance. He looked dispirited, indifferent, weary-eyed.

"I didn't bother to ring up," he said. "I didn't know just when I'd arrive."

I put the dress on its hanger and Eilys began to fold the ironing board away.

"What can I get you, Gordon? Tea? Or a cold drink?"

"Anything that's handy, I don't mind. Is everybody all right?"

"Is this all?" said Eilys tauntingly. "No ardent greeting? Perhaps you're inhibited about passionate embraces in public. Don't mind me."

A line of anger folded itself between his brows.

"Stop it, Eilys," I said, "and fetch Gordon a drink while I put these things away."

"Drink looks to me the last thing he needs. He looks to me like a very nasty hangover."

"You heard what Delia said," said Gordon.

"Oh, get it yourself." She walked out of the room.

"I don't know what's the matter with her," I said, "but don't take any notice."

"I'm not."

"Come in the drawing-room."

I got him a drink, but I felt terribly worked up, the bottle clattered against the glass and the whisky spilled over. I felt his surprised eyes on me.

He took a sip.

"That's good. I've had a trying sort of trip. Everything went wrong, you know how it is sometimes."

"I'm sorry about that."

"How have things been here?"

"All right. I mean—why?"

He put down his glass.

"Am I wrong in sensing that you don't seem actually delighted to see me? What's underneath all this? What have you been up to? Has the cook left? I hope it's nothing worse."

I took a hard breath.

"There is something, Gordon. I've got to talk to you."

For the first time his impeccable self-control seemed to crack. He sat down and picked up his glass again.

"For heaven's sake! What are you coming out with this time? Surely not another dollop of drama. Really, Delia, you sometimes remind me of the woman who comes on in a Greek play and tells you all the filthy things that are going on in the wings."

I winced.

"Shall I fill your glass up?"

"No, you won't. Come along, out with it! Let's have it. I can take it."

"I've got something rather dreadful to tell you."

"You usually have."

I struggled to find some opening words, keeping my eyes away from his splendid sardonic face.

"Gordon, while you were away I made a frightening discovery. Jarzy wasn't alone that last evening he went into the lake."

I toughened up enough to look at him. Apart from a hardening of the jaw he seemed unmoved.

"Frightening? That's an odd word. What frightens you?"

"The implication," I said. "If there was a man with Jarzy, why hasn't he come forward? When Jarzy didn't come out of the water, why didn't his—friend do anything about it?"

"You seem to like questions," he said. "Here's one. What has all this got to do with you?"

"But you must see that it's terribly important."

"I don't see it at all. I don't even know how you thought up this idea. If there was anybody else with Jarzy that evening, he may not have wanted to be mixed up in what he couldn't do anything to help. What makes you think there was anybody there?"

"They were seen. And overheard talking."

I should have looked directly at him then. I knew I should. That was the crucial moment which might have told me everything I wanted to know. But I couldn't.

I waited, looking down at my hands, and my heart thumped.

"Who is supposed to have seen and heard this?"

"Old Siebler."

"Who on earth is he?"

I told him.

"He sounds senile. He must have been dreaming."

"No," I said. "He's a very sound, sensible old man."

"And has he been spreading this story round?"

"No. He didn't want to be mixed up in it either. He only told me."

"Well, who was this other man you're bothering about?"

"Siebler didn't know him. He said he was a tall, dark man, older than Jarzy."

Gordon went over and refilled his glass with cool deliberation.

"And I suppose my sweet, loyal fiancée thinks that the mystery man was me. She would! What sort of a mind have you got?"

I swallowed down the hot lump in my throat.

"Jarzy must have had a number of friends," I said, "who'd answer to that description."

"Thank you very much for realizing that! I'm grateful that you give me a break for once. Yes, Jarzy had a lot of friends and acquaintances. I don't see what all this is leading up to, apart from the fact that I'm supposed to have known all about Jarzy's accident and for some reason of my own kept it dark. That's what you thought, isn't it? I can see you did."

"Gordon," I said desperately. "I know I'm behaving unnaturally, but please try to understand. Just tell me it wasn't you—straight out, please. I only want to hear that. Please!"

"Of course it wasn't me." Rasping anger broke through. "You ought to have the sense and decency to know that."

"You're furious, aren't you?"

"Of course I am. Who wouldn't be?"

I ought to have believed him. I should have been satisfied, and yet—oh how, Gordon, blinded by my passion for you, could I distinguish the truth from a lie? When you yourself had said to me not long before, "When I lie it's one hundred per cent convincing like a lie ought to be."

"Well?" he said. "Is that all? It makes me wonder where we go from here."

"It isn't all," I said. "There was a lot more."

"More what?"

"I have to tell you," I broke out. "It couldn't be harder."

He stretched out in a chair and ran a hand through his hair

"I'm damned tired. I've just had a steamy three days of fruitless work and a delayed train journey. I'm not in the mood for drama. Get whatever it is off your mind if you've got to, but don't expect me to play the part as you wrote it. What's coming now?"

I gritted my teeth. "Old Siebler said that the man with Jarzy was—antagonistic to him. He thought he was Jarzy's enemy. There was a feeling of evil. Jarzy didn't want to dive. This man urged him to, practically drove him to it. He must have had a lot of influence over Jarzy. He knew he was sending Jarzy to almost certain death and—he wanted to. Then he disappeared."

I stopped because I felt too sick to go on.

"Wanted to send him to certain death!" Gordon's voice was incredulous, mocking, reducing everything I'd said to absurdity. "My poor girl! Do you ever think what you're saying? Doesn't this strike even you as corny?"

I jerked my head. "I'm telling it badly. But it isn't corny, Gordon. Something awful did happen that night. The man gave Jarzy a drink out of a flask, and Siebler got a feeling that it might have been drugged. If it was—well, you see—" My voice trailed away.

Gordon's was taut with sarcasm. "Oh, don't stop. Go on, do. This seems to have made a great impression on you."

"It has—it did."

"I can see it did! If you'd believe a yarn like that you'd believe anything. Have you told anybody else this wonderful rigmarole?"

"No! As if I would! But isn't it right that I should tell you?"

"Quite right, if you can stop being serious and laugh it off as the damned lunacy it is. Otherwise keep it to yourself."

"Keep it to yourself—a thing like murder?"

He took a loud, exasperated breath.

"So it's murder now. Delia, if you can possibly bring yourself to be logical, have you asked yourself the elementary question why anybody should want to murder Jarzy? The lack of any possible motive makes the story fantastic. It falls to pieces."

"But somebody did it," I said, stubbornly wretched.

"You can't believe that!"

"But I do. I can't help it. And you don't know what I've gone through since I knew."

He stood up. His hand shot out and fingers of steel clamped my wrist.

"Stop this hedging. I'm beginning to see what's on your mind. If you've screwed yourself up to imagining that I was responsible for Jarzy's death, tell me now. Say it to my face! Put it in as stark words as you can—'I think you murdered Jarzy.' Say it—say it?"

I made one explosive protest. He dropped my hand.

"You don't know what you believe. You've no convictions. It's the Ida business all over again, isn't it?"

"Gordon," I implored, "for God's sake make me see where I'm wrong. Get me out of this ghastly mess of mind that I'm in or I'll go mad."

I, who was too much given to making pictures in my mind, saw as though I were there the secretive lake, steely grey below the thunder-green plantation where the old countryman sat hidden. I saw everything happen as he said it had happened.

Gordon walked over to the window and stood with his hands in his pockets, looking at me coldly and critically.

"You have a talent, Delia, for looking for the unreasonable where the reasonable would fit. Any counsel in court would reduce you to fine ash and blow you out of the window. To examine your story. In the first place, we're aware that Jarzy had plenty of friends and acquaintances in town, tall, dark, and older than he is. We're also sure that not one of these would have the slightest motive for doing him any harm. Who could have? As for this hallucination of evil intent—well! Consider the word hallucination. It's only too clear that old Siebler was seeing things. You've heard of senile delusions? The whole story is a dream or a fabrication, and you're the only person who can't see that. Verdict? Laughed out of court."

"That's what I can't accept," I persisted. "And I don't care what anybody says. If Siebler says he saw that man, then there was a man. Siebler is not senile, he's as sane and balanced as—"

"As you are? Not an awfully good comparison, my dear."

"Leave me out of it," I said curtly. "Listen, Gordon, will you do something? Will you come with me to the spot where it happened, where the old man spends all his time among the larches by the lake? See him yourself—talk to him, ask him the right kind of questions—you should know how. I think that's a fair thing to suggest."

He made a scornful sound. "Not on your life!"

"And why not?"

"Why not? Because I'm not going to help make a fantasy into a fixation. You don't drag me into this sort of thing—by doing so you'd only make it more real to yourself. What with the old fool thinking he was important enough to be consulted, and embroidering his original tale, and you drinking it in, and me standing there for corroboration, you'd be in a worse state than you are now. No, I think I've been extremely patient with you, and if you can't accept what I've said, then I've a low opinion of your intelligence. This whole story is a menace. Nothing can bring Jarzy back. So why pursue a pointless theme that's going to make everybody miserable?"

"And you a lawyer!"

"What's that got to do with it?"

"Isn't it your instinct to follow up suspicion?"

"Not in a case like this, it isn't."

"You mean you're content just to say there wasn't any motive, and leave it like that?"

"Look," he said, "you can put all the responsibility on me. I ought to know about these things, and I say, leave it alone. A few years ago an old man died in Dorfen. Everything was perfectly simple and straightforward. Weeks afterwards a fool of a servant started some story about arsenic. Then all hell broke loose. Eventually there was an exhumation—no arsenic. The whole scandal was a fabrication, all the ballyhoo for nothing. But meanwhile a daughter had nearly lost her reason, a nurse had been smirched and discredited out of her profession, and a husband and wife had split up. See what I mean?"

"I see what you mean. But I'm not making a ballyhoo. I'm simply saying that I think you might go with me to see Siebler. Nobody else need know."

"Considering the state of mind you're in, Delia, I'd be a fool to encourage you."

I was wounded. "I think I'm in a perfectly calm state of mind, and I think you definitely ought to go."

"And I think I'm not going to chase a pack of fairy tales. I know these Bavarian natives better than you do. They're a bit visionary, ready to believe anything. They've got fairies on the brain, just like they got Nazi-ism on the brain. It started round here as you once informed me. I'm not going to encourage this old dotard into thinking his morbid fancies mean anything. Drop it, Delia."

I sat back and shut my eyes. Suddenly I felt his hand on my shoulder, the touch tingled through me. His mood had changed completely, he was smiling down at me.

"Let's put paid once and for all to this kind of rubbish," he said. "Otherwise you're going to make a shocking wife."

At that moment I was half-minded to tell him that it would be better if I never was his wife. I tightened my eyes, trying to resist his appeal, and summoned up the deepness of the chilly lake, the voices on the shore, Jarzy with that shiver of premonition as he took his dive, and somebody—somebody!—on the brink. But not—oh, please not!—the one I dreaded to think of.

My mind screamed danger.

There was a sound of footsteps in the hall, the door opened and Franz came in, took one look at Gordon and me and retreated fast.

The break was a blessing, it brought me back to normality.

"Well, that's settled," Gordon said.

I wasn't sure whether it was. I got up.

"Will you stay for supper?"

"Provided the atmosphere is pleasant, I'd like to."

The atmosphere was in fact not all it might have been. Franz, usually to be relied on for good conversation, had for once hardly anything to say. Eilys on the other hand talked outrageously. There had to be a devil in her that night, just when my head was throbbing.

She came in looking dazzling in a new white silk dress, fine pleats from neck to hem, with a gold necklet clasping her throat and huge gold chandelier ear-rings.

"You two have had a long session." She looked pointedly at Gordon and me. "But you don't seem particularly hep. What's the matter? Aching to get married and wishing I'd go? Well, don't consider me, I can leave at any minute. I'm dying to."

Gordon slid a tight-lipped look at me.

"Are we considering Eilys?"

"Eilys knows I don't want her to leave," I said sharply.

"There you are, Eilys. Don't be a fool."

"Thank you, Gordon. I know when I'm a dead fly in the cup of bliss." She planted her elbows on the table. "Did I ever tell you about Klaus Kleminger?"

"Who on earth is he?"

She rattled off into a highly coloured story about a film director of that name who had taken her for a holiday at Lavandou when she was seventeen.

"He was Jewish, of course, but the aquiline, romantic type, all brow and eyes, not the stodgy Teutonic type—sorry, Onkel, I forgot you were there—and what that man offered me was nobody's business. But I was young and not up to handling things. I didn't know my own value."

"Do you know it now?" said Gordon, stabbing at a roll.

"To the last hormone, darling." She passed her empty plate to Sigrid who was collecting them. "I give by the ounce, by the inch, but never altogether."

"Sigrid understands English," said Gordon, as the maid left the room. "Your tasteful remarks will now go to be mulled over in the kitchen."

"Good. It'll probably brighten them up. I bet nothing I could say would teach that girl Sigrid anything. She's Austrian, did you know? Had a whale of a time in the war, she told me. I wonder what Roumanians are like as lovers? Max Todor gave me a ring, but I lost it. I've always been careless about other people's property."

"General instability of character," said Gordon. "You should watch that."

"I'll know who to go to for lessons."

Under the circumstances I wasn't surprised when Gordon declined coffee, and saying that he had a meeting to attend, went off after kissing my hand formally and giving a curt nod to the others.

Franz also went out.

"What got into you?" I said to Eilys. "You were revolting."

She giggled. "I made all that stuff up as I went on—about Lavandou. I only wanted to see Gordon rise."

"Why do you have to gun for him all the time? It isn't funny."

"It's funny to me. He looked so smug."

"You were beastly rude to Franz, about stodgy Teutons."

She put on a look of contrition. "Poor old Onkel, I'm sorry about that. It just slipped out. And I'm sorry if I annoyed you."

"That's putting it mildly."

She grabbed my hand impulsively. "Deel, you're the one person I respect and really care for. You've got to understand that. In all this time you've been the one I've been truly grateful to. Remember that when I'm gone."

I gave her shoulder a friendly brush.

"I'm awfully fond of you, you know that, Eilys. But why do you have to be such an exhibitionist? Your bad-girl pose wouldn't convince a baby. You're as generous as they come, except to yourself. And I don't want to think of when you're gone."

I looked round the flowerless room into which the grey twilight was creeping, and realized that we hadn't had a flower in the house since Jarzy went. He was the one who brought flowers home. Those empty vases seemed typical of what our lives had become.

Eilys was brightening her lips before the glass.

"Well, I'll be running along, darling. Don't wait up for me, I may be late."

"Oh, you're going out?"

"Just a little date. And a shoulder to cry on."

I wished I could be more like her. Volatile, buoyant. Capable of making the casual date, or running gaily out of sad surroundings into lively ones that kept one from thinking. Eilys proved that it was possible to get through life very well like that, living on the surface, leaving the deeps alone.

I watched her running to the garage to get her car, a white coat slung over her shoulders. And I was left alone with nowhere to go.

9

I WALKED up and down the beautiful room which Ida had planned and created for us all to be happy in, only a few months ago—you could reduce it to weeks! I had never felt so utterly alone as I did now. Before, there had always been somebody in to talk to. Now the sense of everything closing in upon me was appalling.

Make it a bad dream! I thought. Send back the singing and the fun. Ida with her exasperating charm can't really be dead. Nor Jarzy who was so boundingly alive. Any minute they'll be walking in, any minute now. Make me like I used to be, wildly in love with Gordon, and just engaged, and madly happy.

And even if Fate had to strike with those two awful accidents, what's wrong with me that I can't even pick up the bits? Eilys never has a qualm. Franz is like he always was. I'm the dead loss. No wonder everything is breaking up.

The room echoed. I couldn't endure the hollow quiet. I thought, I've got to come to a decision, give Gordon up if that's the only way, close the house, get Eilys to let me join her in Switzerland with the Todors. She would do that, it would help me to get straight with myself to stay with her for a while. Life with Eilys would at least be free of doubt and gloom, and it would be a good sort of thrill to see the Todors made happy. I could help, take some of the duller responsibilities from Eilys.

Alone in that sad room I was desperately trying to get away from that last conversation with Gordon, the one I daren't think about. The implication of it stuck in my throat.

Gordon flatly refused to see Siebler. He was vehement about it. He had excuses, of course. He wasn't going to build up the old man's ego by making his foolish fancies seem important. He wanted to save me from my worst self. He didn't intend to stir up mud which had settled. In short, he would take good care that he didn't meet Siebler. Why?

Why? Why?

Because Siebler would say at once, "You are the man!"

The words tore themselves alive out of my throat and the shock of hearing them was too much for me. I sat down on the sofa and held my hands across my mouth in choking despair.

It must be true. Only Gordon could have persuaded Jarzy to do that dive when he was reluctant to. Only Gordon whom he admired and trusted could have had enough influence over him to make him do it.

But what for? Gordon thought as much of Jarzy as Jarzy did of him. There wasn't any motive. It didn't make sense. None of this horror made sense.

I jumped up and rubbed my hands over my stiff cheeks. I couldn't go on thinking like this, it was too much like the brink of madness. I would go to the kitchen and talk to the maids, listen to the local gossip, just not to be alone.

I heard footsteps in the hall and the door opened.

It was Franz. I was so glad to see him that I could have cried.

"All alone?" he said.

"Oh Franz, I was so lonely. I am glad you've come home early."

"I had a feeling," he said, "that you might be alone and wanting company, so I didn't stay, I came back on the next bus."

"That was thoughtful of you. The silence was getting on my nerves."

"Put a record on," he suggested.

"I don't think that helps when you're lonely and want to escape from yourself." I mustered up a shaky smile. "Some smug woman coloratura-ing away—I always want to throw a shoe at her."

He dropped his strapful of books on the window seat and sat down there. A soft rain pattered suddenly against the glass.

"What have you got to escape from, Delia?"

"My own crazy, crazy thoughts."

His eyes searched my face deeply.

"There's still something wrong between you and Gordon, isn't there? At supper you hardly spoke to each other."

"Eilys did all the talking."

His look went deeper. It seemed to have some power of understanding that reached me like a handclasp.

"Forgive me, but—Delia, you're never going back to that business of Ida's death? That's all finished. Nobody believes the slander any more. You couldn't still be thinking about it."

"Franz," I said explosively, "tell me this truly—what do you think of Gordon? Do you feel anything about him?"

He considered for a minute.

"I think Gordon is one who will always get what he wants."

"Whether it is good or bad?"

"For whom good, or for whom bad? Good and bad are relative. Gordon is what you would call an opportunist. That doesn't of necessity mean a bad thing. Many strong individuals are like that. Never content, they are always striving for something and they will take every chance. Gordon wants much better things than he is getting from life now. He's ambitious—a small-town lawyer in a rut—he wants the big life. But what is wrong with that? You love him, but you do not like his character, is that it?"

I couldn't think of anything to say.

"Sometimes I think you don't even love him." Franz spoke with bold candour.

"Of course I love him! If I didn't love him, why should I be driven mad by the thought—" I bit it back.

"Oh Delia." Franz shook his head. "Why must you admit a terrible idea into your mind and nourish it there?"

"In the first place," I said, "I never did admit it. Gladys thrust it in. And I don't nourish it, it took root and grew."

"If you suspect things about Gordon," he said, "why have you to keep them stuffed in yourself? It does no good. Perhaps I could even tell you how wrong you are."

"I wish I thought that."

He pulled out a big sigh. "It is so difficult. You'll have to decide quickly what you're going to do. I don't think Eilys will be here much longer, and then I shall have to leave also. I can go at any time,

ake over Gordon's apartment, it is agreed."
at the new turn in the conversation.
Eilys will be off to Switzerland very soon.
here and taking the Todor family, you know
great interest for her. I've just been thinking
ased if I went with her. I could help her a lot
e way, Franz, she didn't mean a word she said
e told me so. And she certainly didn't mean to
She was just being idiotic, and she was sorry
enuine really, I don't know why she has these
ed, "I do feel it would be better if I got away
ow—for a time."
he looked quite shocked.
s! You—and Eilys? Oh, that wouldn't do at all.
ldn't think of it. You wouldn't be happy. Eilys
isn't what you think her."

"Is anybody what I think them?" I said with a spurt of anger. "That's what's worrying me. I'm so tired of all this, so sick of it all. Life isn't worth living if you're always warding off shadows. And don't tell me, Franz, that if there are shadows there isn't something behind them!"

He looked grave. "Couldn't you let yourself have more faith in Gordon? That would settle everything."

"I don't want to be tranquillized," I said. "I want the truth. How can I get beyond the limit of my own mind's capacity and see the truth?"

"People see what they want to see," he said with a worried face. "It hardly ever is the truth."

"Oh, I know that Gordon is a friend of yours. He was your friend before I ever knew him."

He gave a twisted smile. "The word 'friend' does not of necessity mean anything at all. It was my brother's friend who betrayed his hiding place in Holland to the Nazis—for five hundred marks. It did him no good. They gave him the money and arrested him the same night, and he and my brother went to Buchenwald in the same truck. No, my head is clear of illusion and I myself believe in Gordon. But if you cannot, you must send him away. But please do not think of going with Eilys. She is not the friend for you."

I must have looked as I felt, bewildered and wretched, because his eyes gave a merry twinkle and holding out his hand he said, "Come! Lift up your head. Up above the clouds, like the mountains do. We will go and visit some friends of mine—yes? That will cheer you up. When you are low you must never sit alone, because bad thoughts grow in solitariness."

10

FRANZ was leaving next morning for a few day's walking holiday in Austria. He and I had breakfast together early, Eilys didn't come down. I hadn't slept all night, and it had been daylight before I heard her car and her steps on the stairs, and the soft click as she closed her bedroom door.

Franz wore *lederhosen* and an Alpine jacket. His haversack was ready in the hall.

"Thank you for taking me to see your friends last night," I said. "It did me worlds of good. And now you're off. I wish I was going with you."

"Why not? You could pack enough in a few minutes. Do come."

"I'd love to. But I don't see how I can."

I got out the car and drove him to the station at Dorfen. The house, when I got back, felt depressingly empty without him.

Eilys didn't come down until noon.

"Well, well!" I said. "Are you wanting breakfast, or can you wait twenty minutes till lunch?"

"I'll wait. Sigrid brought me a cup of coffee while I was dressing."

"You nearly came home with the milk," I said. "It must have been quite a shoulder."

"Quite a what?"

"The shoulder you said you were going to cry on."

"Oh, it was. A pet of a shoulder." She studied a bunch of grapes on the dish, picked one off and popped it into her mouth.

Max Todor! I thought. So it's gone as far as that. I hoped she wasn't starting anything that somebody else would need to be sorry about, but her rather messed-up love affairs seemed trivial compared with what was tearing me apart.

"Franz has left for his walking trip," I said.

"Good luck to him." She picked off another grape. "Only you and me left in this barrack now? Doesn't sound too madly gay."

I gave a small shiver.

"Eilys, I was wondering—I would like to get away from here for a while—"

She looked surprised. "Get away? What for?"

"I just want to go right away."

"Have you told Gordon about this?"

"I'll tell him—don't bother about that. I've been thinking, if you let me go with you I could help you quite a lot."

"With me?"

"Look, be an angel, don't ask any questions. You'll have your house to get ready and the Todors to organize. It's a great deal for you to take on alone and I know I'd be useful. When you find you have to do things alone, after being with us all, you're going to feel very lonely, so if you'd let me come and stay—"

While I had been talking her face had gone completely blank, and now for part of a second a look flickered across it that chilled me. An unwelcoming look, so unexpected that I could hardly believe it. Eilys didn't want me!

Oh no, that couldn't be true. I must have imagined it. And by now she was smiling and sunny.

"But of course, Deel. That would be marvellous."

"You're quite sure?"

"But you know I'd love to have you. After all, I've been your guest all this time."

"Thank you very much."

"I don't even know what you're thanking me for."

I picked up some discarded newspapers and pretended to rearrange them. That look of hers. I must have been wrong—I must have been. But it gives one a shock even to imagine that a close friend doesn't want you.

Sigrid came in to lay the lunch.

"I only want a quick snack," said Eilys. "I've got to go out."

"This afternoon?" I said. "Must you?"

"Yes, I've simply got to."

We ate a hurried meal. Within twenty minutes Eilys had finished and gone up to dress. I wished she hadn't needed to go, leaving me all alone again.

As soon as she had driven away I rang Gordon at his office. I didn't often do that and he sounded surprised when he answered the phone.

"You've just caught me before I leave for lunch," he said. "How are you today? No troubles, I hope."

"You may not like this," I said, "but I had to ring you, to find out if by any chance you've reconsidered what we were talking about yesterday afternoon."

"Reconsidered what? I don't understand."

"Oh Gordon. You must remember. About going with me to see the old man."

"Oh, not that again." His tone was hard. "I thought we'd nailed all that down once and for all."

"We settled nothing," I said. "I recognize all your arguments against going, but I'm not building up a myth, and I am reasonable. It's a very serious matter and I've got a feeling that you couldn't care less. It would be a small thing for you to agree to go with me, and it would make all the difference to me. I can't speak more directly on the phone, but I do think you might be understanding enough to do this for me. I don't often ask anything of you, and—"

"I tell you, *no*." He was quite deliberate. I'd known all the time that he wouldn't go. He went on, "The matter's closed, and I insist that you forget all that nonsense, finally and completely. What are you doing today?"

"Nothing. Eilys has gone off to town. I'm by myself."

"What has she gone to town for?"

"I've no idea."

"Well, for God's sake don't let yourself brood. I don't know if

I can manage dinner tonight, but if I can I'll give you a ring and you can come into town."

"I don't think I want to," I said with a touch of temper.

"What do you expect me to do! I'm tied up all afternoon."

"Good-bye," I said, and rang off.

I can't face him, I thought. I can't see him again. Coward! Fool! And he won't see Siebler. He daren't. He dare not come face to face with that old man. There can only be one reason for that.

It was miserable to be alone like this. Should I go to the camp? I couldn't make myself go anywhere, not in this frame of mind, not with this nightmare hanging over me.

If only Eilys hadn't gone out and left me alone! She might have stayed in, just for once, or asked me to go with her. Why couldn't she have asked me to go with her? The long hours of nothingness stretched ahead.

And then suddenly Franz came home. He appeared from nowhere. I heard the front door open and shut, and then footsteps. I thought it might be Eilys. For a second I dreaded that it might be Gordon. But it was Franz, and when I realized I nearly shouted out with joy, and then with a reaction that must have sounded almost unwelcoming I said, "What's the matter? Is anything wrong? I thought you were miles away."

He looked a bit bashful.

"Are you all right, Delia?" he said.

"Me? I was feeling lonely. Eilys is out again."

"That's what I thought. I couldn't enjoy myself. I kept thinking, Delia is alone and not happy. I'd better go back."

"Franz! You don't mean you've come back because of me?"

He stood smiling at me warmly, but hesitant and awkward as though he wasn't quite sure how I was taking it.

"Well—yes—but—"

"Oh, how sweet of you! You shouldn't. What a thing to do! To wreck your holiday—but you don't know how glad I am to see you. Have you had any lunch?"

"I didn't have time. I had to run to catch the train." He began to laugh. "They had to pull me on it."

"I'm going to get you something at once."

I ran off to the kitchen. The maids were upstairs. I began to prepare a meal for Franz, bacon, sausage and steak under the grill, rolls, fruit, coffee. It was the happiest thing I had done for a long time. The relief, the release from those long lonely hours stretching ahead.

I sat and watched him enjoy it.

"The best meal I've had for years."

"I don't believe you!"

"Eilys had no business to go off and leave you alone."

"Don't blame her, she didn't know I was upset," I said without thinking.

He pounced on the unfortunate word.

"Upset? What about? Tell me, you must tell me."

"Nothing that matters at all."

"But why can't you tell me—why? Anything that troubles you I can surely know. It would help to tell me. Perhaps I could clear it up for you. What do you think I came back for?"

"Just keep me company," I said. "That's all I need."

"Have you told Gordon about this trouble?"

"Yes, I have."

He looked relieved. "What did he think?"

"He thought I had nothing to worry about."

"Well, then—?"

I cleared away, and we sat on the balcony smoking and talking companionably. Like this, everything was bearable. I could hold misery at bay. And I was going away, I was getting out of it all—soon.

"I've got to tell you," I said, "I'm definitely going away with Eilys."

He started to fill his pipe.

"When?"

"This week, I hope."

"What does Gordon think about it?"

"I haven't told him yet, I'll tell him tomorrow. And what he thinks won't influence me—I'm going. I'm only concerned about one thing and that's you. You'll stay here, Franz, the girls will look after you. You'll be all right, won't you?"

He poked thoughtfully at his pipe. "Of course. Don't worry about me."

"I feel guilty all the same. You spoiled your holiday for me to save me from stupid loneliness, and now I'm leaving you."

He suddenly took my hand in both of his.

"Listen—I am well able to look after myself. You don't have to think of me, except as just a friend to help and understand when I can't really know. If it will make you happy to go to Switzerland, you go. There is always home to come back to."

II

EILYS came home in the late evening. I told her Franz was back, but she didn't seem to take it in. She seemed abstracted, a little vague.

"When are we going?" I said. "You said any time would suit you. Tomorrow—the next day?"

She came to life.

"But we can't possibly. I've got things to see to, and you must have too."

"I didn't mean it literally," I said, "but this week—"

She frowned. "Perhaps. But we haven't fixed anywhere to stay yet."

"We could easily do that by phoning."

"But I must see the Todors, and—"

"I don't want to rush you," I said, "but you were saying yourself that you wanted to go."

She relaxed and smiled, throwing me a cigarette.

"Of course I do. You start making the arrangements."

I realized she was right, there were things to see to before we left and I started making my preparations.

Gordon neither came nor rang up. I knew I ought to tell him I was going, but I put off phoning him. I didn't want to see him, I thought I would leave it until almost the last minute. Perhaps he too would be relieved that I was going off. Our relationship was on the rocks in any case, and the future was just a fog. Put it off. Put off thinking, planning, worrying, everything. Walk out on it. Things might look different from a distance.

It was three days later. I was in the kitchen mixing a cake to take to Madame Todor on what was to be my last visit to the camp, while Gerda the Gossip sliced beans at the table.

"We'll have to order some vegetables from the shop," she said.

"From the shop? I thought you bought our vegetables at the door."

"Yes, but the man who brings them says that his father has got himself drowned in the lake. They found him yesterday morning. They're burying him tomorrow, so the son won't be coming with the vegetables."

"What man is that?"

"You know. The one who always comes. His father was a queer old thing, spent all his days wandering about by the lake. He used to live down the valley before they let the water in. He took dizzy fits. They'd warned him."

"What was his name?"

"Johann Siebler. Over eighty. He must have had one of his dizzy spells and fallen in the water—just what they guessed might happen. They missed him at night and went out to look for him in the morning, and there he was with his head and shoulders in the water and the rest of him sprawled on the bank. Dead as a log. He'd been there for hours, the doctor said. Silly old fool. But they get like that when they're old—stubborn. You can't do anything with them. And the funeral's tomorrow."

I dropped the mixing spoon.

"Are you sure about this?"

"Of course I'm sure. The baker told me about it too when he brought the rolls. People are a responsibility when they're old and obstinate. They'd told this old fellow again and again that he'd be coming to some harm, away off like that and liable to fall down heaven knows where. I'll pop out tomorrow and see the funeral, if you don't mind, *Fräulein*. I always like a funeral, you usually come across somebody to have a chat with."

Mechanically I tipped the cake mixture into the tin and put the tin in the oven.

"Could you watch that, Gerda? It wants half an hour. Take it out if I'm not here."

Three deaths. Three accidents. *Three murders?*

I felt so sick I went and sat on my bed with my hands tight on my throat, staring into a pit of black horror.

Old Siebler's tongue was silent now. Anything he knew had died with him. He would never be able to recognize a tall dark man who had stood with Jarzy beside the dangerous water. That story had ceased to exist, it was reduced now to the nonsensical imaginings of a neurotic person like me.

Icy cold, I shook with panic.

I had talked! I had told Gordon about old Siebler, and thought I was doing the right thing.

And he had had a fatal accident. Understandable by everybody—those dizzy fits. Nobody would be surprised that he had fallen into the water, and they would bury him tomorrow, and that would be the end of it all.

This was certainly the end for me. I couldn't think any more. I couldn't work out the implications any more. I was utterly desperate. If I didn't get away out of all this I'd go mad.

I slapped cold water on my face, I rubbed my cheeks to make them look alive. My eyes were like staring pin-points.

I went to Eilys's room. She was sitting on her bed, humming the words of the dance tune which her radio was playing and sewing the back seam of a stocking.

"Eilys!" It didn't sound like my voice at all. "About going away. What's to stop us going now—at once?"

She didn't look up.

"You're a bit sudden, aren't you?"

"I must go. I've got to get away from here, I can't stand it any longer!" I tried to get a grip on myself, fighting off near-hysteria. Eilys bit her thread and hurled the stockings across the room.

"Well, you needn't get in a tizzy. What's the matter with you?"

"I've told you. There's nothing to stay for. You've always said yourself that you wanted to go."

She slid off the bed and began to fiddle with the trinkets on her dressing-table.

"I've got a few things to attend to. Why the mad rush?"

"Eilys, please! We've hung about long enough. Do let's go."

She considered as she buffed a finger-nail. "I'll need to go into town."

"All right. I can start packing while you're gone."

"Good heavens! When do you think we're going?"

"Tomorrow?" I suggested breathlessly.

Her eyes shot open. "Oh, not tomorrow. Have a heart! Perhaps —Friday, if you're so set on it. But I still don't see—"

I was so relieved I would have agreed to anything.

"Friday, then. That's wonderful. I'm sorry to sound worked up, but—"

"Oh, anything you like." She sounded casual, slightly irritated.

I would have given anything to be leaving there and then, but I couldn't rush Eilys without giving any explanation. Friday— only the day after tomorrow. Somehow I'd struggle through, keep busy, stop thinking.

I heard myself babbling, "I'll see to everything, don't you bother. I can pack your things too. Franz can stay here and I'll pay the maids in advance. I must see the Todors too and tell them about our plans."

"Yes, you can do that."

"I'll go tomorrow afternoon. We ought to be ready to send for them in about a month, shouldn't we? Where shall we be staying— Geneva?"

"It's as good as anywhere." She kicked off her shoes and found another pair.

"And what about an hotel?" I said. "I can ring up and book if you'll suggest one."

Eilys hooked down the linen suit she usually wore to go to town.

"Oh, don't bother. I'll ring some friends and they'll fix us up."

"Shall we travel in your car? We could send some of the luggage on."

"Yes of course." She put on her bracelets and picked out a pair of gloves. "You get along with it all, Deel. Only don't get so worked up, you'll be tearing strips off yourself."

"Thank you, Eilys," I said breathlessly. "It's awfully good of you to put up with me."

As soon as her small red car had disappeared I rushed to the telephone. I'd get this bit over at once, before I thought of anything else. The horror was still like a live thing inside me. Even my own hand on the receiver seemed to change under my eyes into that dreadful hand that had once loved me.

I clamped my brows with my fingers and dragged off the receiver. I gave Gordon's number, and for once he answered himself, not the clerk.

"Well, what is it?" His tone was curt.

"Gordon, I thought I'd better tell you. I'm going away with Eilys."

"You're—*what*!"

"I'm going to Switzerland with Eilys. On Friday."

"With Eilys! When was this arranged?"

I hadn't expected him to be so astounded.

"I've been thinking about it for some time, but it wasn't arranged until just now."

"But—When did you say you were going?"

"On Friday. The day after tomorrow."

"I still don't—"

"I want to get away," I interrupted, because I had to get this done with before my voice gave out altogether. "I need a change. So I asked Eilys if I could go with her to help her to settle in her new house. We're going to stay in Geneva. I don't know why you sound so surprised. You know things haven't been right between us for quite a while—I don't want to talk about that—I just feel it would be better if I went away."

"I see . . . Is Eilys with you now?"

"No, she's gone into town, she had one or two last-minute things to see to, but she'll be back soon."

"What have you told her? I mean, about wanting to go off so suddenly."

"I haven't told her anything—just that I'd like to stay with her for a time. And, Gordon, there's another thing. I think it would be better if I didn't see you before I go. It might be difficult for us both. Shall we leave it like that?"

"Just as you wish."

He sounded indifferent, but my tone had been as discouraging as I could make it. The one thing I'd dreaded was that he'd insist on coming over. I was weak with relief that he wasn't suggesting any such thing.

"You understand, Gordon?"

"I suppose I do."

"So—good-bye."

"Good-bye," he said, and I heard him ring off before I put my own receiver down.

I stood for a minute, dizzy, with my hands to my eyes. Now it was over. Now I could get on, I could go and pack.

I found my cases and carried them upstairs, but I was too dazed to know what I was packing.

I would never see Gordon again—never again. I had a feeling that once I was gone he would go too, that he would leave Dorfen and disappear, and then I would be able to come home.

He had done all that—for nothing! For nothing at all. What must he be feeling now?

I took a grip on myself. The next thing was to go down and arrange things with the two maids.

They heard all I had to say in silence, looking awkward.

Then Gerda said, "I don't think I shall care to stay, *Fräulein*. If you will give me my money then I will go when you also go."

"But couldn't you stay?" I said, taken back. "There will only be the *Herr Doktor* to look after. It will be easy. I thought you liked being here."

She shook her head thoughtfully.

"No, I shall go. I would rather work in the town."

"And I too shall go," said Sigrid. "It is not lively here. I like a house with a lot of people, or an hotel."

Nothing I could say would persuade them otherwise.

When Franz came in I told him what had happened.

"Eilys and I are going to Geneva on Friday, Franz. And the awful thing is that the maids don't want to stay on. They say they're going to leave when I go, it's rather an unpleasant snag. What about you? I feel so bad, as if I were turning you out."

He smiled encouragingly. "But that's nothing to worry about, I'll go to rooms in town. I can arrange it today. You do what you feel is right for you, and please don't think about me."

"I know it's best for me to go," I said. "And I won't consider the future yet, anything can happen. I'd like to write to you."

His face lighted up.

"I do hope you will. If things turn out not so good, or if there is something you burst to tell to a friend, it may be nice for you to know you can write, and I shall understand. And then I can let you know what happens here, yes? Would you like me to keep my key, and come in to see that all is well with the house?"

"I'd be so grateful. I'm looking forward to coming back some day. Franz, you're the person I most dislike leaving."

He gripped my hand so hard that it hurt.

"So you must go. But I shall look forward too, and I know you will come back. It will not be good-bye, but only *auf wiedersehen*."

For the first time in all this wretched business I was near to tears.

12

THE night seemed long. In spite of my resolution the pictures built up in my mind.

It couldn't have been difficult for him to do it. Only too easy in the desolate darkness to overpower the old man, to see that he finished up half in the lake and half out of it. It couldn't have taken long.

With the morning light I deliberately blacked all this out. It was the Past I was going away to forget.

Eilys spent the next morning packing, and refused my help. She had a lot to pack, and she went at it like a whirlwind, boxes and cases open all round her room, drawers pulled out, tissue paper flying. Unwanted dresses, shoes, lingerie were flung out on the landing.

"Anybody can have those. Give them to Sigrid, she's the only one they'll fit."

"She doesn't deserve them, for walking out on Franz like that."

"Oh, he'll be all right. He'll probably be better off in a flat in town."

"By the way," I said, "did you fix an hotel for us? I haven't written my luggage labels yet."

"There's no need to. We'll be met. My friends have fixed everything."

"Oh, you rang up from town."

"That's right."

"Will there be anything to be sent on?"

"No, I've discarded a lot of stuff. It'll all go in the car, and I don't suppose you've got much."

"I told you I was going to the camp this afternoon," I said. "Are you coming?"

She looked surprised. "I don't think I can, I still have a lot to do. You don't mind going by yourself, do you, Deel?"

"I don't *mind*," I said, "but the Todors will when they hear you're going off tomorrow without seeing them."

She thought for a minute.

"I could slip round tonight—"

"I'll tell them that."

Sigrid served us a cold lunch. Gerda, she told us, had gone to watch the funeral.

"If you listen," she said with relish, "you can hear the bell tolling."

Loud on a sudden breeze, the mournful dong! came up the valley and faded in the falling calm. The next one was faint and the one after that swelled out, and every minute they came.

"How madly gay," said Eilys. "Who's dead, anyway?"

"An old man from the village."

I gritted my teeth and felt the colour leave my face. Eilys was looking at me curiously.

"They say funerals go in threes," she said, "so that's the lot . . . Eat up, Deel, don't go into a trance . . . *Deel!*"

"Sorry," I said jerkily. "You can take the plate, Sigrid, I'm not hungry today. I think I'll get along."

I brought round the car.

"Can I pick anything up for you in town?" I asked Eilys. "No dresses forgotten at the cleaner's?"

"I might slip in myself." She came out on to the steps and watched me go. The sun in her eyes made her blink as she waved me away.

I had to tell Nora Nixon about my sudden change of plans.

"Going tomorrow? I hope it won't be for long. I don't know what we'll do without you." She sounded sincere, and I felt a pang.

"I'm sorry," I said, "but I have to go, for personal reasons."

She nodded. "I understand. You've had a lot of bad luck with those two accidents in your family. It's bound to have got you down. But I'll be hoping all the time that you'll feel better, and come back soon. We need you a lot."

"I want to come back," I said. "I'll think of you often. Meanwhile I'll be helping Eilys to get her home ready, and then we'll send for the Todors." I handed her a cheque that I'd written that morning. "Please use this while I'm away."

She looked down at it.

"Bless you, Delia, this is wonderful. But I'd really rather have you than the money, and that's the truth. Is Eilys with you now?"

"She's finishing her packing, and coming round this evening to say good-bye."

"It's a fine thing she's doing for the Todors. I only hope the old man doesn't die of excitement before we get him away. Madame Todor and Isold seem wonderfully well. It's amazing what joy can do for the body. Are you in a hurry?"

"I'll stay and help a bit," I said, "and I won't even think it's the last time."

She grinned wryly. "Don't you dare let it be!"

No, it couldn't be the last time, I told myself as the afternoon went on. They needed me here so much, I must come back again.

Even if my personal life folded up on me I would have something to give in this place.

When I had done all I could I went along to the Todors.

"News!" I said. "Eilys and I are leaving for Switzerland tomorrow to get the house ready. We'll be sending for you very soon."

Speechless, Madame threw her arms round me. Isold's eyes shone and she gave a little yelp of excitement.

I disentangled myself from Madame who bustled over to the stove.

"I have ze kettle boiling, I know you are here. We drink coffee for ze last time in zis dirty place togezzer, and ze next time it will be in Swizzerland. What happiness! I nearly burst."

"That's what Mrs. Nixon's afraid of," I told her. "You'd better try and calm down. You see that she does, Isold."

"I'm rather far gone myself," she said, getting out the cups. "I haven't coughed for a long time and I feel wonderful. Tell Eilys never mind about getting the house ready, I'll do all the work."

"What do you think I'm going for?" I said. We laughed and made silly jokes about the amount of work we both meant to do. My spirits went up, I actually forgot my nightmares.

Isold poured the coffee and I carried over the old man's.

"This will cheer you up!"

"Me, I do not need cheering up," he said with great dignity. "Nor do I go mad like zose. I have learn zrough many ups and downs never to go mad, but when ze good sing come it is vair nice in ze heart. Where is Miss Ei-liss?"

"Finishing her packing," I said. "She's coming to see you tonight."

"To say good-bye?"

"Not good-bye. As soon as we get to Geneva we're going to start making arrangements. You'll be with us in less than a month. Max will be there to look after you on the journey."

"Max always look after us, he is a good boy."

"I must fly," I said, putting down my cup. My eyes smarted as I looked at them, still so elegant, so alive after all that the dreary years had done to them. We kissed all round and murmured, *Auf wiedersehen . . . auf wiedersehen*, and I hurried off.

Outside was the clanging passage, the yelling children, the clanking cans, a babble of distraught voices, a drunk shouting ribald curses. If only these could all go to a new life! But one family saved from despair was something.

Nora Nixon walked to the car with me.

"Mind you write to me."

"I certainly will."

"All I have to offer you is this God-forsaken hole, but I think you'll come back."

"Don't," I said. "You'll have me breaking down and howling."

"Get along with you!"

I waved to her as she stood with her hand shading her eyes and that mouldering old Luftwaffe barrack behind her.

I drove home. Franz was in the hall, when I went in. He looked so strange, I halted like a startled cat.

"Delia . . . I have a shock for you."

"What—" I didn't know what I expected.

"Eilys has gone."

"Gone!"

"She's gone without you. Do you understand?"

That was the last thing I'd expected. I grabbed a chair.

"I got home about half an hour ago," Franz was saying. "Sigrid told me that a few minutes after you left for the camp Eilys told the girls to bring her luggage down and put it into her car. Then she tipped them, and drove away."

My heart felt like lead. So she hadn't wanted me! Then anger flared. At least she could have been honest and told me so. How could she tell those lies, deceive me like that, up to the very last minute? It was unthinkable, unbearable.

"I can't believe it," I gasped. "There must be something that hasn't been explained."

"Wait, I shall get you a drink."

He brought me one, but I couldn't even hold the glass. He put it down, and looked at me sympathetically.

"She left a note for you. Here it is."

"I'm sure this will explain—"

The envelope was sealed and had "For Deel" written on it. I

slit it and took out two sheets of paper scrawled over in Eilys's rather flamboyant writing.

Dear Deel,

This is going to be a bit of a bomb for you, but in a way you brought it on yourself.

Here's the simple fact. You're not going to Switzerland with me. I'm not even going to Switzerland myself. You nearly put me on the spot yesterday when you sprang your plan on me. I had to work fast. You see, I'd already made full arrangements to leave *today*, and not for Geneva either.

When you read this I'll have gone. With Gordon, of course. It was always him and me, and where your eyes were not to see it I don't know.

You gave me a bad time. He wanted me from the start, but when I got myself disinherited it had to be you instead. He had to have money. The biggest laugh was when you forced me to tell him I was Daddy's heiress and he realized what he was losing.

Now don't play jilted. You asked for it. You were for ever accusing Gordon of murdering Ida to get you, and a man won't stand much of that. I wonder if you'll now suspect him of murdering Mike to get me? I wouldn't put it past you with your imagination. But I was fond of Mike. I didn't feel good about playing him off against Gordon like I had to, and I was sorry when he died. That's the truth.

When I've time I'll send the Todors a cheque, so you needn't worry about them. They'd probably rather have the money.

If I was as black-hearted as you think I'd have gone off without writing you a word. But I owe you something if only for being—very unobservantly—a friend to me. Buck up, Deel, you've lost nothing.

Where are we going? There's always some island. Wipe us off the slate, forget us. We shan't even be in the same world. Matter of fact, we never were.

EILYS.

I read the letter right through again, taking in the meaning of every phrase. Strangely enough, my dominant thought was, she's taken my particular hell with her and she doesn't know it. It was ironical. And nothing seemed real. Nothing can feel real when this kind of explosion bursts in your face.

I held out the letter to Franz.

"Read it. She's gone for good. With Gordon."

He made a shocked exclamation, read the letter, and stared anxiously at me. I don't know what he expected from me, but I began to curse. I didn't know that I could curse. I didn't think I even knew the words of blistering imprecation which poured out of me now and crashed about the room and ricocheted off the walls.

Franz didn't try to stop me, he let me go on till there wasn't anything left to come.

"I'm not wounded, Franz," I said at last. "I swear to you I'm not injured. But I'm furious—blazing at her filthy treachery. I'm wild with rage that such foul faithlessness can exist. I thought she was my friend, and she lied like a devil while she was smiling at me. All through these days she knew what she was planning to do, it was all worked out, and she let me make my poor little plans, and laughed at me behind my back. Don't ever pity me, Franz, there's no pity needed. I'm glad, with all my heart I'm glad, that they've both gone out of my life for ever."

"I saw it," he said. "I saw that falseness in Eilys and I tried to warn you. I hoped I was wrong. But Gordon—"

Gordon? What did I feel about Gordon's flight? Only a huge, tearing upsurge of relief. I was free. Free, free! Released in one instant from infatuation, the ball-and-chain I'd called love, released from the dreadful dragging at my heels.

"That's nothing," I said. "I mean it! Gordon is less than nothing to me, he doesn't exist any more. He isn't even worth a curse. But Eilys!— Don't you ever think it's what she's done to me that's turning me into a tigress. It's what she's done to the Todors. My God, I can't bear that! I can't think about it—yet. And she's even been having an affair with Max Todor since Jarzy died."

I stopped abruptly, because it had suddenly come to me that Max had never really been in the picture at all. Just another stooge, poor Max. It hadn't been Max's shoulder on the night that ended with daylight footsteps going up to Eilys's room. All those afternoons of slipping into town, all those mysterious evenings, had had little to do with Max at all. It had been Gordon, Gordon, Gordon.

I had been brought up in a world where lovers and friends were steel true and blade straight, and now I was looking into a pit where your closest ones could deceive and desert you, and all with hateful, smiling faces.

The Todors . . . the trusting, hoping, waiting Todors.

I yelled out a few of the things I could do to Eilys, the sort of things I hoped might happen to her.

"Franz, you didn't think she was as bad as that, did you? You couldn't have done."

"If I'd thought she was as bad as that would I have let her get away with it? No! Heartless, I thought. Just selfish and likely to make you unhappy."

He was so anxious and so kind that on top of everything else it was too much for me. I did what I thought nothing could make me do, I began to cry. The tears poured out of my eyes and ran down my face. I wasn't crying for myself. I was crying for the Todors.

I had to explain to Franz.

"I'm not crying for myself—"

"I know—I do know. You're crying about the Todors."

"She'll never send any blasted cheque! She'll never give it another thought. And what would it be, anyway? A filthy insult." I was blazing up again.

After a spell in my room I felt calmer. We didn't feel like supper, so we had some sandwiches and a bottle of wine on the balcony in the soft cool evening air. I even caught a glimpse of peace outside all this murk and fog of treachery.

But there was still something, a lump of ice inside me that both burned and froze. I knew now why Jarzy had died. No longer could I say there was no motive, it was only too clear.

"And now what will you do?" said Franz. "Unpack?"

"I don't think so. Too much has happened in this house to make it possible for me to live here alone. From the little thinking I've been able to do up to now it seems the only thing is to get rid of the house. Put it in the hands of an agent to sell." The very thought of it made me so unhappy I nearly broke down. "Oh Franz, it sounds so brutal—what I've just said. The house that we came into so gaily a few months ago."

"I know, I know." He covered my hand with his. "And you?"

"All I can do is go back to England," I said, feeling like a lump of lead. "And I'm most sorry about you, Franz, because you've lost the most—your home, everything, for the second time."

He said firmly, "You are not to worry about me. I still have good friends and my work, and I'll be comfortable in town. Think about me, Delia, when you're gone, write to me if you can, but never never worry about me. You've had the worst blow, I can't tell you how bad I feel about that."

I took a grip on myself.

"The maids tell me that they're leaving tomorrow. I've a good deal to see to tomorrow myself, and I think I'll arrange to fly to London on Sunday."

"I hope you won't mind," he said, "if I stay on here for a few days? My rooms won't be ready for me before Monday. I can take the keys to the agent for you."

"Of course you can stay. Oh, Franz, I wish we didn't have to talk about such things."

I felt tired out with the reaction from my shock and fury. I felt myself clutching his strong hand which was still over mine.

"Tell me," I said, "tell me what to say to the Todors. I'm dreading it so. I have to face it tomorrow."

"I think you needn't be afraid," said Franz out of a depth of knowledge. "I think they are brave people and they will not scream. You'll see."

13

"My God!" said Nora Nixon. "What I couldn't do to that girl with my bare hands! I thought at the beginning that she was no good. Then I changed my mind. I ought to have stuck to my first judgment, I'm rarely wrong about people. She hadn't the kindness or the morals of a ferret."

We stood at the door of the camp with a rather chilly wind blowing down on us from a grey sky.

"It was awfully good of you, Nora," I said, "to tell the Todors yourself—before I saw them. I was a coward."

She spread her hands.

"Not a bit. You'd gone through enough without that. I'm used to grim jobs."

A few minutes before I had been in the Todors' room. The old man was quite superb in his dignity.

"So we do not go to Swizzerland. When you are as old as me, Miss Delia, one does not cry or make protest. It was all a dream, I say. Zere is only left for one to die, and zat will be a kind sing, never to be feared. You must excuse my daughter, she go in toilet to cry alone so you will not see, she have such pride. Max he can work, he is a strong man, and little Isold we will be gentle to because she is young and ze young have to learn how to suffer. Zose old White Russians zey will laugh and say, 'So you do not go wiz Miss after all, ha-ha! You did have too much trust, wasn't you?' Zen zey will be kind and say, 'Have little sip vodka zat we brew, you feel better.' Zose wizzout hope are best friends of ozzers wizzout hope."

I went and fetched Madame Todor out of the toilet, and it was I who did the crying and she who told me it wasn't the end of the world.

"Zat beetch," she said, "run away wiz your young man. Ze same happen to me in Bucharest when I am twenty, but I get a better young man, and so will you."

"You're wonderful," I said. "What about Isold?"

She patted my hand kindly.

"You leave Isold to me. She will be all right, I see to her. Best nobody else see her just yet."

"I'm going back to England tomorrow," I said. "But I'll come back, I promise! I'll do something—when I've had time to think. Please go on hoping, I'll never let you down."

Yes, I would do something for the Todors, though it wouldn't be the same. When the golden dream is shattered nothing else can quite take its place.

"So you're off back to England," said Nora Nixon as we stood saying good-bye.

"It's all I can possibly do. I'm selling the house. It's been an unlucky summer."

She thrust out her lip. "You've certainly had more than your share of tragedy since you came here. And, Delia, if it isn't indelicate of me, may I say how sorry I am about your—er—fiancé?"

"You needn't be," I said with stony conviction. "He's only after Eilys's money, like he was after mine. She'll take her shot of poison in the end. I couldn't wish her worse than the bargain she's got in him."

It was probably the most uncharitable thing I had ever said in my life, but it did me a world of good to get it out of my system.

"Thank you for all you've done for us," Nora said. "We'll miss you like hell."

"Just now," I said, "I promised Madame Todor that I'd come back. I don't know what made me say it, but I'll stand by it. I don't know when or how—but this isn't good-bye."

Behind us in the passage a child's hysterical crying broke out. Somebody called, "Mrs. Nixon . . . Mrs. Nixon!" The smell of poverty and stew and disinfectant came surging out.

I went to the car and drove home. It was evening, I had been out all day. The house felt hollow and quiet now that the maids had gone. Then Franz, smiling, appeared at the kitchen door.

"Come in, it's all ready."

He had made a hot supper and I realized I was starving. I hadn't eaten a thing all day.

"Oh Franz, you shouldn't have bothered, I could have done it. It was my job."

"But I'm on holiday, and you've had a bad day."

"It hasn't been very nice, I must say."

While we ate I told Franz about the Todors. It was raining hard outside, and we took our coffee into the drawing-room and lighted the fire and sat feeling the growing warmth soothe us and listening to the drip of water in the garden.

"I went to the house agent," I said. "He'll take the keys over when you're ready to leave and arrange the sale of everything. Then—" I felt my voice harden, "—I popped along to the bank with my mind full of negotiable securities. But strange as it may seem, they were all there."

Franz's mouth dropped open.

"What! You even thought that Gordon—"

"Well, wouldn't you?" I gave a cynical bark. "I could believe anything, I've grown so sceptical of outward appearances in the last day or two. But I misjudged Gordon, or else he was too shrewd to start himself off with a criminal black mark—anyway, Eilys has loads of lolly. My money's all right, but I can't say the same for the simple trust in people that I had when I came here."

"Because two were bad out of so many good?"

I thought that over for a minute.

"You're quite right, of course you are. I'll get my sense of proportion back some day when the smarting stops. Don't ever let me slip into making horrible remarks, check me when I begin."

It occurred to me that there wasn't going to be much opportunity left for him to do any such thing.

He went over to the big radiogram and put on a record. It was the *Aubade* from *Le Roi d'Ys*.

"Let us have a little music. We both need it."

"Thank you, Franz, that was a wonderful thought." I went on, "Won't you please take the radiogram and all the records for yourself? I'd so much like you to have them."

He looked at me incredulously.

"For me? Oh Delia, thank you—thank you. What a wonderful gift."

"I ought to have thought of it before. I don't know where my mind was. And if there's anything else you'd like, please take it. What about furniture? You should have all the things from your room, at least."

"I don't really need anything," he said. "I'm going into furnished rooms."

"But you might have a flat some day. Do pick out anything you think you may want before they do the inventory." I went on, heavy-hearted, "I've booked to go to London tomorrow. I haven't let my mother know I'm coming, because I thought I'd spend a few days by myself in London to settle my mind. I can telephone her from there. My plane leaves München at noon. Oh, it all seems so—so—"

I got up. "I'm terribly tired. I think I'll go straight to bed."

He switched off the music to which in fact I had scarcely listened, and opened the door for me.

"Good-night, Franz."

"Good-night, Delia."

I was wretched and exhausted and I didn't sleep until it was light. When I woke I smelt coffee, and dressed and went down guiltily because I had meant to make breakfast myself.

Franz had it ready on the table. It was a morning of clear pale blue rain-washed sky, filled with sunshine. Everything on the table sparkled and shone, the china, the little silver toast-rack . . .

As I emptied it I said impulsively. "I'm going to take this with me. It's such a pretty little thing—to remind me—a souvenir—"

"Yes, it is pretty. Do you remember once Ida—"

He stopped. I sat with the little toast-rack in my hands and remembered too many things.

"I'll be going with you to München?" said Franz.

"No, please! I can't bear public, right-to-the-bitter-end good-byes. I'd much rather say it here. That's why I ordered a car to take me right to the airport."

"If I went to the airport I could help you with your luggage."

"The porters will do that. Please, don't insist. I'd so much rather you didn't go." I got up. "It's time I put my things on."

"Is your luggage ready?"

"Upstairs."

"I'll bring it down."

I went quickly round the house for the last time. It was painful all the way. I should never see it again, and I'd only remember how sad and lost it looked. It should have been a happy house. It started out as one, but now it was tragic, and I must try to forget it entirely. In my room I put on my hat, and as a last gesture slipped the little toast-rack into a drawer and shut it. Best to take nothing away. A clean break.

Franz called up the stairs, "The car is here."

"I'm coming."

When I went downstairs he said, "Your luggage is all in."

"Thank you. So it's good-bye, Franz."

He took both my hands and held them tightly.

"It is hard to say good-bye to a real friend," I said.

"I feel that also—very, very much. Good-bye, Delia, I hope you will some day be happy again. I'm sorry you've been so unlucky here. You take away so little that is good to remember."

"I shall remember you," I said. "You must come to England, perhaps next holidays, and stay with us. Do say you will!"

The sadness lifted miraculously from his face.

"I would love to do that. I feel there is nothing left now that you go, but it will be something to hope for, to look forward to."

"And I mean it. I'll count on you coming. Good-bye, Franz."

"Good-bye, Delia."

The driver was impatiently holding open the door of the car and I got in. Franz stood on the steps alone, outside the desolate house where everything had happened. He was holding up one hand in farewell. He looked so forlorn. I waved once, the car moved away, I didn't look back. I couldn't have seen anything if I had, there was fog in my eyes. I shut them tight and didn't even look out of the window until we had gone through Dorfen and were on the Munich road.

After that it didn't matter so much, this countryside had no significance. I watched it rolling by, the farmlands, the hazel thickets, a village or two with gingerbread barns and medieval cottages, a hillside bristling with rocks.

"The rocks have angry faces"—who said that? Hilaire Belloc? I couldn't have cared less. A stupid, irritating little thing was nagging at my brain. I had thoughtlessly left the breakfast table without even clearing and washing up the dishes, just leaving them for Franz. How could I have done that? Like a bit of grit in a shoe it was going to harass me for days, a last exasperating, regrettable memory.

Deflated, hopeless, biting my lips, I arrived at the airport. The driver handed me over to a porter who took away my luggage and showed me where to go to check my ticket. What bleak, efficient, falsely cheerful places airports were, with their cute steely chairs and fat ashtrays and souvenir shops and blaring amplified voices bossing the scurrying ant-people round.

I checked my ticket. The idea was to go and get some lunch, at leisure, with plenty of time for the plane. On the plane I could sleep, and wake up in London.

I walked towards the restaurant. All I could see was Franz standing alone on those steps with the desolation of the house behind him. The melancholy, betrayed house—and Franz alone. Franz who had given up his walking trip to come back to me in case I might be lonely.

"You selfish clot!" I said to myself. "*You* should have been the last one to leave. How could you walk out on him?"

It was hell. I couldn't go on with it. I didn't even reason with myself or tell myself I was crazy. I turned round and went charging off to the luggage section.

"I'm not going," I said. "I want my luggage back."

There was a spot of consternation and a bit of officialdom, but fortunately my luggage hadn't gone out to the plane, thanks to my being early. If it had, I think I'd have let it go to London by itself.

In twenty minutes I was in another car, headed for home. *Home?* That was an insane thought. This could lead to nothing but a few days' delay, and another departure, but no matter. I owed it to Franz that he shouldn't stop alone in that house till Monday.

The journey seemed long, but my heart was lighter by a ton and half my troubles were gone. At last we drove up to the door and the driver put off the luggage on the steps.

"Shall I carry it in, *Fräulein?*"

"No, thank you. Leave it." I tipped him, I wanted to get rid of him. Now I was back at the house I never expected to see again—or wanted to—and I was so glad I could have shouted.

I tried the door and it opened, I walked in.

It was silent inside, but the hall was full of sunlight.

"Franz!" I called. "Franz!"

Had I come back for nothing? It was afternoon now. Most probably he had gone out, and wouldn't be back till night. I felt suddenly lost.

Then I heard him upstairs. He came to the top of the stairs and stood looking down at me, absolutely bewildered and unbelieving.

"Delia! Is that *you*? What happened? Didn't the plane—"

"I've come back," I said. "You came back to me when I was all alone. I couldn't walk out on you like that. I shook München airport to the core, but I had to come back. I hadn't washed the breakfast dishes."

He came down the stairs like an avalanche. The next minute his arms were tight round me.

"You came back! To me? Oh Delia, my heart's dearest, you did that for me?"

I hadn't meant it to be like that at all. His heart's dearest? Was I really? Did I want to be?

But there was something lovely in the thought, warm, comforting. I heard myself saying, "Don't let me go, Franz. Don't let me go away again."

The sunlight poured over us, the dead air seemed to be coming alive. He and I had just created something between us that could drive the sad horror out of this house.

"You must love me," he said, "or you wouldn't have done it."

"I don't know why I did it. I just couldn't bear the thought of you stuck here alone, with everything finished—"

I couldn't go on. I didn't know what I felt, beyond a confused happiness which had all the time in the world to sort itself out.

"You love me. I shall keep on saying it until you believe it."

He held my face between his hands. I laughed into his eyes.

"Oh, I'm so glad to be back. I can't explain it—not yet. By the way, my luggage is out on the steps."

"I shall bring it in."

"Do! It isn't going out again. I've come home."

"That's a beautiful thing to say."

"It sounds pretty good to me too. Stay with me, Franz."

"You don't have to tell me."

I realized that I was starving hungry. So was he, he hadn't eaten either. We got some cold food from the larder, and made coffee, and ate ravenously, utterly contented. Then we went and sat on the balcony in blissful quiet and peace.

I had to break it.

"I've a lot to tell you," I said. "Don't stop me, don't say 'not now'. I must."

"But need it be now?"

"It has to be."

He sat forward with his hands between his knees.

"Is this anything to do with what has been burning you up?"

"Everything to do with it. I can't keep it from you, the horror and the misery, but when I've told you I hope it'll be finished for ever so far as I'm concerned."

He said gently, "What is it all about, Delia?"

"About Gordon."

"Is there anything about Gordon that I don't know already?"

"A great deal," I said grimly, tightening my hands on the wicker arms of my chair. "There are two stories you've got to hear."

"You're sure it is necessary?"

"More than sure. Before we plan any future, Franz, you've got to look into my mind, even you think I've been harbouring insanity."

"Not that." He smiled and put a hand on my arm. "You mean, don't you? that you've been going back and back to Ida's death? What is it stops you from getting over that?"

"There's more than Ida's death," I said. "I've let myself believe that Gordon killed three people who stood in his way."

His hand jerked away.

"I know how that shook you," I went on. "I don't blame you. I only hope that every word I'm going to say will sound more and more fanciful until I can convince myself that it is imagination—or you can convince me."

"Go on—please."

"This is the first story." My fingers began to dig into my palms and the pain of the pricking nails stimulated me.

Slowly I began to tell the whole thing from the beginning, with all my growing doubt and fear and final horror as the dreadful drama worked itself out to the last tragedy.

Franz only interrupted me once, jumping up with an anguished exclamation when I described how Gordon, to stop Eilys going away with Jarzy, had brought about his friend's death.

I didn't spare myself. I had been worse than ingenuous. Dazzled by Gordon, I had behaved ridiculously and had paid for it.

I gave the story its full value, right up to Siebler's death and my final panic.

"And that's it," I ended bitterly. "Eilys made a fool of me—how she must have despised me!—and I suppose I deserved all I got, but thank God I came off no worse. The huge irony is that she's been fooled herself. A triple murderer! She's taken death in her purse all right."

I had finished. I looked at Franz. His face was dark and furrowed, his lips bitten in.

"Go on!" I said. "Don't be afraid to say what you really think. Tell me I'm out of my mind, I can take it from you."

"I wasn't going to say any such thing." He thought for a minute. "It's a perfectly logical story. Once started it had to work out as it did. But there's another one, isn't there? You said so. Those three accidents. They could be explained naturally. I wonder—is three too many?"

"It needn't be," I said. "When I let my brain cool I can take the whole sequence at its face value. It's a straightforward story of mishap and bad luck. In it Gordon simply emerges as the opportunist you once called him, and the worst thing you can say about him is that he was an unscrupulous fortune-hunter and a liar. Early on I got on the wrong foot about Gordon. Gladys was always dropping little bits of malice to put me against him. There was a probably meaningless incident in the hotel at München—I needn't go into that. But these and other things were preparing my mind for the awful ideas which followed and the ghastly suspicions. If I was wrong, he put up with a lot from me. Oh yes, Franz, that's how it could have been. Which story do I believe—really believe? I don't know what I believe, the mind can do such things to you. You're the one and only person who can save me from spending the rest of my life on a frightful see-saw of doubt, dreading the shadows in my house. You've got to decide! I've put all my horrors into words,